I wasn't in
Helen's. I was aware that the moon was suddenly hidden behind a cloud. I was aware that I seemed to be the only guest in an otherwise empty inn. I was aware that my soft soled shoes were making a lot of noise on the walkway…and that was all I was aware of when an arm shot out of the dark from behind me. The ceramic pitcher went flying into the air and my feet flew out from under me as I hit the ground. It happened so fast that everything became a blur. I didn't have a clue who belonged to the arm or, for that matter, to the fist that slugged me. I remember seeing feet, but the image I had was that of black tennis shoes belonging to neither male nor female. Maybe I should say, belonging to *either* male or female, I had no idea which. I rolled over, clutching my jaw, as footsteps ran away from me, heading toward the street. But my reflexes were too slow. I didn't get as much as a glance at my attacker. I sat there on my tailbone, holding my aching jaw, rocking back and forth, trying to take it all in.

★

MURDER
in the movies

ESTHER LUTTRELL

WORLDWIDE®

TORONTO • NEW YORK • LONDON
AMSTERDAM • PARIS • SYDNEY • HAMBURG
STOCKHOLM • ATHENS • TOKYO • MILAN
MADRID • WARSAW • BUDAPEST • AUCKLAND

If you purchased this book without a cover you should be aware that this book is stolen property. It was reported as "unsold and destroyed" to the publisher, and neither the author nor the publisher has received any payment for this "stripped book."

For Dean who continues to inspire,
for Brooke, whose friendship means everything,
and to the man who is and will always be,
the wind beneath my wings.

Recycling programs
for this product may
not exist in your area.

MURDER IN THE MOVIES

A Worldwide Mystery/September 2010

First published by Hilliard & Harris.

ISBN-13: 978-0-373-26724-8

Copyright © 2008 by Esther Luttrell.
All rights reserved. No part of this book may be reproduced or transmitted in any form or by any means, electronic or mechanical, including photocopying, recording or by any information storage and retrieval system, without permission in writing from the publisher. For information, contact:
Hilliard & Harris, P.O. Box 275, Boonsboro, MD 21713-0275 U.S.A.

This is a work of fiction. Names, characters, places and incidents are either the product of the author's imagination or are used fictitiously, and any resemblance to actual persons, living or dead, business establishments, events or locales is entirely coincidental.

® and TM are trademarks of Harlequin Enterprises Limited. Trademarks indicated with ® are registered in the United States Patent and Trademark Office, the Canadian Trade Marks Office and in other countries.

Printed in U.S.A.

Acknowledgments

A book is not just an idea that comes out of a writer's imagination; it's the result of who we know, what we find to be curious about, and who's willing to answer our endless questions. In the end, it leaves the writer's mind, the writer's computer, and goes into critical hands, to be read by critical eyes. Without all of those willing to play a part in the telling of a tale, the tale would never be told. Here, then, are a few of the people who made this little tale possible, and to whom I'll always be indebted.

A big thank you to the Fresno County Coroner's office, who answered endless questions I posed regarding the forensic detection of poisons.

Once I got the manuscript into some kind of readable form, I first passed it by the sharp eye of my daughter, Brooke, who found page after page of errors and omissions. Thank goodness for her objectivity and her love of detail.

After I "fixed" it, I put it in a drawer and there it sat for a very long time until, one day, I had the nerve to show it to writer and friend, Joanne Bodner, who offered encouragement and gave me the confidence to go the next step in preparing it for the marketplace.

That "next step" was to run it past fellow-writer and close friend, Betty Laird, who offered meticulous editing and sound advice, as did dear friend Helen Cleary.

And then I dared to follow my heart. I had seen books published by Hilliard and Harris and determined that they had to publish *Murder in the Movies,* no one else would do. And so I queried them. And I waited, not so patiently I confess, for seven long months–until one day I got the phone call I had been hoping for. As editor, Shawn Reilly, said, "The secret of *The Secret* worked for you." And so it did. Thank you, Shawn.

Now that that dream has been realized, I want to thank Peggy Johnson for her sharp and critical mind. It is because of Peggy that holes in the story were plugged and gaps filled. Bless her heart.

Kevin Konowalec is a writer I admire more than he knows. He surprised me with the gift of a masterful "Murder in the Movies" web page, for which I'm deeply grateful. And then there's Steven Glen Thomas. My computer guru. Oh the patience that man has shown as he sat on the other end of the phone, walking me through the dozens of steps that kept the manuscript from falling apart as it went (sometimes intentionally, sometimes not) from one format to the other. I could never, never have completed the task without him and his (daily) guidance.

I mention Jock Mahoney in the book. He would be tickled pink to know how much his friendship meant to me when we worked together on an MGM film, and later when he and his wife Autumn became almost family. He's been gone now for several years, but I have a feeling he was watching over my shoulder and whispering in my ear as I wrote about stuntmen, for there was none better than my buddy Jock.

What I write about MGM is mostly from memory and experience. I really did drool over Cary Grant one day as he waved hello; I really did watch a dying Steve McQueen drive through the gate in his old pickup truck, waving a brave hello to our gate guard, Bill Hollywood. And, yes, that really was his name. The house in Sun Beach is real; I lived there. The apartment on Naples Island is just as real; I lived there, too. The streets and places are real, but the murder, sorry, but I made it up.

And now my deepest appreciation, which has been withheld until this moment; it goes to you, dear reader.

ONE

I KNEW WHEN I GOT the call there was going to be trouble. Helen wasn't one to chat on the phone unless she had to and she wasn't going to run up a bill calling from California unless it was absolutely necessary. The storm made hearing her the challenge of the day. Through the crackles I could make out something about "...horrible..." and "...arrested..." and "...please come, Katie."

Please come meant get on a plane and fly to Los Angeles, but I wasn't sure how it fit in with "horrible" and "arrested" until the crackles died down and I heard her cry, "Lanie didn't do it! You know she couldn't do a thing like that!" I managed, "Like what?" And she answered, "They've arrested her, Katie! They say she murdered him!"

Then the line went dead.

TWO

I'M KATIE TO THOSE who know me, Katlin Wallace to bill collectors. I'm older than Rita Moreno, but not by much. I'd been working in Los Angeles doing office type things for my husband's detective agency, although I hated the sound of those words. It isn't like TV detective shows or true crime magazines. Nothing that exciting or dramatic. On the West Coast it's a career that consists primarily of following up on death threats made to movie stars or sitting behind the wheel of parked cars on the trail of wayward spouses, taking notes on where he (or she) is spending the night or a steamy two hours in the middle of his (or her) day, then reporting to the suspicious spouse—the one paying our agency's bills—that their worst fears have been confirmed. That's what we did. We confirmed worst fears. A terrible way to earn a living. I think it's what made my husband change over a period of time, like eroding rock under the steady drip of that one proverbial drop of water. If you're exposed for extended periods of time to people who lie, and those without any sense of moral obligation or honor, it rubs off on you. Frankly, I've analyzed the whole thing to death over the past year and I can't find an acceptable reason for the way things turned out between us.

MacKay was his name. MacKay Wallace. Started out years before as a rookie cop on the L.A. police force, took early retirement and ended up opening his own agency on Sunset Boulevard—and don't let the name mislead you. It's a nasty place, Sunset Boulevard. Palm trees lining the wide avenue are pretty enough, majestically regal, but what's under them is pure slime, I'm sorry to say. The Hollywood Chamber has done their best to clean up the place, but it's like trying to sweep sand off the beach. Prostitutes, male and female, sex shops, motels with bars on the windows and broken glass in the driveways, strip mall shops. We had an office in one of the buildings of yore, meaning that the gingerbread stuck on in the '30s or '40s was still in place. It still had some of the architectural charm of that era though the halls smelled of mold and old plaster and creaked mightily underfoot.

I'd been working at one of the major studios as a production coordinator on a long-running television series when I met MacKay, a man I once described as tall, dark and arrogant. We flirted, we dated, we married. I'd planned to live happily ever after, though I thought it would be just the two of us. See how naive a female can be? Our marriage was enjoyed by him, by me, and by a multitude of women I wouldn't learn of for many years to come.

MacKay often worked traffic control at Hollywood events and on movie sets when they filmed on location around town. He had made enough friends in the Industry (the big 'I' means the Movie Industry to those in the know) that the decision of leaving the police force to open his own detective agency seemed logical. He'd been on bodyguard detail for more than one mega star, and the moonlighting paid a lot better than his LAPD salary. Steady work seemed assured.

Helen's daughter, Lane Allison, was once the darling of the MGM lot, back at the close of their golden era, which was way before Ted Turner made off with its brilliant library of old movies and virtually destroyed the legend. Lane had been a favorite of mine. As a kid, I'd sit in a darkened theater, mimicking her crinkly grin, trying to squinch my eyes up to look cute and innocent the way she did. She had a way of wrinkling her nose when she was tickled, which I imitated ad nauseam. I'd pull my snoot up into a bunny thing that was so adorable on her and so ridiculous looking on me. With the honker that God granted me, my nose wrinkling efforts had more the effect of wadding up a wool blanket and slapping it in the middle of my face. A fact that didn't go unnoticed among classmates. "What's the matter with your nose? How come you keep scrunching it up like that? Why doncha blow it if it itches?"

Lane's star began to fade; ingénues weren't in demand, in fact they became quite a giggle at one point. A *virgin* in her thirties? Ha ha ha. So the Doris Days and the Debbie Reynolds and the Lane Allisons joined the way of the dinosaur and the home-grown tomato. One of her last films brought bad reviews and a man named Glance Debrey. Debrey had been released from prison after serving seven years for mutilating an eight-year-old he'd raped and stabbed to death. He became fixated on Lane after seeing that particular movie and began stalking her.

MacKay was still with the police force then, and was sent to help her out. He ended up guarding her in his off hours and that's how I got to know Helen. I met Lane, who was only a few years older than me, when we were invited to the funeral of her Director of Photography husband. He had died in a fiery plane crash along with the rest of his camera crew on their way to Sri Lanka to work on a picture. Then we met again a few years later at her elaborate Malibu wedding to up-and-coming TV producer, Richard Wagnor. Her two kids were teenagers by then; Caroline, a Grace Kelly gorgeous fourteen-year-old, and Michael, a handsome twelve who would turn the magical teen corner within days of the nuptials.

By the time of her wedding, MacKay and I were ensconced in our Sunset Boulevard digs, chasing those wayward spouses. We didn't see much of Helen and her husband Donne until her family got yet another death threat, from yet another ex-con who planned to kidnap Caroline for ransom. Why Caroline? Because Richard Wagnor had just produced a TV documentary about famous kidnappings, like those of Frank Sinatra Junior, Patty Hearst, the Lindberg baby and the Getty grandson. As this moron ex-con sat in front of his TV, he must have thought who better for him to kidnap than the stepchild of the man who gave him the idea. *Yeah,* he must have thought, *maybe they'll make a movie about me someday, huh?*

This pencil brain had been sending Richard warnings of his intentions. You'd think he might demand money *or else I'll snatch your kid,* but no. His notes rambled on about how he was watching Caroline and knew her every move and that one night, when they least expected it, *bam!*, he'd grab her, and there followed gruesome details of what he planned to do to her. All of this was written—make that printed—in crayon. Three notes sent on three consecutive days.

Helen and the Wagnors were sick with worry and anger and helplessness. The warnings promised unspeakable harm to the entire family if they went to the police. So Helen called me. And I told MacKay. And MacKay was in Richard's office, passing himself off as a production assistant when the mail arrived the next day and, sure enough, there was another note, this time in magenta. Now, I don't mean to boast about an ex-hubby, but MacKay actually arrested the guy within the next hour and a half. How'd he manage such clever sleuthing? The jerk had written this last correspondence on the back of his phone bill! His name and address were on the other side! Being the high caliber detective MacKay was, he went right out and nabbed the sucker. Helen and Donne were eternally grateful and we four became fast friends.

When Donne died of a heart attack about two years ago, Helen called me right after she notified Lane and Richard, who were in Brazil where Richard was trying to raise money to produce what would have been his first feature film. Lane flew back for the funeral, but Richard felt he was too close to a deal to jeopardize it by leaving. That was the last time I had seen my childhood idol, her crinkly eyes red and swollen. Her bunchy nose ran continuously. And, to me, she was still the most beautiful woman on planet earth. I think I didn't really even see her, though. I think I saw an adoring ten-year-old sitting in a dark theater, trying to pull her nose up between her eyebrows in an effort to be cute-as-a-button. Everyone longs for their childhood, even if it wasn't ideal. What I don't know is why.

When MacKay's mother reached her ninety-second birthday, and still hadn't missed a day of work in over forty years, he decided we should move to Florida so he could be closer in case she needed him. I didn't argue. I was tired of smog and freeway traffic that turned into parking lots during rush hour. Mostly, I was tired of the earth grumbling and shaking under me. No matter that it only happened a few times a year; I detested those earthquakes that happen so quickly, so unexpectedly. You're sleeping, or sitting at your desk, your mind on everything but the possible jeopardy of the planet, when all of a sudden the walls begin to creak. I'd look at anything that hung from the ceiling, potted plant, wind chime, anything, to see if it was swaying even the least bit. If it was, then watch out. The world was about to wobble. First would come the tiniest groan. Wood resisting the movement beneath it. Then *crrrraaaackkkkk!* And your mouth tastes suddenly black and evil, and your heart does a boogie-woogie in your chest, and you realize in that instant—my God—there's no place to go! Ditches and basements for tornados, high ground for hurricanes and floods, but nowhere to go in an earthquake. That word becomes a mantra: *nowhere.*

Having agreed on the Florida move, MacKay and I closed the office, bid Helen and a few other friends goodbye, and packed. Five days and two flat tires later, we were in St. Seminole, Florida. I found our house on the Internet, though I couldn't do it again if I tried. It was a fluke. I usually can't find anything on the Internet, but anonymous entities finagling to bill my Visa or MasterCard for dubious unwanted goods. The place is a sprawling affair in central Florida on one of the highest points in an area thick with giant, moss-dripping trees. The city of St. Seminole has the same kind of nostalgic feel as St. Augustine, though more upscale. Our house sits on five acres surrounded by Dinah and Nolan's cattle ranch, which forms an L around our property, and a winding, red clay lane that disappears into a stand of woods behind us, separating us from Terry's place. Terry's an honest-to-goodness rodeo cowboy who earns his living roping Brahmas. He has five horses that give me no end of gazing pleasure.

The house we bought is too big, but MacKay had this notion that we were going to entertain all of the southern relatives he hadn't seen in years and maybe even talk his mother into moving in with us. Turned out he had a couple of chances of that happening: fat and slim. She's married to her job, absolutely loves it. Besides, she has a lot of responsibility as an Executive Secretary. It falls to her to pick up company VIPs when they arrive at the airport. Plus she takes care of their corporate taxes, or at least prepares them for the CPA. And she's very involved with her church. There's no way she'd ever leave Miami, even if she were the only Caucasian left in Little Haiti. It's *her* house, paid for since 1948. Her boy was raised there, she was widowed there, and by thunder she'll bar the windows and doors before she'll even entertain the idea of moving. So MacKay and I rattled around in a four-thousand-square-foot house, trying to get our Florida footing.

Not that we were alone. There's Gracie, the old black lab that was on the property when we got there, and Shadow who stepped in front of a diesel out on the country road beside us. A two hundred dollar vet bill makes Shadow ours, I don't care who birthed her. There's Sparkie, a mixed German Shepherd-Dingo that we rescued from an abusive home; Puggie the Pekingese who belonged to my father before he died, plus Precious and Itty-Bit, the tom cats.

This is the long way of telling you how I came to be in the state (as in emotional condition) I was in when Helen called on that dark and stormy night. I'm working up to present day, so be patient.

MacKay thought he could pick up some detective work, being so close to the Orlando film community, but it turned out the studios there weren't really about making movies. They're about tourists and theme parks, and they have plenty of minimum wage security, thank you. He was all right about it at first. I mean, the fellow had five acres to mow, a pool to clean, and a huge house to maintain, not to mention a workshop where he could whittle to his heart's content. There were constant glitches in the fence that surrounds the property and, as soon as he'd finish mowing the back forty, it was time to start over again. So, it wasn't that he didn't have anything to do; it was that he was bored out of his mind. He wanted to nail somebody. He wanted to lurk in parking lots and follow horny men to wherever they were going. He also missed the women in his life, I came to realize, though I didn't learn about that until after he was gone.

It was nearly Christmas; I was actually longing for the hustle-bustle of L.A. (I had these spells from time to time. Until the garbage truck rumbled by, reminding me of the sounds I associate with earthquakes). MacKay went to bed one night unusually quiet. I lay there, knowing he was awake, and waiting for him to tell me what was on his mind. Finally, in the darkness, he said, "I really hate St. Seminole."

"I know," I said from my place a million miles away from his.

"I really hate this house."

"Well, it's ours now."

"I'm going to Miami."

That wasn't unusual. He was spending about two weeks out of each month there anyway. But then he added, "I'm going to live with Mom."

Oops. Live with? Did I hear live with? I think I gulped. I dunno. I do know my voice came out thinner than I'm used to hearing it when I said, "When were you thinking of doing this?"

"Tomorrow."

Oh. Tomorrow.

We didn't say anything else and I suspect he was as long in dropping off to sleep as I was. Tomorrow. I couldn't even think ahead. My mind went numb. I stared into the darkness. *No. That won't happen. No way would he walk off and leave me with this house and all these grounds. And the* animals. *Nah. We've been married too long for him to do something like this.*

Cut now to dawn. MacKay was up and packing his overnight bag and a larger suitcase. I got up and made coffee. While it was brewing, I walked around picking up this and that of his and saying, "How about this, hon? Wanna take it?"

"Naw. I'll just take a few things for now. Till I'm settled. I'll come back for the rest of the stuff later."

Oh.

An hour after that I was standing out at the front gate, waving as he turned onto the county road and soon disappeared from sight. The last thing I saw of him was his hand out the window, up above the roof-line of the Nissan, jiggling his goodbye.

I stood there, in that tiny spot on those giant five acres, and felt nothing. It wasn't happening. The dogs looked questioningly down the empty road, then back up at me for reassurance. That's when I broke down and cried until my head hurt and my nose was so swollen I couldn't get a peep of air through either nostril.

We had no money to split; it had all gone on the house and the move. I had no job, no income. He's still living at home in the room he grew up in, while Momma works and cooks the meals. *Ninety-two years old,* for cryin' in the beer.

My pool became a fancy shade of slime green, the animals walked through the front porch screens, and I didn't have money enough to fix them. The grass needed the fine touch of a machete. *What to do, what to do,* I found myself moaning as I sat in the middle of the big, empty king-size bed. I became immobile. I was petrified. New state, no friends, no income. No MacKay. And then I found the stack of love letters.

He'd left several boxes that had never been unpacked since our move. They were in a corner of the garage, a place that seemed to be the social center for every black widow within a holler and a shout of our property. I killed seven of them before I decided I'd better move MacKay's things and spray. I trudged to an outbuilding where we stored assorted debris, hauled out a few boxes that were in good condition, and began to transfer his goods from one to the other. And there they were. In a box within a box. Letters from Norma and Renee and Mary and Alice, and great Lord, can you believe it, letters sent to a box rental on Hollywood Boulevard, covering every year of our marriage. The blood drained from my face. My heart wasn't racing; it had come to a standstill.

I went back in my mind to try to find some signal, some clue, some warning. *Oh, the wife knows,* they always say. *She just doesn't want to admit the truth. She's in denial.* That's bull. I did not know, was not in denial. In my honest opinion, MacKay was one of the most upstanding, most decent human beings I'd ever met. I'd never particularly wanted to be married. I loved independence. But when your path crosses the likes of MacKay Wallace, you join hands and happily agree to go the distance together. I'd married my best friend. And now I suddenly realized that he had never been a friend. Friends don't do that to each other. By this time, he'd been gone for nearly a month.

I wasn't even tempted to write him one of those ten page notes like we did in high school when spurned by the love of our short life. I had no intention of pouring out my heart with how-could-you. What would I gain? He knew what he was doing when he did it. If what I thought had mattered, he wouldn't have done it. Besides, the love letters went back years and years and continued up to the last few months, these addressed to a rental box in St. Seminole. It hit me that MacKay had never been married. Never. We'd shared things, but not marriage. And you know what? It's his loss. Not that I'm such a prize, but I realized that he would never know that warm, comfortable feeling that comes with looking at the person you love across the breakfast table. All right, let's not romanticize. He had terrible morning breath. But he was so solid. So *there.* And I was so safe with him. I could do anything because my friend was there to give me a wink or shoulder rub. I pushed away the vision of Alice's shoulder rub. Never mind Renee's and Mary's. Those hands. Those hard-knuckled, soft-palmed hands. I thought I knew them and they weren't even knowable. The knuckles I kissed had plunged under another woman's hemline and the thought made me physically ill.

IT ISN'T JEALOUSY, it's betrayal. Suddenly you have no confidence in your own ability to make judgments. If you can be fooled that long, to that degree, what kind of a dummy are you? I'd ask myself. Myself didn't know. Myself didn't much like me. I don't like stupidity and when I'm the one being stupid, it's especially unacceptable. Ego? Not exclusively. It's deeper than that. The self-confidence is brutally kicked out from under you. I itemized a litany of standard clichés: no one can do to you what you don't give them permission to do (did I send a message that it was okay to cheat on me?), we give off signals to others that tell them how they are to treat us (do I have a doormat sign on me?), we are the most hurt when we have unrealistic expectations of others (oh, s'cuse me…I guess it was silly to expect fidelity and truth from a mate. Where was my head?). In the end, I was left feeling not independent and grandly free, but deflated. MacKay didn't define who I was, but he made me doubt who I thought I was. I thought I was someone who deserved honesty. I thought I was a pretty good someone whom someone I loved would never intentionally hurt. What I thought and what I found out about myself were two entirely different animals.

Over the next few days, as I pondered my future (suddenly so re-arranged! Talk about lack of control over one's destiny), I realized St. Seminole had no art galleries. I paint. A little bit. No training, but Grandma Moses didn't study art either, I've heard. I drove to an Altamonte Springs shopping center fifteen or so miles away and bought a couple of canvases and a few bottles of acrylic and set up shop in the garage among a new generation of black widows. The results weren't too terrible, but I'm still trying to figure who'll buy them. A little workshop on the property a dozen or so steps from the side of the house had once been used as an architect's studio. I'm fixing it up bit-by-bit to become my studio. Think I'll call it something like the Master's Prodigy.

I was out there hanging curtains when the storm broke. The sky had become ominously dark, the wind had kicked up to gale force, and lightning was striking too close for comfort. I got down off a step stool, slapped my hands to get the attention of Puggie, Shadow, Grace, and Sparkie, then we sprinted across the wet grounds to my front door, drenched to the bone. I was still closing windows around the house when the phone rang and Helen asked me to come to Los Angeles.

THREE

HELEN LIVED IN STUDIO CITY, a colony nestled between two famous canyons, Coldwater and Laurel, a stone's throw from downtown Los Angeles. One side of it backs up to the Ventura hills, the other stretches to the monotony of several bedroom communities lumped together in two descriptive words: The Valley. On the other side of the hills, you'll find Hollywood. Heading toward L.A. proper on Ventura Boulevard is Universal City, made up primarily of Universal Studios and the Universal Hilton Hotel. Before you reach that turnoff you'll come to the Barham Street bridge that takes you into Burbank where, despite what you might think, is where the majority of studios are located. Warner Brothers is there, Disney's there, so is Columbia. NBC is across the street from the ivy-covered English-style Tudor mansion that houses dick clark cinema productions (the little letters are his idea, not mine). On the same side of the street as Clark's place is an unpretentious post production house where most of "The X Files" sound effects were recorded.

Johnny Carson used to say on his late night show that he was coming to you live from Burbank, California, "The little town where anything can happen—but nothing ever does." It's changed a lot since then.

Before I married MacKay, I lived on Palm Avenue, not too far from where Debbie Reynolds was born. The cottage has since been torn down and a condo stands in its place. Concrete has replaced the little orange grove in the back.

MacKay owned a house in Sun Beach and that's where we set up housekeeping. One of the few southern California beach towns I find acceptable, it's south of Los Angeles, butted up against Long Beach. Most coastal communities consist of little more than roof-covered mattresses where young adults engage in the noisy ritual of puberty celebration. Sun Beach, in contrast, is a cobble-stoned haven of seclusion for those wanting peace and quiet after a week of coping with the masses.

It took fourteen years of wedded bliss to get us thoroughly sick of the tedious commute to our Sunset Boulevard office. We ended up selling our home to Helen and Donne, who gave it to Lane and Richard as a wedding present, apricot trees and all. Like Fred and Ethel and Desi and Lucy, we moved next door to our best friends, in a modest yellow ranch-style house, balanced precariously on a Studio City hill. Solid as a rock, a geologist said before we bought the place. It'll take more'n an earthquake to knock this baby down. Odd thing about California. In other parts of the country when you're thinking of buying a house, you bring in the termite inspectors; in California, you bring in a geologist to tell you if you're buying on rock or landfill or, God forbid, a fault line (there's actually one that runs through the heart of Hollywood).

A MID-MORNING FLIGHT from Orlando to Los Angeles International Airport was the best I'd been able to book for myself after Helen and I hung up, a flight that put me, at five-thirty on a Monday, April eighteenth, smack in the middle of one of the things I'd gone cross-country to escape: traffic. Mind-boggling, fender-snapping, rear-end bumping, sit-and-wait-in-the-middle-of-a-freeway traffic. Even though I'd spent years doing exactly this same thing, in exactly this same spot, I was feeling anything but nostalgic. I was hot and tired and my stomach was gnawing on my backbone, demanding something more substantial than the two pretzels I'd had on the plane.

I maneuvered the Toyota rental off Ventura Boulevard, turned a hard left onto Spring Drive, and climbed a narrow, winding road that, phony as everything else that has to do with the film community, looked as if I'd suddenly arrived in the countryside. It sounded like the country. It felt like the country. But it was only two blocks back down the lane to heavy commerce, grime and crime.

To my right, the cliff dropped sharply into a field of tree-tops, their trunks far below, buried alongside Coldwater Canyon Drive. To my left, mansions of all colors and descriptions sat back from the road. A castle, straight out of a Robin Hood adventure, perched in the crook of a hairpin curve at the end of the street, but I wouldn't be going that far. Helen's Bavarian-style guest cottage marked the entrance to her property. My old yellow house was beside it.

I turned off Spring Drive and followed a gravel lane behind the cottage to a gigantic gray stucco home nearly hidden by gigantic live oaks. "Gigantic" is a Hollywood word. Everything's gigantic in Hollywood. Movie openings. Restaurant openings. New offices, new office buildings. Five-foot-eight Sylvester Stallone is "gigantic." Al Pacino is "gigantic." Dustin Hoffman is "gigantic." I sat beside Hoffman one day on a concrete bench in the lobby of Columbia studios. I was struck not so much by the girth of his nose, but by the fact that his feet didn't touch the floor. His talent, I have to admit though, really is gigantic.

I parked the car and locked it, because in broad daylight in southern California, even in your own front yard, you're likely not to have a vehicle when you come back outside fifteen minutes later if you don't batten the thing down. Helen's yard man had left a hose slung across the walkway. I pitched it aside and continued on to the front door. There was a stillness in the air that was somehow unnerving. I had the feeling that a thousand secret eyes were on me, watching my every move. I glanced around, half expecting to see yellow eyeballs peering down from the trees. I lifted the brass knocker, let it drop and rang the bell instead. Two ding dongs and the door flew open. Helen looked like hell.

"Thank God," she muttered, pulling me inside and slamming the door behind us. As soon as the chain lock was in place, she said, "You're here" and it was as if she could, at long last, rest easy. Matt Dillon had arrived. The ranch would be saved from cattle-rustlers and bank foreclosure. I opened my mouth to speak, but she pulled me to her so roughly and so close that I could feel her chest starting to rise and fall in advance of an onslaught of tears. The dam broke and I could only imagine how long she'd held it in.

"It's okay," I said, patting her back. It was a lie, of course. I didn't even know why I was there, so how could I tell her it was going to be okay? Besides, horrible and arrested and murdered aren't words to indicate things might be made okay anytime soon.

"Come in, come in," she said finally, stepping away from me. She dabbed at her eyes with the back of one hand and led me to the living room with the other. I followed meekly, suddenly at a loss for words with a friend to whom I could have said anything. If I could have thought of anything to say.

The living room, so familiar to me, covered the entire back of the house. Ordinarily it overlooked a forest of trees, but today the drapes were pulled tightly. The only light came from a Tiffany on a side table near the gigantic white sofa. In front of the gigantic rock fireplace.

"Sit down," she said, indicating a spot beside her on the sofa. I chose, instead, a footstool and pulled it up to face her. Her eyes glistened with fresh, unshed tears. Taller than my own five foot seven, there was a smallness about her at this moment, a vulnerability I'd never seen before.

"I'm a mess," she sighed in a tiny voice. Then she drew in a sharp breath and stuck out her chin. "Tell me about you," she said. "Tell me how you're doing in Florida and wh—"

"You tell me," I interrupted. I nailed her with a look that said to cut the bull; a look she knew, but had never had directed at her before. "Tell me what happened."

"Oh, God, Katie..."

I reached over to pull the chain on a floor lamp beside us, but she caught my hand in midair. "No! No lights." Her eyes darted in the direction of the closed drapes and, farther along the west wall, to a bank of three low windows, also covered. "They sit in the woods and watch," she whispered. "Like preying things."

I didn't have to ask. I knew she meant photographers.

Her hands fluttered in her lap. Her lids sagged over those watery eyes. "They peek over the windowsills if I leave a curtain open. Their cameras are always pointed at the house…" Her voice trailed off. Those were the stares I'd felt out front when I came in. Where were the vultures hidden? Didn't they feel foolish, grown men and women, crouched among the foliage on someone's private property? The answer was no, they didn't. Helen shivered. Her elbows were resting now on her knees, her face buried in her hands.

The room was quiet except for Helen's muffled sobs. I gave her arm a little squeeze and let my hand linger there while I looked around the room in which I'd spent so many afternoons and evenings.

Finally I said, "I'll get us some coffee," and got up, feeling awkward and inadequate. I was there to hold my friend's hand, but I couldn't find a damn thing to say that would give her a moment of comfort.

I flipped a wall switch in the kitchen, which kicked on a ceiling fluorescent. *Immaculate as always,* I thought vaguely as I moved toward the white marble counter where Helen had already laid out two mugs, the pink sugar stuff and a carton of half-and-half. I knew where the spoons were and found two of them. She looked up when I went back into the living room.

"Tell me what happened," I said for the second time, settling onto the footstool. I put her cup beside her, under the Tiffany, and held on to my own with both hands. A scene flashed in my mind, like they say happens just before you die. I saw me sitting on this same footstool not all that long ago, and Helen, face shining with happiness, telling me that Lane was up for a very important comeback role in a movie (it never happened). And, years earlier, this same footstool and Helen's face gray with grief, telling me about the plane crash that took her son-in-law and his crew. I didn't know her very well then. I was there with MacKay. He was in a corner, talking to Donne, sunlight streaming over him from the big bay window, and I was thinking more about how I'd like to jump MacKay's bones that very moment, right there on the rug in front of the fireplace, than I was about Helen's tragedy. Another scene. Same footstool. "Lanie's getting married," Helen beamed to a small group she'd invited for dinner.

"A wonderful man, actually a few years younger than Lanie, but who cares about that kind of thing anymore?" She'd laughed. "Richard's a television producer. He wants to find just the right screenplay for Lanie's return to film. Isn't that terrific?"

We all agreed it was terrific. And now she was staring into her coffee cup and the terrific moment had long since passed. Richard was dead and Lane was accused of killing him.

I'd seen a newspaper at the airport that morning. Richard's demise hadn't made headlines, though it did make the front page, at least in the *Orlando Sentinel.* A small item near the bottom, under a blurred picture of Lane and her husband: *Hollywood Producer Murdered.* The line under that: *Actress Accused of Slaying.* The story had gone on to report that Richard David Wagnor, 48, and his wife, "one-time sweetheart of the American Cinema," Lane Allison, 53, were entertaining in their Sun Beach, California, home on Sunday, April 17th, when an argument broke out between them. The event, according to the newspaper account, ended with Lane shoving her husband down a flight of stairs, which resulted in his death. The shoving part came from an eyewitness at the party, the part about his death from the local coroner. Details were sketchy and the brief article concluded with a list of Richard's producing credits, mostly television, and a longer list of Lane's early films, mostly forgotten. It went on to state that Richard was survived by a daughter, Royalee, 21, from a previous marriage, as well as stepchildren, Caroline, 21, and Michael, 19.

I'm not very good at numbers, but remind me never to let a reporter anywhere near my checkbook. Follow me here. If I'm a tad older than Rita Moreno, and Lane's a bit older than me, that doesn't make her fifty-three. Or if she is, then I'm getting younger every day, and I want some of what she's having.

Who knows how old Richard Wagnor really was?

Hollywood.

"She didn't want to have the party," Helen was saying. I quit counting on my fingers and toes, and tuned back in, waiting for her to elaborate. "It was mainly for Richard's friends—for the garden group at the church. He served on the Grounds

Committee, you know." I didn't know. "He wanted to show his appreciation for the hard work they'd done on the spring planting program."

"Lane..." I prompted, trying to steer her back on track.

"She didn't feel like they were really friends or even that much interested in the church grounds. They made such a fuss about Richard being a TV producer...gushed over him, that sort of thing. It was uncomfortable for her. The fact she'd been a star...not that she ever thought of herself as a star, but they did. They'd introduce her to new members of the congregation like she was the biggest draw in movies today. It embarrassed her. She's another person now. A wife, a mother, a stepmother...and she loves that role better than anything she's ever done. She's told me that a million times. If only she'd met Richard earlier in her life. He was so good to her. They were like newlyweds. But these church people...phonies. That's how she described them."

I nodded and said *ummmmmm* and stuck out my bottom lip like I was thinking heavily but, in truth, I didn't know the people, didn't really know Lane or Richard, and I didn't have anything to add to the conversation. "Richard's sister was there, of course." Helen said "of course" like I should know this. "She practically runs the church. And she's always let it be known how much she dislikes Lanie."

I tried to think if I'd ever met his sister and drew a blank.

Helen said, "Anyway, they got into this big argument—"

"Lane and her sister-in-law?"

"No. Lanie and Richard. I don't know what it was about. I haven't been able to talk to her." Her voice caught. When her eyes fastened on mine there was panic in them. "They took her away and..."

I waited again while Helen sobbed into her hands. When she could catch her breath, she swallowed hard. "They arrested her," she whispered. "It was all over the news last night...handcuffed. Can you imagine?"

I put my coffee cup on the floor and wrapped my arms around her again. No, I could not imagine. After a moment, she took a tissue from her skirt pocket and wiped her nose. "I've got to pull myself together. This is crazy." She drew in a sharp, desperate breath. "You are going to stay and help, aren't you, Katie?"

I didn't have a clue how I could be of any help except to do what I was doing. Be there. Hold her hand. Listen. Beyond that, well, if Lane pushed her husband to his death, then she pushed him and those consequences would have to be dealt with. My heart ached for Helen's loss, for Lane's predicament, but no one except a very good lawyer could do much to help either of them.

"Talk to her," Helen said suddenly.

"Surely if you can't see her, they won't let—"

"Talk to Dorothy."

"Dorothy?"

"Richard's sister."

"Oh, Helen—" If there was an incredulous tone to my voice, it was intentional.

"She's the one who claims Lanie shoved Richard. Says she saw it with her own eyes. But maybe…I mean, it's only her word. Maybe, in the heat of the moment, Dorothy imagined that she saw Lanie push him, or maybe she just saw a chance to hurt Lanie—not realizing the extent of the damage she was doing until later. Dorothy has a flair for the dramatic and a terrible vengeful streak. Don't you see? A little fib and she'd get her own picture in the paper! On television! It would become *her* moment. She'd get attention and, at the same time, punish Lane for marrying her brother. Maybe now that so much has happened, she's looking for a way to take it back, to admit she made it up."

False testimony is serious business. I got to my feet and went to the window, where I pulled the drape back a fraction of an inch. Sunlight bounced off of something deep inside the foliage out there. A camera lens? How much would one photograph of Helen, the mother of the accused, fetch from a sleazy magazine? Not as much as one of a terrified and grief-stricken Lane suddenly appearing at the door. The paper said she had been released on a million dollars bail. I figured that the photographers thought it was worth the wait. I let the drape fall back into place, thinking about Richard's sister. If the woman had already given her statement to the police, she wasn't apt to change it for me.

False testimony. Serious business.

"Have you tried talking to her yourself?" I asked.

Helen shook her head. "I wouldn't be able to hold my tongue. I'd have to tell her what I really think, what I've always thought of her and that wouldn't do anybody any good." She rubbed her temples with her fingers. "I can't face the woman." Then she quickly added, "But somebody's got to."

FOUR

IT'S QUITE A DRIVE from Studio City out to Long Beach where Dorothy and Harmon Ermaling live. He's a retired financial analyst for a brokerage firm that deals primarily in funding major motion pictures. We're talking a firm that finances films of Titanic proportions. A mind like Harmon Ermaling's could probably even figure out how old Lane and Richard really were.

I left Helen's place early the next day, after the morning rush, and took the Ventura Freeway to the 101, otherwise known as the Hollywood Freeway, where I veered south. The traffic was insane as usual. I breathed diesel fuel and managed to elude every non-English speaking driver on the road between Universal Studios and Dodger Stadium, where I swung onto Harbor Freeway, racing at a snail's pace in a southwesterly direction. I knew those folks didn't speak English because of their abundant use of sign language. I was cutting now through a part of Los Angeles that had become famous for its riots. Soon I'd plunge into the stench of Carson, heading toward the Pacific Ocean and a breath of fresh air. As I gained on downtown Long Beach, I made a left onto Ocean Boulevard and drove in the direction of the old Seal Beach Naval Station. A community of new homes had been built in the last eight years near Martial Stadium, where the Ermalings lived. The trip took an hour on good days, two hours on normal days and up to three hours if it drizzled or a truck turned over en route. I had plenty of time to review everything Helen had told me over cold crab cakes the night before. There wasn't much to it, really. Except for the devastating finale.

Helen said Richard had given a party for his church garden group, a grand total of seven people. Not surprisingly, most were women: Henny Thornton, long-time church member and a friend of Richard's since before his marriage to Lane; Joanna and Farley Norco; Belinda, the church's secretary; John and Suzanne Marlowe; and finally, Dorothy, who had come alone. Belinda, the Norcos, and the Marlowes were going on from the party to a play at the Long Beach Civic Center and had left early. At the time of the argument between Lane and Richard, no one was there from church except Dorothy and Henny. Richard's daughter, Royalee, was spending the weekend at the house. She and Caroline, a student at the UCLA-Long Beach campus, were in the family room listening to CDs when they heard the commotion. They didn't investigate, however, until they heard Richard tumble down the stairs, his cries mixed with those of Dorothy and Lane. Royalee reached her father first. He was already dead, having hit his head on the corner of a step. Michael, Lane's son, had been clearing tables out on the patio when he heard the screams. It was Michael who called paramedics from the kitchen phone.

According to Dorothy's statement to the police, and later to reporters, she, Henny, and Richard had been standing on the back patio talking when he excused himself and went inside. Next thing they knew, they heard Richard and Lane screaming at one another from someplace in the house. It sounded like it was coming from upstairs. Dorothy, curious, went inside and was near the bottom of the stairs when she saw Lane shove Richard from the top landing. Dorothy said that Henny had rushed in right behind her and was privy to the whole thing, too. Royalee and Caroline raced from the family room, but Caroline hung back with Dorothy and Henny, while Royalee fell to the floor beside her father. His head was still cradled in her arms when paramedics arrived. There was nothing anyone could do. The police appeared on the scene a little while later.

Helen admitted that things got blurry beyond that point. Yellow police tape went up at the Wagnor home, she was sure of that, and neighbors jammed into the yard while being pushed back by the cops. She remembered seeing a couple of local reporters who arrived seconds after the police (having heard the news on their police scanner, she surmised). It seemed that before anyone could count to ten, especially if it was reporters doing the counting, news vans were racing up the street and parking everywhere, even on adjoining lawns. Meanwhile, Dorothy, Henny, Lane, Royalee, Michael and Caroline were interviewed separately by police detectives. What I gathered from what Helen repeated was that standard police protocol was followed: perimeters examined, body examined, the scene photographed, sketches made. Everything was duly processed. There seemed to be no big mystery. For the police, it was business as usual.

Everyone knows that eyewitnesses can make mistakes, get confused, or withhold information—or lie about what they saw. But the Wagnor tragedy was cut-and-dried. Richard and Lane argued, she pushed him in the heat of the moment, and Dorothy witnessed the whole thing. It was clear that Richard was dead and it was clear he had died as a result of his fall down the stairs.

Lane was taken into custody, booked, and then released on one million dollars bail raised by Helen, who was unable to reach her lawyer on a Sunday night, but did manage to locate one of his junior partners at his home in Sherman Oaks. The Wagnor house was bombarded with media who continued to arrive in a steady stream throughout the rest of the day and evening and into the night. The same night that Helen called me in Florida.

Helen and I turned on all the radios and television sets in the house in an effort to hear what distortion was in the works at any given minute. National news figures were beginning to arrive in private planes. What they thought they'd find was a riddle to me. Caroline moved into the apartment of a friend who was away on a foreign exchange program and whose parents offered her the key. Michael returned to the student film production he was helping crew out in the Mojave Desert near Joshua Tree (he'd been home for the weekend). I doubted he was getting much work done, but at least he was protected from reporters and photographers who weren't allowed on the set. Michael, it turned out, was a student at Long Beach Community College, but he was taking a two month break to work on a University of Southern California film project.

Royalee, interning at a Fresno television station, left for home as I was flying across the country. She lived near her mother.

Arlene, Richard's ex-wife, a botany teacher retired from Fresno City Campus.

As soon as Lane was released from custody, Helen and a family friend spirited her into a van and, under cover of night, took her to a cabin in Onaga Valley, owned by a writer they knew and trusted. It was actually only a couple of miles from where Michael was on location. In case all of this geography is confusing you, Joshua Tree, the Mojave and Onaga Valley are all in the general direction of Palm Springs, only further north, and why anyone would want to live there is beyond me. A passion for scorpions, lizards the size of St. Bernards, the biggest, hairiest, spiders ever created (why'd Noah take two of them on the Ark?), sand that burns the foot and blinds the eye, and heat to melt your teeth, is a must for anyone even traveling through that forsaken land, let alone actually residing there. Mojave Desert. Boot camp for Hell. Horrible place in my humble opinion. Anyway, that's where Lane went, to the cabin of a New York based writer who wasn't using it, anyway. I know if I were a reporter and someone told me Lane was hiding out in Onaga Valley, I'd find another story to pursue.

If you're wondering, as I was, why Lane had to hide, I'll explain it the way Helen explained it to me. After all, Lane Allison hadn't made a movie in several years, and the last one was a bomb. Richard, a television producer of mostly documentaries, wasn't a Hollywood name to contend with either, so why the enormous publicity?

It's easy to explain.

Everyone was so turned on by the publicity generated by the O. J. Simpson case, and Laci Peterson's plight, and JonBenet Ramsey (one aging athlete and two unknowns) that the media had begun looking for more windows of opportunity where an incident could be accelerated into an Event. Books. Movie deals. Magazine articles. Interviews. Talk shows. In other words, there really are times when the media creates not the news itself, but the spectacle around the news. This was one of those times. A lot of low-life leeches would become rich on this one horrific incident.

Lane had once been a very big star. Her stock-in-trade was her innocence. America loved her. What happens when the country's one-time darling retires? She goes nuts and kills her husband out of professional jealously or stifled rage or the pure undiluted need to make headlines. That's what was being tossed around on *Oprah* and *The Late Show with David Letterman* and even on the distinguished *Meet the Press*. Pop psychologists were analyzing Lane's motives, even though they'd never met her and knew nothing about her relationship with her husband. Networks were devoting entire segments to the subject. And what fueled the flame? The fact that no one knew where Lane was hiding. It had become a huge scavenger hunt. A game—with Lane as the prize.

So, you say, why doesn't Lane just come out of hiding? That would chill the interest, wouldn't it?

Think about it. Lane had been stalked twice in her life, both times by nut cases willing to go to any extreme for the publicity. Who knew who was out there, waiting to stalk again? To hurt one of the children? Society is on the high end of madness and now Lane had to face not only the grief of losing her husband, a man who, according to Helen, was the passion of her life, but the added horror of possible imprisonment.

I'd hide, too.

Helen got no further with the story because by then we were both in tears. Mine were tears of rage, hers of unbearable heartbreak. How dare the media do this? Even if Bill Clinton were still the president, and he stuck his arm up another woman's dress, it would be a yawn. Yeah, yeah...been there, seen that. Next. Who'll be next? Lane Allison, of course.

What I couldn't imagine was what I'd say to Dorothy, the sister-in-law. She saw what she saw. What was she supposed to do? Say she didn't see it? Still...Helen needed to know I was there for her and if being there meant a chat with Dorothy, I'd do it.

Things would not be okay, at least not for Helen and Lane, anytime in the foreseeable future—if ever.

I'D HAD THE CAR RADIO tuned to a jazz station, but turned it off when the news came on and the lead story was The Disappearance of Lane Allison. The subject had gone from serious (death and murder are serious) to absurd (she'd kill to get her name in the papers again). What I resented most was the lack of concern for Richard and Lane's children. Royalee was devastated by the loss of her father. She was the apple of his eye; spoiled, according to Helen, but totally devoted to her dad. Caroline and Michael were walking zombies. They, of course, knew where their mother had gone, but they dare not try to get to her for fear of leading the media to her. Caroline didn't even want to go to her grandmother's home, preferring to simply disappear into her friend's apartment where no one would bother her and she could grieve in solitude. Royalee had lost her father, Caroline and Michael lost their stepdad (they'd already lost their real father to a plane crash years before, don't forget), and now they were losing their mother, too. Show me the humor in that. Show me the "game."

I FOUND THE WHITE clapboard Ermaling house just as Helen had described it from her one visit there a couple of years back when she had attended a surprise birthday party in Richard's honor. Lavender, pink and blue pansies lined the flagstone path to the front door. A bird bath sat in a circle of white rock near the front steps, which I climbed before crossing a covered expanse of blue porch where I rang the doorbell. It echoed faintly in three tones inside the house. I turned to watch the progress of a bee as it circled a plant hanging from a porch rafter. I was debating fight or flight when someone said, "Whatever you're selling, we're not buying." The voice was male, had a hint of humor in it, and surprised me since I hadn't heard the front door open.

"Oh. Hello." I smiled brightly, turning to face a man who was short, balding, and not handsome by any stretch of imagination, but not unpleasant looking either. A favorite professor or uncle. I recognized him from the Wagnor wedding and Donne's funeral. We'd never spoken before and I doubted that he would remember me. He didn't.

His eyes were becoming wary. "Can I help you? That is if you're not from the media."

"No, sir. Actually…could I talk to your wife?"

"You won't be talking to anybody if you don't state your business."

"Katlin Wallace." I stuck my hand in his direction.

He made no move to open the screen door that separated us.

I gave it another shot. "I'm a friend of—"

"Who's there?" Harmon Ermaling turned to watch his wife approach in an electric wheelchair. She was heavy-set, actually fat, and, like many overweight women, had a flawless complexion and unlined face. The pushy one at family gatherings. She hadn't been in a wheelchair when I saw her on those other occasions. I wondered what had happened.

When Dorothy reached us, she looked up at me curiously, trying to place the face, I assumed. Her dark eyes suddenly lit with recognition. "Helen Allison's friend?"

"That's right."

She immediately became suspicious and I noticed that Harmon's expression became guarded. The intelligence in his eyes intrigued me. Very bright, this Harmon Ermaling. Not one to be underestimated.

"Did Helen send you?" Dorothy asked.

"To be honest—"

Harmon stepped between us, his hand on the inside door as if to close it. "We don't want trouble with her. We've all been through a lot these last forty-eight hours."

My face felt hot. I was embarrassed to be standing out on a porch, under a droning bee, trying to figure a way to get Dorothy to admit she'd lied. Which I doubt she did. "Well, she just asked if I'd stop by to see if we…you and I…you and Dorothy and I… could talk about—"

"Her daughter killed my brother." It was a cold, harsh statement delivered by Dorothy.

"Well, yes, that's what I'm hearing. Helen had hoped…look,

uh…it's really hard to talk about it out here on the street. Could I come inside for a minute?"

"I don't think so." It was Harmon. "Talking isn't going to make Helen or anyone else feel any better. My wife's said everything she has to say to the police."

"I know, but—"

"Like my husband said, I gave my statement to the police." Dorothy's face flushed deeply with—what? Indignation? Anger? Her lips, already thin, became a straight pink line. The square jaw thrust itself to its full jutting position as she wheeled her chair into a tight circle and drove it out of sight, around a corner in the living room.

"Sorry to have troubled you," I mumbled to Harmon. "It's just that I promised Helen—"

He nodded and interrupted with, "I feel sorry for her, for all of us. But facts are facts." Then he gently—but firmly—closed the door in my face.

FIVE

I DROVE AROUND for a while, trying to decide what to do. I wasn't ready to tell Helen that I couldn't get Dorothy to talk to me. I had the uncanny feeling MacKay was sitting in the passenger seat, watching me with one black brow raised accusingly, giving me the kind of pathetic look he saved for when I attempted to work anything that had an electrical switch—an expression I came to loathe. An expression that drives wives to shout "Then do it yourself, bozo!" which, as I learned, doesn't make for ties that bind.

I decided to grab a sandwich at Hoff's Hut in downtown Belmont Shores, a Long Beach neighborhood cupped alongside the bay. It was only a few blocks from the Ermalings. I was in the mood for a broad umbrella under a sun that had finally burned off the morning smog and a temperature that was stretching toward the eighty mark. I was lucky enough to find a BMW easing away from the curb almost at the front door, slipped into its space, jammed a coin down the throat of a balky meter, and went inside.

I made my way to the upstairs terrace, found a table that was empty once I shooed away the starlings. A disinterested blonde (yeah, sure) waitress took my egg-salad-on-a-hard-roll order, poured a tall glass of tea from a chilled pitcher, and I was left with my thoughts. I squinted, readjusted the umbrella to allow for more shade, but what I was really doing was stalling. Next, when I ran out of busy work, I'd have to think. What to tell Helen, how to tell Helen, and, mostly, how to let her know that I'd exhausted my ability to "help"?

I glanced around to see if there were any familiar faces. Not surprisingly, there weren't. MacKay and I put in ten to twelve hour days at the agency and I wasn't one to join clubs or women's groups. I knew cops and cops' wives and the people down the hall in our Sunset Boulevard office building. That's about it. Wouldn't know my Sun Beach neighbors if I were sitting on them.

Thinking about cops reminded me that I wanted to call Donald Stuart before leaving town. Donald had been a good friend of mine and MacKay's, a career cop who had his knees shot out from under him and took early retirement rather than ride herd on a desk for the rest of his professional life. Last I heard, he was working as a police consultant on the television series *Cop Patrol,* one of those real-life productions with live cameras and live mics and cops being much more copperly than ordinary because they're cognizant of doing their duty while entertaining their kids at home, watching Dad on TV.

The egg salad was obviously going to be masterpiece in presentation; it'd been ten minutes and was still nowhere in sight. I got up, told my waitress I was going to use the pay phone and would be right back.

I found Donald's number in the phone book, dialed, got his machine telling me to leave my name, number, blah blah. I blahed back to it. Told him where I was having lunch if he was home but not picking up, where I was staying if he didn't hear my message until evening.

And then I did the inevitable. I thought about what to tell Helen.

It's a funny thing about thinking. I mean the kind of thinking where you have a definite idea of what you need and want to be thinking about. It doesn't come naturally. When you're driving along and your mind is cartwheeling this way and that and you're letting it play itself out, you can come up with some really good stuff, but try to rope that sucker brain into a corner and examine something under a mental microscope, and it's darned difficult. I'd start to think about what I'd say when I got back to Helen's place and my mind would go scudding off somewhere, conjuring up images of Dorothy's face turning that stunning shade of red. Or the sudden change in her husband's expression, from half-amused, to deeply analytical, to almost hostile. Quick changes.

I realized there was something about the look on Dorothy's face that bothered me, but I hadn't realized it at the time. That's why my mind wouldn't stay still. I wanted to think about Helen and our upcoming conversation. Mind wanted me to center on Dorothy. Like a kid pulling at the hem of my skirt, I finally heaved a sigh of surrender and turned my attention to the woman in the wheelchair.

What was there about it that I was supposed to know? Her eyes had gone hard when she realized who I was. And then, when I asked to talk to her, her face had flared crimson. Anger at my audacity to think I could have a private conversation with her? Me, a friend of Helen's? No...that wasn't the look. So what was it?

MacKay was nagging me, too. I could hear him saying, "Look at what you don't see, Kat. It's what you don't see that tells you everything." He had a great instinct for getting behind words and finding the person's true intention, often the opposite of what had been stated. I marveled at how he did that. I'll hear someone say something and unless it's as blatant as "I sure think you're nice" and they're holding a meat clever, ready to do me in, I'm apt to believe what I hear. I seem to miss the subtleties.

But back to Dorothy. The tugging at the back of my brain... what would MacKay be analyzing if he were here and had this same kind of uneasy feeling? It was as if something had happened right in front of me that I couldn't put my finger on.

Whatever it was would have to wait. I couldn't concentrate. I decided that, as soon I polished off the egg salad, I'd visit the house where MacKay and I had lived and which was now the scene of a crime. It was only a couple of miles north of Belmont Shores.

THE CALIFORNIA COAST is lined with beach communities, each blending into the other, one hardly distinguishable from the next. Belmont Shores crosses a grand old humpback bridge onto tiny Naples Island which serves as a link into Sun Beach. I stayed on Second Street, curved to the Pacific Coast Highway, and followed that to Seventh Street, past the University of Southern California-

Long Beach campus, onto a knoll that made up Bell Park off to one side of the highway, overlooking my old neighborhood. I parked the car and got out.

There was no one around at this hour, nearly one o'clock. Later, when it cooled a bit and naps were over, the playground with its four swing sets would be filled with mothers and kids. Around four-thirty the softball field would overflow with teens. After dinner, before it got dark, overweight dads would play catch with their boys and ride bikes with their families along the path that ran behind a tall stone fence which encircled the entire half-moon of a hundred or more houses beneath me. On the other side of the wall, a channel ran to meet the Pacific.

Even from here, I could see half a dozen news vans parked around my old place. Camp chairs were set up in the cul-de-sac and people I imagined to be bored reporters drank coffee or wrote in notepads on their laps. What did they think was going to happen, I wondered? The house was empty. Lane was out there in no man's land, Onaga Valley; Caroline was ensconced in her friend's Naples Island apartment; Michael was back on the set of the student film in Joshua Tree, and Royalee, Richard's daughter, was home in Fresno. Helen said they had no live-in maids or hired help, so what were the reporters doing? I remembered the same kind of scene during the O. J. Simpson mess. Vans jammed the streets around Simpson's Brentwood house (and, no, it wasn't a mansion. It was a big house on the corner of a neighborhood street), but O. J. wasn't there. Friends and family came and went, but no one gave interviews, so why the same tired report day after day from reporter after reporter? I decided to watch the news when I got back to Helen's to see what in the world they could be saying about this empty house in a tiny community tucked almost under the freeway.

I picked my way down the slope to a gate that opened onto the bike path. From there I followed the stone wall until I came to a wooden gate, maybe six feet high, that opened onto the far curve of the cul-de-sac. I'd planned to use one of the public access gates that opened onto a path leading into the neighborhood then, once on that side of the wall, double back across several backyards until I reached the Wagnor home. That's when it dawned on me that my plan wouldn't work. Not only would people panic, thinking a stranger, no doubt connected to the media, was on their property and maybe dial 911, but also some of the homes had backyard walls that hooked up to the stone wall, boxing them in and making it impossible for me to get past without hurdling someone's fence. Definitely not a good idea.

I went back to a spot along the wall directly behind my old house and looked around for something to stand on so that I could crawl over the wall into the backyard. I found a couple of small boulders, which of course I couldn't lift if my life depended on it. By scrunching down and putting my tailbone against the largest of these mothers, I was able to push against it until it inched closer to the wall. After that, all I had to do was climb up, throw one leg over, hoist myself up with both hands, and sling the other leg along behind me. I'd jump down and, presto, I'd be in the Wagnor's backyard. My old backyard. Problem was I couldn't get my damn leg up that high. I skinned my knee, bloodied my palm, and slammed my nose into the wall, trying to pull myself over. No luck. It was too tall and I was too short. It hit me that I was going about this all wrong. A stone wall is uneven. An uneven wall is bound to have a niche for a toe or two in it somewhere. I squatted down and searched and, sure enough, I saw a lot of possible toe-holes. I took off my sandals, butt-shoved the rock to a place where I could use it to gain some height, then wiggled my toes into the rough surface of the wall and, shazam, over I went.

It was both odd and not odd to be standing there with scuffed toes and a pair of shoes tucked under my arm, looking at the backyard where I'd exhausted myself sodding the grounds. The results were worth it. A yard the size of a postage stamp, bordered by lilies, azaleas and tiny tea roses, went along a path from the swing that hung from a branch of an apricot tree, all the way to the covered back patio. I'd sat in that swing so many times, mainly on Sunday afternoons, reading. The peach tree had finally committed hari-kari. It bore so much fruit, it had snapped off its own limbs. There was a stump now where the tree had stood all those years. One Easter I hung baskets on it and had a patio lunch for several policemen and their families. I guessed that the Wagnor's garden party must have looked similar to the way it looked that holiday with tables on the patio and a buffet set up under the dining room window.

Why didn't I feel a pang of something? Longing, nostalgia. Something. Instead, it was like remembering a movie. I could recall the scenes, but they weren't connected to me. We'd sold the house years back, but MacKay had only been out of my life for a matter of months. I was braced to feel a stab of pain when I saw the home we'd shared. Instead, I saw something I recognized, but no more than that. Maybe it was related to the fact I'd never much liked the place. I was glad when we sold it and moved into Studio City, closer to work and friends. Helen said Lane loved the home though, and so did Richard. That's good. Houses need to be loved; they can sense when it's lacking and so can its guests.

I crossed the patio to cup my hands against sliding glass doors that opened onto the living room. All I saw was the reflection of my face with a freshly-skinned nose. The drapes were closed. The lock and a safety device were firmly in place. I moved to a dining room window and saw me again. I went around to the side, to a window over the kitchen sink and, beside that, to a door that opened onto a tiny patio. Everything was battened down and covered up, and I was being as foolish as the reporters out front. What'd I think I'd gain by being here, I asked myself. I suppose I thought I was doing detective work of some kind, but in reality it was nonsense. I quickly turned around and got my hiney over the stone wall as unceremoniously as I'd arrived.

IT WAS NEARLY SIX before I walked in the door to Helen's house and found her sitting at the kitchen table, her face swollen, her eyes puffy and red. She had on a satin robe. Her hair, ordinarily neatly arranged in a coil at the base of her neck, went a dozen angles from her skull. She was holding a cold cup of coffee. She obviously hadn't heard me come in because she nearly jumped out of her skin when I said, "Helen?"

Her chin quivered. She lifted her eyes to meet mine. "They told me Lanie was in the hospital—" It was all she could manage before she broke down. I pulled out a chair across from her and leaned over far enough to remove the cup from her hands and wrap my own around them.

"Who said that?"

She shook her head as if to clear it. "I was taking a nap, maybe half an hour ago, I don't know…I'm losing track of time. The phone rang and I got up to answer it. A voice, a woman's voice, said that Lanie had been in an accident and was in the hospital, in the emergency room, and that I should come right over." When she ran her hand along the side of her face, her fingers were trembling. "My head was in a fog. I couldn't grasp what she was saying. What emergency room? What hospital? In Onaga Valley? What happened? Lane's out there all by herself and I know she's scared and, my God, I thought, what if she tried to…do…something to herself. She wouldn't do that…she loves the kids too much to do anything like that…but I couldn't understand…" Helen drew in a deep breath and looked at me with the kind of expression I've only seen in television documentaries, like when a baby seal is about to get its brains splattered by a towering humanoid and doesn't understand why.

"Did you call the hospital in Onaga Valley?"

She shook her head. "I'm afraid to. I think my line's tapped. Don't look at me like that, Katie. I hear all kinds of clicking when I'm talking on the phone. I started to go to my neighbor's house to use theirs, but then I realized I don't know if I can trust them. I mean, if they heard me ask for Onaga Valley information, and then I called the hospital there…People do crazy things for money, and magazines will pay top dollar to know where she is."

I thought about it for a second before jumping to my feet. "I'll be right back."

"Where are you going?" she called after me.

"Ten minutes," I said, leaving. "I'll be back in ten minutes."

I drove to the end of the street, where it intersected Ventura Boulevard, crossed over to Jerry's Deli, parked between it and a bank, and went inside. Jerry's is a well-known haunt for movie stunt men. MacKay and I had shared many a breakfast in there with the late Jock Mahoney, one of the most respected professionals in the business, and his wife, Autumn. His stepdaughter is Sally Field, though we never met her. Jock played the bad guy in early Tarzan movies then briefly became Tarzan himself after Weissmuller left films. Tarzan Goes to India comes and goes on American Movie Classics. I've caught it a couple of times.

I realized I was feeling more nostalgic about Jock and Autumn than I'd felt walking around barefoot in my old backyard. I snapped myself back to reality and shouldered my way through the noisy crowd toward a bank of pay phones near the rear exit.

Onaga Valley information informed me that they had no local hospitals. Closest one, a friendly operator told me, was in Palm Springs, some thirty-five miles down the mountain toward L.A. I called the hospital there, asked if Lane Allison had been admitted, and got a bored "no," which I believed. I also believed that whoever answered the phone had more on their mind than movie stars, and that the name Lane Allison didn't even ring a bell. I also doubted the person ever heard of Nicole Brown Simpson or JonBenet or Laci Peterson.

Fifteen minutes later, I was sitting on the edge of Helen's bed while she combed her hair at the dressing table. She was now wearing a casual silk jumpsuit. I told her what I'd found out, or rather what I didn't find out.

She looked at my reflection in the mirror while she continued to try to get her hair into some kind of order. "No…she's not in a hospital. I don't know why I almost bought their story. The woman who called didn't even properly identify herself. If she'd been a doctor or nurse, or even an administrator, she'd have said so. It was a news reporter." She turned to me, hands planted on her knees. This was the old take-charge Helen I'd known for so many years. "They were probably hoping I'd ask if they were calling from such-and-such hospital, which would tell them where she is, or at least give them the general area. Or, what's even more probable, they figured I'd jump in the car and go…and, of course, they'd follow me."

She was on her feet now, pulling an overnight bag from the walk-in closet and tossing it on the bed. Bureau drawers were flying open; clothes were being plopped into the case. She stared into the closet, debated about a raincoat, decided against it, threw in a designer denim shirt instead. "Oh, good grief!" Her hand flew to her mouth. "I was so torn up over that call I forgot all about Dorothy."

Believe it or not, so had I.

"Tell me everything. She made it all up, didn't she? She didn't witness a damned thing."

"Well, actually—"

"You saw her, didn't you?"

"Yes…but through a door."

"You talked to her though, right?"

"I talked at her." I told her what had transpired. When I finished, she frowned thoughtfully.

"That's a peculiar reaction. I would have thought she'd break down just hearing Richard's name rather than get angry. Besides, why would she be mad at you? A temper tantrum doesn't seem like a normal reaction."

What she said was making perfect sense, but the last thing I wanted was to give Helen false hope, so I was careful about how I worded my reply. "This is just a hunch, but I think she got away from me as fast as she could so I wouldn't be able to see the look in her eyes."

"You mean guilt?"

I shrugged, wondering if I should encourage her even more by telling her about the change in Harmon Ermaling's expression when his wife reacted the way she did. I decided to level with her.

"What's it mean?" she asked when I'd finished.

"Maybe he realized for the first time there's a chance Dorothy's not telling the truth. The problem is, one way or another, it doesn't change things. It's what she told the police that counts and, from what I saw of her, I'd bet she's not going to recant her story. By the way, I remember bumping into her at a couple of functions, but she wasn't in a wheelchair. What happened?"

"Probably nothing," Helen said, making a face. "She likes the sympathy it gets her. Supposedly she has some kind of muscular disorder. Doctors are running tests. She's in the hospital so much we've all decided she's confused it with a resort. Meals prepared, back rubs, no responsibilities, lots of uninterrupted soap operas."

"How long's she been that way?"

Helen shrugged. "Two or three months. I'm not sure." She snapped the lid shut on the overnight case. "Why?"

"Curious."

I really was curious. I kept thinking about the hallway in the Wagnor house, the house where I'd lived. It's what they call a shotgun hall, about six feet wide, running from the front door to the back of the house. How'd Henny What's-Her-Name (the other eyewitness), Royalee, Caroline, and Dorothy in that bulky wheelchair fit in there at the same time? Suddenly, I realized that's what had been bugging me all along. My subconscious was telling me there were too many bodies in that tiny space. It wasn't ringing true that someone in a wheelchair could go to the foot of the stairs and see what was happening on the upper landing, and here's why.

When you enter the house from the front door, you come into the narrow hallway. Immediately inside the door to the left are three steps and then a landing. When you get on that landing you're facing a wall, so you have to make a very sharp right to go up a staircase to the second floor. For Dorothy to have seen what was going on at the top of those stairs, she would had to have pulled her wheelchair to a place in front of the door, leaned way over, and angled her head to the right. Her chair would have been wedged into the hallway.

Now, let's say she heard Richard and Lane arguing, and she came rolling in from the back patio. Looking from the front door down that hallway, your view would be across a portion of the living room and beyond that, the sliding glass doors to the patio. So she would have had to wheel herself through the open patio doors (they'd have to have been open for her to have heard them), across that part of the living room, and into the hallway. She would have had to continue past the family room doorway, where Caroline and Royalee were listening to CDs, to the front door where she would had to have parked her chair and craned her neck uncomfortably to the right to see what was going on on the second floor.

Let's say she did that. And she saw Lane standing at the top of the stairs with Richard. Saw her shove him. Let's say Richard tumbled down and fell in a heap on the tiny landing. Now, let's further suppose that Henny came running in from the patio when she heard the commotion. What could she have seen? Dorothy and her chair would have completely plugged up the only space that would have let her glimpse the upstairs.

I shared all of this with Helen who finally said, "But…if you can figure all of this out, Katie, why don't the police see it that way, too?"

That was a good question. But a better one was why did Henny back up Dorothy's story?

"Well," she said, with a resolute sigh, "all of this only confirms my decision."

"What decision is that?"

"To go and stay with Lane until this whole ugly mess is resolved."

Did that mean I was free to return to Florida? I wondered. Maybe the fact that I had tried to talk to Dorothy but couldn't released me from further obligation. My observation of the Ermalings had at least settled things in Helen's mind. Dorothy was lying. Whether or not she really was, was immaterial. At least to Helen. I was relieved, to be honest. I wanted to get home and take care of the menagerie and to see what damage had been done to the property in the storm that was still raging when I'd left for the airport. Was it really only yesterday? I was just getting around to wondering how Helen was going to get to Onaga Valley without leading reporters to Lane's hideout when she said, "You don't mind driving me up there, do you?"

Forget that it was eight o'clock at night or a little after. Forget that it was a two hour drive across a barren stretch of desert, then grueling mountain roads that reach up to four-thousand-plus feet, heading into the constellation Orion. Forget all of that. What about the reporters?

When I asked, Helen sighed with exasperation and said, "Oh for heaven sakes, Katie. All of those cop shows you worked on with MacKay, and all of those stunt drivers you worked with, and you're telling me that you don't know how to lose a couple of obnoxious reporters?"

SIX

LOSING A COUPLE OF obnoxious reporters and having coffee on a movie set with stunt men are not one and the same. Keep in mind, however, that I'd never seen a photographer or a reporter around Helen's house, except for that brief glimpse of something metallic glinting in the foliage out back when I first arrived. I didn't see news vans or an unusual number of cars on the street. I took Helen's word that the media lurked in every crevice, but I had no firsthand knowledge of that as a fact. I didn't doubt that it was a reporter who'd made that cruel call about Lane being in the hospital, and probably for the reason Helen stated: to follow her to wherever Lane might be. I didn't doubt news hounds were contriving methods of learning Helen's secret, but their physical presence wasn't in evidence.

We drove to Ventura Boulevard, where I made a turn to the right. Jerry's Deli was doing a landslide business and traffic jamming into their parking lot was heavy. Maybe that's why I didn't recognize the signs of danger right away. The deli shares space with a bowling alley in the rear and a community theater upstairs, so not everybody was out for pastrami on rye. The tennis court next to the parking lot was lit; a couple of players were going at it like they were in training for the national playoffs. Beyond that, businesses were dark until we got to the heart of Studio City. Art's Deli, arguably Jerry's biggest competition for the Hollywood clientele, had a line waiting to get in. Further up on the left was the entrance to CBS-Studio City, across from McDonald's and a shopping center. This CBS, as opposed to the corporate structure on Beverly Boulevard in what's called The Miracle Mile, was where shows like *Gunsmoke, Roseanne* and *Seinfeld* were produced. Beyond that point, more dark businesses, with only the occasional rehearsal space or bar showing any signs of life.

At Mario's Italian Restaurant, I made a left onto 101. That's when I realized the traffic behind me was made up of some of the same traffic that had been behind me since turning onto Ventura Boulevard from Spring Drive. I noticed because one car in particular had a headlight that swung up into the trees, like a wartime searchlight on the lookout for bombers. I'd seen it in my rearview mirror almost as soon as we got past Jerry's Deli. It was still there, maybe four cars behind me now, as we zoomed past the turnoff to the Universal Hilton Hotel. I changed lanes, trying to lose them. The driver of the whacky-eyed vehicle changed lanes too. I increased my speed. So did they. I changed lanes again and dropped my speed at the same time, hoping they'd sail on past, but no such luck. They changed lanes and dropped their speed to correspond with mine.

Helen was searching the car radio for news. She stopped where an announcer was saying, "…America's Search for the Missing Lane Allison…"

I was listening, but I was also watching the rearview mirror, trying to decide my next move.

"Tonight we have with us in studio Doctor Phyllis Ambrose of the University of Clinical Studies in Palo Alto. Doctor Ambrose's book, *Celebrity Impact on Star-Struck America,* chronicles the careers of well-known personalities and the impact their lives have had on the American public. She's here to talk to us about the Wagnor murder and, more specifically, about Lane Allison herself. What would turn a former actress, now aging and out of the public eye, into a cold-blooded killer? Or was it only an accident with death the result rather than the intention? In a moment, Doctor Ambrose."

During the commercial break I made a decision to leave the freeway and veer onto Highland, which would take me through the heart of Hollywood. At this hour, I knew it would be a hopeless tangle of cars and pedestrians. Traffic inched past the Hollywood Bowl, congested because of a Broadway extravaganza. I eased up to an opening where I could get the Toyota onto the shoulder of the road and crawled past the line of cars waiting to turn into the Bowl. By the time the commercial was over, I was on the far side of the Franklin turnoff. I tried to ignore the purple-haired spooks and the spaced-out girls with white spikes coming out of their skulls and black spikes strapped to their feet.

When I reached the intersection of Hollywood Boulevard and Highland, male hookers were on every corner. The most attractive of those who appeared to be female were, for the most part, transvestites. On to Sunset Boulevard, then finally to Wilshire. I didn't get far onto Wilshire, however, when I spotted the cross-eyed auto half a block behind me and gaining. There wasn't anything I could do about it, so I tuned back in to the radio station where Doctor Ambrose was expounding on the plight of poor neglected former star Lane Allison and what had, quote, pushed her over the edge, end quote.

"We often see this kind of acting out," Ambrose whined over the airwaves, "in adults who had once been child stars. They can't seem to make the transition from the fantasy world, in which they've spent most of their life, to the reality of the world around them."

I glanced at Helen. I was thinking that Lane had been in the real world about fourteen years now; odd that she should go to pieces at this late date. I don't know what Helen was thinking, but it was probably somewhere in that same ballpark. How absurd could the good doctor get, I wondered. As the program opened its phone lines to take calls from the public, I realized that another car, a Jeep Cherokee from the looks of it, had also been on my tail since somewhere around the Hollywood Bowl. I noticed it because it had edged up onto the shoulder of the road to make its way around the choked artery of vehicles just as I'd done. I figured they saw me do it and decided that if I could, they could, too. But here we were, several miles from the Bowl, and they were still keeping pace a couple of cars behind the walleyed monster. Had someone signaled them by cell phone to tell them of our approach so they could pick us up en route? If so, the chase was being professionally orchestrated. This called for action.

Helen's attention was on the radio and a string of what I considered mostly idiotic observations and comments called in by listeners. I don't think she noticed when I swerved onto a one-way street going the wrong way. A wide alley runs behind the Beverly Wilshire Hotel. I used it to get to their entrance, where I executed a fast U-turn and headed back the way I'd just come, now going in the proper direction. Somewhere in there, Helen began making little gasping sounds and clutching the armrest with white knuckles. I greeted the startled drivers of goofy-eyes and the Cherokee with a saucy salute as I sailed past. A motorcycle cop swung out from under the dark portico of a closed shop and nailed the Jeep. By the time he'd pulled them to the curb, I'd turned toward Pico Boulevard, still on my way to Highway 10. The cross-eyed auto was nowhere in sight.

"What the hell was that about?" Helen asked when she could catch her breath.

"You said to use what I'd seen the big boys do," I replied, eyeing the rearview mirror.

Then we broke into gales of laughter. It wasn't especially funny, but we needed a chuckle and it felt good to giggle again.

IT WAS A TEDIOUS DRIVE to Palm Springs with traffic heavy most of the way. The scenery used to be mostly uninterrupted barren hills and scrub grass. In the moonlight it tended to soften into something more acceptable, but recent years have brought developers who have destroyed even that hint of natural landscape. Now it's cars and heavy traffic, smog and heavy trucks, mile after mile after mile.

When it started to thin out, somewhere on the other side of Banning, the view became bleak again. We listened to the radio, gnashed our teeth through umpteen sound bites from Doctor Ambrose's hour long call-in show, and let country music wail over us the rest of the way along Interstate 10.

At the juncture of 111, we saw far off to our right a fairytale setting of lights cupped at the base of gigantic mountains. This time Hollywood-be-damned, those mountains really are gigantic. It was Palm Springs, home to the stars, watering hole for the rich and famous and tourists with a taste for desert-in-pastel. Bob Hope's house is outside the village proper. The late Gene Autry's club is there. Frank Sinatra's home was there, too. But, of course, none of them are visible from the junction. What you can see are little Christmas-like lights and a skyline of windmills, all pumping away for no apparent reason.

We continued past the Palm Springs road and began climbing again. As the mountain pass became narrower, we saw fewer big rigs. It was as lonely as it's possible to imagine out there. When I'd see an occasional light flickering from inside a trailer or shack or, once in a while, a mansion perched atop some dark cliff, I'd wonder where they went for a loaf of bread and what they did at night. And then I'd picture the scorpions and rattlesnakes they had to endure and couldn't understand why anyone would choose to homestead in the middle of them. People. Go figure.

"I don't think they expected that," Helen said, breaking the stillness.

"Who?"

"Those reporters that were chasing us."

I grinned. "MacKay'd be proud."

She turned to look at me. "Do you care?"

For the first time, I actually felt something. I got a lump in my throat and it made me furious to think his name could do that to me. I shrugged, but I doubt Helen was fooled. The radio was picking up nothing but static now, so she turned it off and went back to staring out the window, gazing at a milky-blue sky dotted with silver stars. The Indians must have loved this place when it was peaceful and theirs. The lump came back to my throat, but this time it had nothing to do with my ex.

I made a left onto Highway 62 and climbed some more. There were no mansions now, only scrub brush and cactus.

We were passing scraps of what might have once been a little town, but was no longer anything except shells of wood and tin structures. Then we leveled out to face a carpet of lights a few miles straight ahead. Onaga Valley. I had passed through it a couple of times on my way to an art show in a Twenty-Nine Palms gallery owned by the late James Cagney's daughter (or is it stepdaughter?), but I could see the place had grown two, maybe three, times in size since then. A couple of miles farther, Helen nodded and pointed to a convenience store. "Turn here," she said.

A zig to the right, a zag to the left, and we were on a bumpy unpaved road called Wolf Cave Trail. I couldn't determine where it ended except somewhere at the foot of a mountain I guessed to be half a mile or so in the distance. It had grown as dark as a Halloween cat despite the hangnail moon and the starlight. Crickets clicked their heels and an animal howled in the distance. Just like in the movies, I found myself thinking.

"That's it," Helen said, pointing. "Past that shack. On the other side of the vacant lot."

I couldn't have missed it. It was the only building around, unless you count the lean-to Helen called the shack, which I didn't, mainly because it didn't have a front on it. All it had were posts that sagged and held up what looked like a corrugated tin roof. Not likely to find Lane Allison in there, I was sure.

Before I'd even pulled into the dirt yard, Helen was out of her seatbelt and had her hand on the door handle. I switched off the headlights, and then the ignition, as a window shade was pulled back on the porch of a long, narrow house that looked like something the next quake might bring tumbling down. An outside light went on and the door was thrown open as Helen literally waded ankle deep through sand to reach her daughter.

Lane Allison. She stood in the open door, framed by a bare bulb hanging from the ceiling behind her. Even from here I could see her blonde-white hair shining like a halo around her head. She grabbed her mother and they cried into each other's arms. I tried to make myself as inconspicuous as possible. Finally, Helen took a deep breath, held Lane back to inspect her, and obviously liked what she saw because she gave her another quick hug. She then turned to me, one arm still around Lane's shoulder.

"You remember Katie Wallace, don't you, honey?"

The smile, the wonderful smile that had lit a million theaters and the heart of an adoring ten-year-old, beamed at me. "Of course I do!" Her nose crinkled. It actually crinkled. "Come in. Oh, my goodness, Momma, I didn't know you were coming. This is wonderful. Come in, come in."

The place was owned by a writer, to be sure. Papers and books and magazines were everywhere. They were stacked on the floor, leaning against walls, taking up every surface in the place. "The place," by the way, consisted of the enclosed porch, a living room-bedroom combination, a teeny alcove of a kitchen and, behind that, as I would learn in a moment, a closet-sized bathroom with a shower. While I excused myself to make use of the facilities, Lane hurried into the kitchen to fire up Mister Coffee. By the time I returned, she was perched on one end of a love seat with Helen on the other. Their hands were clasped together in the space between them.

"So," Lane began as I came into the room, "Momma tells me you're going to help us." She leveled such an appreciative look at me that I was unnerved. "Thank you for being here with her," she said. I told her she was welcome. Then she asked about MacKay, but a look from her mother stifled further inquiry.

Even though I'd been in Lane's company before, this was the most intimate we'd ever been. The other occasions had been group-oriented. Now, sitting in a chair with the stuffing falling out of it, in front of an empty fireplace, I faced the two of them and felt like an intruder.

I couldn't help but see that the years had been kind to Lane, and it wasn't about plastic surgery. There was a glow to her, a sweetness. I'd chalked it up to good makeup when I'd seen her in crowds, but up close it was evident there was more to it. There was an innocence in her eyes that lingered even after all these years. My mother would have hated her. "Sickly sweet" was what she used to say about people who smiled too easily. But it's what had caught America's fancy all those years ago and what made me adore her as a kid. I could feel the schoolgirl in me taking over, though I was fighting it. After all, I'm older than Rita Moreno. Though not by much.

Helen said, "Guess where Katie went today?"

Lane looked at me expectantly.

"I saw Dorothy," I said, uncomfortably.

Lane swung her gaze from me to her mother. "Does that mean—?"

"She wouldn't talk to me."

"Katie thinks she's lying, too, sweetheart," Helen said.

"Thinks?"

"Knows, darling. She knows Dorothy's lying. Don't you, Katie?"

"Well, I don't know it, but it seems pretty obvious she was reacting to something other than my simply being there."

Helen went on to explain what had taken place. By the time she was finished, the smell of coffee had overtaken the room and Lane was on her way to the kitchen.

"Sugar?" she called over her shoulder.

"The pink stuff, if you have it," I replied, getting up to handle my own coffee chores. I towered over her at the plastic-covered table. It was the first time I noticed that her hands, mottled with age spots, were shaking. "Here," I said, taking a carton of milk from her. "I can do that."

She looked up at me, again with that air of gratitude that left me feeling like a fake and a fraud. These two were expecting something from me over and above a chat with Dorothy.

We went back to the living room where Lane handed her mother a cup of coffee and took a seat closer to her this time. I returned to the sagging chair.

"Have you seen Caroline?" Lane asked her mother. "Is she okay? I didn't get a chance to even—"

"She's fine, honey. She's at her friend's apartment. On Naples Island."

"Sara. That's good. Nobody'll bother her there. Is she holding up all right?"

"She's strong. Like you."

Lane's eyes misted and she looked away. "It's so hard on the kids." Her face brightened suddenly. "Michael was here this morning. He couldn't stay long. They're shooting that student film he's working on just up the road a few miles. He said the press has been trying every trick in the book to get onto the set, but kids today are pretty savvy." When she smiled, the sun broke over the horizon. "He's so funny. He came to the door in a long wig—you know, the kind with a pony tail—and a big cowboy hat, and boots! He was driving a grungy pick-up truck with the paint half off…I didn't recognize him when he knocked on the door. We just stood there, staring at each other, then all of a sudden he broke out laughing and we…oh, my goodness, we howled until tears ran down our cheeks. But you know what? No reporters followed him, that's for sure."

She shook her head and when she did, her grin faded and the sun went back behind a cloud. The hand not wrapped around a coffee cup went to her temple. She made little pressurized circles with her index finger.

Helen said, "I'm going to stay with you until this is over."

"You can't do that, Mom. This is a terrible place. It really is." She answered Helen's surprised look with a chuckle. "I've already killed two scorpions."

My feet seemed to leave the floor of their own accord. I tucked them beside me in the chair.

"They make a clicking noise on the hardwood floor," she said to me. "You'll hear them if they're coming toward you."

I felt much better. My feet stayed where they were.

Lane's expression became somber. "What are your plans, Katie?"

My plans? My plans were to go home as fast as I could manage it, but I couldn't say that. Not with Lane and Helen watching me with so much misplaced hope in their eyes. I got as far as, "I don't really…" before I decided to try another approach. "What's your lawyer say, Helen? You haven't told us much about him."

"Not much to tell. He's in Europe, not expected back 'til next week. His partner—"

"*Junior* partner," Lane put in with a dour expression. It was obvious she didn't much care for him.

Helen patted Lane's knee. "He'll do until Harold gets back.

Anyway, Katie, I posted bond and it's all rather routine right now."

"When's the hearing?"

"In two weeks." It was Lane again. She sat back, letting the rim of her coffee cup play against her lips.

Helen said, "What I don't understand is how, if Katie can see that Dorothy couldn't have possibly witnessed what was going on at the top of the stairs, the police couldn't figure that out as well."

They looked at me again. That expectant look that let me know they thought I had an answer. I could conjure up all kinds of theories, but I couldn't know, of course. I could assume that the Sun Beach police force, small and understaffed and unaccustomed to media attention, was anxious to get this behind them with a minimum of controversy. I said as much and took a long sip of coffee while they thought it over.

"As long as Dorothy sticks to her story," Helen was saying, "I don't see what we can do, do you?"

I shrugged. "Not really. But tell me this, Lane, why would Henny-what's-her-name?"

"Henny Thornton."

"Why would Henny Thornton substantiate Dorothy's version of what happened?"

Lane shook her head. "I've tried to figure that out, too. I can almost understand Dorothy's motivation. She never liked me and this is a great way to show it. But I don't understand Henny doing a thing like that."

"Are they friends?"

"They go to the same church. They're even on the grounds committee together, but I never thought they were especially close."

Helen scoffed. "You should hear what they say behind one another's back."

"Momma." Lane smiled softly, then turned serious again. "If the police believe Dorothy, I can see where Henny might not want to make trouble. Maybe she agreed just to keep out of it."

"So you don't think she actually saw anything?"

Lane lifted one hand, palm up. "What was there to see?"

That gave me the opening I was looking for; to ask the question I'd wanted to ask in the first place, of the one person who could tell me. "What *did* happen, Lane?"

She hesitated a moment, then put her cup on a chipped and scratched coffee table. "You mean just before the accident?"

"Yes."

She hesitated only a second, organizing her thoughts. "Richard came in from the patio where he'd been talking to Dorothy and Henny. Everyone else from the church had gone by then. Michael was helping clean the tables and—"

"Caroline and Royalee were listening to CDs in the family room," I said, wanting to get past what I'd heard and had no reason to doubt.

"Yes. Well, Richard was in the kitchen when I came in with a tray of dirty dishes from the patio. He'd made me a cup of my favorite tea. When he handed it to me, he said it was a peace offering."

"For what?"

"He'd been snippy with me all day. For a couple of days, actually."

"That was unusual?"

She nodded. "Then he kissed me on the cheek and went back out to the patio. Next thing I know, he sticks his head in the kitchen door again and says he wants to see me upstairs. He was standing at the top of the stairs, on the landing, when I got there. As I started up, he began yelling at me."

"About what? I'm sorry. Maybe I shouldn't—"

"No, it's all right. It helps to talk about it. I want to try to keep it as clear in my mind as I can for when I have to...tell a jury." She lowered her eyes again, collected herself, and looked up. "I couldn't figure out what he was saying. Something about me taking too many pills...and that was crazy. He knows I don't take any pills, not even aspirin. I saw so much drug abuse in the movie business that I—well, anyway, I didn't know what he was yelling about, but I went on up and when I got to the top, he grabbed my wrist and twisted it…" She stopped, cocked her head to one side, remembering.

"Had he ever been physical with you before?"

"No." She shook her head emphatically. "Never. We almost never even argued. That's why it was all so insane. Anyway, he was yelling and jerking my arm, then, all of a sudden, he got this…this stricken look on his face, and his knees buckled. It happened so fast. Just like—" she snapped her fingers "—that. He…kind of…crumpled over…and fell down the stairs. That's when I screamed."

"And Dorothy came charging down the hall in her wheelchair?"

"I could see Richard was going to topple down the stairs…I grabbed for him, but he'd already started to collapse—"

"So, what Dorothy saw was you reaching for him, not pushing him."

"If she saw anything that's what she saw because that's what happened." Lane made a tent of her fingers and rested them under her chin, thinking. "Richard screamed, I remember that. It seemed like the house was vibrating with screams. I screamed, Richard screamed, Dorothy was screaming, and then—I don't know where she came from—Royalee was at the bottom of the stairs, holding him in her arms, but she wasn't screaming. She was…sort of…moaning."

Tears had been building; I could hear them in her voice. After she said that about Royalee, she buried her face in her hands and cried softly as I watched, feeling helpless. Helen held her and whispered *shhhhhhh* while patting her on the back. After a bit, I said, "Where was Henny?"

Lane shook her head. "I…I…didn't see her. I don't know. I mean, she was at the house, but I don't remember seeing her around Richard, or anywhere near Dorothy when it all happened."

I didn't get it. Why hadn't the police investigated it as an accident? Why murder? It all came back to Dorothy's word. If Lane pushed him, it would either be murder one or murder two. Premeditated, accidental, or murder without premeditation. A jury would have to decide. Back to square one. Only now square one had another peg in it: Was Henny lying, too?

The conversation came to a standstill. We were worn out, emotionally and physically. It'd been a long day. Lane handed me a couple of sheets and we began the bedding down process. Having come to Onaga Valley directly from the police station, Lane didn't have anything to sleep in, so Helen had brought her a couple of her own gowns and robes. I'd left Helen's without giving a thought to pajamas and stayed in what I'd worn all day.

I was relieved to learn that they weren't planning to sit up the rest of the night visiting. Helen asked if I'd take care of her house until she got back. I didn't like the sound of that. My neighbor, Terry, the Brahma bull rider, was looking after my place and tending the animals. Problem was, I'd told him I was only going to be gone for a couple of days. I'd have to call him right away.

Helen shared the single bed with Lane. I scrunched up on the love seat, making sure the bed sheet I was using for a blanket didn't drag on the scorpion-infested floor. One scorpion is an infestation as far as I'm concerned and Lane had already killed two.

The house was quiet. Far away, a coyote howled and an owl hooted.

"Lane?"

"Ummmm?"

"Wasn't there an autopsy?"

"Yes, of course. Why do you ask?"

"Is it possible he had a heart attack?"

"That was the first thing I thought of, too, but they checked. His heart was fine." Her voice caught again. "He died of a massive head wound."

Something was very wrong. Dorothy was lying, I was sure, but she was in a bind. She'd made such a fuss over what she supposedly witnessed that it was almost impossible for her to back down now. Maybe, like Helen said, it had been her opportunity to get in a good lick at Lane, never initially realizing the extent of damage she was causing. I had the feeling that her husband had believed her without question, until today, though it's possible

I was misreading him. Maybe he still believed her, but I didn't think so. Or at least I think that Dorothy's reaction to my visit may have planted the first serious doubt in his mind.

The question was one of getting Dorothy to admit she saw nothing. Without an eyewitness to Lane having pushed Richard, it would be ruled an accident, pure and simple. And what was Henny Thornton's motive for lying? Why would she back up Dorothy's account of the incident? What was in it for her?

I wondered if my old friend Donald Stuart had heard anything. He lived in Sun Beach. Cops tend to stay friends even after they leave the department, and friends talk. Maybe he'd heard scuttlebutt about findings not yet made public.

I jammed the pillow over my head and tucked my feet up tight against my rear end, willing myself to sleep. As I dropped off, I was making a mental To Do list: call Donald Stuart again, see Henny Thornton, phone Terry to see if my house was still standing and if the animals were still kicking, and change my airline ticket to extend my stay another twenty-four hours. I'd give it twenty-four more hours, but then I was going home, come hell or high water.

What I didn't know was that the dam was about to break and water was going to run higher and faster than any of us could have imagined.

SEVEN

SUN STREAKED IN THROUGH a window beside the empty fireplace, dazzling me awake. It took a second for me to figure out where I was. I had knots in my knees, in my butt, in my shoulders, and I spent a full minute unraveling myself. A person who's five-seven doesn't do well on a love seat nearly a foot shorter. Lane was already in the kitchen making coffee. I could smell fresh baked muffins tinged with the scent of orange. I fished around under the sofa for my shoes, found them, and walloped them against the floor. Good thing I did. A spider came out of one of them, lickety-split. In a knee-jerk reaction, I threw the thing half the length of the room. The shoe, not the spider.

"Lizard?" Lane inquired, like a lizard in your shoe is the most natural thing in the world. She brought a plate of muffins to a card table that, last night, had been weighed down with magazines. Now they made an uneven column on the floor, and three paper napkins served as mats for plates and coffee cups in their place.

"Spider," I mumbled, stumbling toward the bathroom. I grabbed my purse off of the coffee table where I'd left it the night before. It had my earthquake emergency kit in it: toothbrush, toothpaste, small jar of cleansing cream, box of Band-Aids, and the ever important whistle. If a freeway or a concrete wall falls on you during a quake, a whistle can save your life. Assuming, of course, the concrete wall didn't take it.

"Coffee's ready," I heard Lane say from the other room.

I looked in the cracked and yellowed medicine cabinet mirror. A very unhappy face stared back at me. As I dug toothbrush and toothpaste from my purse and scrubbed away the gritty taste of sand, I tried to decide how I was going to spend the day. I remembered the To Do list, went over it again while gargling tap water. Talk to Henny. Why'd you say you saw something you couldn't possibly have seen? That would be the gist of the conversation, but I'd have to think of a better way to put it.

Games. I hate games.

Call Donald Stuart.

"You know," Helen said, looking up from an orange muffin when I returned to the living room, "you should probably change the rental car for something reporters don't recognize."

"I was thinking about that." I sat down across from her at the card table, sloshed coffee onto my napkin, and watched the paper disintegrate. Lane handed me another on her way back from the kitchen.

"You should have seen this woman ditch reporters last night, honey," Helen chuckled. "If you ever need a stunt driver, she's the person to hire."

Lane tried to smile, but I could see that the effort was enormous. She pulled out a folding chair and joined us at the table. Her eyes were red. I was certain she'd been crying in the night. I had a feeling she'd just as soon be alone. It couldn't be easy, facing what she was facing, and having to put on a cheerful face for a worried mother at the same time. "What's the next step, Katie?" she asked, stirring sugar into her cup.

"After I trade in the Toyota at the airport, I'll go see Henny Thornton, though I doubt she'll be any more inclined to talk to me than Dorothy was."

Helen said, "Can't you just tell her that you're a friend of the family and that something's been concerning you, then tell her what you told us—that she couldn't possibly have seen Lane push Richard? After all, the fact is—"

"The fact is that no matter how I dress it up, I'm calling her a liar. She's bound to get defensive."

We ate in silence, or near silence. Whatever kinds of birds were perched on power lines outside the window, they were noisy. A couple of neighborhood dogs barked. The vroooom of a motorcycle started up, then roared into the distance. I was anxious to be on my way, knowing that the sooner I faced Henny and phoned Donald, the sooner I could get back to Florida. The thought caused an unexpected knot in my stomach. No one would be there when I got back. No one was waiting for me to walk through the door. Animals would wag tails and purr and bark, but the man I'd thought—

"Anybody know what time it's getting to be?" I asked, interrupting my troubled thoughts.

Lane glanced at her watch. "Nearly eight. Traffic's going to be horrible going back toward L.A. Maybe you ought to wait a while."

Commuters living in Onaga Valley and Palm Springs make the trip daily into Los Angeles, clogging highways and byways, but I didn't see any point in waiting. I pushed my chair back and got to my feet. I'd combed my hair and straightened my denim skirt as best I could. The tee shirt was good for another day at least. I was ready to strike out. If I waited for traffic to thin, my outfit would go out of style.

"Do you need anything before I head back? Milk? Bread?"

Lane shook her head. She was still in her mom's housecoat and slippers. "Katie?" She watched me for a long moment with that peculiar intensity that made me uncomfortable. When she spoke, her voice was husky with emotion. "Please try to get Henny to tell the truth. If she'll do that, Dorothy'll have to back off. My sister-in-law's loud and she's pushy, but I don't think she'll stick with her story if there's no one to back her up."

"I'll do what I can, but I can't promise anything. It just doesn't seem reasonable that she'd confess something to me after she's already given her statement to the police."

"Who?" Helen asked from behind me. "Dorothy or Henny?"

"Both. Either." I pushed the front door open and stepped into a blast of desert heat. The sand that got in my shoes was already hot as tiny embers. I hip-hopped to the car, unlocked the door and, as soon as I got the Toyota started, turned the air conditioner up full blast.

Helen and Lane were waving goodbye as I pulled onto Wolf Cave Trail. I pot-holed my way back to the highway and traffic that reminded me of what would happen in the event of a nuclear holocaust. This one road, the only one in or out of the mountains, would look exactly like it looked on this hot and smoggy Wednesday morning. Everyone would burn to a cinder, log-jammed on this solitary escape route. Nuclear threats and earthquakes. Traffic and smog. Welcome back to California, Katie Wallace.

The car exchange at the airport took longer than I'd hoped, but not longer than I'd imagined it would take. Between the two hour drive from the mountains and the desert, and the wait at the auto rental facility near LAX, it was lunch time before I reached Helen's house. I didn't see a Jeep Cherokee anywhere around and wouldn't have known which car had goofy headlights unless it was dark, but it appeared the coast was clear as I pulled up behind Helen's guest cottage and into her circular drive. I let myself in with the keys Helen had given me, casting a furtive glance over my shoulder to see if I was being observed. To the best of my knowledge, I was of no interest to anyone. I entered the place feeling grungy, gritty-eyed, and very much out of place.

I'm not a detective. I did paperwork for MacKay at the office. Learned to pick a lock in case I was ever called on for an emergency break-and-enter, but I never carry a gun, and don't intend to carry a gun. I'd probably blow my toes off if I did. I don't know the subterfuge necessary to get an unsuspecting soul to reveal information I might want, but which they might not want to divulge. MacKay was great at that sort of thing.

I flipped on lights as I went from one room to the next. The heavy drapes were still closed in the living room. Venetian blinds were shut at all of the other windows. The place felt cool, even though the air conditioner wasn't running. Plush carpeting underfoot made my trek as silent as a submarine on the ocean floor.

I went to the kitchen where I remembered seeing an answering machine beside the telephone. Its red light was flickering. I pushed the Play button and skimmed through thirteen messages, seven of them from reporters. Someone claiming to be from *Entertainment Tonight* asked Helen to return their call. Somebody else said they were working on a deadline and needed a statement from her before noon today. Like their deadline was Helen's problem. Two female voices, in two different messages, identified themselves respectively as Minda and Beverly, and wanted to know if Helen was holding up all right and if they could do anything. They ended their calls with "God Bless" and "You're in my prayers." The thirteenth call was from Donald Stuart.

"Hello!" Chuckle, chuckle. "My goodness, I haven't heard that voice in a while," he said. "Didn't get your message until I got home about ten this evening. Sorry I missed you. If you want, you can call me back tonight. I'll be up until midnight or so. Or you can phone me at the studio tomorrow, 818-555-6262. That's the direct line to our production office. Just ask for me. Hope you guys are going to be in town for a while. Maybe we can have dinner tomorrow night if you're free." Click and dial tone.

I'd jotted down the studio number as he'd rattled it off. Now I dialed and waited through several rings before a male voice barked, *Cop Patrol*. I asked for Donald Stuart and waited some more. Finally, he picked up and said, "What can I do for you?"

"Is that how you greet everybody?" I asked, laughing.

"Might as well. Nobody calls unless they want something. How are you, Katie?"

Old friends are like coming home. His voice felt good. I pulled a stool out from the kitchen counter, kicked off my shoes and wiggled my toes as I sat down, pulling the phone closer. "I'm a fish out of water, Donald," I replied.

"Oh? How so?"

"It's a long story. Can I tell you about it over the dinner you mentioned in your message?"

"I've got a production meeting starting in about an hour. It'll probably drone on for the better part of the afternoon, but I'm free for early evening. Where'd I call you, anyway? The message machine said Allison residence. Lane Allison?"

"Helen. Her mother."

There was a frown in his voice. "Is MacKay working the case?"

"That's part of the long story."

"I've got all night. How about we meet at—?"

"That German place you like so much." I didn't want him to say the name of the restaurant in case Helen's phone really was tapped. The last thing I needed was a reporter seated at the next table with a concealed listening device aimed in our direction.

"The inn over on—?"

"That's the one," I said quickly, hoping he'd get the hint. He did.

"See you about six?"

I mentally tallied up my plans for the afternoon and said that six would be great. We hung up and I ran, feeling better for no good reason, to the bathroom where I showered and changed clothes. Helen had asked me to stay in the main house, rather than in the guest cottage. The night I arrived, I'd settled into the spare bedroom down the hall from hers where I'd unpacked my two shirts and two skirts, underwear, and shoes, and now I was faced with wearing either the denim skirt again with a fresh tee shirt, or the old tee shirt with a fresh skirt. Instead of either, I shook the wrinkles from the beige trousers I'd worn on the plane and pressed the brown short sleeved turtleneck blouse with the flat of my hands. Tan sandals completed my fashion statement and I was on my way out the door, heading for an address Lane had given me.

Henny Thornton would probably be home, she'd said. "She's a widow who'll never need to work again. If she ever worked at all. Anyway, gardening's her passion. You'll probably find her poking around in her backyard jungle."

I'd traded the Toyota for a Chrysler Le Baron convertible. The only difference between it and the one parked in my garage in St. Seminole was five years and several thousand miles. The newer one handled fine; I felt right at home behind the wheel. It didn't escape my attention that the charge was going on my Visa card and that the payment would have to be made somehow, some way, but I couldn't do anything about it now. The request for a replacement car was nearly denied, even though I swore the Toyota kept overheating and I was afraid to drive it on the freeways. A lie, granted, but a good one. I really needed a car that reporters didn't recognize. The rental agency had one vehicle they could let go of, they said, at a slightly higher daily rate: the Le Baron. I suspect they had others, but this was their slap on my wrist for causing them extra paperwork.

Once on the freeway, I was looking at another hour before I'd reach my destination. I gave up trying to listen to the radio. There was nothing on it but coverage of Lane Allison's disappearance.

HENNY THORNTON'S ADDRESS put me back in Belmont Shores at a dark timber house on a finger of land that jutted into the bay, along with about ten other equally expensive homes jammed against one another with only a path to separate them. There was no front yard. Roses formed a solid bank under the windows and climbed a trellis over the entrance.

I knocked twice before I spotted the ornate doorbell nearly hidden under thorny stems. I lifted one back enough to jab my finger onto a mother-of-pearl button and was turning to watch a jet skier doing death-defying maneuvers on a sliver of water visible between two houses across the way when the door was thrown open by a very angry woman I took to be Henny Thornton.

"I told you to call first!" she screeched. Suddenly, her brows shot up into her hairline and her eyes squinched narrowly, like blinds snapping shut. Slices of blue peered at me. "You the shuttle driver?"

I looked around to make sure she was talking to me, which was pretty silly since I was the only other person in sight and she was looking directly at me. "No, I…uh—"

Her red mouth clamped angrily. "Where th' hell's that shuttle!" It wasn't a question and I knew that she knew I didn't have the answer. "Ah! Well! It's about time!" Her glance had moved past me to something over my shoulder. I turned to see a van, with Land-to-Sky Shuttle Service scrolled on its side, pull to the curb in front of the Le Baron. The driver, a kid no more than nineteen or twenty years old, was studying the house number and checking it against a scrap of paper in his hand.

"You Thornton?" he called.

At about five-foot-one, Henny Thornton was a teeny tower of

fury. "I certainly am and just where the hell have you been? I told your dispatcher to have a van here forty-five minutes ago!"

It seemed I was the forgotten man here, so to speak. Henny had turned on her heel to snatch up a carrying case inside the door. When she wheeled back around, she was still barking at the kid who had gotten out of the van to open the back hatch. He was loping up the sidewalk when she nearly crashed into him. "Get those two bags in the living room and shut the door behind you."

I was wondering if I'd become invisible. But then the kid looked up from hooded eyes that had been fastened on the sidewalk beneath him. "S'cuse me," he mumbled as he pushed past me and through the front door. While he was grabbing up the suitcases, I turned to Henny who was pulling herself into the shuttle, using the door handle as a grip.

"Mrs. Thornton!" I called.

She'd managed to haul herself into the passenger seat. Grappling for the seat belt, she looked at me as if seeing me for the first time.

"When will you be back? I need to—" I could have bitten my tongue. It was a stupid question that I knew she wouldn't answer. You don't sing out "I'll be gone for two weeks" to a California neighborhood at large. Might just as well sing out "Would you like to rob me? I'll be away for a while!"

She didn't even grace the question with a reply. She simply slammed the door shut and stared ahead. The poor driver, who was about to endure an hour's trip with her to the airport, trudged past me again, eased her suitcases into the back of the vehicle, closed the hatch, and went around to the driver's side. He'd left the motor running and, in seconds, they were on their way. I could hear Henny screaming at him even as they rounded the corner.

I could only guess that, once she determined I wasn't the shuttle driver, she dismissed me as a door-to-door salesperson. Or the deliverer of *Watch Tower* pamphlets. Whatever she thought was immaterial. She was gone.

I stood there feeling dumber than dumb and totally at sea about what to do next, though in hindsight I don't know what I found so puzzling. There wasn't anything to do but leave. I was getting back into the Le Baron when a plump grandmotherly soul pulled her car up beside mine and rolled down the window.

"S'cuse me, dear," she said pleasantly. Probably not a California native. "Your rear end is just a tad into my driveway. Could you pull up a bit so I can get in?"

"Sure," I said. "Sorry."

I started the engine and moved forward as she eased her sedan into the driveway belonging to the house next to Henny's. The lady smiled at me in appreciation. I smiled back. And then I left.

EIGHT

SO FAR I'D LOST two out of two chances to help my friend Helen. That's it, I told myself, driving away from the Thornton house. Dinner with Donald, then pack up and go home tomorrow. It dawned on me that Helen would have no way to return to Studio City if I left her out there in Onaga Valley. Then I argued with myself that her lawyer would soon be back in town and would need to talk to them. He'd probably make the trip to the mountain hideaway and bring them back with him when he returned. No problem. Clear conscience. After all, I'd flown to California, tried my best to talk to Dorothy, and attempted to talk to Henny Thornton. What more could I do?

Listen to what you don't hear, Katie...

You can remove a man from the place he once nagged, but you can't remove the nagging. MacKay's voice followed me out of Belmont Shore and into a neighborhood café near my old house in Sun Beach. I saw that the strip mall where the eatery was located had fallen the way of most strip malls; half the shops were closed, leaving only an insurance agency, a travel agency, a convenience store and this family-run café. I'd only been in a couple of times and didn't expect anyone to recognize me. No one did. Nor did I recognize them. The West Virginia husband-wife team who'd opened the establishment had obviously sold out to a Vietnamese couple who smiled broadly while scampering around, filling my order of fries and salad. I got my own Snapple out of the cooler and found an empty booth overlooking the boulevard. Two tables were filled with men chowing down and talking loudly. At both of the tables, empty chairs held camera equipment and film bags. I tried to see if there were station logos on the bags, but couldn't from where I was sitting. About the time my lunch arrived, a disheveled woman came in lugging a monstrous satchel over her shoulder. She made her way to one of the tables where the media men were seated, grousing about what a boring morning it'd been and why the hell did she have to schlep all the way out here to babysit a damn empty house, anyway? My thoughts exactly.

The logo on her satchel was turned toward her, but when she swung it off her shoulder to toss it into a chair I caught the letters KVAZ-TV.

KVAZ? Never heard of it. But then channels are springing up all over the country faster than anyone can keep track. Maybe it was the new gay and lesbian channel I'd heard was in the works about the time we left California. Why would an issue-oriented station be interested in the Wagnor case, I wondered.

As if reading my mind, the woman was grumbling, "Who th' hell's this dumbass anyway? Some wanna-be TV producer and a washed-up old movie star that nobody remembers. I told Dory, I said 'you send me on this cockamamie assignment and you can find yourself another field reporter'." The men nodded sagely. Good for her. Spoke right up. Told old Dory just what she thought. This gal had gonads.

She got up then to put in her order at the counter. When she got back, I guess the steam had run its course because their voices lowered considerably. What was obvious was that none of them wanted to be there, yet all of them wanted to be the one to find Lane Allison. The first one to find her. A beer drinking guy, with the traditional ten-month-pregnant belly, tilted a brown bottle toward his mouth and bellowed, "*National Enquirer*'s offerin' a ten thousand dollar bonus for anybody comes up with the broad first." Then he guzzled while the others at the table made *no shit* sounds of approval and the woman scowled.

"Hey!" This voice belonged to a scrawny little guy wearing dark-rimmed glasses. He was sitting next to Beer Belly and directing his remark to the Vietnamese woman behind the counter. With wide, jet black eyes she turned to Scrawny Guy. "Yes?" she said in that whispery tone that only Oriental women can master.

"You know the Wagnors? Richard and Lane?"

The Vietnamese woman frowned as if she didn't understand.

Scrawny Guy spoke louder. "The fellow who got himself murdered in the next block. You know 'em?"

The woman shook her dark head. "No. I not know him."

Beer Belly wasn't buying it. "It's just a block away. You sayin' he never came in here to buy anything? His kids never came in for takeout?"

She was still shaking her head. The shake was getting more adamant by the second. "I don't know, I don't know," she murmured, turning her back to them and busying herself with trays and straws and plastic forks. I was certain she knew who they were talking about, but she wasn't about to get dragged into it. I was proud of her. I left her a great tip. Especially considering that I was getting dangerously low on funds.

After that I got back in the car, still undecided about what to do next. It would be another three hours before I was set to meet Donald. That's when it hit me that I should at least say hello to Caroline, since I was only a few blocks from her Naples Island apartment. Helen had provided me with emergency numbers and addresses. Caroline's temporary quarters headed the list.

Sun Beach connects to Naples Island by a two-lane bridge. It has one major thoroughfare, Second Street, which continues past about a mile of tiny California bungalows and immaculately-kept gardens. At the end of that stretch, you come to the grand old humpback bridge I mentioned earlier, that leads into Belmont Shores. You can drive the entire distance from Sun Beach in less than five minutes.

Naples is probably seven streets wide, on either side of Second. Each street features a little bridge that spans canals sometimes dotted with gondoliers. At dusk you can hear guitars strumming, a feature of their popular sunset champagne cruises. Built along the Naples side of the marina is a new tropical hotel and a row of two-story apartments, circa 1940. It was in one of these apartments, actually a triplex, where Caroline was staying.

I parked at the curb in front. The street was almost empty

of cars. There were no garages or driveways on this part of the island. Curb parking was all that was available and, at this hour, most everyone was at work. There were two doors on the front of the triplex, one on either side of an open arch leading to a staircase. Helen had said that Caroline occupied the top floor, over the duplexes. I went up, knocked on her door and, in a moment, heard muffled footsteps, saw the peephole darken, then heard a young female voice ask who was there. I told her. A chain clinked on the other side of the door, then it opened a crack. A wary green eye studied me briefly before the door opened further, revealing one of the prettiest women I'd ever seen.

Like her mother, Caroline had a glow about her, a cleanness and beauty that needed no makeup for enhancement. Her gaze was steady, her oval face natural and unflawed. Although she was close to my height, when she smiled I saw the childlike quality that had charmed the world in her mother.

"Mrs. Wallace," she said and seemed genuinely pleased to see me. She stepped back from the door, but not without first glancing cautiously down the stairs. "Please, come in." She closed the door behind us. "Grandmother called after she talked to you in Florida. She said you were flying out."

I was standing in a large room where a bank of windows overlooked the street on which I'd parked. Ahead of me I could see onto a terrace that wrapped around the back of the building, overlooking the marina. To my left, was a small kitchenette and a dining table for four. I assumed that the bedrooms were at the far end of a hallway that ran behind me. Everything about the place was light and airy, the floral sofa, wicker tables and chairs, hardwood floors gleaming in the sunlight. Caroline was leading me to one of the chairs and taking another for herself. She wore jeans and white tee shirt. No shoes.

"Michael called a while ago. Said he'd managed to phone Mom at the cabin this morning and that you'd taken Grandmother up to be with her." She stopped for air. "I'm rattling, I know, but I'm so grateful you did that. Just being here for us is...well, it's more important than you'll ever know."

Omagawd, here we go with gratitude again, I thought, depressed. "Well, I can't really do anything, Caroline—"

The dark blonde head was swinging urgently from side to side. "No, no. You don't understand." She leaned back and tucked her legs up under her. "When my dad died, I was seven years old, but I remember that almost no one came to be with Mom. All those parties she'd given, all the people who'd gushed over her...they were gone, nowhere to be seen. I was a kid and I was just...stunned. I couldn't believe it. So, when this happened with Richard, the first thing I thought was that Momma would be alone. And Grandmother, too. And then when I heard you were actually here for them..." She smiled quickly and sincerely.

"I'm surprised you didn't go to Onaga Valley with her," I said without realizing how much it sounded like a judgment.

Her eyes clouded. "They took Momma so quickly. I was... it was all a blur...I was trying to comprehend that Richard was dead when all of a sudden Dorothy was screaming that Momma killed him and I was trying to understand *that* and then, before Michael or Royalee or I knew what was going on, Mother was in handcuffs and we were so...helpless. We followed the police car to headquarters—"

"We?"

"I drove my old Volks. Michael and Royalee went with me. Michael had the presence of mind to call Grandmother from the police station. I think she broke every traffic law on the books getting there. Anyway, we were at the precinct for I don't know how long, trying to grasp it all. It was like...walking under water...you know? Everything felt surreal. Like this can't be happening. We didn't see Mom alone, not for a minute even. Then they took her into a room for questioning and, next thing we know Grandmother's lawyer, well, not her regular one, but someone from that office, came and bond was posted, and by then it'd become a mad house. Reporters and television cameras and, when we tried to go outside, the press tore at us and..." She stopped to collect her thoughts, unable to go on.

"Sun Beach isn't used to that much attention," I reminded her.

She nodded. "My girlfriend, Sara, is in Europe on an exchange program, but her parents, George and Millie, heard about what was happening—"

"So fast?"

"You've heard of 'breaking news'? We were the breaking news. Anyway, they'd heard about it and came to the police station and pulled me aside to offer Sara's apartment. They had keys in case of an emergency, of course, and said it's what Sara would do if she were here."

"Not many people have friends like that." I meant it.

"Grandmother urged me to go, then everyone was busy trying to get Momma out of the police station, to a safe place where no one would know where she was. Grandmother made a couple of calls and they ended up with the New York writer's cabin in Onaga Valley. Michael said he was going back to location; that he'd be pretty well insulated from the press out there, and Royalee was so distraught she didn't know what she wanted to do except to get home."

"Home is where?"

"Fresno."

I'd forgotten. Richard's daughter was an intern at a Fresno TV station. Lived near her mother, Arlene. Retired botany teacher. Got it.

"I try to watch television and then I try not to watch television." She pulled her legs from under her and stretched them out across the coffee table. "It's like I'm drawn to it. These stupid talk shows and hours of pop psychologists analyzing why Mom did this and why she did that...and there's Aunt Dorothy's face all over the news. I can't believe it."

I told Caroline about going to Dorothy's and asked what she made of her behavior.

"Of course she didn't see anything. She couldn't have seen anything if there had been anything to see. It'd be impossible from a wheelchair."

"Did you tell that to the police?"

"No one would listen to me. They said I was in the family room, so I couldn't know what was going on."

"What about Henny Thornton?"

She gave me a level, thoughtful look, then asked if I wanted a glass of tea. "I just made fresh mango herb," she said, getting up.

I followed her into the kitchen, a three-sided box that opened into the area holding the dining table, where I pulled out a chair and sat down while she found glasses, ice, and the pitcher. "Henny Thornton is…how do I describe the woman…?"

"I stopped by her place before I came here."

Caroline's eyes widened. "You did? You talked to her?"

"Well, about like I talked to Dorothy. No, actually, not even that much. I think she thought I was a peddler. She was waiting for an airport shuttle. It came, she went."

"She's a piece of work." She shook her head in irony. "Cornerstone of the church she and Richard attend. Attended," she corrected herself.

"Who was it that said there's been more mischief done in the name of Christianity than by the very Devil himself?"

She smiled ruefully. "I sure wasn't aware Henny had any animosity toward Mom. Guess I didn't know how wrong I was." She handed me a chilled glass. "Want to sit on the balcony?"

No, I didn't really want to because I'd never adjusted to California smog. People sit around in it like they think it's fine and natural to breathe what you can taste. Orange gunk hangs in the air and scums up the rim of the horizon. Makes you feel like you're at the bottom of a dirty tub. Nevertheless, we ended up in striped canvas chairs with a wrought-iron table between us, facing a line of yachts. The orange gunk watched us like a diseased eye.

"Tell me something," I said when we were settled. "Your mother's going to be trying to convince a jury that she was reaching out to keep Richard from falling and that Dorothy mistook the gesture as her pushing him. On the other side of it, the jury's going to hear arguments that she and Richard had been fighting—"

Caroline was moving her hand back and forth in a gesture that said no more, no more. "I've heard it and I don't understand. Richard adored my mother. And Momma—" she sighed, looking for the right words "—even after seven years of being married to him, she was like a young bride. They never argued."

"Except on this day."

Caroline frowned and nodded. "And a couple of days before that."

We fell silent for a time, each with our own thoughts. Gulls cartwheeled overhead. Starlings hopped around on the banister. Somewhere along this row of apartments, someone was listening to Andy Williams sing "Moon River" on an oldies-but-goodies station. It seemed more than coincidental that I was sitting here, talking to the daughter of my childhood movie idol, and someone else's head was in that timeframe, just a few doors down, yet we were totally unrelated in action or in thought.

"Do you suppose your mom misses having a career?"

Her laughter was so soft I had to listen carefully to hear it. "Lord, no! I don't think she ever really cared about acting in the first place. I think Grandmother wanted it for her. She was so proud of her…and it all sort of happened by accident…being discovered in a school play right there in Burbank, practically in the studio's backyard…then MGM put her under contract and it was just a fluke. There wasn't any reason to quit films, but she'd never struggled to get in and that made it, I guess, easier to walk away when the time came." As if to explain "when the time came," she added, "When Dad died in the plane crash, Mother forgot all about work."

I remembered the scene at the cemetery. No actress could feign that kind of grief.

"Grandmother helped her through that one, too. Took care of Michael and me. Momma couldn't face anyone or anything, not even us kids. Not for months. And then, afterward, she tried to make up for it by nearly smothering us to death with affection." She thought for a long moment. When she spoke again it was to a distant mast. "We were her miracle children." Then, to me, "All those years she'd been told she couldn't have kids."

A smile flickered at the corners of her lips. "I was a Christmas surprise. And *what* a surprise, at that point in her career." The smile vanished. She was silent another moment, remembering. "No one offered her any roles for years after the plane crash, but I think she was glad. She wanted to be with us. Family meant more to her after Dad died than it ever had before. We became everything to her. And she to us."

"And then she met Richard?"

"Well, a few years later. And it was high time. Michael and I used to try to fix her up with our teachers and anybody else we could think of, but when she met Richard, it was absolutely right."

"You kids liked him?"

She nodded vigorously. "And we love Royalee. She's the sister I've always wanted."

"How about the rest of Richard's family? Dorothy, for instance."

"She's not really his sister, you know."

Hold everything. I replayed that and tried to comprehend what she was saying.

Caroline went on. "Dorothy's parents died when she was about five and Richard's folks took care of her from then on. She wasn't formally adopted, but she and Richard have called each other brother and sister ever since."

Bells were ringing in every direction. Good grief, was it possible that Dorothy had always been in love with the man everyone accepted as her brother? Could that be the root of the problem? It sounded as melodramatic as anything ever concocted by Danielle Steel or Nora Roberts. Did I dare mention something like this to Caroline? I decided not to. Not now. I had to digest this new bit of information. Was Richard's death the trigger that let Dorothy finally admit her feelings, if only to herself? Did it motivate her to try and destroy Lane by swearing to something that never happened? And when Dorothy reacted to me the way she did, did Harmon Ermaling realize for the first time that his wife felt like more than a sister to the dead man? Or...was my imagination in overdrive?

Even if any of that were so, why would Henny Thornton lie, too?

I don't wear a wristwatch; something about the chemistry in my system stops the mechanism, so I'm always asking people for the time. Caroline's chemistry was fine. She informed me that it was nearly four. If I intended to meet Donald at the German restaurant at six, I'd have to get on the road.

When I got to my feet, Caroline took my glass and walked with me back into the apartment. As I picked up my shoulder bag from beside the wicker chair where I'd dropped it, she said, "You asked about Mom's career. Did Grandmother mention that Richard was putting together a film deal that would bring Mother back to the screen?"

"No, she didn't."

"Well…it's bad luck to talk about deals before they're in stone, but he was going to Puerto Rico for financing and to scout locations. He'd been concerned about this for some time now. On edge, jumpy. He'd come so close to putting together a couple of movie deals in the past and they'd always fallen apart before anything really happened. This one was, I don't know…sort of like his last chance. I think he felt like he'd reached an age where it was either going to happen this time or it never would."

"Think that's why he'd been snapping at your mom the past few days?"

She nodded.

"Was she looking forward to the trip?"

"She wasn't going. His idea, not hers. In the past, potential investors were always people who'd been fans of Mom's. Their interest was in simply being around her. Then they'd get to know Richard and, for whatever reason, it seems like they ended up losing faith in him. They didn't have confidence that he could pull a major motion picture together, and they'd back out. This time he wanted to go it alone. No fans, just business. And Mom was fine with it." Her eyes suddenly clouded. "What day is this? Wednesday? He was set to leave this afternoon. And maybe it would have been the big break he'd wanted for so long. Who knows? Timing. Funny, huh?"

I knew she didn't mean funny ha-ha. I nodded and mumbled something about life being like that and knew I was being mealy-mouthed and jabbering clichés, but it was funny. Damn funny. A thought was churning around in my mind and I couldn't grab hold to see what it was. *It's right in front of you, Katie,* MacKay was saying in my head. This time I didn't invite him to shut up. Instead, I said *"Where? Damn your sneaky hide, MacKay, where?"*

THE DEUTSCHLAND INN sat in the middle of a busy block near what used to be MGM studios in Culver City. Back in the late '80s the little town had a family-run market that enjoyed a thriving luncheon business delivering subs across the street to workers in the Thalberg Building, MGM's administrative center named for early film pioneer and young movie-making genius, Irving Thalberg. The downtown portion of Culver City had dusty, musty buildings that had been standing since the turn of the century. After Ted Turner finished with the once grand movie lot, it was sold to an Italian, then it became Sony and so it remains today. *Wheel of Fortune* spins from one of its sound stages. The family-run market is gone and, in its place, a brick pyramid houses offices for industry executives. The quaint, old buildings are mostly gone now, too. Nondescript concrete bunkers are headquarters of bustling commerce, strip malls abound, and crime is as brisk here as any place else in greater Los Angeles.

Backlots filled with African villages and western streets and Middle America neighborhoods have all been sold off. Developers have built condos in their place and hidden them behind a high wall so punks have someplace to practice writing in spray paint.

For years I loved getting to work at the studio as the sun was sneaking over the smog-obliterated horizon. Even at that hour, the lot was already coming to life. Prop men and scenic painters were hauling flats from one sound stage to the next, or from the big carpenter mills out back. Wayne, MGM commissary manager, would be standing in the kitchen door, taking his morning smoke, watching the activity, greeting people as they passed. One morning Steve McQueen came along in his pick-up truck while I was coming through the guard gate. He was bearded; the medication for the cancer that would soon kill him had left him blotchy faced and bloated. Wayne waved his usual, "Mornin'" to him. McQueen nodded his reply. Then Cary Grant came striding briskly from between two buildings and I almost had a heart attack. He was wearing an expensive blue silk suit and he looked downright gorgeous. That was only a few months before his death, but I gotta tell you, he was one handsome fellow right up until the end. Anyway, Wayne puffed on his cigarette there in the kitchen doorway and said to Mr. Grant, "Mornin'" and Cary Grant gave him a little salute and a grin and I said, "Morning, Mr. Grant" and kept walking like it was something I did every day. He called out behind me, "How are you today?" and although we both knew it was a rhetorical question that didn't require an answer, it was all I could do to keep from wheeling around and jogging along beside him, telling him what I'd been up to the last week or so. Wayne saw me stop and stare after the man and he grinned a huge grin like two friends do when they know each other's secrets. It broke the spell and I laughed, too, as I hurried on to my office.

If I sound like a star stuck fan, let me set the record straight: Two movie stars have my respect and admiration and have had since I was a kid: Lane Allison and Cary Grant, though Jimmy Stewart's right up there with them. I wish I'd been around when Grant was in his heyday. By the time I got to the studio, he hadn't made a film in years, though he was on the studio board. He'd come on the lot from time to time for business meetings, only to be seen briefly and in passing.

While I'm talking about studio life, let me quickly dispel any notion that having an affair with a producer gets a woman to the top. An executive producer I worked with (never mind which show) had six mistresses on the set, each thinking they were his One and Only, and all it got them was a laugh behind their back from the crew and a few days work as extras. There really is a glass ceiling in Hollywood—don't let anyone tell you differently. It is a good-ol'-boy society, and the boys are getting younger every day.

All of this was playing around in my mind as I drove past the studio once touted as having "more stars than are found in the heavens!" *Good Lord,* I thought suddenly, *have I really become an ancient dame muttering about the good old days?* If you think about it, our lives are made up of complete plays within plays. Each play has a beginning, a middle, and an end. Each play has its own cast of characters and seldom do they become involved in the plays that follow or went before. Every marriage is a distinct play. When the curtain comes down, it's over. Our childhood, college years, new jobs, new neighborhoods, new states, every one of them a play with their own cast of characters and events and locations and settings. My last play had starred MacKay Wallace. It was set in contemporary Hollywood. I loved that role, but it was over. This new play now stars Katie Wallace in a solo role set in central Florida on five rolling acres. It's the plot I'm not sure about, let alone the last scene. I guess I'll learn the part as I go.

By the time I'd worked my way through the sticky wicket of nostalgia and philosophy, I'd reached the parking lot behind the German inn which was joined on either side by a Chinese laundry (specializing in cleaning feather boas!) and a costume rental shop. It took a moment for my eyes to adjust to the dimness inside.

Donald Stuart said from behind me, "Late, as always. Some things just never change."

I turned to find his handsome, craggy face brimming with good humor. I laughed, too, and we hugged as he put his arm around my waist, guiding me to a corner table. Rock walls, German travel posters everywhere, very hushed oompah-pah music piped in the background. Little individual lamps with hunter green shades centered each cloth-covered table. A plump waitress, with the appropriate blonde braids coiled over each ear, handed us oversize menus even before we were in our chairs, but Donald took mine and set it aside. "First," he said, "I want to know about MacKay."

"He's all right, if that's what you mean."

He nodded. I could sense relief.

"He just decided he'd rather live at home with Momma." I realized he was waiting to hear more, so I added, "He really hated the house we bought, and his mom's getting up in years."

"She in Florida?"

"Miami."

Donald shook his head sadly. "Rough town. I did some consulting work for *Miami Vice* their first season. Not any place I'd want to live. 'Course South Beach has gone topless and there's a nude beach down from that, but..." He grinned, saw I wasn't grinning back and grew serious again. "Want to talk about it?" he asked.

I shook my head. What could I say that wouldn't sound like I was whining? Which I would have been.

He sighed decisively and picked up his menu, handed mine back to me. "All right then. We won't. Try the *kurnoodles*. It's exceptional."

We had wine rather than the traditional beer, *kurnoodles,* potato bread steaming and soft, red cabbage with white potatoes, and a sticky dessert made of pastry pockets jammed with apples and sauce. I hadn't seen Donald in nearly two years, but neither of us seemed to notice the gap. It was as comfortable as feet in front of a fireplace. We made it all the way to after-dinner coffee before he mentioned the Allison-Wagnor case. He wanted to know what I was doing staying at Helen's and I told him. I also told him everything else that had transpired, ending with, "I realize the police have to follow up with an investigation when an eyewitness claims it's murder, but I can't understand why someone doesn't look into the stories Dorothy and Henny are telling."

"They will," he said, refilling his cup from a pot left on the table. "It's going to trial, I'm sure." He held up the hand with the coffee urn in it. "More?"

I shook my head. "If it were proven that the women out and out lied, wouldn't that be the end of it?"

"Sure, but from what I've been hearing, it's an open-and-shut case."

A three-piece band was taking its place on a little stand near an empty fireplace. In a moment, conversation would be impossible. Even tuning up, we were forced to lean close to one another, and I had to practically shout, "I can't stop thinking about the possibility that Wagnor could have had a heart attack."

He frowned in concentration, trying to hear over a rowdy trombone. When I stopped talking, he looked up. "Wasn't there an autopsy?"

"Came back negative."

"What?"

I shot the musician a dirty look. "I said, his heart was just fine."

Donald leaned closer and shouted, "Did you—?" then sighed and got to his feet, grabbing me by the arm. "Unless you want to polka, let's get out of here."

NINE

WE FOLLOWED Venice Boulevard to where it ends at the ocean, in the heart of the village for which it was named. I don't know California history well enough to have even an inkling of what the place was like before I first saw it in the '80s when it was hippy haven, but whoever coined the phrase "where the slime meets the crime" must have had Venice, California, in mind. Tattoo parlors, sunglasses stands, shaved-ice wagons and body-piercing shops line the walkway facing the beach, alongside herb tea and specialty coffee houses. Skaters and skateboarders take precedence over pedestrians. Under the swaying palms that separate sand from concrete, drug deals proliferate behind the backs of beach cops lunching on hot dogs and Slurpees. It's also where talent gets a shake at being seen and heard. A juggler who works with a chain saw and three eggs performs on the sidewalk every Sunday of the world. Except during monsoon season.

New condos and apartment buildings face the wide boulevard leading to the beach, but across the way can still be found interesting little cafés and ancient seafood houses. For years Tony Bill had his office in Venice. So did Roger Corman. Behind the business section, tiny houses follow the curve of a chain of canals that, like Naples Island, are sometimes choked with enterprising gondoliers. The place is so picturesque that photographers from around the world can be found snapping away at most any hour of the day or night. Jane Fonda and her second husband, a California politician, had their home on one of these waterways.

You can follow a bike path all the way into Santa Monica to the north or, if you're energetic enough, can continue on that path clear into Malibu, farther up the coast. We didn't go all the way into Santa Monica or Malibu. We stopped when Venice

Boulevard ran out of asphalt and became a beach. The public parking lots were jammed, but we were able to find a place in one of the narrow alleys that ran behind a one hundred-year old, two-story office building. Donald took my elbow and I felt like a little old lady being helped across the street by a Boy Scout. Porgie's Pig Out was two doors down once we reached the sidewalk. The pungent aroma of their famous barbeque sauce peppered the air. Inside, I noticed Mary Crosby at one of the tables with her husband. We waved at one another. I'd met her when she was on *Dallas* (she shot J.R., remember?) and later we shared a studio lot when I was production coordinator on a badly directed, quickly forgotten, feature film.

Donald went to the counter and ordered drinks, which we took to the patio out back. Smog had finally disappeared. Palms were silhouetted against a sky going from lavender to midnight blue. The salty breeze smelled good. I felt like a young girl on a very special date. The feeling lasted approximately fifteen seconds. This was Donald Stuart! Nine years my junior, many years my friend. Where was my friggin' brain?

"So," he said, easing back in his chair and crossing an ankle over one knee. "Are you going to stay in Florida?"

"We bought a house. There's no equity. Do I have a choice?"

"We all have choices, Katie. MacKay made one when he left. You make one every day that you stay."

That was a hell of an argument. MacKay took bankruptcy and thumbed his nose at the mortgage. I couldn't do that and didn't even want to. If I said it though, I'd sound like I considered myself grand and noble while MacKay's a jerk. Which he is. I, on the other hand, am not so much grand or noble as I am simply stuck. I couldn't live with the guilt of walking out on a mortgage. Besides, I had two head of cat and four head of dog. What would I do with them if I decided to bail? It was out of the question.

"Tell me this," I said, changing the subject. "What if Lane's telling the truth and Richard had an attack of some kind, maybe a stroke? Shouldn't an autopsy have identified the problem?"

Donald thought a moment before saying, "Not necessarily."

I sucked my glass dry and pulled out the straw. "Nobody doubts that hitting his head on the corner of the steps killed him, that isn't an issue, but I'm inclined to believe Lane when she says that something happened to him to make him fall. Her description had all the classic symptoms of a heart attack, but—what? Why are you grinning like that?"

"Still the gullible and trusting Katie, aren't you? For such a feisty broad, I never understood that side of your nature, charming as it is. If memory serves me right, I think you once told me that Lane Allison was your childhood idol."

"I don't have a damn idol," I scoffed indignantly. "I thought her nose was cute. Anyway, I was a kid." I ran the straw between my lips and looked out over the water. And I wondered for one one-hundredths of a nanosecond what MacKay was doing that moment.

"When are you going back?"

I looked at him gratefully. Saved me from the brink of thought. My hero. "Tomorrow."

He was oddly quiet, as if considering something. Finally he said, "Belmont Shores is a little town, Katie."

"What's that supposed to mean?"

"I used to go to the same church that Richard and Henny attended. Years ago. Before Wagnor met Lane Allison. They were an item then, Richard and Henny. She was pretty sure he was going to marry her when his divorce from his first wife became final."

"Where are you going with this?"

"Richard was just breaking into the business. Did some production work for a local television station here. We used to talk a little. We weren't buddies or anything like that, but we were on a couple of church committees together. I was still with the Long Beach police force, picking up a little movie work in my off-time, like MacKay, handling crowds and traffic when companies filmed on location around town, that kind of thing."

"Which is how we came to meet you," I reminded him.

"Henny Thornton had her sights set on Richard. I mean, she

was relentless. They dated for, oh, I don't know how long then, all the sudden, he got a break at one of the big studios."

"And met Lane Allison," I said.

"Right. But he didn't drop Henny. Richard was the kind of guy who'd wait to see which side of the bread had the best tasting butter, if you get what I mean. Henny had money, but Lane Allison had the potential of making a come-back in films. Richard got the idea that, if he could find the right role for her, he could produce a movie and they'd be on easy street for the rest of their lives. Sort of like Bette Davis with *Whatever Happened to Baby Jane*."

"And Don Ameche in *Cocoon*. But wait a minute. He did find her a come-back script and he *did* produce a movie. Years ago. It was awful."

"Television movie. Cable television movie." He said it as if a cable TV movie was the lowest of low. "Richard wanted to make feature films. Being important was high priority for him. Actually, it was because of that cable deal he was able to raise funding for the documentary he did next."

"The one about celebrity kidnappings."

"And he was finally accepted as a bona fide producer. Of sorts."

I wiggled my hand back and forth in a so-so gesture.

Donald laughed again. "Game shows, low budget cable. Nasty work, but somebody's gotta do it."

"And Henny. Sounds like everybody stayed friends after Richard made his decision in favor of Lane. So, why'd she lie the other day?"

He shrugged. "Who's to say she did?"

"You know her. *Would* she lie?"

"No, I don't know her particularly well. I broke with the church about the time she and Richard started going at it hot and heavy. He was still married to his first wife. Too much hypocrisy for my blood. Now I sit under a tree on Sundays and watch God's handiwork in the clouds and the sky."

"That's downright poetic," I said, but I wasn't making fun of him and he knew it. I thought back to the times MacKay and

I had been with Donald and his wife, Kendall, before she died in a boating accident. I didn't remember him mentioning that he knew Richard Wagnor. But then again, why would he have mentioned it? I asked if he'd ever met Lane.

"Nope. Saw her a few times around town, shopping, driving the kids here and there, but I never met her."

"So, Richard divorced, then he dropped Henny and married Lane, and they moved into the house MacKay and I sold to Helen and her husband." I bit back a grin. "You follow that?"

"Yep. But you missed a big step in there."

"I did?"

"After Richard's wife went to Fresno with their kid, he moved in with his sister and her husband. The sis, Dorothy, was tight with Henny from the church work they did together. Dorothy was pretty sure Richard was going to marry the gal."

There went my theory about Dorothy loving Richard and wanting him for herself when he was free. I debated about telling him that she wasn't really his sister and decided against it. I'd just listen for now.

Donald added, "I don't think Dorothy ever took to Lane. At least that's what I heard."

"What in the world did Richard ever see in Henny Thornton?" I wondered out loud. I couldn't see how any man could find her attractive, though obviously at least two had: her late husband and Richard.

"Dollar bills," he said with a grin. "When Henny's husband kicked the bucket, Richard was right there to carry the pail to the cemetery."

"You make him sound like a fortune hunter."

He shrugged. "Opportunist's a better word. Hey, a woman's nuts about you and she just happens to be left a very hefty insurance policy by her late husband, what's a poor guy to do?"

"Yeah, poor guy," I said sarcastically. "Screw the shrew, that's what you do."

Donald threw back his head in laughter. "You do have a way with words, Katie. You surely do."

"So you think Henny's still sulking because Richard married

Lane, and when she got a chance to get revenge, she took it. A good lawyer will make mincemeat of her story on the witness stand."

"Depends on how strongly she feels about sticking to it. And, like I say, we're not positive she *is* lying." There was that look again, that questioning look that was making a decision about whether or not to tell me something. He decided to. "He never stopped seeing her, Katie."

Suddenly, I was getting Richard and MacKay mixed up in my head. Richard was sneaking around, seeing Henny. MacKay was sneaking around, seeing everybody. Lane didn't suspect? I know Katie sure didn't.

"I didn't know whether or not I should say that," Donald went on, uneasily, "and I don't think it has a damn thing to do with Richard's death, except maybe as a motive to back up Henny's account of events the afternoon Richard died. Assuming she didn't see what happened firsthand. She obviously still cared about him. Anyway, you seem hell bent on getting to the truth, so let me add that grain of fact to the pot," he said, reaching for his wallet.

"How do you know he was seeing her?"

"Like I said, Katie, it's a small town. And I have eyes. Well-trained eyes." He motioned for the waitress. "Now, let's get you back to your car. I've got to be at the studio at five in the morning. Sure you have to leave tomorrow?"

When I got back to Studio City it was well past midnight. I'd spent the entire trip going over what I knew, what I'd heard, and what I'd seen. I'd seen a very emotional Dorothy, who was not Richard Wagnor's sister. I'd seen her husband react in a way I couldn't define. I'd seen Lane Allison tell me about the man she adored and the fact she tried to catch him before he fell down the stairs as a result of something that happened to him on the upper landing. Something physical. I'd seen a mean-mouthed Henny Thornton, a beautiful young daughter who adored her mother, and an old friend who confided that Richard Wagnor was cheating on Lane with the horrible Henny. But now a new thought crept in. What if Lane found out that Richard was still seeing Henny?

What if she'd never confronted him with it until last Sunday when something happened, some look, some word between Richard and Henny that confirmed what Lane had maybe only suspected until that moment? What if Lane and Richard argued, just as everyone said, and she accused him of infidelity? What if he admitted it?

What if…Lane really did shove him down those stairs, so furious in that instant that she wanted him to break his philandering neck?

What if…the second the deed was done, Lane was horrified by her own actions and, out of lifelong habit, went into performance mode?

What if…it was so traumatic for her that, afterward, she convinced herself that Richard fell of his own accord and now actually believes it?

My heart sunk. Every fact indicated this was the true scenario.

I mulled all of this over, wondering at the same time about the junior law partner who was supposed to be helping Lane. Why wasn't *he* out here talking to all of these people? Not that I'd want him to find out about Henny, but it *was* his job to dig for facts.

Jerry's Deli was dark and deserted. Even the theater upstairs was closed. I turned off of Ventura Boulevard. Spring Drive was so dark I could scarcely make out the cliff's edge to my right. Headlights cut into the blackness and I missed the turn onto Helen's property. Cursing under my breath, I made a point of not looking at the yellow ranch style house separated from Helen's place by a wall of Italian Cypress and went all the way to the end of the street where I made a hairpin curve around the castle and wound up another level on the hill. Then I began the corkscrew drive down the far side of it, to Ventura Boulevard again.

I turned left, followed the empty street back to Spring Drive and made another stab at finding the gate beside the Bavarian cottage that marked Helen's entryway. I parked under the trees, locked the car door behind me, then crunched through leaves and gravel to the back entrance. I was fishing inside my purse for the key when I realized that the door was open a crack. Hair stood up on the back of my neck. I drew in a quick breath and stepped back into the shadows. What the hell was going on? Over the thunder in my chest, I made some quick calculations. I could close the door and get back in the car and drive to a motel to spend the night. But if I did that then whoever was in there, assuming they hadn't left yet, could clean out the place and I would have done nothing to stop it. Not good.

Next option: I could get back in the car and drive to a pay phone and call the police. But what if whoever had been in there was still crouched around somewhere and, when I left, they followed me? Then, when I got out to use a pay phone on one of the dark corners in Studio City (there were no brightly lit ones at this hour), "they" sneaked up behind me and—I stopped the thought process right there and dismissed that option also.

I could go to a neighbor, but all of the houses were dark. A lot could happen while I was standing there pounding on a door. The owner of the house probably would be too scared to open up anyway. They'd no doubt be dialing 911 while I was fighting off an assailant on their doorstep. Then the cops would arrive. They'd want to know what was going on. If I told them, they'd demand the whole story and Lane's whereabouts would be revealed. Also, there was a chance I'd know some of the guys conducting the investigation. They'd expect me to level with them.

Meanwhile, I was still crouched in the shadows, about to asphyxiate myself in foliage, my ears throbbing with the sound of my own heart. If I'd had a gun I would have chanced putting my toes in mortal danger and gone into the house like Batgirl. I told myself to calm down and asked the question, *what would MacKay do?* I knew the answer, of course. He'd pull out his gun and charge inside. He'd take his six-foot-four frame and pit himself against whoever was lurking in there. Forget MacKay. What the devil was I going to do?

I looked around. I didn't see cars other than the Le Baron, though it was possible that a dark colored automobile could be hidden under trees at the deepest part of the lot and I'd never notice it. While I was standing there, turning all of this over in my mind, a figure burst through the back door and sprinted to the stand of trees I'd been considering. An instant later, a car engine sprung to life and headlights came on. I ducked behind a tree and watched as a dark, two-door sedan gunned past me and disappeared through the gate beside the guest cottage, making an abrupt right onto Spring Drive. I had no idea who it was, but I sure as the devil recognized the cross-eyed headlights.

I came out of my hiding place and hurried to the back door. Inside, I fastened the double chain behind me. Not the easiest task I'd ever accomplished the way my hands were shaking.

I was in the utility room. I slid my sweaty palm along the wall until I located the light switch and flicked it on. Nothing seemed disturbed.

I moved cautiously into a long hall, to the kitchen, where I turned on the fluorescent and saw that nothing was out of place there either. In the living room, the stereo and television set were still in evidence. No drawers were pulled askew; nothing was missing that I could see. Now more curious than scared, I ventured into Helen's bedroom.

This had been the intruder's destination. Her writing desk was a mess, with papers strewn everywhere. Bureau and dresser drawers had been riffled through in a hurry. However, Helen's jewelry box was still filled with rings, bracelets and necklaces. The television set and her computer on a stand next to the closet were still there.

I was puzzling it out and growing more confused by the second when I realized that the family albums we'd gone through on my first night were missing from the shelf where she kept them. Photos of Lane as a child, her wedding pictures, pictures of the children, photos of the kids' dad, the funeral, Lane's wedding to Richard...photos of Helen and Donne with MacKay and myself on backyard picnics and lake outings...gone. Every single scrap-book (there were four of them) was gone.

My God, I thought with a sinking heart, how far will the idiots go for a story?

I was still shaking, well, actually I was shaking even more than before, but this time it was in fury, not fear, as I retraced my steps through the house to turn off the kitchen light. From there, I went into the utility room, intending to do the same thing when I saw how entry had been gained. The skylight over the washing machine was open. A sprig of stars stared down at me.

I climbed up on the appliance to investigate. Someone had managed to pry it up enough to get in. The same person who was preparing to leave by the backdoor when I arrived. When I didn't come in, they must have decided to chance running to their car, hoping I didn't carry a weapon. Granted, it was a relief to think I'd nearly confronted a reporter and not a rapist or worse, but still…the whole thing was unnerving and I knew it would be a long time before I'd drop off to sleep. As it was, the sun was just coming up behind an orange blob in the sky when my eyelids snapped shut.

My final thoughts were on Dorothy and Henny and the question of how they could live with themselves if everything they were swearing to was a lie, and that Lane would no doubt spend years in prison because of them. Then I remembered the ill-humored, bible-thumping Henny the way I'd seen her earlier in the day, and it made even less sense than before that a man with a family like Richard's, with an adoring wife like Lane, would risk it all for the likes of her. Why?

By now I was so sleep-drugged that my muddled brain morphed images of Richard into one of MacKay, and Henny became a composite of Alice…and Mary…and Norma…and Renee…

TEN

MY FLIGHT WAS SCHEDULED for three-ten out of LAX the next day. Allowing the two hours now required for check-in, and the hour it took to get to the airport, plus another half-hour to return the Le Baron, I figured I should leave Studio City no later than noon. Conceding the fact there might be trouble on the road, like an accident that could hold up traffic, or long lines at the car rental, I decided to make it eleven-thirty.

Since I hadn't gotten to sleep until dawn, I was feeling pretty groggy. My spirits were about as low as they could get, too. A lot of good I'd done Helen. All I learned that she and Lane didn't already know was that Richard Wagnor was a cheat. And I couldn't tell them that.

I was thinking about that and about how good it had been to see Donald when the phone rang and I answered it.

"You okay?" he asked from the other end of the line. Interesting how many times things like that happen.

I fibbed and said that I was fine. "Except," I added, "for a little excitement when I got back here last night." I told him what happened.

"Damn media," he said, disgustedly. Then, "If I forgot to mention it last night, Katie, I'm sorry about you and MacKay. It can't be easy for you right now."

"Thanks," I said, and meant it. "You might want to give him a call in Miami. He'd like hearing from you."

"Maybe another time. Right now my sympathies are with the missus."

Believe it or not, I didn't have an answer and felt myself get flustered. "I have to leave for the airport in a few minutes," I said, "but I'm glad you called. I enjoyed last night. Maybe we can do it again the next time I'm in town."

"I'm going to hold you to that," he said. "I don't get around much outside work. Knees are a mess and the psyche's not so hot, either. Divorce and death. They're a lot alike, Katie. Well, you take care."

"You too."

And we rang off. I sat there at the kitchen counter, not wanting to move. He'd said something, I don't know exactly what, that took out what little wind was left in my sails. Which, granted, hadn't been much to begin with. Divorce and death...maybe that was it. All I know is that I felt even more like I'd just returned from a wake. MacKay was dead. Dead in my life, dead in my future, and I didn't even know he'd been sick. The marriage was dead. I had no idea it was going to happen, but suddenly, I broke down and cried like I haven't cried since I was a kid and my Boston terrier got hit by a truck. I cried for the years I'd wasted on a sneak and a liar, the years I'd spent wearing blinders, thinking they were *good* years. I cried for myself and my miserable state of affairs and the animals that trusted me to take care of them when I didn't even know how I was going to take care of myself. I cried for the years MacKay wouldn't share with me and I cried, most of all, dammit it, because I was so blasted mad at myself for giving a rat's rear.

Finally, when I ran dry, I got up and trudged into the guest room where I grabbed my purse and put on my sandals. In ten minutes I was back in those beige pants and the brown shirt, tearing down Spring Drive in the Le Baron, but I wasn't going to the airport. I was going to Belmont Shores to learn something about the woman who allegedly sneaked around with the husband of my childhood idol.

There was, of course, every possibility that Donald was wrong about them, but I knew this for a fact: if a woman's in a relationship, there's going to be something in her personal belongings to confirm the fact.

I didn't have a plan beyond getting my airline ticket changed to something open-ended, which I did from Jerry's Deli where

I stopped long enough to wolf down the world's best omelet and to use the pay phone. When I got back in the car, my morale was up and so was the sun. It had broken through earlier than usual, leaving a circle of sky so blue it dazzled. It's weather like that, rare as it might be, that gets photographed for postcards which, in turn, bring thousands of out-of-towners to add to the freeway mess. Someone once reminded me that the homeless are in such numbers along the coast because, "Well, where would you rather sleep? In a snow bank or under a palm tree?" In any case, not even the traffic could darken my mood. The cry was good for my soul, the eggs were good for my stomach, and the sunshine was good for about anything I could think of. *Now let's hope the ground doesn't wobble,* I thought as I pulled onto the approach into downtown Belmont Shores.

I parked at the curb in front of Henny Thornton's house and was debating my next move when the grandmotherly soul on the adjoining property came from around the far side of her house carrying a garden hose. When she saw me, she broke into a wide smile and waved. "Good morning," she called cheerfully.

I got out of the car and started up the walk to Henny's house. "Morning," I replied, opening my purse and rummaging around. "Oh, for heaven sakes," I groaned, loud enough for her to hear. A sneak peek told me that she was watering a bed of fern, but also watching me. I glanced up, met her eyes and grinned foolishly. "My sister's going to kill me," I said apologetically.

"What's that you say?" she called, leaning my direction.

"I'm supposed to look after things while Henny's gone, but I went off and left her keys on my dresser." I shrugged helplessly. How else could I justify the fact I was about to go through a window or jimmy a lock? "Boy, do I feel stupid."

"Henny's your sister?" She had lowered the garden hose and was turning off the water at a spigot near the corner of her house closest to me. She was a good foot shorter than me. Everything about her was round; her eyes, her bottom, her enormous boobs, her arms. Even her white hair made a soft white halo around her little round head. She was of such good cheer I doubted I could stand being in her company for very long at a stretch.

I took a step toward her and stuck out my hand. "Hi. I'm Jenny."

She grinned and frowned at the same time, then said, without a hint of suspicion, "You certainly don't look like your sister." She took my hand in hers, pressed it rather than shook it, and let go.

"She favors Mom. Tiny. Red hair, just like Mom. Everybody on that side of the family has red hair. Irish, you know."

The lady found that fascinating. Like any good actor, I was encouraged to embellish.

"Dad's side's Scottish. Dark hair. Tall."

"You sure take after him," she said, marveling. "Henny won't be back for a week, but I guess you know that."

I was nodding vigorously. Sure, know all about Sis being gone for a week. "She's got some plants that—"

"You going to feed the cat, too? She likes him to have his Tabby Tummy twice a day."

I snapped my fingers. "Tabby Tummy! Darn. That's what I was supposed to pick up at the store today. Thanks for reminding me."

"Wonder why she asked you to water the plants? I usually do it same time I'm in there feeding Mister Tom."

Having been married to a detective for a very long time, and having observed his remarkable powers of detection at work, I deduced that Mister Tom was the cat. "Well, she knew I was going to be in town so she asked me…" I stopped because I was beginning not to believe me. I thought I'd better slow down while I was ahead. "Anyway, I left the key back at my place, so—"

"Well, land sakes, if she wants you to take care of things, use the spare she leaves with me when she goes away. Hold on. I'll get it for you." And the darling disappeared into her house. *Damn,* I was thinking, *lying's hard.* How do the MacKays of the world do it and sound so convincing? Just think about it: if I were in town then I must live out of town, but if I lived out of town why wouldn't I be house-sitting for my sister? And if I were from out of town, why would I have a place? Wouldn't I have a hotel or motel room? Fortunately, the neighbor was more trusting than

Donald gave even me credit for being. And fate was very kind to place this lady just where I needed her to be, when I needed her to be there. I took it as a positive omen. I was still thanking the gods of good-sneak when she returned with a key in her fist.

"Here you go," she said, handing it over. "Just leave it under the mat when you're through. I'll get it later."

"Oh, no trouble. I can bring it to—"

"I'm off to a church meeting, dearie. Late, as usual. It'll probably last all day. Just put it under the mat, that'll be fine. It's a pretty safe neighborhood."

"Well, I certainly thank you for your help. Henny'll be appreciative, too."

She frowned uncertainly for a moment, then the cloud disappeared from her features and she smiled her pink smile again. With a wave of her plump little hand, she headed back across her yard, to her front door. "You have a good day, Jenny!" she called over her shoulder.

I promised to do just that and let myself into Henny's house.

IT WAS A STRANGE FEELING, standing in someone else's living room. I wondered if the reporter who stole Helen's scrapbooks didn't have a tinge of guilt when they broke into her place. Maybe not. Maybe, like MacKay, you can get hardened to things dishonorable. After all, it's a reporter's job to get a story by any means they're bright enough, and wicked enough, to devise. It's a detective's job to get whatever is needed to make a case. But I'm not a reporter and I'm not a detective. I'm not, I was thinking, even a detective's wife—not that that would cut much ice if someone found me breaking and entering.

Henny's home was small and ultra contemporary. The tiny square of a living room had no windows other than one on either side of the door, over the rose bushes. The fireplace looked fake and unused against a panel of dark wood. Two steps led down to a conversation pit, where a built-in sofa followed the contours of the wall. There was just enough room for a piddley little coffee table. Straight ahead, the dining room was so scrunched that the round table for four took up the entire space. By sucking in my hips, I was able to move into a dark kitchen that made trailer living seem luxurious. Off of it, a bottle-glassed bathroom featured only a toilet, sink and shower. No tub. I spun around slowly, trying to figure where the blazes the bedroom could be when I noticed a ladder-like staircase back by the front door. It disappeared into a hole in the ceiling. I retraced my steps and ventured up the apparatus, slowing emerging onto an enclosed loft. It was lighter up there, even though the ceiling was so low I cracked my head on it twice. I guessed it had once been an attic. A double window looked out over the grandmotherly neighbor's house and, beyond that, to the Pacific, or rather to the bay that fed into the Pacific.

A bed was crowded in under the slanting eaves, covered by a spread heavily decorated with vines and roses. The pink and green theme continued into the curtains and onto the cover of the one chair beside her built-in dresser. I felt like a giant in a toddler's playhouse.

Crossing the carpet to the dresser I asked myself what I'd kept when MacKay and I were dating. A diary? Never. Who had time? Anyway, it didn't seem realistic to expect that I'd burst in, looking for evidence that Donald's report was accurate, and there waiting for me would be a written account with all the lurid details. Maybe in the movies, but not in real life. In real life, I was standing in a stranger's home, sniffing through her belongings when only last night I'd been in a rage because somebody had done the same thing to Helen. Of course the difference was that I wasn't going to remove anything from the premises. *Oh, really? Even if you thought it would clear Lane, or give her justification for pushing Richard in a moment of passionate fury?* Well, okay, so maybe I'd take something, but I wasn't going to sell it, for heaven's sake. *Oh, really? Hasn't it crossed your wee mind that if Helen's lawyer is going to get megabucks for you doing his work, that maybe you wouldn't argue if she saw her way clear to reimbursing your airfare and paying a few expenses?* It's terrible to be cursed with a conscience.

I closed the dresser drawer, having found nothing but underwear so skimpy I could have worn them for ankle warmers.

Nightstand, ah-ha! I opened the drawer and found a roll of Tums, package of tissue, a bible and a pencil.

Love letters. Shouldn't she have a bundle of them somewhere? Maybe she wasn't as sentimental as MacKay had been. Maybe if she got love letters, she had sense enough to burn them. Then again, why would she? She wasn't married. She could have a trunk full of love letters and who'd care? I couldn't find a trunk and I couldn't find any love letters. I couldn't even find any photos or photo albums or old Christmas cards. This was one cold broad.

I turned around at the opening in the floor and inched my way backward, down the stupid ladder to the living room. Nothing there, either. Built-in sofa and a dinky coffee table with no drawers. The mantel held only one brass holder and a half-burned candle. No place to stash so much as a hanky.

Back I went through the dining room to the kitchen. Clean as a model home. Where'd this lady sit? Where'd she relax? This wasn't a place that screamed comfort. No magazines, no books, no clutter anywhere. It was unreal. And then I spotted it. I moved a partially open louvered door back all the way, half expecting it to lead into a hidden room where I'd find a rumpled sofa, scattered newspapers, and maybe even a footstool and television set, but no such luck. All I found was a closet bigger than the bathroom that held a vacuum cleaner with its cord neatly wound around the handle, a broom with all its bristles in place (this woman was a disgrace), a pastel feather duster, and...*well, well, what have we here*...a wall calendar.

It was a big square pad, taking up about two feet of wall space, one of those where each page represented an entire month. April was up there now. I clicked on an overhead light and leaned in closer to study what was written in black marking pen. This was set to be a busy thirty days (months prior to this one were torn out). In the various squares, beginning with April 2nd, large block letters spelled out "Tom—vet—10:30," "hair—2:30," "Lit. Guild—library—7:00 p.m."

I'd gotten to the tenth of the month when something black and furry swished across my ankle and I broke into a rain dance, leaping out of the closet, thinking I'd been attacked by a hairy snake. Mister Tom ambled out from behind the vacuum and stretched. He gave me a bored glance as he moseyed on to an empty dish beside the refrigerator. Guilt kicked in when he turned those accusing blue eyes on me. I went to the cupboard, found a stash of Tabby Tummy, flipped the tab to open it, and dumped a heap of the fishy slop into his bowl. He gratefully, if disdainfully, proceeded to curl himself over his meal and purr as he ate. I went back to the calendar and puzzled over the April 18th square: "Meet RW San Pedro rm 210." I didn't want to jump to conclusions. Maybe she was to meet a telephone company representative named Roberta Wright in conference room 210 of the San Pedro Communications Building to discuss her phone bill. Or a Doctor Raymond Williams to go over her mammogram results in hospital room—who was I kidding? She was going to meet Richard Wagnor on Monday, April 18th, in room 210, in San Pedro. My guess is that the room would be found at the Sleep Tite Hide-a-Way, or any of the other sleazy motels in the little village perched on a cliff top, twenty minutes south of Long Beach. The only thing that interfered with their rendezvous was Richard's death the afternoon before.

On that date, April 17th, the square on the calendar read "2:00 p.m. garden party." Under Tuesday, April 19th she had written "keys to Dolly/stop paper delivery." Yesterday, Wednesday, April 20th the entry was "shuttle pu—flt 3:15 Galleria Hotel SJ." The squares after that, up until Wednesday, April 27th, were marked through with a diagonal line. On the 27th it read: "return home."

SJ. San Juan? Was she intending to fly to Puerto Rico with Richard? Lane was staying home, Caroline had said. He wanted to go it alone. It looked like he wanted to go it with Henny. But why would she have gone ahead and taken the trip under these circumstances?

I was thinking about how she must have figured that the ticket was already purchased, why waste it, when I heard a car pull up out front. I sprinted to the window and pulled the Venetian blind back a couple of inches. A cabbie was helping Henny Thornton unload her bags from the trunk of his taxi when a man on a bicycle, coming from the direction of the beach, called to her in passing, "Thought you were in Puerto Rico."

"The damn flights were canceled out of Miami," she yelled. "Spent the night in a flea bitten hotel listening to drunks curse each other in Spanish."

The cyclist made a wide turn in the street to reply. "Freak of nature, that's for sure. Who ever heard of a hurricane in April?" then he completed the circle and, with a so-long salute, continued on his way.

"I told you to be careful with that bag!" Henny screamed at the cab driver as he set a suitcase on the grass. I couldn't see what the guy was doing to warrant her wrath, but I wasn't about to hang around to find out. I lost no time unlocking the back door and getting my rear out of there.

I bolted across her backyard through a tangle of vegetation into the backyard of the house behind hers, facing the next street. Once at the sidewalk, I slowed to a leisurely pace, turned left at the corner, then made another left onto Henny's street as if I were strolling in from the main boulevard. I fiddled around in my purse, pulled out the Le Baron keys, got in, and casually eased away from the curb as Henny was lugging her suitcases through her front door.

I was heartsick to find that Donald was right about her and Richard. For Lane's sake, I didn't want it to be so. For Helen's sake, too, of course. I had to face the possibility that Lane probably really did shove her husband down those stairs, and that Dorothy probably really did see the whole thing. One fact remained clear, however: Henny could not have seen it, too. Hers was the lie that would be exposed at trial, yet it wouldn't alter one tiny bit the fact that Dorothy had witnessed the incident. And Dorothy's statement, not Henny's, was the incriminating factor.

I decided to call Caroline. I had to know if she had an inkling that Richard was unfaithful and if so, did she believe that her mother knew. I stopped at a pay phone outside Border's Books on Second Street. Caroline answered on the first ring. When I asked if I could come by, she was hesitant. It crossed my mind that she might have a male visitor, but I dismissed the notion. Caroline was too distraught to think about much but her mother and their situation right now.

"I don't mean to sound paranoid," she said into the phone, "but the media, they're so damn crafty. Are you sure they don't know your car? Are you positive you aren't being followed?"

I told her that I was absolutely, one hundred per cent sure, but she still wasn't convinced. "To be honest, Mrs. Wallace," she added, "I don't feel up to having company right now."

I told her it was urgent.

She sighed while I waited. Then she said, slowly and reluctantly, "Do you know the Tropicana?"

"The new hotel beside the Second Street Bridge?"

"That's it. They have a terrace in back, on the beach. It should be pretty empty at this hour. Take a table as far away from anyone else as you can. I'll come in off the street side."

"How long?"

"Where are you?"

I told her.

"You're only a couple of minutes from there. I'll be right behind you."

I knew she could walk from her apartment, cross Second Street, and be at the hotel before I could even get the car started. Less than five minutes later I was parking in the guest lot at the front of the luxury hotel. The plush lobby was nearly empty except for a couple of bellboys and preoccupied desk clerks. I crossed to the triple wide exit directly ahead of me and onto the back terrace.

A few customers were lounging around tables, sipping drinks brought to them by waiters in pink trousers and white shirts. One of them hurried to seat me, but I waved him away with, "I'll sit over there. I'm waiting for a friend."

"Would you like something while you—?"

I shook my head and settled into a pink wrought iron chair at a pink wrought iron table, facing the water. Kids were playing Frisbee on the yellow sand and muscled hunks strutted their stuff in front of the few girls sashaying by, almost wearing swimsuits.

"I feel silly, sneaking around like this," Caroline said, slipping into a chair beside me. Her hair was tucked up under a wide-brimmed straw hat. She wore sunglasses that looked like red-framed snow goggles. All we needed now was for 007 to race in on a jet ski. Her back was to the other customers.

"I apologize for not asking you to the apartment, but I have this nagging feeling that reporters are lurking behind every doorway." She shivered involuntarily. I told her that the feeling wasn't unwarranted.

Pink Pants returned and we gave him our order. Ginger ale for me, Perrier for Caroline. Then she leaned back, removed the glasses, and shook her head wearily. "I've spent all morning finalizing plans for Richard's funeral. It's so…" She left the sentence unfinished. Her eyes clouded and she looked away.

I hadn't thought about his funeral. I don't know why it didn't dawn on me that he'd have to go, well, somewhere.

"When is it?" I asked.

"Tomorrow. I thought you knew."

I didn't, but then who would have told me if she didn't mention it when I saw her yesterday, which she didn't.

"Will Lane be there?"

"Of course."

"Well, with her in hiding and all…" I shrugged, unable to think of anything else to say. It seemed to me that Lane had gone to a lot of trouble to keep from facing reporters and a funeral would be the one place they would congregate. When I commented on it to Caroline, she said, "Harold's back. Grandmother's lawyer. She'll come in his limo, surrounded by police and bodyguards. You know, Mrs. Wallace. Like your husband used to do for us."

I felt ancient when she said Mrs. Wallace like that. "Katie."

Her cheeks flushed. "Katie."

"You were pretty young the last time he worked for your mother."

Accepting her drink from our waiter, who bowed deeply and

left, Caroline said, "I remember him really well. Mostly that he was so tall. He looked like somebody you could trust with your life, which is what Mom did, of course. He just gave you the feeling that, no matter how bad things were, he could make them right again."

That was him. Good ol' trustworthy MacKay. Yessir. Which brought me to the subject I wasn't sure how to broach. Fidelity. I thought I should go at it slowly. "Can I ask you something pretty personal?"

"If it will help Mom, sure."

I looked up at the blue, blue sky. A small plane pulled an ad for a Russell Crowe movie behind it. I watched it climb into a steep turn, its banner whipping in the wind. Finally, I said, "Is there any possibility that Richard would...cheat...on your mother?"

She fastened those green eyes on me as if deciding whether or not I was trying to bait her. "Why do you ask?"

"I need to know." I could see that didn't satisfy her.

She leaned back in her chair, exasperated. "It's impossible to have a private life if you've been in the public." She rubbed her forehead. "There are no secrets."

"Should there be secrets?"

"Everybody has them, Katie."

"Did Richard have them, you think?"

She leaned in closer to me and lowered her voice to little more than a whisper. "Please, please don't tell my mother. It would kill her."

"It's true then?"

"It's true."

"How can you be so sure?"

"I caught him."

"You actually walked in on them?"

"Nothing like that." She leaned back again and spread her elbows on the arms of the chair, lacing her fingers together in front of her. "I was in Pasadena one evening with a friend. We were going to a play. We got to town early and had about forty-five minutes or so to kill, so we stopped at Starbucks for coffee. And...there he was. There they were."

I put my hand on her arm, but quickly withdrew it. As gentle as she appeared to be, Caroline wasn't someone who sought sympathy. I started to say, "Maybe it wasn't what you thought" but she cut me off.

"It was obvious. The way they were looking at each other. He had his arm across the back of her chair and he was watching her…so attentively. He was fastened on her, like she was the most remarkable creature on earth. That's when I noticed her hand on his knee. Katie, women don't put their hand on a man's knee unless they're intimate. We just don't."

I tried to picture ugly Henny with her hand on a man's knee. Not hardly. Not unless she was holding a knife and moving it up his thigh with foul intentions. I couldn't make the image of a romantic Henny stick in my mind. "Did he know you were there?"

Her face clouded again. "I wanted to get away before he could see me, but it was so crowded. Starbuck's has mirrors behind the counter, you know…I was trying to shoulder my way out of there when I saw Richard's reflection as he glanced up. Our eyes locked. It was so peculiar. His face…you should have seen him. He looked stricken."

"What'd he do?"

"He got up and came after me. Caught up with my friend and me out front. I didn't want to talk to him. Didn't want to hear his lies." She stopped for breath, then went on. "He begged me not to tell Mom." She shook her head in irony. "If he'd just said something like 'Hi, Caroline! Bring your friend on over and join us!' I would have dismissed it as him having coffee with his secretary. But it was the look on his face and the way he was begging me not to mention it to Mom that cinched it."

Secretary? Who the hell was *that* and where'd she come from?

"Marcie Garner," Caroline said. "She's been with him for years."

The rest of our visit isn't worth repeating. Most of what we said was lost on me because I was hung up on trying to figure out who the devil this man, Richard Wagnor, was. I found it hard to believe that Lane really didn't know, but then I found it hard to believe that I really didn't know about MacKay. I didn't mention Henny's name and pretty soon Caroline looked at her watch, said she had a thousand more details to attend to regarding the funeral, and that she'd see me the next day.

"Where?"

"St. Theresa's on Hollywood Boulevard. Two o'clock."

I asked if I could bring someone and she said it would be fine, but not to plan on talking to her mother as it would be almost impossible. I couldn't imagine that I'd walk up to the lady at her husband's funeral to announce what all I'd found out. I promised Caroline that I'd keep my distance. She started away, then turned back as if she forgot something, and surprised me by giving me a kiss on the cheek, brief and heartfelt. Then she dashed across the terrace to the side street. Last I saw of her, she was hanging onto the wide-brimmed hat against a sudden stiff breeze coming in off the bay. And I was holding onto an even wilder image of the man Lane and Helen exalted as the wonderful Richard Wagnor.

ELEVEN

I PAID THE BILL AND stepped into the lobby, to the bank of pay phones. I called information for the number of the studio that produced *Cop Patrol* only to learn a few minutes later that Donald was out to lunch and not expected back until around two-thirty. I said I'd call back, hung up, dug my long distance calling card out of my billfold and used it to call home. No answer. On the sixth ring I heard myself on the machine asking me to leave my number and I'd get back to me as soon as I could. I left a message asking Terry to please call me, keeping in mind the time difference. I left Helen's number, even though it was written on a bulletin board beside my phone in the St. Seminole kitchen. Then I went into the hotel gift shop for a package of mints.

That's when I saw the row of newspapers screaming headlines about the Allison-Wagnor murder. I snatched up a copy of the *L.A. Morning Edition*. The front page featured a picture of Lane Allison taken on the day of her first husband's funeral. I knew that, but the public wouldn't know it. In the photo, Lane was ashen, her eyes swollen and bloodshot. The banner slanted across the picture read: My God! Richard's dead! What have I done! as if the photo were taken in the aftermath of Wagnor's death. That picture had come out of Helen's scrapbook. A strip across the bottom of the page screamed: Exclusive! Never before seen photos of Lane Allison! Disgusted, I slapped the paper back into its stand, wondering how it had gone to print so quickly.

The *Los Angeles Times* featured a news photo of Miami beaches under attack by hurricane Abby. I bought the paper and took it to the coffee shop where I ordered a tuna sandwich and iced tea, and turned to the follow-up story of Abby on page five. The unprecedented storm had cut across the Atlantic, leaving a path of destruction in Puerto Rico, then moving along the eastern rim of Miami. It was headed toward the Carolina coast at fifteen miles an hour with winds gusting up to a hundred and ten. That meant St. Seminole would get heavy rains, possibly even a spin-off tornado or two. Rather than dissipating, the article indicated that Abby seemed to be gaining in strength. I looked around at the people in the coffee shop wearing shorts and sunglasses. Nobody cared about a Florida storm or the fact it wasn't even hurricane season. If it couldn't be measured on the Richter scale, it didn't count. After all, this was California. Southern California. Center of the Universe.

By the time I finished with the paper and polished off my lunch, it was nearly two-thirty. Quick trip to the sandbox, then back to the pay phone. This time Donald came on the line when I asked for him.

"Well, what's this?" he said, good-naturedly. "Your flight canceled?"

I hadn't thought about that. No one said it was when I called the airline to change my reservation earlier in the day. Maybe planes were still flying into Orlando. "No," I replied. "I stayed to take care of some unfinished business. Richard's funeral is tomorrow."

"Oh?"

"Care to attend with me?"

He thought for a moment, or I guessed he was thinking. Anyway, he was silent for a bit, then asked what time.

"Two o'clock. St. Theresa's."

"On Hollywood Boulevard." He knew the temple. Seemed like most celebrity services were held there, just as most of them seem to prefer burial at Forest Lawn in Burbank, next to Warner Brothers Studios. "Let me see if I can shuffle a few meetings around," he said. "Can I let you know over dinner?"

I was surprised at how receptive I was to the idea. "I've got a lot to tell you, Donald. And a lot to ask."

"Where are you now?"

I told him. I also told him about meeting Caroline, but I didn't go into details.

"Why don't I pick you up where you are? I want you to see my new place."

"How'd you like a home cooked meal?" I hoped it didn't sound coy.

"Well, uh…"

All right, so cooking wasn't among my creative skills and he knew it. "We can grab some sandwich makings." I said. "I put together a mean sub."

"It's—what? Almost three. I've been here since five this morning, but I've got a feeling we're in for a long day on the set."

"Problems?"

"The star's sucking his thumb in the dressing room. Won't come out till the company agrees to give him a new toy."

That could only mean a new car. Exotic new car. Imported. Studios find most star tantrums amusing, yet annoying. Their demands are usually met about the way you'd toss a plaything to a child squalling in its crib. It keeps them occupied so you could get on with business.

We agreed that he'd pick me up at the hotel in an hour and a half, which left me with time to kill and thoughts to think. I went back into the gift shop and bought a writing pad. I found a table under a window in the lobby, pulled out of my purse the pen I keep clipped to my checkbook, and began making a list.

1. Dorothy is not RW's sister. Did she have feelings for him beyond family?
2. Did Harmon Ermaling realize Dorothy may have been lying—because of those feelings?
3. Did Henny back up Dorothy's story simply to hurt Lane?
4. Did Lane push Richard, or did she try to keep him from falling?
5. If she didn't push him, why did he fall?
6. Did Lane know RW was cheating on her with Henny?
7. Did Lane find out RW was cheating on her with secretary, Marcie?

8. If she knew, did she shove him down the steps in a fit of rage?
9. Harold, the lawyer, would surely try to substantiate Lane's version of events by verbally whipping Dorothy—and Henny?—into admitting on a witness stand that they saw nothing and had a personal grudge against Lane.
10. But the prosecutor will try to prove that Lane had reason to kill her husband.
11. When the probing starts, RW's affairs with Henny/Marcie will be revealed.
12. Proving that will be a lot easier than proving Dorothy's a liar.
13. Proving that will even be easier than proving Henny didn't see anything.
14. Once the affairs are exposed, probably neither Dorothy's testimony nor Henny's, will be challenged.
15. The question then becomes one of plea bargaining to get Lane the least amount of prison time possible.
16. Harold will argue either temporary insanity or manslaughter.

I got up out of the chair half an hour later more depressed than ever. Helen had no idea what they were in for.

I decided that the tan slacks and brown shirt could stand alone in a corner by now, I'd worn them for so long. Reluctantly, I pulled out my trusty Visa card. No way would I pop for hotel boutique prices. I left the car in the parking lot and walked to a shop I remembered being on a side street, behind the library, across the bridge. It was more hiking than I'd done since I was about ten. I hated the sweat it generated under my arms. I have an aversion to sweat. The express lane at the grocery store is about as fast as I want to move.

I found the shop, and a skirt that didn't make me look like I'd left the hanger in the hips, along with a blouse that fit just fine. The clerk slid my Visa across a machine that took a chunk out of my dwindling credit card balance, then I returned to the hotel to change in the ladies' room. When Donald pulled up at the front entrance, I was freshly sponge bathed and newly clothed. My spirits lifted the minute he leaned across the front seat to open the passenger door. "S'cuse me for not getting out to open this thing, Katie," he said. "The knees are acting up again."

We stopped at the Marketplace, where I ran in with a twenty dollar bill he'd pressed on me and bought cold cuts, cheese and Italian bread, skipping tomatoes because there's no such thing anymore. There are only orange pods with gas pumped into them for artificial color. Wet cardboard is not how I remember the taste of tomatoes from my youth.

Going against evening traffic, we continued on toward downtown Long Beach. When I asked where we were headed, he said, "You'll see," and grinned mischievously.

I was surprised by the number of new buildings along the boulevard near Pine. To our left, Catalina Island, twenty-six miles out at sea, looked like a misty humpback whale. We turned onto St. Thomas Bridge, a dramatic span with enormous cables and ropes of steel overhead, and emerged in San Pedro. It struck me that Donald might be taking me to see where Henny and Richard used to meet, but then we curved back, under the bridge, and bumped along a rough road bordering a community of houseboats and second rate yachts. It was tacky in an interesting sort of way.

Donald parked the car and we got out, toting the groceries across a muddy embankment to a creaky dock that tipped dangerously to one side, and onto a plank leading to the deck of a houseboat covered in shake-shingles. He unlocked the door. I stepped into his bachelor pad.

I was impressed. It was homey, unpretentious, cleverly decorated with items that couldn't go thump on a stormy night. Chairs, tables, even oil lamps, were battened down. It was clean, smelled of brine and Lemon Pledge and I loved it. I was also anxious for us to get to a point where I could show him the notes I'd made back at the hotel.

We small talked about the studio, stubborn actors, the impending writers strike that threatened to put everyone temporarily out of work while it was negotiated, and his choice of a houseboat for his new home. "Couldn't take the memories any more, Katie. Besides, a split level and bum knees aren't particularly compatible. Next you'll ask why I didn't get a suburban house and I'll have to admit that I'd a lot rather scrape barnacles than mow grass." Finally, subs washed down with cold ale, we settled onto a long sofa under open windows to talk about Lane Allison's situation.

I dug the notes out of my purse and, while I was spreading them across the oversized tool chest serving as a coffee table, explained what I'd learned about secretary Marcie and from the calendar in Henny's house. When I came up for air, he got up to refill our glasses.

"Seems like the more I do to try to help Helen and Lane, the more damage I cause," I said.

He returned from the galley and settled back onto the sofa. "Have you talked to her lawyer?"

"He's been in Europe. Due back this week, but to be honest, I haven't wanted to talk to him. Everything I've found makes Lane's case even weaker. If she had even an inkling that Richard cheated on her, they're never going to be able to convince a jury she didn't shove him intentionally."

"Off the record, I'm hearing that her defense will be passion provocation manslaughter."

That didn't surprise me. I nodded and swished cold ale around in my mouth.

"I've got another theory," he said. "Let's say, for the sake of argument, that Wagnor grabbed his chest and his knees buckled just the way Lane described it before his fall. What's it sound like besides a heart attack?"

I thought, shrugged, sipped ale. "I dunno."

"Sure you do. You just don't want to say it. I didn't either. But the more I think about it, and the more you tell me about it, the more I'm convinced it's a possibility."

"You plan to share this possibility with me?"

"Poison. And you've got three people at that garden party with a damn good motive."

"Murder? I mean, we've been talking murder all along, but accidental murder, not *murder* murder. You're talking about plotted out, thought out, deliberate murder?"

He crossed his ankles in front of him. "I am."

"Wait a minute. An autopsy was performed on Richard. Why wouldn't poison have shown up if—?"

"Supposing you suspect that someone's been poisoned. There's an autopsy. When tests are run for poisons, the results come up on a computer screen as patches of color. Certain colors indicate the test is either positive or negative—for those particular *kinds* of poison. So, even if the patches show negative, it doesn't rule out all poisons."

"I'm not sure I follow what you're saying."

"There are literally thousands of kinds of poison. Insecticides, household chemicals, drugs—prescription and street—lethal raw food combinations, tainted foods, fumes, poison berries and plants." He waved his hand impatiently. "The list goes on and on. The range is enormous. In order to find out if poison killed someone, you have to know which kind of poison to test for."

"So, if no one suspected anything like that—?" I raised a brow and waited for him to finish the sentence.

"Lane brought up the possibility of a heart attack. But the postmortem examination showed his heart to be perfectly sound. Frankly, I doubt anyone seriously considered his heart, though her lawyer would have torn the prosecutor to shreds if a medical examination for heart failure hadn't been performed. They wouldn't have searched further, since they already knew actual death was the result of massive head injuries."

I was trying to sort it out. "So, you're suggesting there are three people with motives."

"Two mistresses and a sister who isn't a sister. But—what if Lane found out about one or both of the women? She'd be the most likely suspect, so we're back to square one. She killed him, only with poison, not with a mighty shove." He took a long drink, watching me over the rim of his glass. "It's possible," he said.

"Yeah, but why would she poison him at a party where there are witnesses? That doesn't make sense."

"Maybe she wanted the blame to fall on others. Or maybe she poisoned him, thinking it wouldn't affect him until everyone was gone, but it kicked in a little ahead of schedule. She sees what's happening to him, he buckles, she instinctively reaches out to catch him. That part of her story would be the absolute truth. She tried to stop the fall, Dorothy saw the whole thing and swore Lane pushed him for all the personal reasons you already suspect."

"And Henny?"

"Henny has her own reasons for attesting to Dorothy's story. It gets rid of a woman who's been her rival for a very long time. Revenge."

"Okay, okay. What if you're right...what if he was poisoned? And what if Henny found out about the secretary?"

"Good point," he interrupted with a wicked grin. "Now you're thinking like a detective. To think like a detective, you have to be able to think like a criminal."

I mulled that over. Somehow a thank you didn't seem to be in order.

He went on. "Henny could have done it knowing Lane would be the first one the police would investigate. The shoving part would have been dumb good luck, a bonus for Henny that would help throw suspicion right where she wanted it in the first place. On Lane."

I tried to get a mental picture of Henny as a killer.

"It's a rule, Katie dear—you can cheat on your wife, but you can't cheat on your mistress."

I didn't like the rule, but I wasn't through hypothesizing. "What about Marcie?"

"That doesn't work. Not unless she was there that day."

"Haven't I read about slow-acting poisons? Women who give their husband arsenic over a period of years until the cumulative effect finally does them in?"

"I was thinking about the day of party, but you have a point."

"So," I said slowly, "you're right. They each have a motive. Marcie, Henny, and Dorothy."

"And Lane." He leaned forward to set his glass on the tool chest. "Personally, I favor the notion it was Dorothy. She found out Henny was still seeing Wagnor, and it was the final insult to a woman who'd loved him like more than a brother for a very long time."

A foghorn sounded somewhere out on the water. Waves lapped at the sides of the houseboat as it rocked gently under us. It should have been a pleasant evening, but it was turning into something I wasn't prepared to face. Lane was nowhere near off the hook, even with all of our other theories. I drained my glass.

"Why didn't the police think of this, if it's so logical?"

"Because they aren't going to keep this alive any longer than they have to, Katie. They don't have the manpower or the resources to devote to that kind of investigation. And I can tell you right now, they'll be damn glad to see the media get out of their jurisdiction. Nobody likes that kind of national scrutiny, especially a small precinct like the one doing the investigation."

"Why don't they change the venue? Take it downtown?"

Donald shook his head. "Don't you remember what happened when they moved the Simpson trial from Santa Monica for exactly those reasons? They're not about to repeat that mistake."

"What kind of poisons would cause the symptoms Lane described?"

He shrugged. "Hard to say. We'd have to do a little research."

"Can't we tell the police what we suspect and let their fingers do the walking?" I could see me not getting back to my menagerie for another thirty days. Sixty days. This year!

"Like I say, Katie, they're not going to pursue it. They have an eyewitness and a dead man. That's good enough for them."

I saw his point.

"Tell me this," he said. "You believe Lane, don't you?"

I had to admit that I did.

"So, if she didn't push him, and I'm not saying she didn't, but if she didn't, what else could have happened to him—besides poison?"

There was no answer. He knew it. I knew it. He changed the

subject. "I rearranged meetings so I can pick you up around eleven-thirty in the morning. I thought we'd grab a bite to eat at Jerry's Deli. You probably won't feel much like dinner after the services."

"The funeral. I almost forgot."

"There's even a good chance you'll get to meet the secretary." He got to his feet, stretched and yawned. I got the hint and pulled myself up from the sofa. "Ex-wife, too, I suspect. Good thing she wasn't around last Sunday or we could add her name to the heap," he said, digging car keys from his pocket. "What'd MacKay used to say? Watch for what you don't see. It's what you don't see that tells you everything you need to know."

"He said that to you, too?"

"All the time."

It was half an hour to my car, another hour and a half back to Studio City, and around one in the morning before I laid my weary, reeling head on the pillow in Helen's guest room. Tired as I was, there was too much to think about to even consider sleep.

TWELVE

I WOKE UP WITH the feeling that something ominous was happening. Or about to happen. The house was too quiet for me. I slipped out of bed, did the morning bathroom ritual, and glanced in the mirror. How come men wake up looking like they did when they went to bed, but women deteriorate overnight? I hoped the bed sheet wrinkles in my cheek were temporary.

Helen needed a cat. Maybe a dog. Even a bird. She needed life in the house. In the kitchen, I put together enough coffee for two cups and returned to the guest room to finish dressing while it dripped. The aroma was welcome. Almost as good as a living thing, but not quite. *Good Morning America* popped up on the screen when I clicked on the remote. Diane Sawyer was interviewing a child who had rescued a grown man from a fire. Some people save people, some people kill people. And Diane Sawyer always looked unruffled and nice. I wondered if she was really that nice and laid a bet with myself that she is. I want to be more like Diane Sawyer. Never upset, never ruffled. And always nice. Life would surely be less complicated.

National network news followed the Sawyer piece. Hurricane Abby was the focus of attention. A journalist did his best to stand his ground on some Florida beach as giant waves crashed in around him. He was yelling over the wind and I wondered why he had to be there. The words "raging," "gusts up to a hundred and twenty-five miles an hour," and "mass evacuation" carried plenty of impact. Why'd we have to see an idiot out there being whiplashed by a storm? The ultimate show-and-tell.

I dialed my house remembering that although it was seven-thirty in California, it was later in St. Seminole. The phone rang four times before the answering machine picked up. Static was so heavy I didn't attempt to leave a message. A ringing phone told me that at least the house was still standing. Surely the phone wouldn't ring if the walls were gone. Would it? Poor Grace, the old black lab. She was terrified of lightning, trembled violently when wind howled. I hoped Terry remembered to leave the doggie door open so that she and the other furry kids could get inside.

I dressed quickly, downed the coffee, found a bagel that had seen better days and a dab of cream cheese with only a dot of green in it. I remembered that the local library used to open at eight in the morning on Mondays and Fridays. I hoped that was still the case. I had no idea how to begin researching poison, but I intended to find out. Letting myself out the back door and heading for the Le Baron, I noticed a helicopter flying dangerously low. And then I realized they were tipping to one side as they passed Helen's rooftop. Photographers! I cupped my hand to my forehead and squinted upward without stopping to realize the photos they'd have were of a woman just a tad older than Rita Moreno with her neck craned back, a puckered frown between her eyes, and her mouth wide open in amazement.

THE MAN AT the library's research desk suggested I start with Deadly Doses, an easy-to-read, layman's language book on poisons and their effects. "Great for research if you're writing a mystery," he added, scribbling down the number of the volume and handing me the scrap of paper. I thanked him, made my way to the proper section in an otherwise empty building, and found not only the book in question, but several others on the subject. It was eight-thirty. Donald wasn't to pick me up for another three hours.

I read, I noted, I read some more, then I noted some more. There wasn't enough time to digest it all. The possibilities, as Donald had pointed out, were vast. Where to begin? What would someone use in a common, everyday murder? Something not too exotic. Something that could be obtained easily, without involving a pharmacist or doctor. Something you could slip to someone without detection...but how? *In* something? In *what?* Where's

Sherlock Holmes when I need him? By ten-thirty I had a yellow pad filled with scribbles and scrawling that I hoped I could decipher once I got back to Helen's guest room at the end of what was bound to be a long and difficult day. Despite the filled notebook, I still didn't have an inkling of the kind of poison that might have done in poor Richard. The choices were just too extensive.

I bundled up my bulging notepad and stuck it my purse, then headed back to Helen's, where I changed into my newly acquired boutique outfit with a gold belt. Sandals seemed inappropriate, so I pulled a pair of Helen's dress shoes from a rack and managed to curl my toes under the balls of my feet so they'd squish into pumps at least a full size too small. How did Oriental women endure the pain of bound feet? It hurt like hell.

At exactly eleven-thirty, I heard a car horn and I wobbled to the front door. To my horror, the entire street was filling with news vans and a crowd of people carrying cameras and sound equipment and recorders. Donald had managed to ease his car into the drive and was frowning angrily as I limped down the walk toward him. Before I could open the car door, a female reporter jammed a mic in front of me saying "…not sure who this is. Perhaps a family member or friend of Lane's mother. Excuse me—Jane Robertson, Channel 16. Could you just tell us if Lane Allison will be making an appearance at the funeral this morning? Do you know—?"

I hobbled past, jabbed an elbow toward her midsection, and watched her bounce back, hissing the word "bitch" between her teeth while maintaining a smile for her TV audience. I jerked open the door and slammed it shut behind me.

"Get us outta here," I growled needlessly.

Donald already had the car in Reverse. A man holding a TV camera crouched to get a better view inside the car and ran along beside us, taking pictures, until Donald swerved dangerously close to the drop off. The guy had no choice but to back away. We inched past media vehicles parked recklessly along the narrow road. Once at Ventura Boulevard, he gunned the engine and we shot away from the gaggle of pursuing automobiles.

"Damn," he cursed under his breath.

I held on and kept my mouth shut.

"Forget lunch at Jerry's," he grumbled, glancing into the rearview mirror.

"This is crazy. What're they going to do with pictures of us?"

"They probably thought I'm Helen's lawyer coming to pick her up. I suspect they figured Lane would be with us."

"If this is any indication of what's ahead, the funeral's going to be a mad house."

"More like a house of horrors," he admitted ruefully.

"Turn left here."

"Can't. It's one way."

"Turn anyway."

He grinned like a naughty kid as he made a sharp left, into oncoming traffic. Like the Red Sea, traffic parted ahead of us as we rolled through, waving royally. Not a single media car followed. Donald whipped into an alley and followed it to the back entrance of a Chinese restaurant. After parking beside a take-out van, we ducked inside. "Hope you feel like Mandarin," he said, guiding me with a steady hand on my elbow past the kitchen toward the dining room. I limped beside him miserably, counting the steps to a table where I could plop down in a chair and pull my scrunched up tootsies out of those infernal size six's.

Fortified with egg foo yung and every batter-fried, greasy, vegetable-pork-chicken combination you can imagine, we returned to the car. I'd made the mistake of removing Helen's shoes. There was no possibility that I'd be able to jam my swollen feet back inside them. "What size do you wear?" Donald asked, opening the door on the passenger side of his car as I slipped in, barefoot.

"Why?"

"Just tell me."

I suspected what he was up to, but my feet hurt too much to argue. "Seven," I said, then felt my face get hot and added, "and a half. Well, actually eight." He was back within ten minutes with a shoebox containing a pair of black, sensibly heeled dress pumps in my proper size. Flashing a pleased grin, he backed out of the alley and onto Laurel Canyon Drive, headed toward Hollywood, St. Theresa's, and a media circus I could never have imagined possible.

While we'd eaten lunch, I'd shared some of the things I'd learned about poisons that morning at the library. He'd listened, nodded, chewed. Most of the stuff I told him, he already knew from his years on the police force. When I ran out of material, we ate in silence. It takes a lot to impress my friend Donald, and this morning's effort didn't even come close.

STREETS WERE ROPED OFF in a four block area around the church. There was not just one helicopter over us, there were three, all of them from news stations. Crowds lined the streets much as they line them for the Hollywood Christmas parade. I even saw a few people holding autograph books. I guess they were hoping to capture celebrity signatures as recognizable personalities came or went from the service. One entire side of the street across from St. Theresa's was filled with news vans and satellite dishes. Cables and electrical extensions snaked across asphalt and under parked cars. Men and women with press passes clipped to their lapels barked orders, spoke into microphones to the unblinking red eye of a camera pointed at them, ignoring police orders to move back. I wondered what gave them the idea they were special. Parking ordinances, decent manners, civil obedience or disobedience—none of these things had anything to do with them. They were above it.

The parking lot was surrounded by uniformed police. I noticed several off-duty officers that MacKay and I had known also working the ropes that held back fans and the curious. One policeman was blowing a whistle furiously, motioning for cars to move forward and turn into the parking area designated for family and friends of the deceased. I was surprised to see so many actors and actresses from Lane Allison's career days among the arrivals. I wondered, too, if they used a precious sum out of their social security checks to hire a limo for the occasion. There was something sad, almost pathetic, in the sight of them huddled grandly in the backseat of a chauffeur-driven Town Car. Most people aren't aware that a limo and driver can be hired for as little as twenty-five dollars an hour in Los Angeles, their use is so common among movie folks. Still, twenty-five dollars, times three or four hours, is a hunk out of a pension.

A roar went up from the crowd as Donald followed a fellow police officer's directive and parked in a space near the back of the lot. I turned to see what had caused the commotion. When a black stretch limo pulled to the curb in front of the church, a uniformed driver hopped out and opened the rear door. A man with Popeye's biceps and the torso of an Incredible Hulk stepped out and scanned the crowd. He leaned back to the car and nodded. A tall gentleman with iron gray hair and a neatly trimmed mustache emerged. The word "distinguished" had been created so there would be a way to describe him. He stood erect outside the car, took a deep breath with his nose tilted slightly skyward, and bent over to offer his hand to whomever was coming out of the automobile behind him. It was Helen. Bulbs flashed in her face, but from a distance. A line of police had jumped into action to restrain the media the minute the limo had come to a stop. Helen's face was ashen. There was a slope to her shoulders I'd never seen before. As she stepped out, the distinguished gentleman offered his hand to another passenger.

Lane Allison could not have appeared more delicate, more innocent. She glanced gratefully at the throng, which generated a tremendous cheer and scattered applause, even an inappropriate chorus of whistles. Holding on to the man I was pretty certain was Harold, their attorney, Lane moved between him and her mother, on their way to the sweep of stairs that led to the temple entrance. I counted four bodyguards and another four off-duty policemen around the trio. Invited mourners crushed in around them, protectively, as flashbulbs went off and a babble of voices could be heard speaking into microphones.

"Lane Allison Wagnor has just arrived, accompanied by her mother Helen and family attorney—"

"As you can see, hundreds of fans and well-wishers have lined the streets of downtown Hollywood to see this—"

"...out on one million dollars bail, Lane Allison Wagnor,

widow of television producer, Richard Wagnor, has just entered St. Theresa's for her husband's memorial service. Ironic that the woman accused of killing him less than a week ago is wearing widow's weeds and appears to be genuinely grieving...but let us not forget, acting is her business..."

The voices were blurred and mixed. I wasn't sure who was saying what, except for that last voice. I knew it belonged to the most popular announcer on local TV. I thought the words were petty, beneath the dignity of the station, but then nobody asked for my opinion. Donald shook his head sadly and squeezed my hand as we struggled among the masses toward the concrete stairs.

Once on the landing, we stepped aside to let others pass. I wanted to see who would show up. I didn't have long to wait before getting a glimpse of Henny Thornton dressed in gray and looking dour. I was wondering how Dorothy was going to manage with her wheelchair when someone tapped my shoulder. "Mother wants you to come down front with us," Caroline whispered. Donald put a protective arm around my waist as we followed her to a side entrance. A row of officers stood against the wall. Donald nodded to several of them.

The church was filled nearly to capacity, though guests continued to arrive. Helen and Lane were seated in a front row, facing a casket banked—nearly hidden, actually—in carnations. Helen looked up gratefully when she saw us approach. She patted a place on the pew beside her to her right. On her left sat a clean-cut young man of nineteen or twenty who I was sure was Michael. Lane, seated next to him, kept her face averted. One hand held tightly to her son's arm. Caroline left us to slip in on her mother's right so that Lane had her children beside her, one on either side. Their attorney sat erect beside Caroline.

When Donald nudged me, I followed his gaze to a rear door where Dorothy Ermaling was being brought in, her wheelchair pushed by her husband. I thought that Dorothy looked smug and defiant. I glanced at Donald, realizing that he was probably thinking the same thing. Harmon Ermaling seemed somewhat embarrassed. An usher indicated a place where they could sit so that the wheelchair would be out of the way, yet still allow Dorothy to be privy to the activity. I wondered if it was my imagination, but I thought I saw Dorothy shoot Lane a quick, hostile glance. Harmon kept his attention riveted on the casket.

Henny Thornton was seated directly behind us. I could hear her sniff, but I wasn't sure if she was crying or if she had a cold. A young girl, rather tomboyish, in a tailored pale blue suit, leaned over Caroline's shoulder to kiss her on the cheek. Caroline twisted around enough to return the gesture. Probably her step-sister, Royalee. I took a quick peek behind me and saw that a large-boned woman with conservatively cut gray hair and a kindly face was settling in beside the girl I took to be Richard Wagnor's daughter. This was no doubt Wagnor's ex-wife, Arlene.

The auditorium was animated, as if a party were in progress. It didn't grow quiet until a man in a black robe entered from a room behind the pulpit. He surveyed the crowd slowly before letting his attention settle on Lane Allison. "Beloved," he began, directly to her. She looked up then, met his compassionate gaze with tearful eyes and the crowd fell to a hushed silence. If this had been a scene in one of her movies, there wouldn't have been a dry eye in the house.

IT TOOK AN HOUR to thread our way to the cemetery, following a mile-long line of cars. Forest Lawn sweeps up grassy knolls, rolls down into shallow valleys, yet is surrounded by the heavily congested Barham Boulevard on one side, a freeway behind it, and a giant studio dead ahead of it. Despite that, it somehow manages to convey the impression of total serenity. A huge monument stands over Al Jolson's burial spot, seen by everyone who drives by. Tombstones etched with the names of other famous personalities dot the immaculately tended grounds. If you don't make it to heaven, Forest Lawn is the next best place to spend eternity.

Again, there was a multitude of bodyguards and policemen on duty and off. Again, mass parking. And again, Helen's attorney in attendance, one arm around Lane's shoulders, another around

Helen as we all made our way to the place Richard Wagnor would be laid to rest. And, from what I'd learned about him in the last day or so, the guy needed to rest.

Henny Thornton pressed in behind the family while, once more, Dorothy and Harmon Ermaling kept their distance. After the brief graveside service, Caroline and Michael greeted sympathizers graciously, shaking each hand and thanking them for coming. Donald and I remained seated in the front row of the two or so hundred white folding chairs that had been provided. No need to hurry. It would take a very long time to ease out of the parking lot once we made it to the car. Might as well sit and observe.

Lane and Helen were secluded from the press as long as they stayed on the grounds; even air space overhead had been kept clear of media helicopters. We could see the vans lined up along Forest Lawn Drive and we knew that long-lens cameras were focused in our direction, but at least we could pretend they didn't exist, even if only for a few minutes. Ropes kept the crowd at a respectable distance. Forest Lawn personnel know how to let families of celebrities grieve. Not that Richard was a celebrity. Oddly enough, the occasion itself was the celebrity; everyone involved was simply a character in that play. Even Helen and Lane Allison.

When the last guest had walked away, leaving only a few dozen security officers around them, Helen motioned for us. Caroline, Michael, and Lane had drawn into a tight huddle. We could hear their sobs. Helen said in a voice so soft I had to strain to hear, "I'll be going back with Lane. Please don't leave California just yet." Her eyes, so bleary with fatigue and sorrow, pleaded with me. How could I go? She held out her arms and gathered me to her. I let her cry for as long as she needed to. Donald waited patiently. Finally, Caroline pulled away from her mother at almost the same moment Helen stepped back from me. Helen looked at her daughter and, on some unseen cue, they moved toward one another. Their embrace was tender, almost too tender to witness. I had to look away.

"Katie," Caroline said, startling me, "I'd like you to meet my sister, Royalee."

I turned to see the girl in the pale blue suit approaching us. She had intense blue eyes that were direct, a rather long face and, like a good race horse, strong white teeth that were visible when she said, "Hello. I've heard a lot about you." A girl who rode horses, swam like a fish, and probably played a mean game of softball. She didn't seem comfortable in a dress and I imagined that she could hardly wait to get home and be rid of the thing. This was a blue jeans girl if I ever saw one. Caroline put an arm around Royalee's waist and their heads touched.

"Mrs. Wallace?"

Michael was just under six feet tall. His green eyes met mine as he held out his hand for a firm handshake. "Thank you for being here for Grandmother," he said simply. The blonde good looks and rather delicate features hadn't prepared me for the deepness of his voice. I liked him on sight.

"Michael." It was the attorney.

"Yes, sir?"

The man took a step closer, glanced at me as if to gauge whether or not to speak in front of me, and must have decided it was all right. "We're taking your mother to the Stratton," he said cautiously. The Stratton Hotel is on a par with the Bel Air Hotel and, in case you don't know what par that might be, let's just say that a cottage on the grounds goes for around thirty-five hundred dollars a night. Secluded, beautiful in an old-world way, there would be no way the press could reach her on those hallowed grounds.

Michael glanced at his sister who said, "We'll be right behind you."

"No," the older man said. "I think you should let her rest. We'll get her back to Onaga in the morning. A decoy will make it appear that she's going to your old house, but she wants to wait it out at the cabin."

Caroline leaned to him and kissed his cheek. "Thank you, Harold. Tell her I'll be up as soon as I can figure how to get there without—"

The attorney cut her off with a quick nod. No need to say it. He knew. He acknowledged Donald with a curt inclination of his head, bid me goodbye, and wheeled away, taking Lane and Helen firmly by their arms and leading them to the waiting limousine. Caroline, Royalee and Michael watched Lane until the car was out of sight. Then Caroline sighed heavily, as if a weight had been removed from her shoulders.

"Can you come to dinner tonight, Katie? You, too, Mr. Stuart."

"Caroline!"

We all turned to find a short woman of about thirty-five or so making her way toward us. She was rather squat with a ring of dark curly hair protruding out from under an old-fashioned hat. The kind you'd buy at a retro shop. When she got to us, we could see that her eyes were rimmed with red, her nose almost the same hue. "I'm—so sorry."

Caroline looked at the ground. I had a feeling she was taking a moment to compose herself before she said, "Marcie, this is my grandmother's friend from Florida, Katie Wallace. Donald Stuart. Richard's secretary, Marcie."

The secretary! No wonder Caroline needed a second for composure. I said hello, but her discomfort was apparent as she shifted from one foot to the other. "I'll be…closing out the office. If there's anything you'd like…or if you want to come by—"

"Just put his personal things in boxes, Marcie," Caroline said. "I'll have someone pick them up later in the week."

Marcie couldn't think of anything else to say. She began to back away. "Well, goodbye, kids."

The kids, Michael and Caroline, didn't reply.

I hated to be catty, especially at a time like that, but between Marcie and Henny I had to conclude that Richard had a problem with choices. Being unfaithful to someone like Lane for those two was simply beyond my comprehension.

Caroline mentioned dinner at her place again, but Donald had a night shoot he couldn't get out of. I promised I'd be there by six. Then we trudged toward our cars. I felt a pang of anger when the media swarmed around Caroline's old Volks as they pulled onto Barham. The press was so intrusive, they actually blocked it from negotiating the freeway entrance while they snapped picture after picture.

We were behind them several car lengths. There was nothing we could do. Donald eased out of the line of automobiles to head for a side street.

"What'd the guy use for taste?" he asked wearily.

"What?"

"The secretary. What'd he see in her, you suppose?"

I shrugged. What'd MacKay see in Alice or Renee or…I stopped myself. I was so tired of playing that same damn tape in my head.

Donald sensed my mood. He reached across the seat to lay a hand over mine. "It's times like this I wish I were eloquent," he said.

"It's times like this a friend knows that words aren't necessary," I told him.

We were out on the freeway now, having gained access by taking several back streets away from Burbank. The drone of helicopters following the stretch limo that carried Helen, Lane and their attorney filled the air. I looked behind us and could see news vans veering off toward the Stratton exit.

It was still only mid-afternoon.

THIRTEEN

WE DROVE BACK TO Studio City in relative quiet. The afternoon had been a nightmare, but I had to think that, as bad as it was for me, it must have been even more horrible for Helen and Lane. For the kids, too. I found myself picturing Henny in her gray mourning suit. The nerve of her, coming to Richard's funeral. What a slap to his widow and children. And what a nasty little secret she had, though in reality it wasn't much of a secret with Donald, and probably half the people at their church, knowing about their affair.

And what about that secretary? Marcie.

I felt my pulse rate jump from whatever it usually is to something almost audibly swishing through my veins. Richard and MacKay. MacKay and Richard. Marcie and Henny. Renee and Alice. Damn damn, men, damn 'em, and damn us women for letting it hurt so much. And for being so stupid. Damn us for that, too.

"Hey."

I'd forgotten about Donald. When I glanced at him, he was watching me with an odd look of concern in his blue eyes. Then he turned his attention back to the traffic. "Your fists are in a ball. Don't want you to punch out my window."

"Sorry."

I don't have long nails, so I had to have had quite a clinch to have cut into my own palms the way I did.

He reached over, put an arm around my shoulder. For all the damning of men I'd been doing, that arm sure felt good. I brushed my lips against his knuckles and didn't even bother being embarrassed by the gesture. He patted me in a good-old-girl sort of way and grinned. Then a low rider slammed around us, signaling the driver's single digit IQ.

THERE WERE NO REPORTERS at Helen's house when we got there, or so we thought. As soon as Donald eased the car into the drive, a helicopter rose up over the rooftop and swooped in over us. I could see camera flashes from its dark interior. Donald said he'd call me in the morning as I leaped from the car, cursing the reporters again under my breath. Once inside the house, I felt my heart hammering in my chest. I couldn't help but wonder if someone was going to jump out at me from a closet or from behind the drapery. I realized once again how disturbing it was to think that if anyone decides they'd like to earn their livelihood entertaining us, they'd better be prepared to give up everything of their own. All the money in the world wouldn't make this kind of life acceptable.

I took another shower just to get rid of the stench of reporters, wrapped myself in Helen's long terrycloth robe and lay across her bed. The TV remote was on her nightstand. I clicked to a news station and watched the horror of the day unfold on the screen. Only it didn't look like what I had seen and experienced, not even remotely.

Helen was shown getting out of the limo on Harold's arm, looking thin and worn. Then Lane emerged from the car. She smiled bravely, waved shyly at the crowd. She looked tiny. And vulnerable. An off-screen announcer was saying in a somber tone, "Lane Allison arrived with her attorney and her mother, the first time the aging actress has been out of hiding since the death of her producer husband, Richard Wagnor. This woman, hardly five feet tall, has been accused of attacking her six-foot three spouse with enough passion to hurl him to his death—"

I clicked off the set in a new state of fury. Convicted! The media had already convicted Lane. Who needs a judge? Who needs a jury? Save the tax dollars, America; we've got the almighty media to decide guilt or innocence for us. The devil with MacKay; I'd found a fresh thing to damn: TV news.

There was no use trying to rest. Caroline had asked me to be at her place for dinner at six; might as well get ready. I decided my boutique outfit was too gussy for the occasion and went back to the beige pants and brown turtleneck which I'd tossed in Helen's washer, then in her dryer, before heading out to the library that morning. They could have used the hot side of an iron, but I couldn't justify the time it would take.

I ducked out of the house and sprinted to the Le Baron parked under a tree in the backyard. No helicopter. No camera lens bouncing off of sun rays. Just squirrels and birds and a strange quiet. The day was coming to a close with shadows gathering in the deeply shaded yard. MacKay used to say he could smell trouble and he could sense when the coast was clear. I sensed the coast was clear, but then what did I know?

Ventura Boulevard was thinning out as much as Ventura Boulevard ever thins out at the golden hour. It was equally clear of heavy traffic out on the freeway as I drove toward Naples Island with one eye on the road, the other on the rearview mirror, leaving me to look a lot like the headlights on the cross-eyed media car that had followed me the other night. I arrived at the triplex without mishap and, surprisingly, at exactly the appointed hour. Zori's Pizza truck was pulling away as I crossed the walk to the arched entrance.

Michael opened the door quickly, almost furtively. His good-looking features were gray in the fading light. Caroline glanced around from the dining table, where she was opening a large pizza box. Forks, napkins, a bottle of wine and long-stemmed glasses were laid out on the coffee table.

"God, what a day," Michael said, snapping a dead bolt in place the moment the door was shut. "Was there any trouble at Grandmother's when you got back?"

I told him about the helicopter. By now Caroline had slipped large wedges of pepperoni and cheese onto our plates and was bringing them to the living room. "We weren't able to lose the reporters for hours. Get the chips, will you, Michael?"

He disappeared into the kitchen, returned with an oversize bag of potato chips and tossed them unceremoniously on the coffee table. Then he pulled a chair around to sit in front of his plate.

Swallowing pizza, he said, "We had to leave the car at the hotel over on Second."

Caroline poured wine into our glasses. "We ducked inside, then slipped out the side door and walked to the apartment."

I was imagining reporters hovering around the Volks, waiting for Caroline and Michael to return, when I dropped a blob of sauce on the front of my shirt. It reminded me of what MacKay used to say when we'd be on the road and I'd want to stop for lunch. "Why don't you just suck your shirt, Kat? It's got half your breakfast on it." Funny man, that MacKay.

Caroline lifted her glass. "A toast. To Mom."

Michael added, "To the truth. May it set her free."

I joined in, toasting the legal system. Next we toasted each other. I felt at home with these youngsters, like I'd always known them. That's what disasters do: they draw people together, like those Florida hurricanes managed to do when I was a kid. Mom would make bowls of potato salad, Dad would fill tubs of water, and we'd head off to the highest and sturdiest place in the county, a rock church at the top of a knoll. While adults huddled around battery-operated radios, following weather updates, we kids romped about in candlelight, then napped on mattresses and blankets strewn around the sanctuary. Outside, the wind howled and rain pelted, but inside it was safe and warm. Strangers when we came in, friends while clustered under the church roof, hiding from the big, bad storm, like children in a closet. Despite everyone's vow to keep in touch once we were given the all clear to return home, no one ever did. But we were sure buddies during the course of the emergency. I hadn't thought about my childhood in that way in a very long time.

Polishing off the last scrap of pepperoni, Michael said, "Think we ought to take a look at the news?"

Caroline reached for the remote on the arm of the sofa and gave it a click. The screen came to life and there was Lane Allison again, emerging from the car at the cemetery. "She looks awful," Caroline said softly, studying her mother's face.

"I think she looks damn good, considering," Michael said defensively.

"That's Henny," Caroline said as Henny Thornton was seen maneuvering her way through the crowd. I glanced at them, watching their reaction to the woman. Like Caroline, Michael was riveted to the action on the screen.

"How well do you know her?" I asked.

"As well as we want to know her," Michael mumbled, watching the scene change to that of a news anchor at her desk at the local station. I couldn't tell whether or not the kids had a clue that Henny was Richard's mistress at the time of his death. I suspected not or I'd probably have seen more response from them. My thoughts were cut short by the sudden realization of what was being said by the newswoman.

"We have here, footage of a woman we've now been able to identify as Kathryn Wallace." And there I was! On the screen! With my name misspelled, superimposed under me. My face was scrunched up, brows knitted, hand to forehead, shielding my face from the sun in Helen's backyard. It was me looking up at the helicopter that had dipped over Helen's roof so unexpectedly. I felt my cheeks flush.

The newswoman continued. "We have also learned that Wallace is divorced from private detective, MacKay Wallace, who in the past headed up security detail for Lane Allison." But it wasn't her words causing me embarrassment and alarm. It was her tone. As if she *knew* something...something ominous in the relationship between protector and protectee. Nothing she said, mind you, but implied nevertheless.

And now the camera angle switched to include a newsman at another desk, facing the female anchor. "Sources close to the family," he said, "speculate that Wallace may be here as something other than simply a supportive friend."

The female news anchor frowned dramatically. "Do we have any idea exactly what that means, Frank? Why would the family hire a detective? I don't believe there's any question as to who murdered Richard Wagnor. I think the question at this point isn't *who,* but rather *why.*"

Frank tapped a pencil against the desk, reflecting on his co-worker's questions. "To the best of our knowledge, Wallace isn't actually a detective, though it's been confirmed that she's had numerous secret meetings with a former member of the L.A.

police force who knew Richard Wagnor before he made it big in Hollywood."

Caroline groaned and pulled a throw pillow over her face. Michael balled up a napkin and threw it at the screen. "Bull bull bull," he growled through clenched teeth.

So, someone knew I'd seen Donald...but wait. He was with me at the funeral and, later, at the cemetery. In public. In front of cameras. Why'd this Frank and what's-her-name try to make it sound like we were rendezvousing inside the Kremlin?

Caroline snapped off the set and leaned back on the sofa, thoroughly disgusted. Michael took our plates to the kitchen and, from the clatter, must have practically thrown them in the sink. When he came back to the living room, he sprawled across the wicker chair, rubbing his forehead.

"Man, oh, man," he groaned. "Why'd they have to drag you into this?"

I said it was okay and for them not to worry about it, but it wasn't okay. No wonder the public stays confused on major news issues; they never get a straight story from the media. When I said this aloud, Caroline was quick to defend the profession. "It isn't everybody, thank God. The few who do this sort of thing make it hard for those who do their damnedest to get it right."

Michael reluctantly agreed. "We actually have reporters call to check the facts before they go public. It's just that the ones who are irresponsible muddy the waters so much that people don't know what's true and what isn't."

"Tell me about your stepdad," I said, changing the subject.

They looked at one another with "what's to tell" expressions, but it was Caroline who replied. "Well, you know about him and his secretary."

I glanced at Michael. "You knew?"

"Caroline told me."

"And?"

He shrugged. "I wasn't that surprised."

The fact he wasn't surprised surprised me. "Why not? I keep hearing about how wonderful he was and how devoted he was to your mom."

Caroline ran a hand through her hair and let out a long sigh. "Truth is, Katie, Michael and Richard never got along very well."

Michael elaborated. "I never said anything, but he was pretty much a jerk when we were alone. I think he was jealous of our relationship—mine and Mom's."

"What about you, Caroline? You said the other day that you liked him, that when they first met you even wanted him to marry your mother."

"I did. But, like you say, that was at first. Richard could be charming."

"Does his daughter know the truth about him?"

"You can't say anything against Richard around her," Caroline replied.

"Their relationship makes me sick," Michael said. "He spoiled the hell out of her, pardon my French. Anything his little girl wanted, his little girl got."

"That's not fair," Caroline countered. "Don't blame Royalee."

Michael leaned back in the chair, elbows on the armrests, fingers laced over his middle. "Anyway, he knew that I was on to him."

I looked at Caroline. "And he knew that you were on to him, too. So, he must have been pretty scared one of you would tell your mother what was going on."

Michael shook his head. "Uh-uh. We'd never hurt her. He was depending on that."

"So...Lane didn't know he cheated on her?"

"She still has no clue," Caroline said adamantly. Michael, equally adamant, agreed.

"Your mom swears she was trying to catch Richard, not push him, when he fell."

Michael nodded. "That's what she told me when I saw her at the cabin in Onaga Valley."

Caroline was puzzled. "Why do you think he fell?"

I didn't know how else to say what was on my mind except to simply tell it all, Donald's poison theory, and then what I'd learned about Henny and Richard. They listened carefully, letting it sink in for a few seconds before Michael, hardly able to keep the optimism out of his voice, said, "You mean Henny might have slipped something into his lunch? Is that what you're saying?"

But Caroline's reaction was gender oriented. "He was going to Puerto Rico with her?"

Michael shot her an impatient glance. "We're not talking infidelity, Sis, we're talking murder."

Caroline shook her head. "He sounded so…convincing…when he said he wanted to go alone…the details…why it was important to him. All a lie…"

It was another glance from Michael that kept her from going further. I remembered a quote attributed to Sharon Stone: "Women may be able to fake an orgasm, but men can fake an entire relationship."

Caroline's eyes had the faraway look you get when you're thinking back on something. "Let's don't forget Aunt Dorothy. I've always suspected that she was secretly in love with him. What if she noticed Henny and Richard looking at each other in, you know, a certain way at the party and she just snapped? What if—?"

Michael turned sarcastic. "You think she went around with a vial of poison in her purse just in case she ever needed it?"

"Maybe she came to the party with the intention of killing him," Caroline offered, but Michael wasn't buying it.

"That doesn't make sense. You said it. Dorothy loved Richard. And more than any damn sister, let me tell you."

The question dawned on me for the first time. "Did he return the feeling, you think?"

They both laughed. "Not hardly," Michael said.

Caroline added, "Frankly, I don't think he could stand the woman."

We were quiet for a time, letting all this new information sink in.

Finally I said, "Let's recap. There were three people, and only three people, at that party who had a motive and the opportunity to kill your stepdad—your mother, Henny and Dorothy."

Michael shook his head slowly. "Actually, Royalee never forgave him for divorcing her mom."

Caroline nodded. "Yes, but she'd never hurt him." And then, as an afterthought said, "Of course, I'm not so sure his ex-wife wasn't still in love with him. In fact, from what Royalee says, I'm almost certain she was."

I stifled a yawn. The day had been long. "We've got to stay focused on those who were there that day."

"But she *was* there," Caroline said.

That woke me up. "Her name isn't on the list."

Michael got up and walked toward the kitchen, calling over his shoulder. "She stopped by on her way to Long Beach Harbor."

Caroline picked up the explanation. "She and some of her friends from the college where she used to work were taking a three day cruise to Mexico. Royalee had been trying to get her to meet Mom ever since the marriage. Said she wanted a civilized relationship between everyone."

Michael came back into the room with a pitcher of ice water and three glasses. "I think Royalee had begged so much that Arlene finally gave in and came by."

"Did she stay for lunch?" I asked.

He filled the glasses, handed one to Caroline, one to me. "She met Mom, said a few words to Richard, then kissed Royalee goodbye. She wasn't there—oh, I don't know. How long do you think she was in the house, Caroline?"

"Five, ten minutes at the most."

How long does it take to dump a lethal dose of something into a drink? I wondered. Unlike the improbable theory about Dorothy arriving prepared, an ex-wife certainly might. Caroline lifted her water glass to her lips. "Why would she wait seven years to kill him?"

"Maybe it was her first opportunity," Michael suggested.

Another long silence was punctuated by the sound of traffic on Second Street. I got to my feet. "You guys sure there's no one else you've forgotten to mention? Somebody who came to the house while the party was in progress?" I said it halfheartedly, not expecting a reply, but Michael suddenly jumped to his feet and snapped his fingers. "Harmon!"

Caroline looked at him as if he'd lost his mind.

"When he dropped Dorothy off, he came in for a while," Michael said, remembering.

"I'd forgotten. He brought some extra ice," Caroline concurred.

We looked at each other for a long moment. Harmon Ermaling didn't strike me as a killer. "I think that notion's pretty farfetched," I said. What I didn't say, but was thinking, was that the strongest suspect, the most reasonable one so far, was still Lane Allison.

FOURTEEN

I LEFT NAPLES KNOWING that I couldn't face Helen's place. Not tonight. Couldn't drive into that unlit backyard, park the car, crunch through leaves under giant umbrellas of black trees to unlock the door to that lonely, shadowed house. It gave me chills to think about it. I turned the Le Baron toward a side street and wound my way to a bed and breakfast, the only one on the island. Fortunately, a vacancy sign was lit and within five minutes a matronly lady in jeans and work shirt was unlocking the blue door to room 102.

"You can open the windows if you want," she said, unfastening shutters and throwing me a questioning look.

"Fine. Thanks."

"We're walled in pretty good. Safe enough. Even at that, we still get a stiff ocean breeze. You need anything, pick up the phone and dial 0. That'll get you the switchboard for another few minutes. After that, it rings through to my apartment."

She lifted the window and, like she said, a stiff ocean breeze floated in, disturbing the fresh flowers in a clay pot in the center of a tiny table. The lace cloth fluttered.

She looked around to see if everything was in place. Satisfied, she returned to the open door. "Ice machine's down the walkway. Turn left to the alcove." She stepped onto the threshold, turned back to me a final time. "Breakfast's served from seven to nine."

I like B&Bs. I like the homey atmosphere. A rapist wouldn't dare brave the potpourri to do his dirty deed. It'd be downright un-American. It felt safe in here, safe as a kangaroo's pouch to her young. I realized I was dog tired and dying to dive into the pile of fat pillows and what looked like a down comforter, but the woman had planted the seed of ice in my mind and now all I could think about was a long, cool drink of water. I grabbed up a ceramic pitcher, cream colored with hand-painted roses, and tromped down the walkway as she'd instructed. Sure enough, the path led to my left and there I found a lit alcove and the ice machine, along with soda pop and snack dispensers. I shoved the pitcher up under the lever, which released an avalanche of shaved ice, then headed back to my room thinking about nothing in particular except how good the cold water was going to taste. I wasn't in my alert mode, as I would have been at Helen's. I was aware that the moon was suddenly hidden behind a cloud. I was aware that I seemed to be the only guest in an otherwise empty inn. I was aware that my soft soled shoes were making a lot of noise on the walkway...and that was all I was aware of when an arm shot of out of the dark from behind me. The ceramic pitcher went flying into the air and my feet flew out from under me as I hit the ground. It happened so fast that everything became a blur. I didn't have a clue who belonged to the arm or, for that matter, to the fist that slugged me. I remember seeing feet, but the image I had was that of black tennis shoes belonging to neither male nor female. Maybe I should say, belonging to *either* male or female, I had no idea which. I rolled over, clutching my jaw, as footsteps ran away from me, heading toward the street. But my reflexes were too slow. I didn't get as much as a glance at my attacker. I sat there on my tailbone, holding my aching jaw, rocking back and forth, trying to take it all in. When I finally got up, I retrieved the pitcher, or what was left of it, and staggered back to 102, where I locked the door behind me. Then I closed and locked the window, snapping the shutters closed, too. After that I sat on the side of the bed, trying to decide my next step.

I couldn't call the police for all the reasons I'd never called them up to this point. I wouldn't call Caroline and Michael. No need to upset them, though I would tell them about the incident in the morning. What I needed was to talk to Donald. A production assistant located him on the set. I didn't give him the details. I just said that I'd been attacked, that I was fine but shaken, and could he come out when he could get away. I unlocked the door and waited. He arrived within the hour.

In the interim, I'd taken a shower and washed my hair with that pretty bottled stuff B&B's always provide for guests. I smelled like a gardenia. I looked like I'd dozed off in my Mix Master. The lower half of my face was turning a snappy purple, and my rump had a knot on it that felt like a boulder when I tried to sit on anything but the down comforter. That was the picture that greeted Donald when he knocked and I called for him to come on in.

"What the hell happened?" he said, crossing the space between us.

"Shut the door."

He closed and bolted it before returning to me. His face was crinkled with concern. "Who did it?"

I shook my head and patted the place beside me on the bed. Instead, he pulled a white wicker chair up close, sat down, and took my hands in his.

"Well," he said, "we can rule out rape and robbery for motive."

"We can also rule out tiny woman and woman in wheelchair."

He leaned back, studying me. "You sure about that?"

"I don't know, Donald. I don't know anything. I don't know if Lane killed Richard, I don't know why the jerk was screwing Henny and his secretary. I don't know what I'm supposed to be doing to help Helen, and I sure as hell don't know what I'm doing here." I could feel tears building. More than anything in this world, I didn't want to cry. But cry I did. Not big weepy globs, but little wet trails of pure frustration. Donald moved close beside me and put his arms around my shoulders. I don't care who says what; right then it was good to be female and it was extra good to be southern. I rested my head against him until the waterworks closed down and I could take a deep breath. It wasn't until then that he got to his feet and began to pace.

"A warning."

I scoffed. I'm a really good scoffer.

He shrugged. He's a really good shrugger.

"So, who do you think decked me?"

"Dorothy's husband?"

"Why?"

"You said he gave you an odd look when you confronted his wife. Maybe he doesn't want you bothering her anymore."

"Couldn't he just tell me to go away? He doesn't look like the physical type. Besides, how'd he know I was here?"

"How'd anybody know you were here?"

"Somebody must have followed me."

"Looks that way."

Somebody who was watching Caroline's apartment in the first place. But who knew she was staying at her friend's apartment? Or was it somebody who followed me from Helen's, then waited for their chance to let me know I wasn't welcome in California?

Donald moved to the table and perched on the side of it, watching me. "Who considers you a threat?"

"Well...Henny."

He nodded. "She's probably found out by now that you were at her place."

I knew he was referring to the next door neighbor and the likelihood that she told Henny how her Scottish sister, Jenny, stopped by the house. Henny would have seen the news reports and put two and two together. She'd know from those reports that I was staying at Helen's and could have followed me tonight... but, damn, she was so tiny! She couldn't clobber me like that.

"Taking you by surprise," Donald reminded me when I said as much, "she could probably do a little damage."

I rubbed my jaw again, feeling the little damage grow larger by the minute.

"What about Richard's secretary?"

I'd already considered Marcie. If she saw the news, and I was sure she had since the entire world was following non-stop reports, maybe she'd want me to cease my snooping. I remembered the wide hips and swimmer's shoulders and knew that she could indeed deliver a wallop if she put her mind to it. But why would she go to such lengths?

Donald sighed and got back to his feet. He put his arms around me again and, when he looked down at me, his blue eyes were clouded with fatigue and concern. I realized for the first time how much he'd aged since I'd been gone. I wondered if I'd gotten that much older, too. He patted me on the back, kissed my cheek.

"I think you're safe enough tonight," he said. "If they'd wanted to do you real harm, you wouldn't be here to tell me about it." He let go of me and unlocked the door. "I tell you one thing, though, Katie…this cinches it for me."

"What do you mean?"

"I'll bet my next year's bonus Wagnor was poisoned, and not by Lane Allison."

"You think I've opened up a can of worms and someone's afraid of what I'll find while I'm out fishing?"

He grinned, that great wrinkled grin I had always found such comfort in. Then he opened the door. "Go on back to Florida and tend to your animals. It'll all come out at the trial."

"You think I should go to the police?"

"There's not enough for them. They'd chalk up the night's incident to random violence, not unheard of even on this island anymore, I'm afraid…or else they'd try to blame the media for attracting some nut off the street who followed you and made you a target for who knows what reason. No, Katie…for you to tell them everything you know would only help to put another nail in Lane's coffin."

"But what if it doesn't come out at the trial?"

He mulled the question over for a bit, then looked at me with a troubled expression. "You're not going back to Florida any time soon, are you?"

"No."

His chin nearly touched the collar of his shirt when he shook his head and sighed. "I didn't think so." He stepped onto the threshold, looked across the courtyard, then in both directions. Everything was quiet. "Lock up behind me and plan to move out of Helen's place as soon as you can."

"I can't really afford—"

"I'll stay with friends. You take the houseboat." He dug into his pocket, removed a key ring, took a set of keys off it and tossed them to me. "Think you can find it?"

"San Pedro. Under the bridge. Out past the old naval shipyard."

"Good girl. Go straight there tomorrow. I'll stop by after work."

"It's Saturday."

"This is the movie business, Katie. Nothing like the real world, remember?"

And he was gone.

I DIDN'T SLEEP very well that night.

Who slugged me and why? Forget those questions, because they have no answer. Try one that does: Who was at the party?

Henny, the ex-girlfriend. Make that *current* girlfriend. She was on her way to Puerto Rico with Wagnor. Why would she kill him a day before departure? If she were going to do it, she could easily have done it on their trip and made it look like an accident. What was her motive? Did she know about Marcie?

Dorothy, the non-sister in a wheelchair. Would she murder him if she couldn't have him and then see that suspicion fell on Lane, thus killing two birds with one poisoned stone?

Harmon, her husband, stopped by to bring ice. Killed Richard because…I struggled a bit here. Because…he was sick and tired of the guy hurting Dorothy? Or was he aware of Dorothy's true feelings toward this brother who wasn't a brother? Harmon certainly didn't look that passionate, but then you never know.

Arlene, the ex-wife, still in love with Richard. Why?

Royalee, the daughter, still upset at her father for having divorced her mother. That's no reason to kill the guy. Especially seven years after the fact.

Michael. Stepson. He was on to Richard and Richard knew it. How much would Michael hate his stepfather for lying to his mother? Enough to kill him? Even if he'd done it, there's huge doubt he'd let his mom take the rap. It was obvious their relationship was deep and mutual.

Caroline. Now I was really stretching it. Of all the people I'd encountered so far, this girl had the most common sense, the least reason to want her mother hurt so badly.

Who was left?

Look at what you don't see…it's what you don't see that tells you everything you need to know…

I WAS REALLY getting paranoid now. I took the Le Baron back to the airport and traded it for a Honda. The Le Baron overheats, I told the bored clerk at the counter. Afraid to take it out on the freeway. The girl scrolled down her computer screen, frowned. "Didn't you have a Toyota?" I confessed that I did, but that it, too, had overheated very badly. Smoked. Not good on L.A. freeways. The girl gave me a dubious frown and used her five inch nails to type something on the keyboard that, in turn, got me another suspicious glance before she tossed me a key from a peg board and said, "Honda, space 23. White. Bring it back filled."

And there I was, perking along in my little white Honda, tooting back toward Long Beach, Naples Island, Belmont Shores, Sun Beach and all points south, my jaw stiff and puffy, the color purple barely concealed beneath foundation makeup, and not a clue what I should do next.

Breakfast was a blueberry muffin I sucked on until it dried out and flaked into my lap, since chewing was out of the question. My stomach was growling. I wondered if I should call Caroline and ask her to join me at some beach hideaway so I could fill her in on the night's activities. I went all the way to a place called Pirates Bluff and pulled into a lot facing the marina. It was a short order shanty on the sand, given mostly to oversized glasses of tropical teas and pita sandwiches. Lots of avocado and bean sprouts poking out of the pocket lunch. It had been one of my favorite haunts when I lived in the area.

I tromped across the blistering beach to a pay phone outside the building, digging in my purse for Caroline's number. I poked coins into the slot, heard the automated operator's voice ask me for more coins and cursed under my breath. The apartment I was calling was less than five minutes away! Caroline answered on the third ring and said she'd be right there, but first she'd have to go back to the hotel to claim her car. If reporters were staked out around it, she might be a while getting to me. I told her I'd wait.

Reporters must have given up on their vigil. Caroline was sliding into a seat across from me, under a giant multi-colored umbrella, in less than ten minutes. There weren't any waiters at Pirates Bluff. You had to get what you wanted inside and bring it to your table. I thought it made sense for Caroline to show her face as little as possible and did the honors myself, bringing us both iced tea and chicken stuffed pitas. While I was waiting at the counter, I'd noticed a couple of men staring in my direction. Either I was awful cute today or had something I wasn't aware of hanging from my nose, judging from the intensity of their interest. Then I remembered the news coverage. They were trying to place my face. Grabbing up the pitas and our drinks, I threw a twenty dollar bill on the counter and made a hasty exit.

After Caroline told me that Michael had gone back to the desert to work on the student film, I answered her inquiry about the rearrangement of my jaw by relating the events of the night before. She said nothing, nor did she offer sympathy. We ate in silence. Well, she ate. I sucked the chicken out of the pita and rolled it around in my mouth until it was tough, then spit it into my napkin and went for another chunk. The day was hot, climbing up to the high ninety mark according to the outdoor thermometer hanging on the wall. I dug my feet into the sand to find a cool spot and washed down chicken juice with tea while Caroline squinted at the gulls and yachts. I could tell that her mind was on other things. Finally, she rummaged through a large shoulder bag and pulled out a tablet which she lay in front of us, opened to a page filled with scribbled notes.

"I made a list of people at the house that day," she said. "I'd forgotten a couple of things that didn't seem significant until we started talking about it last night at dinner. Now, with this happening to you at the inn..."

I glanced at what she'd written and found all of the names I'd been mulling over the night before, plus a new one. I glanced at her.

"Who's Erik?"

"He was my fiancé."

"He was at the house, too?"

"Just for a few minutes."

"And you think—?"

"You said you wanted the names of everyone there. Erik was there."

I could tell there was more to this story than met the eye. I waited. She avoided looking at me, then finally dabbed her mouth with a napkin and said, "He hated Richard."

"What'd Erik have against him?"

I could see her mind working. She was editing whatever it was she was thinking of telling me. "He's a student at the same university where I've been studying. We dated and I liked him. He's a foreign exchange student from Colombia. I'd never realized how poor the country is, or how limited the opportunities are for young people. Well, actually, for everyone. I felt terrible that he had to go back when his visa was up...and..."

"Are we talking green card here?"

She nodded, embarrassed. "I didn't realize we were talking green card at first, I really didn't. I thought Erik...loved me." She stopped to blink back sudden tears, which she quickly wiped away with the back of her hand. "Oh, Lord. I feel so stupid."

"He wanted to marry you so he could stay in the country... and Richard saw through him."

"Yes, yes, exactly. We got into huge arguments over it—"

"You and Erik."

"No, me and Richard. I was so sure he was wrong about Erik. Mom would try to make peace between the two of us—"

"You and Richard?"

"No, Erik and I."

My head was starting to hurt.

"I'd tell him what Richard was saying and he'd accuse me of

listening to people who didn't have my best interest at heart and we'd go 'round and 'round."

"How'd you learn the truth?"

"I caught him with another woman. A student from his country. Oh, that's a lie, Katie. I caught him with another man." She turned a delicate primrose and covered her face with her hands. When she'd gained composure again, she continued. "I thought he was just...artistic. I loved his gentle qualities. Richard kept telling me that Erik's a fag and he was using me for a green card." Her lips came together in a tight line. "I hated it when Richard said that word. I've got friends who are gay. I can't stand for them to be called fags. But the other part...about him using me..."

"You said you 'caught' him." I was curious because she'd also "caught" Richard with his secretary, remember? Maybe she should be on her mother's case. She was better at this kind of work than I was proving to be.

"Richard arranged it. Erik was a member of our university acting troupe. Richard called for auditions. Said it was for a new television series. He encouraged Erik to try out and, when he did, Richard paired him with a fellow named Alan that we all knew was gay. They were supposedly rehearsing and had been for a couple of weeks before I knew anything about it. I knew about the auditions, and I knew that Erik was being considered for a part, but I didn't know that Richard arranged for him to rehearse with Alan—privately. About two weeks later, Richard invited me to the studio. My major is journalism, but I plan to write screenplays and Richard said he had a project for me. When I got there, he was busy. He told me to go on in the other room—that a script he'd like me to take a look at was on the desk. He said that maybe I could do a rewrite for him. I was so naive. I opened the door and there was Erik—with Alan."

"In a compromising situation?"

"No, not really. But I could tell. There was...I don't know...a kind of intimacy in the way they were sitting. They really were going over their lines, but—I just knew, Katie. When I saw them together, I realized that everything Richard had been saying was true." She looked away, remembering scenes I couldn't even imagine. "Well—" she sighed at last "—that was that. Erik came by that night and tried to smooth things over. Said it was all my imagination, but it was no good. Richard chased him off. Later, I started getting phone calls from Erik telling me he was going to fix Richard—but good."

"Fix?"

Her head bobbed once, emphatically.

"Why was he at the house on the day of the garden party?"

"He'd been by on several Sundays, trying to get me to talk to him, but I refused. On this particular Sunday, he just wouldn't go. He said he was going to have it out with Richard once and for all, that Richard didn't like the fact he was Colombian, which is silly. Richard didn't like the fact Erik never loved me and was feeding me a bunch of bull."

Now, if anybody should be able to recognize bull, it'd be Richard.

"I was in the kitchen getting sodas for Royalee and myself when Erik drove up. Mom said something about uh-oh, here comes trouble. I looked out the window and saw him get out of the car. When I went to the door, he pushed past me and went straight to Richard, who was coming in from the backyard. Richard took him by the elbow and they went out to the patio. I couldn't see them out there, but I heard Richard tell Michael to go in the house, and then I heard him ordering Erik to keep away from me. A few seconds later, Richie left him standing out there and came into the kitchen, shaking his head and half-grinning. He said something like that kid's sure got a hot temper…something like that, but he didn't seem worried about it. Pretty soon, I guess Erik got tired of standing out on the patio by himself and he could see I wasn't going to join him, so he stormed out of the house."

I tried to imagine how the young man would have an opportunity to poison Richard under these circumstances.

"Well," Carline said, "the punch bowl was already out there. On the buffet table. Guests hadn't arrived. It was about ten minutes until they were due, and we hadn't put ice in the big bowl yet, but the punch was in it."

"Then everyone would have been poisoned."

She frowned. "Richard has a glass he always uses…he may even have had a drink in it when he was talking to Erik. I'm not sure."

I thought the Erik theory was stretching it a bit. He may have had a motive, but it didn't seem logical that he had the opportunity. When I told her this, I added, "Besides, I doubt he was the one who clobbered me last night."

She pinched off a piece of the pita and chewed on it thoughtfully. "You're right. I guess Erik isn't a suspect after all. But he was there that day. And he really did hate Richard."

FIFTEEN

THE ADDRESS CAROLINE gave me for Erik was off Third Street in Belmont Shores, four or five minutes away. It was one of those half addresses, which meant it was either upstairs over something or it was behind something. Turned out it was both. The main house, on a residential corner, was white stucco with peach colored trim. Bright cherry-red bougainvillea climbed up an entire side of the two story structure, white wrought-iron lawn furniture sat under a graceful tree I couldn't identify, and the grass was manicured to the point it looked as if it had been spray-painted green. A winding walk led to a slender garage apartment between the central house and an alley. It, too, was whistle-clean. An old van in the open garage seemed out of place, especially with its driver's side covered in primer and rust.

I climbed the stairs to a landing, knocked on the frame of a screen door. A male voice, young and heavily accented, called, "It's open."

I went inside cautiously, craning my neck to see over a kitchen counter where the door to the refrigerator was open, concealing the voice coming from behind it. I cleared my throat.

He popped his head around the fridge door and gave me a hard, surprised look. Erik Perez was dark-haired, in his twenties, and handsome beyond all reason. "I was 'spectin' somebody," he said.

I shrugged and grinned my most innocent grin, which isn't all that easy to do with a jaw protruding halfway into the room. "I'm somebody."

He slammed the refrigerator door shut with one foot and brought two beers into the living area. He was short, maybe my height, which isn't short for a woman, but you get what I'm saying. His striped tee shirt was clean and short sleeved, the jeans worn, but not a disgrace to his forefathers. The jet black hair fell into eyes I was tempted to describe as "smoldering," but which I knew instinctively came from reading too many romance novels before puberty. They were dark, however, and focused and, if eyes can frown, that's what they were doing.

"You sellin' somethin'?" His head was cocked to one side, waiting for an answer. Hadn't Harmon Ermaling said the same thing? Didn't Henny mistake me for a solicitor? If I couldn't make it painting canvases back in St. Seminole maybe I should consider a job at Freddy's Used Ford Lot. "You been in a fight?" He set the beer cans on a side table and folded his arms across his chest, tucking his hands into his armpits. His feet were spread, but there was nothing belligerent in his attitude. I think he was more curious than anything, probably wondering what an old broad with a dinged jaw was doing standing in his living room if she wasn't peddling something.

I stuck out my hand. "Katie Wallace. I'm a friend of the Allison family."

He frowned at first. Then the light went on. "Oh, yeah! I saw you on television this morning." He took my hand, grasped it, let it go.

"Last night," I corrected.

"This morning. Local news in the middle of the *Today Show*." He glanced around like he was going to offer me a seat. The room was neat for a bachelor. Sofa and two recliners were free of clutter. He shifted his weight, then jammed his hands in his jean pockets. "So...what can I do for you?"

"Could we sit down?"

He thrust out his lower lip and shrugged at the same time. I perched on the edge of the sofa. He parked himself on an end table. "I'd offer you a beer, but I've only got two and I'm waitin' for a buddy. Gonna watch the game today."

I had no idea what game he meant and I didn't really care. My butt was sore and my jaw was starting to throb. All I wanted was to ask a few questions and get to Donald's houseboat for a long nap, an early semi-pureed dinner, another run-thru of the list of party guests, motives, and speculations, then maybe an old June Allyson-Van Johnson video, and bed. Erik glanced at his watch, waiting for me to explain my presence.

"Despite the impression the news may give you," I began uncomfortably, "I'm not a detective. I'm just a friend of Lane Allison's mother, doing what I can to get at the truth about the death of her son-in-law."

A puzzled expression clouded his dark eyes. "I thought the truth was that Caroline's mom pushed Wagnor down the steps, where he cracked his skull and died. You know somethin' I don't know?"

I leaned back. It set my tailbone on fire. I sat up straight again. "What would you think if I told you that Wagnor might have been poisoned?"

"Well, first, I'd wonder what it matters what I think, then I'd ask who did the world the favor."

"Someone said you hated him. They must have been right."

He pursed his lips and looked at the toes of his shoes. "Must have been."

"How come?"

I thought he was going to clam up, but instead he shrugged. "He caused trouble. Between Caroline and me."

I decided not to reply. I was there to listen.

"What we had was special. She's a beautiful girl. Smart. Then this hotshot producer dad of hers decides I'm after a green card and he puts the whammy on our relationship."

"So you went to the house on the day he died to have it out with him?"

"I'd been over there a couple of times before, to try and talk some sense into Caroline, but he wouldn't let me anywhere near her. This time I decided to confront her old man and let him have it with both barrels."

"How'd it work out?"

He swung his head from side to side and spread his hands across his knees. "I cornered him on his back patio and I told him, I said, look, why don't you just butt out of our business, mine and Caroline's? I reminded him that she's a grown girl, almost twenty-damn-one years old."

"And he said?"

"He said that as long as she was living in his house and he was paying her way through college, he'd make the rules. Then he walked away from me." He sighed again. "Man, don't nothin' make me madder than for somebody to walk away from me when I'm talkin' to them, you know?"

"What'd you do then?"

"What could I do? He went back in the house, and I didn't want to take on the whole frickin' family. So I left. And that's the last they'll ever see of me. Ain't no woman worth that kind of bull crap."

I was getting to be less of a judge of character by the day. I couldn't tell if he was faking the depth of his feeling for Caroline or not. If I had to make a wager, I'd say he probably really cared about her, but then I thought MacKay really cared about me so there you are. About that time I remembered the accusation about Erik being gay. It didn't seem likely to me. Muscles under the tee shirt told me that he worked out, probably at a gym, or else he had a physically demanding job. And the deep voice belied any trace of feminism or affectation.

He regarded me for a long moment. "What's the bull about him being poisoned? The news says he cracked his head after Caroline's mom pushed him. How come nobody's talking about poison but you? Where'd you get an idea like that anyway?"

I turned my mouth down at the corners in an expression I hoped would look knowing and mysterious. "Just a thought."

"Yeah, well, it's a damn good one, 'specially if it'd get Mrs. Wagnor off the hook."

"You like her?"

"I don't think she's any murderer, if that's what you mean. I think the press and the police are all nuts. And that eyewitness aunt of Caroline's..." He didn't finish the sentence, but hung his head and shook it slowly. "She acted like she owned Wagnor. I never could figure why he let her treat his wife the way she did.

Dorothy gave me the creeps. But then so'd he, so they made a pretty good pair, eh?"

Suddenly, his glance went to the door. His face lit as he sprang to his feet. "Hey, Alan, my man! Come on in. You're late. I was beginning to think maybe you forgot. Uh, this is Miss Wallace. She was just leavin'."

I turned and rose at the same time. The tall, graceful man at the door was about as swishy as anyone I'd ever seen. Alan opened the door and stepped through, carrying a McDonald's sack that smelled of onion rings and hamburger. His wide mouth smiled and his eyes held a doe-like gentleness I couldn't help but respond to. A child in a man's body. His eyes flicked from mine to Erik's.

"Sorry to keep you waiting," he said, thrusting the bag at Erik. "Just a couple of yummies while we watch the game. Hope you haven't eaten yet."

At the screen door, I turned back to them. A short, gorgeous Hispanic with an Adonis look-alike Caucasian. They made a handsome couple. I was going to say goodbye and thank Erik for his time, but they were already in the kitchen, dumping their McDonalds meal onto plates and popping open their Miller Lites. I was about as forgotten as a person could get.

IT WAS NEARLY two-thirty. I'd managed to waste most of the day. Nothing new, nothing resolved. No clue as to who socked me last night, or why; no clue as to whether or not Richard died as the coroner reported or from poisoning. I hadn't accomplished even one thing that would help Lane out of her predicament. I decided that since the day was already pretty much of a wash, I might as well make matters worse and confront Henny.

The car air conditioner went on the fritz and smoke began to curl out from under the hood of the Honda. Great. How could I call the car rental place and tell them the Honda was smoking? Talk about the woman who cried wolf.

I pulled to the curb on a side street and let the engine cool before I lifted the hood. Like I knew what I was looking for, sure. Actually, it didn't take an ace mechanic to see the problem.

A squirrel was fried on top of whatever the gizmo was called, that black thing with tubes running out of it, under the hood. Guess he'd crawled up from under the car while I was parked at Erik's, a curious little guy who'd never have to wonder about anything again. I wasn't crazy about the idea of lifting his tiny carcass and tossing it into a nearby trash container, but on the other hand I couldn't just stand there with a dead squirrel on my engine, waiting for it to disintegrate.

I slammed the hood shut and was trying to decide what to do when a kid in his late teens approached. He was slowly maneuvering his bike along the crowded street, dragging one foot on the pavement, cutting away from pedestrians and autos. I waited until he was directly in front of me to step into his path. He shot me a surprised, then disgusted look, and started to edge around me.

"S'cuse me," I said in the most defenseless voice I could muster. "You know anything about engines?"

He did that incredible male thing of puffing up when you've touched on their point of pride. "My dad's a mechanic. What's the problem?" He climbed off the bike, pushed it to a niche behind my car, kicked down the stand, and ambled to the hood, which he lifted and locked into place. All the while I was saying, "I don't know. It just started smoking and—"

The kid was pointing to the squirrel remains. "Well, there's the trouble right there. Squirrel crawled up under the hood. He was hitchin' a ride on your motor." He lifted it gingerly by its charred tail. "Poor guy." He held it at arms length in front of him, took it to the public trash container and dropped it in. Then he brushed his hands together briskly and returned to his bike. "Should be okay now. Might stink for a while, but it'll wear off."

I thanked him as he peddled out of sight. As I said before... it's good to be female and even better to be Southern. I couldn't have picked up that rodent cadaver if my life had depended on it.

Fifteen minutes later I was at Henny's house. I parked the car across the street and started to her door when the grandmotherly neighbor pulled out of her drive and waved to me. She leaned out of her car window with a big smile. "Hullo there, Jenny! How are you today?"

I waved as she drove on to the end of the block and turned to the left, disappearing from sight. Was she the only person on earth who hadn't seen me identified as Kathryn Wallace on television news?

I could hear movement inside the house as I rang the bell a second time. Finally, the door opened and the petite redhead was staring up at me with an expression about as friendly as the last time I saw her. Her eyes narrowed suspiciously. "Oh, it's you, is it?" I wasn't sure who she thought "you" was; the woman passing herself off as sister Jenny—or the woman everyone but her neighbor was recognizing from TV news. Or...the person who was at her doorstep the day the airport shuttle arrived to pick her up. Hard to believe it was only three days ago.

"I'd like to talk to you, if you have a minute, Mrs. Thornton." I liked the Mrs. touch. Showed respect. Her grim little mouth got grimmer.

"You're Kathryn Wallace."

Was it an accusation? Should I admit it or should I correct the error and tell her that no, I'm not Kathryn anybody; I'm *Katlin* Wallace? Nah. It wasn't important. Instead, I said, "Can I talk to you? Inside?"

The bird-like head tilted back, I supposed to get a better look at me. From her low angle, she might have been wiser to simply take a step back if she wanted to see me in perspective. She kept her hand on the doorknob but, surprisingly, she moved aside, allowing me to enter.

The room looked just the way it looked when I was here before. Not a string out of place. She made no effort to lead me down to the conversation area, but instead leaned against the closed door with her arms folded, studying me. Like a bug under glass.

"What the hell are you doing snooping around behind everybody's backs?" she asked in an icy voice.

"Helen Allison asked me to snoop."

She pushed away from the wall and bounced down the two

steps to the pit. Her size three butt was squeezed into black stretch capri pants, her skinny chest was encased in a tropical halter. All of this was on top of spindly feet the width and length of half a ruler, snug in gold lamé slippers. When she got to the built-in sofa, she sat down and indicated that I should do the same. I chose a place along a far curve, away from her. Then I stared into her pinched face and wondered again why Richard Wagnor would jeopardize his family for the likes of this bad-tempered woman.

"S'cuse me if I don't offer you something to drink."

Such charm.

"I'll only be here long enough to ask a few questions."

"Why should I tell you anything?"

She had a point.

"Henny—"

"Mrs. Thornton."

I felt my face go hot. The last thing I wanted was attitude. I knew that kind of mindset would get me nowhere. "Mrs. Thornton…I don't want to get into he said-she said, but it's not exactly a secret that you were seeing Richard."

"We used to date. Everybody knows that."

This was definitely not going well.

"I heard you were seeing him up until the day he died."

I didn't expect her to practically leap up from the couch, but she did. She hopped like a bird on hot sand across the room, to the door, and threw it open. Her face was as red as her frizzy hair. "Get out of here!"

I didn't move right away. I simply looked at her. When I spoke, my voice was calm and cool. "You were having an affair with him, weren't you?"

She glared at me with so much hatred it made my heart beat double time. I hadn't seen a look like that since Momma rushed Janet Leigh with a knife in the shower. Finally, she drew in a long breath and slammed the door shut. When she came back to her place on the sofa, whatever fury she'd felt was spent. She crumpled into a skinny little ball and sobbed into her bony hands.

It wasn't in me to feel compassion, but it also wasn't in me to interrupt.

She looked at me at last, tossed her head back and said with quiet defiance, "Does this have to come out?"

"If it has anything to do with his death, yes."

"Well, it doesn't."

"How do you know?"

Her eyes blazed again. She was certainly capable of mood swings. "Because I didn't push him down the damn stairs."

"You think Lane was on to you and Richard and, in a jealous rage, shoved him?"

"How the hell do I know what she was thinking? That's for the investigators to find out."

"You plan to stick with the story that you saw her push him?"

"I..." She stopped and looked at her hands, twisted in a knot in her lap. "Of course I saw her. Plain as everything. So'd Dorothy."

"Mrs. Thornton, I used to live in that house. There's no way on God's green earth you *and* Dorothy Ermaling could have seen her at the same time. The hall's too narrow for both of you plus that wheelchair."

Henny turned away as if she'd been slapped. She closed her eyes and bit her lip. It was pretty dramatic, but I think it was real. When she looked at me, she was again fighting tears. "She had no right marrying him. He didn't love her. He married her because he thought he could make her a star again. He felt sorry for her. She was old and he felt sorry for her."

"Maybe it was more that he wanted to become a big film producer by making her a star again."

She shrugged. "What's wrong with that? Anyway, he would have divorced her eventually."

"And married you?"

She couldn't meet my eyes. "Who told you about us?"

"It doesn't matter. What does matter is that if I found out, so will the prosecutor and the jury and—"

She leaned her head back on the sofa cushion for a moment,

thinking. Then she said, "It happened so fast. Richard fell, Dorothy screamed, and I was right behind her. When Dorothy yelled something like *did you see it, did you see it! She pushed him...*I honestly, in that moment, thought I had seen it. Maybe it's the power of suggestion. Maybe it was the confusion of the moment—"

"Maybe it was wishful thinking."

"Yeah. Maybe. Anyway, when the police came, Dorothy was hysterical and describing what she saw, then she turned to me and said *ask her, ask her what she saw! She saw it, too,* and the police asked me if it was true and I said yes, I saw it and I...I swear to you, I felt like I *had* seen it. Later, I got to thinking about it and I realized that I couldn't have actually seen it. I may have visualized it the way Dorothy said, but I didn't see it with my own eyes." She rubbed her forehead and tucked one leg up under her. "I didn't want to recant my story after the fact, though. There's so much publicity. If I draw that kind of attention to myself, our relationship will become public knowledge, and then...oh, God. It's all such a mess. Anyway, what's it matter now? Richard's dead."

"It matters a lot if he fell, rather than being pushed."

She frowned deeply as she watched me. "What do you mean, fell?"

I lifted my shoulders, let them drop again.

She squirmed on the sofa, turned another direction and studied the mantel before she faced me. "He was seeing his secretary too, you know," she said.

Her eyes brimmed once more, but no tears fell. The hands were wrestling each other in her lap. "I was there for him before Lane or Marcie. I was there when he was having problems in his first marriage. I've always been there for him."

"You were going with him to Puerto Rico."

Her eyes widened in shock, but only for an instant. "You're pretty good."

"I'm not a detective. Whatever I find out, anyone can find out."

"Want to know why he was taking me to San Juan?"

"Something about a film deal?"

She shook her head. "There wasn't any film deal. Richard was breaking up with me. The final goodbye and all that crap. We were in Puerto Rico years ago, on a sneak holiday, while he was still married to Arlene. It was the perfect place to end it all, he said."

"I don't understand."

"Neither did I. He said we were old news. History. But that, out of respect for our years together, he wanted it to end on a sweet note. Where better than the hotel we stayed in years before, in Old San Juan?" Her laugh was bitter, but brief. "And I was going. How stupid can a woman be? I was going! To my own funeral, it felt like, but I was willing. If it meant a week alone with him, I'd do it. I guess in my heart I was thinking that, if I could get him some place where we had wonderful memories, maybe he'd change his mind."

The tears exploded out of her. I wasn't sure why she confessed as much as she did, but I knew it was time to go. There was no more to be learned from the terrible Henny Thornton who, it turns out, was also very female.

When I let myself out the door, I could still hear her sobbing. I doubt she even knew I was gone. I drove to a pay phone with a new plan and a shaken opinion of the woman I'd just met. If Henny knew about the secretary, and if Richard was indeed breaking up with Henny, she was more of a suspect than Lane Allison ever was. There were a lot of *ifs* in there, and the biggest one was if Richard was even poisoned in the first place.

SIXTEEN

WHEN WE WERE AT Forest Lawn for Wagnor's burial, Caroline had instructed Marcie to pack his belongings for someone to pick up later. I planned to be that someone, but I thought it only right to let Caroline know of my intentions. I let the phone ring six times. There was no answer, not even a machine or service. I debated about driving to Wagnor's office in the hope Caroline hadn't already taken care of his things, though I don't know when she would have had time. I decided to make the trip and take my chances. Subterfuge. I was getting pretty good at it.

Helen had mentioned that his office was in Sherman Studios in Van Nuys, one of those bedroom communities collectively known as The Valley. Not the most glamorous place in the world. I was familiar with the lot. I'd once been production coordinator on a commercial taped on one of its smaller sound stages. Actually, it only had two stages, one big enough to hold a couple of standing sets, the kind you see on sitcoms where the same interiors are used repeatedly, and a much smaller one used almost exclusively for commercial shoots. There was a mill for building things on the grounds, plus a prop department, space from which they rented out camera and lighting packages, limited editing facilities, and a main building which housed the administrative offices. The second floor was leased to independent producers like Richard Wagnor.

Traffic was thick and slow on the 710. Probably a home game was letting out at Dodger Stadium. Smog formed a gray lid over the city, stinging my eyes. I rolled up the car windows and tried the air conditioner. No luck. I put the windows down and squinted into the filthy air.

Although it only takes an hour to get from Belmont Shores to

Van Nuys, the difference in communities is remarkable. Belmont Shores, on the edge of the Pacific, is a clean, upscale beach town where an ocean breeze, however faint, usually manages to blow away the bulk of pollution by noon. Van Nuys, on the other hand, is inland, jammed between other similar neighborhoods. Huge apartment complexes and businesses are protected by heavy steel gates, and window advertisements can be found in almost every language. Teens hang in groups, their headbands and baggy pants nearly identical from one culture to another.

I'd veered from the 710 onto Interstate 5 in one of the worst areas of Los Angeles. I stayed on it until I could swing onto the Hollywood Freeway northwest where, and for a split second it looked as if the scenery was going to improve. Like Hollywood itself, it's just surface stuff. It only looks better. Underneath, it's just as dirty, just as crime infested, as those streets which are more obviously so. I skirted West Hollywood to my left and avoided cars hurling along at ridiculous speeds all the way to the Victory Boulevard exit, where I jug-eared around to face due west again. I could tell by the fact that the temperature had soared at least fifteen degrees in the last thirty minutes that I had officially arrived in The Valley.

Sherman Studios sat behind a redwood fence off of the major thoroughfare. Unlike its more important contemporaries, there was no guard shack, no stringent security. I drove in, passed the western front central building and nosed the Honda into a space beside a sign that read *Coffee Room*. It was closed, its window shades down. I remembered that it was Saturday, no doubt the reason the lot was almost empty. I got out and went up two steps to a wooden porch, past a couple of windows that looked onto executive offices, or at least that's what they were when I was on the lot several years ago. The entrance consisted of a set of saloon doors. I pushed them forward to find myself in a foyer, facing an empty reception desk. The staircase to the top floor was on my left. There was no sound of life in the building.

The second floor corridor was dimly lit. My footsteps were muffled on worn gray carpeting. There were only five doors on either side of the hall, all closed. I found the one with a wall plaque beside it that read Wagnor Film Enterprises and tried the knob. To my surprise, the door swung open.

Marcie had a lot of work yet to do, it looked like. The room was in disarray with half-filled boxes scattered around, file drawers open, manila folders spread across her desk.

"Anybody here?" I was tiptoeing for no good reason. The name Wagnor Film Enterprises was bigger than the office. Off of this room, where I assumed the desk belonged to Marcie the secretary, was another room, larger and more elegant. That door was standing open.

I paused on the threshold of Wagnor's suite, taking it all in. His desk was monstrous and mahogany, its surface covered with a green felt pad, a glass dolphin, and a magnetic paperclip holder made to look like a miniature director's chair. A cup with a border of film strip graphic held several pens. The maroon leather chair behind the desk looked new. This was the room of a man intent on making an impression. The carpet was soft and deep, the wallpaper masculine with designs of sailing ships outlined in maroon and navy on an off-white background. Navy striped drapes framed the one double window overlooking a manicured courtyard.

Stepping further into the room, I saw that the walls on either side of the door were filled with floor-to-ceiling bookcases. I wondered what a man like Wagnor read. *Playboy? Hustler?* If so, they weren't on these shelves. Most of the volumes were on famous kidnapping cases, no doubt what he used to research his earlier documentary. Three shelves held Hollywood bios on every top film director, producer and studio head ever to grace the industry. I was tempted to grab a couple and make myself at home behind his desk but, instead, I continued to browse, discovering another two shelves filled with bios of Bogart, Grant, Brando, Dietrich, Bergman, and dozens of other famous actors. Another entire section was dedicated to unsolved Hollywood murders. I was reaching for the paperback version of *The Curious Life and Death of Marilyn Monroe* when I heard someone coming down the hall. I stuck my head back into Marcie's front office as she entered the room. She stopped in her tracks when she saw me. I could see the wheels turning as she tried to figure where she'd seen me before. A reaction I'd noticed a lot this past week.

"Sorry to barge in," I said, not sorry at all.

She frowned, then smiled, revealing a whole face full of gleaming white. "Mrs. Wallace," she said, crossing to her desk. "I was in the restroom. Come on in."

"Caroline asked me to pick up Richard's things," I lied. I couldn't help but notice how much easier it was getting to be.

She glanced around at the half-packed boxes. Her eyes were swollen and red. "I'm not through yet. She didn't say when you were…well, it doesn't matter. I couldn't have gone any faster even if I'd known you were coming." She reached for a box of tissues beside the phone. Tears were forming. I could hear them even before I saw them. "I finish a couple of boxes and I…I break down." As if to prove her point, she broke down.

After a moment, I said, "You've worked for him a long time, haven't you?"

She nodded, then blew her nose. "Oh, crap…" She groaned miserably, fanning herself with her snotty Kleenex. She dropped it into a wastepaper basket. "Can I have a little longer? Maybe I can do it all by tomorrow if I stay late tonight."

"Sure," I said, but I wasn't happy about it. I wanted to go through his things now. This minute. "Maybe I can help you," I said, thinking that at least I could pop some of those books into crates.

Her no thanks was too fast to suit me. She seemed suddenly flustered. "I…I can do it. I want to do it. Besides, some things aren't worth keeping—notes, papers he'd have thrown away himself when we got around to it."

As she said this, she was walking to a packing box maybe three feet high and wide. She took a few folders out of it. When there were five or six in her arms, she took them to her desk where she dropped them in a heap. "I've got to eliminate some of this mess…so hard to do. To throw things away, I mean." I couldn't help but wonder why the folders were in packing boxes in the first place if they were meant to be thrown away. Why put them in only to take them out? The whole situation was out of sync. What'd it mean? Maybe nothing.

"How are the kids?" she asked, shoving the folders into a top desk drawer and closing it. "They doing okay?"

"Yeah," I replied. "Seem to be. What time tomorrow can I get his belongings?"

"Well, let me see." She looked around as if calculating how long it would take to complete the task. "Maybe three or four in the afternoon? Would that be okay?"

"Tomorrow's Sunday."

"I'm leaving Monday for three days in wine country, Sonora, Calistoga…reservations are already made, so, yeah, I'll have to be here tomorrow if I plan to finish up before I go." She drew in another deep breath and squared her shoulders. "If I've already gone by the time you get here, just come on in. I'll leave a key to the office on the desk downstairs. I'll get my own stuff out of here and take it all with me when I go home this evening."

Marcie was one of those women who have a pretty face, but from there on down nothing fits. Her shoulders were too wide and masculine. Her hips were enormous, as were her calves. I pushed away thoughts of those ham hocks locked around Richard Wagnor's nude body in the throes of passion. The man certainly liked variety, I had to give him that. Skinny Henny, barrel-hipped Marcie, and the darling of the lot, Lane Allison. Marcie seemed to be reading my thoughts. Her features bloomed crimson and she looked away, fussing needlessly with papers on her desk.

I said something about seeing her later, which we both knew wasn't about to happen, and left the building. The traffic out on the boulevard was subdued, the lot hushed in the dying light. As I got in the car, I could hear Marcie sobbing. I eased out of the gate, realizing that I'd left two of Wagnor's lovers in tears in only a matter of hours. Were there really just two…or were these the only two I knew about?

If nothing else came of my meetings with Marcie and Henny, I realized how we women had weeping in common and I, for one, was tired of it. I had serious doubts that Richard Wagnor or MacKay Wallace shed so much as a teardrop over an affair of the heart, or even of the flesh, so what's with us women? That we're more sensitive is probably a gross understatement, but what was it my mother said about that? It's one thing to be softhearted, another to be softheaded. Watching tough Henny Thornton fall apart, then seeing Marcie come unglued over the same male, gave me the strength I needed to see myself objectively. From here on in I was going to buck up, shake away the past, and maybe even learn the lyrics to "I Will Survive."

Five days into my California trip and all I'd done was get my jaw practically dislocated, my name in national news, and dig up all kinds of dirt on the dead husband of the woman I was supposed to be helping. Now that the press knew I was somehow in the picture, learning the reason would become their secondary game, right after the main objective of uncovering Lane Allison's whereabouts.

From The Valley, all I had to do was get on a main north-south street and I'd end up back on Ventura Boulevard. A left turn would put me only minutes from Studio City and Helen's house. I got as far as the Spring Street turnoff, across from Jerry's Deli, but I couldn't bring myself to go up the hill. As much as I dreaded the isolation of Donald's houseboat, it made more sense to go there, at least for the night.

It was dark now. Saturday night traffic was as heavy as any other night. I braced myself for an hour of travel time and headed for the Harbor Freeway, which would take me through several inland cities to San Pedro, sitting on a cliff that overlooked the Pacific. The town is old. Once known as a sleepy fishing village, it fell prey to gangs and drugs, though recent years have brought changes for the better and it's working its way back to drowsy respectability.

The section of the harbor where Donald kept his houseboat was hardly anything that would interest the yacht set. The rutted road that paralleled the coastline made driving the car difficult. I imagined that, when it rained, it was darn near impassable. A few houseboats other than Donald's were moored several hundred feet apart, the last one visible this side of the toll bridge. I could hear their creaking and groaning, and seawater slapping at them. Music from a ghetto-blaster came in loud and clear, though I suspect the source was a quarter of a mile away. At least that was the only houseboat fully lit. It looked as if a party might be in progress.

I stopped among a field of wet rocks, where several other automobiles and trucks were parked, doused the headlights and got out, locking the car door behind me. It was pitch black. I threw my arms out in front of me like a blind person trying to grasp the darkness, feeling my way along with my feet. Donald's houseboat rocked ahead of me; I could make out its silhouette against the blue-black sky. All I had to direct me was a dim light coming from inside.

I twisted my ankle and cursed. A man's voice came from somewhere to my right: "I tole you I don't wanna go and I'm not goin' so that's that. Shut up about it." A female voice squeaked back at him, but I couldn't make out her words. He didn't answer. I felt like it took me as long to get from the car to the houseboat as it did to get from The Valley to San Pedro, but finally I was walking the plank, or whatever it's called. I bucked a sudden wind and lunged for solid footing on deck. Clinging to a chair bolted in place, I found the key I was looking for and managed to unlock the door. Once inside, I kicked off my shoes, lit a lantern on the kitchen counter, then flopped down on the couch. It had been one devil of a day.

I don't know how long I stayed there, waiting for my jaw to stop throbbing and my ankle to mend, before I realized how hungry I was. Donald's refrigerator was pathetic, even for a bachelor, but I wasn't about to retrace my steps to the car to go looking for a mini-market. Crackers and cheese washed down with red wine would have to do. I don't really like red wine, but the choice was between that, Jack Daniels, or bottled water. I shaved the green stuff off the cheese, fixed myself a platter and took it back with me to the sofa.

The wind was making eerie sounds, ushering in a fog I could see when I got up on my knees to look out of the window. Or is it a port hole? Anyway, I looked and there was a rolling gray blanket hurrying across the water, closing in fast. I heard the distant sound of a foghorn and wondered where the lighthouse was located. In a moment, there would be nothing to do but listen to the wind and hope the cheese stayed in my stomach as the houseboat pitched and rose and fell again, accompanied by the protest of board versus rope.

I tried the phone and was surprised to find it still working. I dialed Helen's number to check messages and heard my neighbor, Terry, telling me the hurricane had blown itself to sea and that my cat, Precious, was missing. The house, he said, made it fine, though the roof of the equipment shed had torn loose. He said he'd try to fix it the next morning. Then I dialed my own special code to check messages on my machine in Florida. The last voice I expected to hear was that of MacKay.

"Hi, honey. I was thinking about you and wondered how you made it through the storm. We got quite a bit of wind damage here in Miami, but otherwise everything's fine. Well, I just wanted to say hello and let you know you're on my mind. Hope you're out on the town, having a great time. Call me sometime...whenever you get a chance."

I frowned as I punched the button that let me hear him again. I was appalled that he'd call so casually, sounding like he was leaving word for a fishing buddy. I was saddened that he didn't say he missed me or was sorry that he left me alone on the Ponderosa. And I was furious with myself for listening a second time—just to hear his voice.

The wind rocked me to sleep. Between fatigue and wine I don't think I even turned over in the night. I mostly don't think I dreamed.

SEVENTEEN

SUNDAY MORNING, WELL, to be honest, I missed morning entirely, so never mind. It was nearly noon when I was finally able to open my eyes. I saw rain pelting against the window, heard it rat-a-tat-tat against the roof and the deck. Unlike southern states, there's almost never any lightning in that part of California. It seldom rains, but when it does, it comes in unbelievable torrents. All or nothing at all, as Sinatra used to say. I rolled over on the clammy sheets and asked myself why I needed to get up. Myself remembered this was the day I was to pick up those boxes of Richard's things at the studio.

I found enough of what I needed to put together a decent cup of coffee, but I couldn't get used to walking on a floor that rolled beneath me. I wondered what it felt like to be in the houseboat in an earthquake. Blowing steam from my cup, I pitched forward to the window over the sofa, where I sat on my knees to watch waves build and crash against rock pilings. Visibility was probably quarter of a mile or less. I was speculating about getting dressed and going out in the weather when the phone rang. It was Donald wanting to know how I slept. I told him, then added a report on yesterday's trip to Sherman Studios. I didn't mention the call from MacKay.

"How about lunch in Beverly Hills?" he said through heavy static.

I didn't feel like getting dressed up for lunch. In fact, I didn't feel like going into Beverly Hills for anything. He was understanding and opted instead for a seafood place near the pier in Sun Beach. I said I'd meet him there after my jaunt out to pick up Wagnor's belongings.

Never mind how I got across the deck of the houseboat or

across that plank to the rocky yard where the car was parked. Never mind how I slipped and slid outside the car, then managed to drive, still slipping and sliding, out onto Pacific Avenue and, finally, onto the 110.

California drivers have no clue how to operate a vehicle in the rain. None. They either go too fast or too slow. They slam on brakes in front of you, not realizing that you have to allow for skid time or else smack against their bumper. They dart out in front of you, careen around you and cut in too close. They pass on the right and make life miserable for whatever time it takes to get from point A to point B. On top of that, city engineers never counted on rain. A smidgen of moisture soon becomes a flood, because there's no proper runoff.

So I splashed and fumed and did some fancy stunt driving, getting myself back to Sherman Studios. Once parked on the deserted lot, I sprinted to the covered porch of the administrative building, darted inside and found the key on the reception desk where Marcie said she'd leave it. I sloshed upstairs to Wagnor's suite and let myself in, flicking on the wall switch as I closed the door behind me, shaking off water like a hound dog in from the storm.

Marcie'd done a decent job of packing and cleaning. In contrast to yesterday, ledges were vacant, file cabinets empty, desks cleared. Curious about those file folders she removed from the packing box while we were talking, I opened the desk drawer where she'd dropped them, but nothing was in there except an empty candy wrapper and a couple of rubber bands.

Wagnor's desktop was also clean, as were his bookshelves. She had thoughtfully left a small dolly for me to put the half dozen boxes onto, to get them to the car. It sounds easier than it was mainly because there was no elevator in the two story structure. I had to maneuver the dolly and heavy boxes down the stairs. It was nearly two-thirty when I started, close to three-forty when I finished. Drenched to the skin, I made two trips from the porch to the Honda's trunk then, when it was filled, began struggling to get the rest of the boxes into the rear of the car. No way. I had to dump the contents of four boxes into the backseat. Books, files, loose papers, the glass dolphin, everything went everywhere, but at least it was all in. I slammed the door shut, returned the dolly and Marcie's key to the reception desk in the foyer, and inched my way through blinding rain back to the freeway.

Donald was standing under the portico of the seafood inn when I pulled the Honda to the curb in front of a placard that warned Tolby's Sea House—Customer Parking Only. When I dashed from the car to his arms, he wrapped them around me and turned me to the warmth of the little restaurant. He'd already gotten us a table in front of a bank of windows overlooking the pier. A fireplace glowed nearby. Tolby himself greeted Donald, who introduced us. The big Greek proprietor gave me a friendly, but puzzled, stare. "You've never been here before? Donald tells me you lived in Sun Beach, yet you never came here? I'm offended." His grin said otherwise.

"That's what makes tonight so special," I said, feeling glib.

"Then I choose what you have. Special menu for special people on this special night." He whisked away the unread menus and bowed as he headed for the kitchen.

There were only a handful of customers, most of them at the bar. It was quiet enough that we could hear the rain outside. Donald poured white wine into my empty glass, lifted his in a toast. "Special," he chuckled. It was an inside joke; he knows how I hate that word.

We small talked, no-talked, ate some of the best lobster I've ever tasted, purred contentedly as the rain gave way to heavy fog. Soon the pier was gone from sight. Tolby joined us for a dessert he created himself, made us laugh with a couple of halfway-clean ethnic jokes, then left. Donald and I sat back and stared at one another. "Damn it's good to be with you, Katie," he said at last.

I said, "Damn if it isn't, Donald," and he chuckled again.

"How'd you like the houseboat?"

"Everything's damp. Papers, bed linen, everything. Doesn't it get moldy?"

"I'll take mold over dust any day."

"It's like living on a waterbed."

"Suits me fine." He regarded me for a long moment. "Bring me up to speed. What have you been up to?"

After I told him, he shook his head gravely. "I worry about you, Katie. You're stirring things up. It could get dangerous." I started to protest, but he stopped me. "You're on to something, and someone's scared you're about to figure out what. The bed-and-breakfast incident was only the beginning, not the end."

"Time for police?"

"Time for you to go back to Florida. I told you that already."

I leaned across the table to cover his hand with mine. "I can't. I've got to get to the bottom of this. You're right. The police won't pursue it or, if they did, they'd only use what I've found to further incriminate Lane. What I can't figure is who socked me the other night. If I could just understand that, I'd have the key."

Donald leaned back in his chair reflectively. "Who knows about our poison theory?"

"Well, there's Erik, Caroline's ex-boyfriend, and Henny—no, I take that back. I only told her that Richard may have fallen rather than having been pushed, but I didn't elaborate. So, let me think. Erik, Caroline, Michael and…that's it. Nobody else."

His brows came together over the bridge of his nose. "What if someone poisoned him, but they don't know you've even considered the possibility? What if they're scared you'll learn about it, or cause the police to investigate further, thus exposing them?"

"Are we talking about those at the party, or are we back to long term effects from—?"

"Who knows? Maybe it's someone you don't even know, but they know from news coverage that you're poking around and they want it stopped."

I leaned my elbows on the table and put my chin in one hand, watching fog tumble across the dark beach. He had a point. I'd been on television news. People I didn't know knew about me. An unnerving proposition. "So, what do you suggest?" I asked.

"I suggest I come back to the boat with you. I'd feel better staying close if I can't talk you into going home."

I felt my cheeks flush with a warmth that I suspected was more than the effect of wine. As he helped me from the table, taking my elbow like a gentleman of days gone by, I felt my knees go weak and I said to myself, *He's nine friggin' years your junior, idiot girl.*

I followed him in the Honda back to San Pedro, though, with the weather the way it was, it was hard to keep his car in sight. I knew it was dangerous to negotiate the narrow road along the water with fog so thick even the headlights did little to penetrate it. My heart was in my throat as I inched along the rocky yard and parked beside what I hoped was Donald's automobile. I turned out the lights and sat there a moment, getting my bearings. The sound of rough surf pounded ahead of me, but I could no longer see it.

He opened the door and stood there in the light from the dome. "That's a drive I don't want to make twice in my lifetime," he said, grinning. But it was a tight grin without humor.

Grabbing onto his arm, we picked our way cautiously to the slick deck and, finally, to the safety of his living room. Once the light was on, even with all of the pitching and rocking under us, I felt a flood of relief. He put his arms around me. I lay my head on his chest, gratefully. Then he pressed his lips to my wet hair, let me go, and spanked my butt. "Get in there and change into my robe before you catch pneumonia."

An hour later we were both in robes after he'd managed to lug in most of the stuff from Wagnor's packing boxes. We dumped everything out on the floor and sat, like children around marbles, going through the files. Most of them concerned scripts other people had submitted to Richard's company, and his responses. Some of the files were intended to be parts of packages used to raise film financing. We didn't find anything the least personal.

Donald yawned and shrugged. "Do you really think his secretary would have let anything you'd be interested in seeing get past her?"

I was plowing through massive folders in a box labeled *Future Story Ideas.* Why I bothered, I couldn't have told you. It wasn't that I was reading any of the material, but I was flipping through it when it dawned on me that I'd been seeing a particular reference fairly consistently in all of the files.

"What have you got?" Donald asked, reading my expression.

"It's more what I *haven't* got. I just realized that certain files are referred to over and over, but I haven't seen them."

"Like?"

"Well, like this one." I pulled a fat folder from the others. "Wagnor has a memo in here that says, quote, refer to Zelena's notes, end quote."

"Okay."

I pulled another file from the batch. This one had a yellow sticky on the inside cover. Scrawled in what I'd come to recognize as Wagnor's handwriting were the words, "Refer to Zelena's notes." I showed Donald, then closed that file and dug through the stack for two others. They, too, had notes referring to Zelena.

Donald shook his head. "I don't see what you're getting at."

"I don't find a single file on Zelena, whoever that is."

I don't think he considered it as important as I tended to think it might be but, like a good sport, he began combing through his stack of files in search of the mysterious Zelena. Five minutes or so later, he held up a slender folder with the heading *Kirk Zelena* written on its tab.

"Who's Zelena, do you suppose?" I said, feeling a stirring of excitement. "What's this about?"

Donald already had the folder open and was scanning through the pages. "Ummm...not sure. I think he's a researcher Wagnor worked with. Lots of notes on various topics, most of them from journals or reference materials." He put his finger on a line to hold his place, searched through several folders for something he obviously wasn't finding, and frowned. He repeated this process on two or three more folders before he gave up.

"You're right. Whatever files Zelena compiled for Wagnor, they seem to be missing. All we have is this one with a dozen or so papers in it, mostly about the death of Natalie Wood. Maybe Wagnor was planning another documentary."

I was disappointed. A producer would naturally hire a researcher on any project he was working on. I myself had assisted dozens of producers in finding just such a person to do research work for us when I was production coordinator, B mac (before MacKay). But...where were the missing files? What were they about? And why were they missing? I wondered if maybe they were what I saw Marcie take out of the box and put in her desk drawer. Maybe she was afraid I'd see them. Why? She was packing those boxes for me, or whomever Caroline was going to send, to pick up. Or was she? Maybe that particular box was never intended to go to anyone but Marcie. Maybe she was packing it to take with her, but when I came in, she was afraid I might see those papers, and she removed them, at least until I was gone.

I stretched out on the carpet. The floor felt odd, gently rolling under me. Donald lay on his stomach beside me, propped up on his elbows, looking down at me. He seemed so familiar, so... good...or was it the magic of lantern light at midnight?

"I think we're drawing a fat zero," he said.

I agreed. Then I yawned and turned on my side to him. It was as if we'd been here, like this, a thousand times before. It was the most natural thing in the world to feel him kiss me, for me to kiss him back. When he pulled away, his face was solemn. "Should I apologize?" he said softly. I murmured "yes" as I held his face and pulled him to me again. I don't know where this would have gone if he hadn't gently removed my hand and gotten to his feet.

"Let's get some sleep, Katie. I've got an early crew call, and you've got about a hundred files to finish going through tomorrow."

I was grateful he stopped us. I'm not sure what he stopped us from—who am I kidding? Of course I know what he stopped us from. And he was wise to do it.

He took my hands and lifted me to my feet, where we hugged briefly then parted, him for the sofa, me for his bedroom.

I wanted to think about Donald, about how good his lips felt on mine, but my mind was playing tricks on me. It wanted to know about those missing Zelena files.

EIGHTEEN

I WAS UP BEFORE the gulls the next morning. Donald was already gone. He'd left a note by the coffeepot: "Just hit the On button. Have a great day and, for God's sake, Kat, be careful."

While I dressed and the coffee brewed, I made plans. There was no time to waste. I told myself I was anxious to finish up and get back to Florida—and I almost believed me. I was putting on my shoes when I had that thought, and it brought me up short. I was getting so good at lying, I was even lying to myself. What I wanted, if I were honest, was to stay with Donald. I didn't want to go to a huge empty house in the middle of nowhere, a house that reminded me of the fact I was someone's reject. It wasn't the aloneness itself. I like being alone. I like independence, but I don't like my nose smeared in bad smelling stuff. Rejection has a stench of its own. I shoved those thoughts away to concentrate on what lay ahead.

There was nothing on the other end of the line but a fast busy when I dialed Caroline's number, which meant the circuit was down. I opened the shutter at the bedroom window to find the kind of day that brings out-of-towners to California by the droves. The whole world looked picture perfect. Last night's wind and rain had blown away any hint of smog. The sky was clear as crystal, the water calm and deep turquoise, sparked here and there by the silver of sun. Gulls were showing off for each other, giddy with high-flying performances. I could hear a distant radio coming in across the water, mellow music for a mellow morning. I knew it wasn't apt to stay mellow once I hit the street in search of those elusive Zelena files.

I figured that Marcie probably got an early start for wine country in an effort to complete most of the trip before the temperature soared. If those files were at her place, I'd have to get her address. I'd already looked for it in Wagnor's belongings, but he didn't seem to have any contact sheets, no phone numbers or addresses other than correspondence with banks, private investors and a gargantuan list of script writer wannabes. There was an outside chance Caroline might know Marcie's address or at least have an idea what area she lived in so that I could find her in the phone book. That's another problem with Los Angeles. There are so many communities and so many area codes you have to have a clue where someone lives in order to get their phone number from Information. I dialed Caroline's number again and got the same fast busy.

A quick cup of coffee to help get the blood swishing and I was in the Honda, headed toward Seaside Boulevard. I hugged the Pacific coastline, went through the part of Long Beach that moors the Queen Mary, and within twenty minutes was on the far side of the humpback bridge that connects to Naples Island.

Birds twittered in trees along Caroline's street as I parked the car at the curb. Her Volks was in front of the triplex, which I hoped meant she was home. She was. She was wrapping a belt around her housecoat as she opened the door. I was pretty sure I'd awakened her.

"Sorry," I said, and this time I meant it.

She ran a hand through her hair, padding toward the kitchen. "Time to get up anyway. Let me get some coffee going. Sit down while I throw on some clothes."

She finished in the kitchen and disappeared into the back of the apartment, reemerging seconds later in jeans and tee shirt, barefoot as usual. We took our coffee to the living room where she sat on the sofa. I faced her from the wicker chair. It took under half an hour to fill her in on what had been happening. When I told her that I'd picked up Richard's belongings at the office, she seemed surprised, but not upset. I ended my recitation with the need for Marcie's address.

"I don't believe I have it," she said, setting her empty cup on the coffee table. "I can't think why I would."

"Any idea what part of Los Angeles she lives in?"

She snapped her fingers. "Oh, for heaven sakes. What's wrong with me? Three or four years ago she gave a barbeque for everybody working on a game show Richie was producing. I was a p.a. on the pilot so I was invited, too."

Translation to English: p.a. is a production assistant, which is another name for fetch-coffee-and-Xerox-this-while-you're-at-it. A position often reserved for nepotism and usually requiring a college degree. It pays just under poverty level, but a lot of grunts have gone on to run major studios from that starting point.

"Let me think. Where was her place?" She leaned over, elbows on her knees, head in her hands. Then she looked up. "Oh, yeah, I remember."

And there I was a few minutes later, heading back to The Valley along a bustling freeway. Palm trees dusted the underside of white scudding clouds. A slight tinge of salt filled the air. I rolled the car windows down, turned up the radio and hummed an off-tune ditty. I felt free and almost happy, though I would have been wise to remember what my mother always said about happiness. She said, "This, too, shall pass away."

Marcie's condo was part of one of the larger complexes along Sherman Way, not far from the studio where she worked. The curbs were bumper-to-bumper with parked cars. As I squeezed the Honda into a spot a block away, an unseen tower bell chimed the morning hour of nine. I doubled back along a winding walk to a lane bordered by colorful flocks that cut into the center of the development. Caroline said that Marcie was in an area designated as "D." I passed "A" and "B" before I found a directory of the grounds on one of those glass-encased signs standing in a circle of pebbles. I studied it from the red star, *You Are Here,* and found that to be *There* I'd need to turn to my left, pass under a rose arbor, skirt one of four pools and there it would be: Pod D.

The numbers 121 were prominently displayed on hand-painted Mexican tiles under shake shingle eaves at her front door. Blinds were drawn at all of the windows, upstairs and down. I crossed the tiny expanse of lawn to a tall fence that ran around the side of her unit. She was on a lot catty-corner from...*uh-oh*...the security guard shack. From his vantage point, he'd be able to see anyone coming in or going out from either her front door or the side gate. A white-haired gentleman in a blue uniform was sitting inside his station, watching me closely. I waved. He nodded.

I wasn't above breaking into Marcie's place so long as I didn't have to smash a window, but I couldn't think how to get past the scrutiny of the guard. How about saying something to him like *Gee, sis asked me to watch her place while she's up in wine country, but I can't seem to find my key.* Somehow I knew not to even think about it. In this part of town, every crooked game in the world's been tried. In an effort not to look suspicious, I knocked on Marcie's door. I waited what I deemed to be a reasonable amount of time to rap it with my knuckles again. Then I turned and walked away, trying to take in as much as possible, using my peripheral vision. No big trees to hide behind, eliminating the notion of me returning to wait, undetected, for the guard's potty or lunch break. The only windows visible on the first floor of Marcie's place were the two beside the front door. The fence connected to the corner of the building, lining a walkway to my left. I figured there was probably a patio behind the fence coming off of Marcie's dining room or kitchen. I couldn't very well jump up to see over the six-foot tall enclosure, at least not without being observed by the watchman.

I tried to imagine what it would look like at night. There was an old-fashioned three-globe lamp almost at her door, but I didn't see any source of illumination over on the side. Maybe I'd come back after dark.

I was more determined than ever to find the Zelena files.

I GOT BACK IN the Honda and drove to the closest service station, where I spent my last three bucks on a California state map I used to get for a quarter. Locating an ATM machine at a bank near Denny's, I winced as I withdrew sixty dollars, and used six of it to get myself some breakfast. Over scrambled eggs and biscuits drowned in ham gravy, I studied the route I needed to take to get to Fresno. When I paid my bill and made an inquiry, the cashier informed me that I was looking at three and a half, four hours on the road. A busboy breezed by pushing a cart. "Sure hope the air conditioner works in your car, lady," he cracked.

It was nearly ten. It seemed reasonable that I'd pull into Fresno somewhere around two in the afternoon. How hot could it get by two? I'd soon find out.

Traffic was getting heavy. Cars, trucks, school and tour buses clogged the freeway up to where I angled inland, making my way toward Interstate 5. It wasn't until I passed Santa Clarita that I could relax behind the wheel with a minimum of other drivers to contend with.

Cutting between the Angeles National Forest on the east and the Los Padres National Forest on the west, I began to sweat. The car fan only kicked up hot air, so I switched it off and tried to think of something other than the fact I was roasting alive. The Honda's engine labored to negotiate the steep incline up the Grapevine. Dusty little Gorman, population of he and she and a few thems, sat lopsided on the side of the highway at over four thousand feet above sea level. Motors strained to pass me in an almost endless cavalcade of big rigs. Tehachapi Mountain range soared to nearly seven thousand feet up near Golden Hills, but I wouldn't be going that far inland. At Mettler, I switched to Highway 99 and coasted downhill all the way to the hot, rocky flatlands. By the time I got to Pumpkin Center, I was wishing I'd rethought the journey. Damn, I was sweltering.

I sailed past Tulare and Visalia, and almost missed Goshen when I blinked. I felt I was making real progress when I saw the Kingsburg city limit sign. Half an hour later, sweat making my thighs slimy, I crossed Highway 41. Caroline, having been to Royalee's apartment dozens of times since Royalee had moved out of her mother's house, had drawn me a map from that point to her stepsister's place on Ashlan Avenue.

Fresno's downtown is like so many others across the nation. Commerce relocated west of the city and new houses are going up at a tremendous rate further out toward Herndon, which used to be nothing but vineyards and cherry and almond orchards. Settled originally by German, Chinese and Russian immigrants, there is, even today, a small Oriental settlement, which tourists occasionally stumble onto on their way to Yosemite. Fresno's history is rich and colorful, though little remains of that heritage.

I turned north on West, west on Ashlan, and took it almost all the way to Victoria Canal. Houses here were mostly old, though a good many had been bought up and razed to make room for apartment complexes, desperately needed to take care of the soaring population.

Caroline had said she'd call ahead to let Royalee know I was on my way, but she couldn't do it until her phone service was restored. I hoped she'd been able to reach her step-sibling by this time.

I slowed to check addresses against the slip of paper in my hand, found the double story complex with probably no more than twenty units, sitting on well tended grounds. I parked in the guest parking lot. Even from here I could make out the number 4 on a center unit. She must have seen me coming, because she was standing in the open doorway by the time I was out of my seatbelt. I was struck again by her tomboy demeanor. Tight jeans, boots nearly to her knees, and oversize work shirt didn't do much to soften the image. Her blonde hair was cut into a '50s style ducktail. She wore no makeup. Her blue eyes were sharp and, I thought, hostile or, at the least, guarded. She stuck out her hand as I approached.

"You look hot," Royalee said in a way I would come to realize was indicative of her entire persona: direct. I don't think it was meant as a come-on. I think it meant she noticed that my hair was plastered to my head and my blouse was soaking wet. "Come on in."

She closed the door behind us and turned to lead the way into a small, rather dark, living room. "It's not usually this hot in April," she said. "Fresno nearly kills you in the summer though, that's for sure." She went directly into a kitchen that was no more than an extension of the one room we were in. "I've got Diet Pepsi and Tab. What'll you have?" As thin as she was, I couldn't imagine why she'd drink chemical fizz, but then again, maybe that's why she was thin.

"Water's fine." I sat in one of two leather recliners. My legs stuck to the chair. I peeled myself loose and moved to the sofa while Royalee pulled a bottle of the distilled stuff from the fridge, along with a tray of ice cubes. "Caroline just called, 'bout five minutes ago. Her phone was on the fritz." She returned with a can of Tab for herself, glass of ice water for me. Then she sat on a footstool, knees spread, elbows resting on them. Her narrow face was pretty in an odd way, but it was those blue eyes that unnerved me. They cut straight through the bull. Caroline had said that she and Royalee were the same age, but those eyes had to be at least a hundred years old.

"I'm not sure I understand what you're supposed to be doing," she said without preamble and took a slug of Tab. That was the best description I could come up with. Slug. Tossed it back the way a guy would toss back a gulp of Budweiser down at the tavern.

"I'm not sure myself, Royalee. Caroline's grandmother asked me to try to get to the bottom of what happened, and I'm doing my damnedest." Something about her encouraged me to curse.

"Call me Lee. Caroline and Michael say my whole name but nobody else does. It's a stupid handle. I don't know what my folks were thinking."

"Combination of names?"

"Yeah. Roy Albert was my granddad's name, Lee was Grandma's." She belched, changed the subject. "I don't understand something sis said the other night on the phone. She said you think my dad was poisoned." And suddenly this tough kid had to look at the floor. Her face drained of color. I could see her knuckles go white around the can of Tab. She took a moment to pull herself together, then looked back at me with that direct stare that pins you to a chair.

"I don't know that he was poisoned, Lee. Caroline's mom—"

"Lane."

"Well, yes…anyway, Lane said he fell down the stairs. She was trying to catch him when he fell."

Royalee frowned. "Aunt Dorothy told the police that Lane pushed him."

"You believe her?"

The blonde head swung slowly left then right. "She's nuts. She's so damn dramatic it makes me sick. I think she wanted some attention and she got it."

"Was there someone around that day you think would be capable of doing something like that to your father?"

She thought about it, then she took another drink of Tab and shook her head again. "I don't know. I don't think so, but I don't know."

"What about Erik?"

The grim mouth curved upward just a modicum. "That geek? You think he poisoned Richard?"

Richard? What happened to Daddy?

"I don't know him," I said. "I only met him once. He didn't strike me as dangerous, but then Scott Peterson looked pretty decent, too."

"Erik's okay. Richard gave him a hard time, but I think he cared about Caroline. I really do. 'Course that doesn't mean she should have married him. But I don't think he'd hurt a fly."

"Harmon was there that day, too."

She threw back her head and chuckled loudly. "Oh, my God. Now we're really reaching." She leaned forward to meet my eyes. "He's the biggest wimp on earth. Aunt Dorothy has him so wound around her finger…" She sighed and clamped her lips. "Besides that, he and Richard got along great. He used to live with 'em. Right after him and Mom separated, when we first moved up here."

I could tell by the way she said the word "separated" that seven years had done little to ease the pain. Maybe that was why she didn't call Richard "Dad." What was it Michael had said? That she'd never forgiven him for divorcing her mother?

"Who else was there that day?" I asked.

"I dunno. I don't pay much attention to those creeps from Richard's church. A bunch of leeches. They're only around because he's in the entertainment business, in my opinion." She was still speaking of him in present tense.

I got up to take my empty glass to the kitchen sink, and also to get a better look at the place. No frills to be found in this apartment, no cute refrigerator magnets, ruffles at the windows. It was less than clean, but not so bad anyone needed to notify the Health Department. Going back to the sofa, I said, "You were close to him, weren't you?"

She couldn't answer. Instead, she studied the floor again and nodded.

"Can I ask you something?"

"Isn't that why you drove all this way? To ask me something?"

"Where were you Friday night?"

She stared at me for a long, incredulous moment. "You sound like somebody from *Law and Order*."

"That's where writers get their dialogue. From real life. *Law and Order* sounds like real life. Sometimes."

"Friday…I'm not sure. Why?"

"Somebody turned my jaw this interesting shade of blue last Friday night."

She squinted. "I don't see…oh, yeah. You've got makeup over it. Good job."

"So? Where were you?"

"You think I did that?" She shook her head and chuckled wryly. Then she pulled herself to her full five-foot seven or eight and took her empty Tab can to within pitching range of the trash can beside the stove. She tossed it in with enough deftness to give Michael Jordan pause. Taking a box of snack crackers from the counter and coming back with them in her hand, she said, "Friday I was…oh, yeah. There's a Woody Allen Film Festival over at Fresno City Campus. That's where I was."

"You an Allen fan?"

"After what he did with his own daughter? Hell, no. But I like Diane Keaton. I thought *Annie Hall* was brilliant."

"That what you saw?"

She opened the box of crackers, passed them to me. I shook my head. She sat back down on the footstool and put the box on the floor beside her without taking anything from it. Leaning back to rest her elbows on the chair behind her, she crossed her ankles in front of her. "Maybe the fifth or sixth time I've seen it. It's kind of a campus cult film now. You think whoever decked you may have poisoned my father?"

"Makes sense, doesn't it? There's been a lot of news coverage that's included me. Somebody might think I'm close to finding out something they don't want me to know."

"Why didn't they just shoot you?"

"Assault's a lot less serious than murder."

"What's it matter, if they already killed Richard? What's another body, more or less?"

Her tone had gone bitter, but she had a good point. Why hadn't I thought of it myself? Could it be that whoever punched me was protecting someone else? Someone they thought might have killed Wagnor? The notion opened up a whole new set of possibilities.

Royalee was on her feet again, checking her wristwatch. "I hate to rush you, but I've got to be at the TV station in an hour, and my wash is almost finished over in the utility room."

I got up, too, and offered her my hand. She took it in a bone crunching grasp, released it almost instantly. "I think you're off base, Mrs. Wallace. I think Richard fell. I'll buy that part of it, but I don't think anybody poisoned him."

"Then what made him fall?"

"Why does anybody fall?"

"He was just standing there, a big, healthy guy—"

Her tone became angry. "He was yelling at Lane. Who knows if he was just standing there? Maybe he was moving around. Maybe his foot slipped off the step and he lost his balance. Look, why don't you just let it all come out at the trial? Aunt Dorothy won't be able to keep up the pretense once she's on that witness stand."

"What if she doesn't break?"

"She will."

Royalee was already at the door. She swung it open and turned to me. "Don't do this to everybody," she said. "It won't bring my father back, and you're hurting a lot of people by keeping this stirred up."

I didn't bother reminding her that national news was featuring stories about the whole affair nonstop, day and night, and that I wasn't responsible for that. I knew there was no use arguing. I hesitated outside the door. "I'm going to stop by your mom's house before I—"

She nearly flew at me, stopping inches from my face, eyes blazing. "Don't you dare go to my mother's! You stay away from her! She loved my father—she still loves him. Leave her alone!"

Her breath was actually hot on my face. I could see veins throbbing in her neck. I backed away, not out of fear, but out of surprise.

"Lee…I promised Helen—"

But I was talking to a closed door.

NINETEEN

DESPITE ROYALEE'S OBJECTIONS, there was no way I was going to leave Fresno without talking to her mother. Caroline knew where she lived because she'd been there several times before her stepsister got her own place. I also knew that Caroline liked Royalee's mom a great deal. She, too, had always wished their mothers could know each other and maybe even get to be friends, but no such meeting took place until that fateful Sunday.

Clovis is little more than a Fresno neighborhood, though I doubt residents would like to hear that. Antique shops and quaint cafés give it an old world flavor, and the houses run mainly to turn-of-the-century except for new developments like those on the west end of Shaw Boulevard. Three blocks from where I was to make a turn, I passed Fresno City Campus. A marquee out front proclaimed April 22-29 Woody Allen Film Festival Week.

I pulled in behind the Sierra Vista Shopping Center, made a sharp right, and found the single-lane drive marked by a mailbox with the words A. Wagnor inscribed on it. I was told that it would lead me to Arlene's cottage inside a stand of trees about a hundred yards in the distance. She'd sold the bigger house several years back, Caroline said, when her divorce from Wagnor became final. A divorce she never asked for, never wanted.

Like most stories, this one also had two sides. She may not have wanted a divorce, but she also made it clear, or so I was told, that when Richard landed a position as producer on a studio lot, she felt she'd lost him. Caroline said that Royalee often lamented that she would never understand why her father felt it was so important to be a Hollywood hotshot. Caroline also told me that she herself often wondered why a wife wouldn't support her husband in whatever career decision he made. It sounded like a standoff with no clear winner. *How could their marriage have ended in anything but divorce?* I wondered.

The cottage was pale green with a wrap-around porch. Two white rockers looked inviting and even more hominess was added by window boxes filled with red geraniums. Altogether, the house was probably no more than fifteen hundred square feet. It looked cozy, but I couldn't imagine Royalee there. I parked the car and walked to the porch where I rang a bell. I cupped my hands to the glass inset and peered inside. It looked dark. I'd about decided no one was home when I heard a car pull in behind me. The same pleasant-faced, gray-haired woman I'd assumed to be Arlene Wagnor at the funeral was parking in front of the garage. Her expression was filled with questions.

"You looking for somebody?" she called, getting out of the car.

"Mrs. Wagnor?" I saw that she had two bags of groceries in the back seat. "Hi," I said. "Katlin Wallace."

She let that sink in for a moment, nodded, and opened the back door of the car. I hurried to take one of the sacks then butt-bumped the door shut. Walking toward the house, she said, "I remember you from Richard's funeral." We reached the porch. She balanced her grocery bag on the banister railing, fished for the house key on a ring, unlocked the front door, held it open with her hip while she retrieved the sack. "I don't have a lot of time, but I suppose you'd like to come in."

A wirehaired terrier raced from the back of the house, yipping happily, and scratching her with his front feet. I followed Arlene from the small foyer to a kitchen equally small. We set the groceries on the counter, where she began digging around for frozen items to get into the refrigerator.

"I saw Royalee at her apartment a while ago," I said, uncertainly.

She glanced at me as she stuffed butter pecan ice cream into the freezer. "I'd just as soon you didn't do that."

"Well—"

"This whole thing has been too much for her. She couldn't reach me to tell me what happened until I got back. Those

Mexican villages, at least the ones my friends and I could afford, don't have phones in the rooms." Frozen fish sticks and mixed vegetables completed her immediate work. She went next for the perishables.

"When did you hear about it?" I asked.

"I got back Wednesday morning. Lee was practically frantic by then." She slammed shut the refrigerator, wadded up the plastic bags, and jammed them into a wire holder on the pantry wall. "May I get you something cold to drink?"

"No, thank you. I'm fine."

She sighed and walked ahead of me to a family room that I guessed was once a second bedroom. Probably her daughter's. The dog leaped onto her lap when she settled into a recliner. "Good boy," she baby talked, chucking him under the chin. To me she said, "Have a seat, Mrs. Wallace."

"I don't really know how to begin this conversation," I confessed.

"I don't really know that I want to have this conversation," she said in a tone without attitude. Her eyes darted to a shelf over a desk, lingered there a moment, misted up. She looked away. When I turned to see what had caused such pain, I found a framed photo of Richard Wagnor. I, too, looked away.

"I hear you used to teach at the same college your daughter attends." It wasn't important; neither the question nor the answer served any purpose whatsoever. It was simply something to say.

"Yes, though she's dropped out since this happened. I hope she goes back."

"What was your subject?"

"Botany. Not very interesting to anyone outside the field, I'm afraid." She patted the dog, held me with a gaze as firm as Royalee's. "Tell me what I can do for you."

"I wish I knew," I said. "I thought that—"

"Why do you think Richard fell down those steps? It's very important to me. What brought you to that conclusion?"

"Where'd you hear that?"

She waved her hand impatiently. "Caroline told me and,

frankly, I called Dorothy. If this woman is going to claim she saw something she didn't see, I want it to come out."

I was startled. "You called Dorothy? Did she stick to the story that Lane pushed him?"

"Oh, of course she did. She's so full of it. I never could believe anything out of her mouth. She loves the dramatic. Always exaggerates."

"Why do you think she'd lie about it?"

"She hates Lane—at least that's what the kids tell me. But it doesn't surprise me. She hated me. She hates anybody who cares about Richie—Richard."

"You think she's getting back at Lane?"

Arlene's broad shoulders rose and fell. Her blue eyes had none of the fire and directness of her daughter's. Nevertheless they were the eyes of a woman who would put up with no nonsense. Probably the result of having dealt with students over a period of years. "I wouldn't say 'getting back at.' I think it'd be more that, after all those years of Richard getting attention and all those years of Lane being in the limelight, she wanted her moment of glory. That'd be more in keeping with the way she thinks."

"Even if it put an innocent person in prison?"

"I don't think she's capable of empathy."

"Then the truth will come out at the trial."

She cocked her head, pursed her lips. "I'm not so sure. I think she's such a pathological liar that, like all pathological liars, she'll pass inspection with flying colors. That's the tragic part. They believe their lies. It's hard to crack their stories." She rubbed her forehead, patted the dog again. "She just may get away with this."

It didn't matter that I was stuck for anything to say next, because her phone rang. She excused herself and went back to the kitchen where she picked up the receiver from a built-in desk. I heard her say hello, then she listened. "Oh, good grief," she finally sighed. "Well, tell them to give the distributor what-for. We paid good money for that film and now we've got angry students demanding a refund." She listened again, then: "I know one of his movies is just like the next, but try telling that to a dyed-in-the-wool Woody Allen fan." She paused, then said, "All right. Let me know. I'll see you at the meeting in—" she glanced at a clock over the sink "—about forty-five minutes."

She returned to the room with a wry shake of the head. "Just because we're a small campus…" She shooed the dog off the recliner, brushed hair from the cushion, but she didn't sit back down. "I'm chairman of the film committee and, unfortunately, we had a mix-up in reels while I was gone. Volunteer students aren't what they used to be, I'm sorry to say."

I got to my feet.

"I don't believe you answered my question, Mrs. Wallace. What makes you think Richard fell down those stairs as opposed to being pushed?"

"What'd Caroline tell you?"

"That her mother was reaching for him when he stumbled."

"That's what I've heard, too."

"Well, all I know is that Harmon grabbed the phone from Dorothy when I called and chewed me up one side and down the other for causing his darling such grief." She glanced back at the clock. "I've got to get ready for the meeting in a few minutes over at the school." She was walking toward the front door as she spoke, which left me with not much else to do but to go along with her. "I don't know Lane. My daughter thinks the world of her, and she loves Caroline and Michael. But I do know Dorothy Ermaling and, in my opinion, there's not a more wicked woman on earth. Totally selfish. I apologize if my call upset things even more, but I wanted to hear with my own ears what she had to say for herself."

"And you determined what from the call?"

"That she's lying, of course. No doubt about it."

She opened the door. I paused with the intention of shaking her hand, only I didn't shake it. I was going to, but something compelled me to clasp her on the shoulder instead. "I'm sorry for your loss," I found myself saying.

She glanced down quickly, then looked up again. This was no sentimental sob sister, but it was all she could do to blink back tears. "He was a good man," she said softly. "A fine man.

I wished him and Lane all the luck in the world, and I meant it. All I ever wanted was the best for him."

I nodded while my mind raced in dizzying circles. Didn't this woman know the extent of his deceit? Didn't she realize that he played around with Henny Thornton while he was married to her? I delved into those wise blue eyes and I knew that she had no clue. He'd died a hero in her mind. *Let it be,* I told myself, let it be.

I'd nearly reached the car when I turned to find her still watching me from the porch. "Mrs. Wagnor, you say you're on the film committee over on the campus?"

She nodded.

"The movie they were showing on Friday, *Annie Hall,* what time did it start, do you know?"

"What do you mean?"

"When did it start? How long does it run?"

She shrugged. "I don't recall. Anyway, that's what all the fuss is about. The distributor sent us *Bullets over Broadway* instead of *Annie Hall* and we've got semester ticket holders madder'n sin. Demanding their money back. *Annie*'s our most popular Allen film. I can't imagine what happened that we got short-changed like that. Why do you ask?"

I told her it didn't matter, that I was just curious, but it mattered a lot. All I had to do now was figure out why it mattered so much that Royalee felt she had to lie about it.

THE DRIVE BACK to Los Angeles went quickly. Miles do that when you have a lot on your mind, a mind that, in my case, was quickly turning to mush trying to remember all the players and to determine who knew what.

I'd told Caroline about the poison theory, yet Arlene didn't mention poison. It appeared she only knew that there was talk that Richard had fallen accidentally. She was upset with Dorothy for lying, probably because it rehashed old memories of things Dorothy had done to come between her and Richard when they were married.

I wondered why Caroline didn't tell Royalee about a possible poisoning. I assumed they confided everything to one another… but then again, maybe she did and it was Royalee who decided not to mention it to her mother. That made sense. After all, it was only a theory; there was no hard evidence for that hypothesis. Or was there? Wasn't my getting clobbered at the B&B evidence that I was on to something? Royalee and Donald had a point when they said whoever did it obviously didn't intend to kill me, that they only wanted to scare me. That being the case, they most likely weren't Wagnor's murderer. If there was a murderer. A murderer other than Lane. Unless Lane did the poisoning. Which I doubted.

That brought up points, such as:

Henny said Wagnor was about to break up with her, and she knew about Marcie. Opportunity and motive, big time.

Marcie was having an affair with Richard, but I had no idea how much she knew about him. Did she realize he was also seeing Henny? Motive, but no opportunity.

Erik didn't know squat, and I don't think gave a prune how Wagnor died, so long as the man was dead. I eliminated him as a suspect. In fact, I placed him outside the loop entirely.

Michael and Caroline knew the whole story, everything. Wagnor and Michael didn't get along. Caroline was disappointed in her stepfather, however, both of them kept up appearances for their mother's sake. Opportunity and motive, but an even stronger motive to protect their mom from the truth about her husband. New thought: Would one of them have killed him to keep her from learning the truth, which was bound to come out sooner or later? Now there was a notion worth pursuing…

Never mind. There was a major flaw in that line of thinking. How could they know their mother was going to do something that could be interpreted as a shove, resulting in a fall that cracked his head open? If one of Lane's children had poisoned Richard and there had been no fall, his death would have been blatant murder—and, once again, suspicion would have fallen on the wife. It's definitely not her children.

Royalee said she saw a movie she didn't see. Why lie about that?

Lane: Same old questions. Did she know about Henny and/or

Marcie? Her kids said no. I wasn't sure. Opportunity and motive, but—?

Dorothy: Since neither Caroline nor Royalee mentioned a possible poisoning to Arlene, then Dorothy wouldn't have any way to know about that theory. She was upset because people were starting to question whether or not she actually saw anything. Opportunity, yes. Motive?

Harmon probably knew as little, or as much, as his wife knew. Unless Richard had confided to him about his affairs during the course of man-to-man conversations. Somehow I doubted Wagnor would share that kind of information with a person everyone considered to be his brother-in-law.

By the time I'd gotten all of this straight in my head I was breezing past Gorman, heading up the Grapevine again. It was dark. I hadn't had anything to eat since Denny's that morning. As I wound down the southern side of the mountain range, Santa Clarita stretched out ahead of me like a thousand strands of Christmas lights thrown on the valley floor. It looked clean and magical. I pulled into the first Wendy's I came to and helped myself to broiled chicken on a bun at the drive-thru. Mustard oozed down my chin, plopped onto my chest, and it didn't dawn on me until later that the pain in my jaw had disappeared. My mind had turned to those missing Zelena files.

I chewed and thought, proving that I'm capable of doing two things at once. I had no idea how it all hooked together, or even if it did. What I knew beyond a doubt, however, was that Marcie didn't want Wagnor's family to get their hands on those folders. I wouldn't stop until I found out why.

The Honda was running on fumes. I refilled at a Shell station and bought myself a cola. The clock behind the counter told anybody who was interested that it was eight thirty-four. I decided to check in with Donald to let him know I'd be at his place around ten. Using a pay phone, I dialed his number on the houseboat, got his answering machine, left a message, and hopped back in the car, bound for Haven Croft Estates, Marcie's apartment complex. I took the Van Nuys Boulevard exit off of Interstate 5 and followed it to Sherman Way.

Curb parking was at a premium. I circled the block, in fact several of them, before finding a spot. I parked and began approaching Pod D from what I believed would be the back, rather than from the front as I'd done that morning. If I remembered the complex map correctly, this route would take me to the side of Marcie's unit, where a row of hedges would conveniently keep people from seeing me sneak alongside her fence. Lights were on in most of the condos, though I was the only one on the sidewalk. I was struck by the absence of trees and the proliferation of shrubs molded into the shape of jungle animals and dinosaurs. For a second I thought about what fun it would be to be a kid living there. With a vivid imagination, it'd be like living in Jurassic Park.

I was emerging from Pod C, going into Pod D, when I spotted the guard shack ahead of me. It was brightly lit. A uniformed woman was reading a paperback behind the window. I slowed my pace, keeping my eye on her. I didn't want her to hear my footsteps and glance up. What I wanted was to get as close to Marcie's place as possible before I crouched behind bushes. I don't like bushes. Bushes not only have thorns and bristles, they also have spiders. I have a spider phobia. Friends tell me there are courses you can take to overcome such fear, but why would I want to? It's good to be afraid of spiders. It's even better to avoid them and, if you can't avoid them, then it's fine to kill them.

I didn't see the dog until it was at my heels. The little bugger raced up, barking like a border patrol hound treeing a drug smuggler. Worse yet, it was a Chihuahua. Domestic mouse. Now, I love dogs. I like dogs more than I like most people, but I don't think a Chihuahua is a dog. I can't find any evidence of it. An elderly man came huffing from a side path, carrying a pooper scooper and a plastic bag.

"I'm sorry," he apologized. Then he leaned down to the critter. "Shame on you, Samson, shame." Samson ducked his head and allowed his owner to sweep him into his arms. "He didn't nip you, did he?"

I assured him I was fine, which I would have said even if I'd been ripped apart by the beast. Who wants to go to an emergency room claiming to have been mauled by a Chihuahua?

The lady guard had heard the commotion. She'd put her book down and was squinting into the darkness. Samson's wrangler called out, "S'okay, Judy. Just me and Samson." She gave him a thumbs up and went back to her book. The man said goodnight to me and shuffled back the way he'd come, cooing to his rat-dog.

I stood where I was for a long moment, waiting to see if Judy realized I was there. She was engrossed in her paperback. I glanced around to see if anyone else was watching before I stepped into the shadow of something I guessed was meant to be a grassy elephant, but more resembled a manatee. My heart was pounding furiously. I gave it a few seconds to settle into a normal rhythm, then I made a run for it. I managed to wedge myself between Marcie's fence and the row of box hedge and crept along to the gate, where I used my Shell credit card to try to unlock the thing. Rotten luck. It was bolted, not latched. I felt for a loose board in the fencing, but nothing was weak enough to give. I squatted on my haunches with my forehead on my arms, trying to figure what to do.

I tried to visualize MacKay on this assignment. How would he have lured the guard away from her post long enough for him to break into Marcie's place? What would he have said about it when he came into the office the next day?

I could picture him in our Sunset Boulevard suite…could see him going to his desk, stopping to bring me a cup of coffee, kissing me on the top of my head. Then he'd sit down, lean back in his swivel chair, and say, "That apartment was like trying to get into Fort Knox." I'd have said something like, "How'd you finally do it?" And he'd have said…what would he have said? *Think,* Katie…He'd have said, "Used the old Lucy and Ethel trick of going to a phone and calling to report a broken window in my apartment. Someone obviously tried to break in while I was gone. Nothing missing. Something must have scared them off before they could get in. I need to make out a report." And then I'd marvel at MacKay's cleverness, while he'd have said,

"Of course she wanted me to come to the guard shack, but how can I do that when I'm recovering from a broken foot? Just got back from the emergency room. That's where I was when the incident took place." Judy would take a report and go to look for the apartment, leaving Marcie's door unprotected. That MacKay was a smart one.

I'm probably the only person in the civilized world who doesn't carry a cell phone. I hate phones. I'd have to locate a public phone somewhere on the grounds. It seemed likely the complex directory would give some indication where they could be found. However, to get to the one I used that morning, I'd have to pass the guard shack, so that was out. But wouldn't there be maps like that in every Pod?

I hurried, hunched and feeling absurd, to the end of the hedge. I stuck my head out to make sure the coast was clear, then stepped onto the walkway, heading back to Pod C. Turns out there were pay phones located near each of the four pools. I chose the closest one. Big red letters on the call box gave me the number of the security shack. I dialed, Judy answered. I told her the story the way MacKay would have told it, right down to the broken ankle. Judy, God love her, said she'd be right over. What was my name again? That's when it hit me that she probably had a tenant list. I didn't know who would be in the unit I was about to tell her I was in. *Think fast, Katie.*

"Carol Riemen."

She made *hmmmmm* sounds, no doubt checking her clipboard. "What unit did you say you're in?"

"192-C."

"I don't—"

"My name won't be on your roster. I'm house-sitting."

"Tenants are supposed to let us know when that happens. Who are you house-sitting for?"

Damn. Stuck again.

I slammed the phone down and stood there feeling foolish. Good thing I wasn't thinking of earning my living as a detective; I'd starve to death. MacKay would have gotten hold of a tenant list before tackling something like this. I walked away from the pool area discouraged and furious with myself.

As I ambled along the sidewalk, going in the direction of Pod D, I saw Judy run from the guard shack to meet two watchmen coming toward her from the opposite direction. She must have called in reinforcements. I could see her gesturing as she no doubt repeated the suspicious phone call. The men listened, nodded, glanced in all directions, but all they saw was a woman about the age of Rita Moreno sitting quietly on a park bench, contemplating the moon. Pretty soon they moved off together in a huddle, still talking, still looking disturbed and serious. I took the opportunity to hustle my buns to Marcie's front door, where I could use my lock picking expertise. I can get inside a house in twenty seconds flat.

I STOOD IN the living room, letting my eyes adjust to the darkness. The only light was filtering in from the street lamp through slats in Marcie's closed blinds. I'd come prepared and took a slender, high-powered flashlight from my purse. I kept it aimed low, sweeping it across rose colored carpeting to the dining room, where three packing boxes took up most of the space not occupied by a table, six chairs, a loveseat, and a hutch. I put the flashlight on the table, focusing its light on the first box I was going to cut open with my trusty pocket knife.

It took ten minutes to go through every file in the box and still I came up empty. It was all standard secretary stuff; books, calendars, production schedules. Nothing of any interest and no mention of Zelena. The second box held more personal items; a pretty bowl filled with paper clips of all sizes, coffee mugs, vases, a coffee pot, boxes of crackers, facial tissue, hair clip, bars of wrapped candy, a jar of M&Ms. I figured that packing box number three had to hold the jackpot—and it did. In a way. I found several folders with Zelena's name on them. Kirk Zelena. All of the folders were empty. It didn't make sense. I went back through the first box, where I'd seen a card file, and thumbed through it.

I found his name and phone number under "R," which I guess

stood for research. I slipped the card into my pocket and looked around a final time. Plastic throwaway gloves kept me from leaving fingerprints in case Marcie realized someone had broken in, though I doubted that would be the case. MacKay had taught me to open and reseal containers in a way not even the police could detect. I put everything back the way I'd found it, snapped off the flashlight, and made my way to the door.

I walked out of Marcie's apartment with an air of confidence, as if I lived there. Judy was back on duty. She was standing at her desk, talking on the phone and checking something on her clipboard. As I closed the door behind me, she glanced up. I waved jauntily. She frowned, peered into the darkness with the phone still clamped to her ear, and nodded in what passed for an acknowledgment of my presence. I hoped the shadows were deep enough that she wouldn't realize I wasn't the tenant she was used to seeing. It must have worked. I didn't hear a police whistle, sirens didn't go off, and God did not part the clouds with a bolt of lightning.

Now to get to Donald's houseboat and give the mysterious Mr. Zelena a ring-e-ding.

TWENTY

THE STRETCH OF Interstate 110 as you come into San Pedro near Peck Park was difficult to negotiate at that time of night. I have trouble with night blindness anyway, always have had, but with a couple of burned-out streetlights the going was even tougher. I jockeyed the Honda onto 9th Avenue and curled back up the coast, where it was black as coal. I could hear the surf crashing on acres of rocks along the shoreline. I left the main road and negotiated the rutted trail to where Donald's houseboat was moored. There were a couple of other automobiles parked across the grounds that I assumed belonged to owners of the occasional yacht or houseboat down the way.

I found a spot next to Don's car, killed the engine, and doused the lights. I was facing the rocky footpath that led to the short pier where I'd board *Donald's Dynasty.*

There was no moon, not even stars. The glorious day that had segued into a glorious evening was dissolving into yet another fog shrouded midnight. Visibility would be reduced to zero by then. Such is the climate in Southern California.

I was stumbling my way along the path when I thought I heard a faint sound behind me. I kept going, dismissing it as imagination or, at worst, a stray dog. I could see the light in Donald's galley. It was like a beacon, urging me on, saying *you're almost there...just a few more steps...atta girl...* That's when I heard the sound again. Soles against rock. Whoever it was closed the distance between us in a couple of quick sprints. Something solid slammed into my head when I turned to face my attacker. I threw my hand over my face, but the surface beneath me was slick. I went down to my knees with enough sense to grab at the legs of whoever was knocking me stupid, but I had the disadvantage of surprise. I couldn't get a grip on them. Then the lights went out all over the world.

When I came to, the first thing I saw was Donald hovering over me. "Oh, thank God," he sighed under his breath. I groaned. This detective crap was getting out of hand. In all the time I'd been married to MacKay, not once did I see his jaw slapped catawampus or hear him complain of a dinged tailbone. This was getting damn old. I was getting damn old.

"What the devil hit me?" I tried sitting up, but abandoned the notion as a rotten idea.

"Take it easy, Katie. It's not as bad as it looks."

I didn't give a pig's rear how I looked. I was concerned about how I felt, and he was saying, "Head injuries always bleed a lot, doesn't mean a thing." Doesn't mean a thing to whom? Not the person whose head is bleeding, I can tell you.

"Did you see who did this?"

I was going to shake my head, but it seemed like I was full of bad ideas tonight.

Donald stood up then, and I was able to determine that I was lying on his sofa with a wet towel on my head. Red sticky stuff clung to my neck. I don't mind red sticky stuff as long as it's in the form of rope licorice or Christmas candy, but it's not so good when the mess is coming out of the vicinity of your brain. I tentatively touched my temple with my fingers. Another bad idea.

Donald was pacing the room, hands on hips. He went to the galley window and peered out into the darkness. That particular window faced land. All he'd see would be his own reflection. Even if we turned off the lights to look out, we still wouldn't have been able to see anything but a field of black rock. He stopped peering to sit beside me on the edge of the couch.

"Not even a glance at him?" he asked.

I closed my eyes and thought back to when I had parked the car. I remembered getting out of the Honda, hearing something, dismissing it as imagination, hearing it again, and getting clobbered. I went down, grabbed at legs…but whoever it was started kicking at me, and then they hit me with a rock or something hard and flat. Twice. I repeated this to Donald, who pressed my hand in his.

"You're going back to Florida. First thing in the morning." His voice had a no-nonsense inflection I found offensive. I sat up, held my head in my hand to make sure I caught all the pieces, and looked him in the eye. Actually, both eyes.

"Donald Stuart, hear me and hear me well," I said with as much passion as I could muster. "I am not going back until I find out what the hell's going on. If I'd even been thinking about going back, all of this would cause me to change my mind."

He started to say something, but I put my fingers to his lips.

"Nobody chases me away," I said. Whatever passion I'd mustered had petered out. I could hardly raise my voice over a whisper. "I don't run scared."

He glared at me disapprovingly, then softened and pulled me into his arms. Oh, how gratefully I went.

When he leaned away from me, he studied me with eyes so filled with concern I nearly turned to goop. "I'm going to stay home tomorrow. We're going to start working on this together. It's our fight now, Katie."

I shook my head. Sort of. "You've got a job. At the studio. I can handle this." Oh, yeah. I was handling it just fine. Maybe I should open a school for detectives and teach my outstanding techniques.

He lifted my hand to his lips, kissed my knuckles. "You gonna live? I think you're gonna live." He took a deep, resolute breath and got to his feet. "Now I'm thinking it's time to call the police. It'll go hard on Lane, but that's her problem. She was married to an egotistical jerk that cheated on her left and right, but we're not going to jeopardize your life to protect hers."

"You will *not* call the police. No. Absolutely not." The words were stronger than the voice. I lay back down and watched him freshen the cloth with more tap water. When he came back, he pressed the towel against my head, then resumed pacing.

"Didn't you hear anything when all of this was going on?" I asked at last.

"That's why I came outside. There was a scream and what

sounded like a scuffle; then I heard footsteps running through the muck. By the time I got out there, whoever it was had made it to a car parked almost down to the toll bridge. I saw the lights come on, then the engine started and they took off toward Old Clipper Trail. That's when I heard you moan. Damn, you scared me, kid. I like to have never found you in the dark."

"Who screamed?"

"You."

"Me? I did not."

"You were in shock."

"Old Clipper Trail...I wonder how they knew about that?" I recalled that Donald had given me the two-cent tour of the area on my first trip to the harbor the other evening. Old Clipper Trail, he explained, used to hook up to a commercial pirate cruise line that went belly-up some years back. Now the road is overgrown and forgotten. Almost no one knows it still exists. If you are brave enough to ford the ruts and potholes, you'll eventually come out in the vicinity of Cabrillo Beach where, a few miles farther north, you could hook up to Palos Verdes Drive, a major link to a coastal highway that, with only a couple of jogs and inconveniences, would land you on State Road One. At that point you'd be on easy street or, I should say, on easy road. SR1 goes all the way up to where it connects to Interstate 101 and from there you could scoot straight on to Oregon.

"Let's put it together, Katie." He sat across from me in an overstuffed chair. "Whoever it was hit you on the head, so they had to have been taller than you."

"Or else they were standing on a rock that gave them height."

"Too slippery. Let's say whoever it was is taller than you. What's your height?"

"Five-seven."

"Can you remember anything about the trousers when you grabbed the legs? Work clothes? Suit pants? Fat legs? Thin legs?"

I let out a sound that was distinctly disgruntled. "Jeez, Donald, I grabbed *moving* legs. Legs that were kicking me. I didn't feel 'em up. That really wasn't on my mind. I wasn't really thinking about it."

He sighed impatiently. "But you must have had an impression."

"I had the impression he was trying to kill me."

Donald stretched back in the chair.

I felt ashamed. I was being smart-mouthed because I didn't know how to handle the depth of his caring. I reached across the coffee table to offer my hand, which he took. "I don't mean to be difficult. But it happened so fast, I couldn't see him, honest."

"Do you have any sense that it was the same person who attacked you at the inn the other night?"

I felt my eyes go wide as I considered that there could be two different attackers. It never crossed my mind.

"Hey," he said softly, "you okay?"

"Couldn't be better. At least not in this town." I let go of his hand and laid my head against the back of the couch.

"How'd the rest of your day go?"

"Better than my night."

He was on his feet, heading toward the galley. "Want some wine?"

"You've only got the red stuff."

I didn't open my eyes, but I heard the refrigerator door open, then close.

"Bought you some white stuff."

I opened one eye. He half-grinned as he handed me a glass. "You do have an evil mouth, Katie Wallace." When he'd settled on the sofa beside me again, he said, "You're lucky."

"I was just thinking that."

"Really. If the guy had gotten a better grip on the rock, he could have killed you. As it was, the surface was too wet. Scared the hell out of me when I saw you lying there in a puddle of blood, but it really is a superficial wound."

"So was my jaw. So's my tailbone."

He grinned again. "You're not cut out for this life, that's all there is to it."

"Gee," I said, sipping wine. "Why would you say that?"

"You can stop now. Nobody'll blame you."

I took a deep breath, pressed the wet towel to my head, and told him about my day.

"Good grief," he said at last. "What a tangled web."

"How's it all tie together, Donald?" I was serious. No more wisecracks. "How's Zelena and his files fit with somebody trying to scare me out of California? And how does any of it fit in with Wagnor's death?"

"We're in agreement that he was poisoned?"

"How can we deny the obvious?" I stared across the room, feeling my head turn into one major throbbing machine. "What I don't get is how we're ever going to prove it."

TWENTY-ONE

WHAT'S THAT OLD country-western song about something being achy breaky? I'm here to tell you the lyricist knew nothing about aching and breaking. I was now the world's authority. I'd tossed and turned all night, listening to the foghorn in the distance, someone's music down the coastline, and Donald snoring from the sofa. My head hurt, my rear end hurt, my feelings were hurt. I came to do good for my friend and I was being used as a punching bag. I was feeling about as sorry for myself as I could get, and I could hear MacKay saying, "Want some cheese to go with that whine?"

I rolled over and stared at the predawn shadows in the room. I didn't want to hear MacKay's voice. I wanted sleep. I wanted to go…I wanted to stay…I wanted…what did it matter? I was here and that was all I could deal with at the moment. Actually, I wasn't even dealing with it that well. I could hardly face today, let alone the future. I had no idea what either had in store.

I was thinking these thoughts when suddenly I heard kitchen sounds. The sun was streaming across the bed, so I guess I'd fallen asleep. I glanced at the clock on the built-in dresser. It was after nine. Donald made good on his promise, or threat, depending on one's point of view, to stay home from work. I sat up, waited for the room to stop spinning, fished around the floor with my toes, searching for my shoes. No way was I going to lean over to look for them. I knew if I did that, my brain would fall out of my nose.

"Ready for coffee?"

Donald was at the door, holding an oversized mug. He was wearing jeans, a white knit shirt—and black tennis shoes. My eyes fell to them and stuck there.

"Katie?"

I rubbed my forehead and sat up to lean against the headboard. By that time, he was standing beside me. "One packet of sweetener and a little cream, right?"

Black tennis shoes. The person who attacked me at the bed and breakfast was wearing—but hold on. I called Donald out on the set right after the attack and he came racing to me that night. No. I called his office and they put me through to him. On his cell phone. He said he was on the set. I hadn't questioned it.

"How are you this morning?" He took a sip from his own cup.

I mumbled something about being fine while he shoved back the short canvas curtains at both windows. "Beautiful day." Backlit like that he had a halo around his head. My angel or the devil's advocate?

"Where do you suggest we start?" he asked.

"The retired-detective-movie-police-consultant is asking a novice old broad from Florida?" My sarcasm didn't escape him.

"There's that mouth at work again." He pulled a straight-back chair from the built-in desk and turned it around backwards to straddle it. "Tell me what you were thinking you'd do today and I'll do it. I want you to stay in bed and mend."

He'd hardly gotten the words out of his mouth before I was on my feet. A little shaky, granted, but upright nonetheless. He sprang out of the chair, nearly tipping it over.

"Hey, hey…" His arm was around my waist, steadying me. I lay my head against his shoulder, just to get my bearings, mind you…but in that moment I realized what a ridiculous thought I'd had. Millions of people wear black tennis shoes. Where was my head that I'd even entertain the idea that Donald could attack me? Where had my head been when I was married to Mr. Wonderful and didn't think he could do what I later learned he did? I brushed thoughts of MacKay from my mind. This was today. Now. Donald was my friend. I hadn't been suspicious of MacKay who betrayed me, yet I was allowing myself to be suspicious of a man who'd done nothing but try to help me.

"First thing we're going to do is get you some decent clothes," he was saying as he handed me my shoes. "I think you were looking for these. You got any others?"

"The ones you bought for me. For the funeral. They're at Helen's."

"What else is there that you need?"

"I only thought I'd be in California for a couple of days. I didn't bring much."

"You've worn the same thing ever since you've been here, far as I can tell. Time for a change."

"You've stood downwind?"

He chuckled. "I've stood downwind. I haven't shopped for a woman in a few years, but if you don't mind, I think I'll make a trip to the mall. Write down your sizes and I'll be back with the goods in a couple of hours." He was leaving the room, but turned at the doorway. "Lock up behind me when I go and don't let a damn soul in till I get back."

"Oh, for pity sake's, Donald."

"I'm serious. Nobody."

I sighed heavily and did what Atlas did: I shrugged.

Half an hour later he knew I wore a size twelve dress, twelve long trousers, twelve medium blouse and, if he remembered from his last purchase, size eight shoes. Not that I wanted him to buy me anything, but I went ahead and made a note that I hate red and I won't wear gray. No sense wasting his money if he was going to be hardheaded and spend it anyway.

I watched his car ease out of the rock field, then I headed for the shower, pulling his sweatshirt that I'd used as a nightgown over my head as I went. He was right about one thing. My clothes were pretty much the worse for wear. I was grateful I'd washed the beige pants and brown turtleneck at Helen's the last day I stayed there, but that was Friday and this was Tuesday. I'd managed to rinse my underwear each night before going to bed—except for last night, of course, but the trousers and top were another matter. I wasn't sure if I'd ever be able to get Wendy's mustard out of the turtleneck.

I was surprised that Donald's clothes fit me so well. There

were a couple of good possibilities in his bureau. The navy blue tee would work, but so would the white cotton button-down. I chose the latter to go with his white duck jeans. Donald's legs weren't that much longer than mine and my own belt tucked the waist in just fine. I turned the cuffs up two turns on the button-down and wore it on the outside. Rummaging around a little more, I stumbled across a yellow plaid bandana, which I tied around my head, knotting it at the base of my neck. The lump on the top of my head was completely hidden.

I was dressed to kill.

Before leaving *Donald's Dynasty,* I phoned Caroline to ask if she'd ever heard the name Kirk Zelena. She said she couldn't place it, and yet it sounded familiar. I told her that he was a researcher.

"Oh sure," she said. "There are several research services in town, but he has the reputation of being one of the best independents. I've heard about him, but I've never met him."

"Your stepdad's company seems to have used him quite a bit."

"I didn't realize, but it makes sense they would."

"Do you know anything about a new project in the works?"

"Other than the Puerto Rican deal, I'm afraid not. Why do you ask?"

I told her about the books I'd found in Richard's office and that were now here with me, in packing boxes. I also mentioned that there were at least a dozen files on mysterious deaths that included Natalie Wood, Marilyn Monroe, the Black Dahlia (Betty Short), and MGM's Tom Ince. Most of those files made reference to Zelena.

"Well," she said, "that's right up Richie's alley. The most successful thing he'd ever done was the documentary on notorious kidnappings. A subject like mysterious deaths would be similar, so it wouldn't surprise me if he had something like that in development, but I never heard anything about it."

"Would you necessarily have known?"

"If it'd gotten far enough along that it was actually going into production, I would have. You know how long these things take,

Katie. It'd be hard to be in the same house and not know about something that major." She added quickly, "On the other hand, it's not unusual for any producer to have six or seven projects that they're trying to get off the ground simultaneously. They don't like to talk about them until it's a sure thing. Afraid they'll jinx it." I was aware that trying to find Zelena might add up to nothing more than a wild-goose chase, busy work to make me think I was being productive.

When I asked if she'd spoken to her mother or grandmother in Onaga Valley, she said no, but that Harold, the attorney, was keeping her posted. Lane and Helen seemed to be doing as well as could be expected under the circumstances. I was anxious to make my next call and to get on the road before Donald returned from the mall. I started to ring off, telling her that I'd phone again with a progress report either later that night or first thing in the morning.

"Katie...Mom's hearing begins next week, you know."

"I know, honey."

I heard the catch in her throat.

"I'm working on something, Caroline. But I don't want to get your hopes up."

"Can I help?"

"I'm not sure yet." Then I repeated all of those clichés that people mouth to one another in rough situations, when they're not wise and don't know what to say: "Keep your chin up," "It'll all work out," and even the ever-empty "God bless."

As soon as the line disconnected, I dialed the number on Marcie's index card. The phone rang four times before a machine picked up and a male voice said, "Hello, this is Kirk. Sorry I'm not here to take your call, but if you'll leave your number at the sound of the tone, I'll—" Another voice, slightly out of breath, interrupted. "Hullo!"

"Kirk? Kirk Zelena?"

"Yeah. Who's this?"

"My name's Katie Wallace. I—"

"How are you?"

"You know who I am?"

He chuckled, but not like he thought anything was funny. "You'd have to live in a cave on a remote island not to know. What can I do for you?"

He'd rattled me. I wasn't used to being famous. I told him that I was going through Richard Wagnor's office files for his wife and family, and that I had a couple of questions that needed to be answered. When he said he'd be happy to help me out, I explained that I had to do this in person. He sounded suspicious, but I wasn't sure why. Or of what. He said he had a deadline on a research assignment, but that he'd try to finish in time to meet me at the Laurel Canyon Coffee Shop before it closed.

"What time's that?"

"Never mind," he replied. "I'll take a break and see you whenever you get here. It's only down the hill from me."

I told him I was on my way.

I took the 110 to the 101, north all the way, a fast right at the Sunset Boulevard exit without looking at the building that once housed our detective agency, straight to Laurel Canyon Drive, then turned right again. The old Schwab Drugstore, where myth has it that a teenage Lana Turner was discovered sipping a soda, is gone now. The glitzy Virgin Mall is across the street from where it used to be. Which brings me to how I come to be a tad older than Rita Moreno despite the fact she was born long before I was so much as a glint in my father's eye.

During one of my studio stints, I ran across a press release on a proposed film project that would star Moreno. In it they gave her age as thirty-one. Obviously a newspaper reporter authored the release because last time I noticed, Rita Moreno was some years my senior. However, if this studio fantasy were to be taken seriously, I'd suddenly slipped ahead of her by more than a year. Over wine that evening I shared this miraculous bit of information with MacKay who, on my birthday the following week, sent me a dozen yellow roses with a note that read, "To my sweetheart who shall ever remain only a tad older than Rita Moreno." The talented and eternally young Moreno is not thirty-one, Lana wasn't discovered sipping sodas at Schwab's and Cary Grant's real name was Archibald Leach. Ah, Hollywood!

Half an hour after I left Sunset Boulevard I parked in the gravel lot of a rustic grocery store built on a Laurel Canyon incline. MacKay and I knew several people who lived in this area, and the café where I was to meet Kirk was a place we often came for lunch. Built a level beneath the grocery store, it's like visiting your best friend's kitchen. I found a seat near the door and waited for someone who looked like they might belong to the voice of Kirk Zelena to arrive. I was late, he was later.

After ten minutes of wondering if I was being stood up, a lanky young man in his early thirties came in, looked around, and spotted me. He wore jeans and dingo boots with a denim shirt and tan suede vest. His expensive haircut was styled to make his longish blonde hair look casual and untended. He nodded to the waitress as he walked toward me. She called him by name, asked how he was doing. He was doing fine.

I stood up to greet him, offered my hand. I had the feeling he was the kind of person who didn't stand much on ceremony, a loner, which is probably why he chose research writing for his profession. His intelligent eyes expressed the same wariness I detected in his voice on the phone. He stood until I was seated, then folded his rangy frame onto a chair opposite me. "How's Lane Allison doing?"

I assured him that she was holding her own.

"Good, good." I couldn't help but be reminded of a young Jimmy Stewart. "Tell me what's so urgent that you had to drive all the way here to see me?"

He seemed to want to cut right to the chase, so I accommodated him. "Have you been doing research for Wagnor Film Enterprises recently?"

The waitress came to our table. "You wanna order now, Kirk?"

He shot me a questioning glance. I nodded. "We'll take whatever herb tea you're selling today," he said.

"Hot or iced?"

"Cold."

I should have offered to buy the kid a sandwich, but my billfold was getting thinner by the hour. I waited until the girl was gone to ask if he was working on something at the time of Wagnor's death.

"Actually, it was finished. I'd handed it in a month or so before."

"Background information on deaths of famous personalities?"

He shook his head. "No, nothing like that."

"He had so many books on the subject I thought maybe—"

"He was developing material based on a screenplay he'd found. The writer wasn't very good, but he felt the spine of the story was there, so he bought the rights with the intention of having a pro come in to polish it."

"You?"

"Not hardly. I'm not a screenwriter, I'm just a researcher. You want to know about the Civil War, certain kinds of ships, anything that requires details, I'm your man. But I'm afraid it all comes out pretty factual and dry in my reports."

"I saw your name in the files a lot. Some of the references were in folders about Marilyn Monroe and Natalie Wood. Everything with your name on it was missing, except the empty folders themselves."

"Natalie…she died a long time ago." He bobbed his head. "I did something on that for Wagnor. It was a devil of a job. I practically lived at the library for a few weeks, pulling together clippings from headlines around the world. Magazine stories. Wagnor wanted it all."

"When was this?"

"Six, maybe seven months ago."

"What about Marilyn Monroe? Tom Ince? The Black Dahlia?"

"Yes, I got information on all of them together for him. Usually when I'm hired it's to provide background for screenplays or novels. The writers don't always have time to dig into the details, so they hire me. Let's say someone wanted to produce a film, or write a novel, about Blackbeard."

"Was he a real person? I thought he was fictitious."

"Oh, he was real all right. He headquartered in Florida. Not too far from where you live, as a matter of fact."

"How do you know where I—?"

"Haven't you seen this week's *International Confidant?*"

"Don't tell me you read that rag?"

He got up from the table and went to a stand by the front door where flyers, announcements, limited interest newspapers, and locally published magazines were stacked. He picked up a thin tabloid and returned with it. When he tossed it in front of me, I saw that Lane's photo was on the cover. Richard's picture was in a jagged edged frame at the bottom of the page, and a banner ran across the top: *Private Detective Uncovers Horrifying Details.* Under that was the picture of me taken from that helicopter over Helen's house. *Exclusive! Kathryn Wallace, Florida Private Investigator—Secrets the Family Friend Discovered!*

I shook my head incredulously. "I'm not a private investigator."

"I know." A smile played around the corners of his mouth. "I did a little research." Our tea arrived. "Maybe I shouldn't say this," he said, offering me a bowl of natural sugar packets, "but Wagnor was having financial problems. He couldn't pay for the work he'd asked me to do. So I did something I've never done before. I agreed to take a percentage on the other end."

"Like an investor."

He toyed with his glass. "It really was an investment—of my time—which I consider valuable."

"And now you're worried that the project will never get finished and you'll never get paid."

"Wagnor was quite the charmer when he wanted to be. He was excited about the script he'd found. He believed in it and, in the end, so did I."

"Is there a chance someone would steal your notes, maybe even the screenplay? Plagiarize the story, produce it themselves? Could that be why everything that has to do with you is missing from Wagnor's files?"

"Certainly possible. It's the Hollywood way of life, I'm afraid."

It occurred to me that maybe Marcie removed those folders with the idea of going ahead with the project on her own, or selling them to another producer.

"Do you have copies of what you gave him?"

"Certainly."

"Would you trust me to take them? Just to read. I'd give them back."

"If they've been stolen from Wagnor's office, it doesn't much matter. My work is only protected when it's a part of a screenplay that's been registered with the Writers Guild of America. Research is just a matter of finding public records. Anyone can take what I come up with, that isn't plagiarism. It's just unethical because of the amount of time I put into compiling notes and records, but it still isn't plagiarism. On the other hand, if they took the screenplay, too—"

"That would be plagiarism since it's original work."

"Exactly."

He glanced at his watch, finished off his drink.

"Why don't you follow me back to the house?" He took several bills from his trouser pocket, lay five of them on the table.

I wondered if he expected me to pay him for the files and made a quick calculation. I only had about three hundred dollars in the bank back home. That would pretty much be it until my next social security check.

I don't know much about cars, but the Jaguar he was driving looked like pictures I'd seen from around the '60s. We passed an elementary school and climbed higher into the narrow road that wound through a pine forest with houses sitting far back among them. These are the kinds of hilly one-lane roads where you pray you never meet anyone coming at you from the opposite direction.

His place was low and modern, mostly wood and glass, accessible by parking below and walking up a steep embankment of stone steps lain in at odd angles. I counted fifty-three of them, though I'd nearly passed out on the twentieth. When we finally got to the top, a couple of golden retrievers barked their greeting and ran to meet him. He tousled their fur and waited for me to catch up with him.

His living room looked out onto a half acre of oak and pine. An aquarium took up most of the wall to my left. I recognized angel fish among the collection. Purple shells, starfish and seaweed were artfully arranged, along with a miniature pirate ship and several treasure chests. The large room was airy and comfortable, the furniture in earth tones. A girl of maybe twenty stuck her head in from a doorway to my right. She was drop dead gorgeous, barefoot, wearing a pair of Spandex shorts. Size forty triple D boobs made a handsome shelf for the ceramic necklace that hung from her neck. She grinned, said hi, and disappeared again.

Kirk's office off the foyer was the epitome of organized clutter. It was crammed with books, magazines and stacks of notepads. A computer sat on a desk nearly buried in mounds of writing material. Each mound had a colored Post-it on top of it, detailing the subject and date. He shooed a kitten from a chair and invited me to sit down. After pulling a number of folders from a cabinet, he opened the lid to his copy machine and began feeding pages into it.

"I've never let anyone I'm not working for see my notes."

"I appreciate what you're doing."

"Wagnor was a good client. You say you're gathering this for his wife and family, that's the only reason I'm going along with your request. I'm going to trust—and that's a word I don't use much in this profession—that none of you have any interest in producing the material or using it for any other project."

"My word."

He stared at me for a long moment. I think he was trying to decide what my word was worth. Then he went back to feeding the copier and stapling pages together. He wasn't one for idle chatter and I'd found a book on ancient myths, causing the next forty-five minutes to pass rather quickly. When he handed me the complete stack, he said, "I hope you can find the script this was to have been used for. I never saw it myself. Wagnor wanted the polish writer to clean it up before he showed it to me. I think he was afraid I'd be disappointed if I saw it before it was as close to perfect as he could get it." Zelena grinned a handsome grin and ducked his head the way Jimmy Stewart once did. "He was the pro. He had it all worked out, book deals, miniseries, foreign market, home video, DVDs, television, feature film, the works."

"Must be some screenplay."

"He thought so. And he convinced me of it."

"Who wrote it?"

"I don't know. I guess that sounds odd, but it's not unusual to buy a rough idea from some aspiring writer and take it to a professional to put in screen form. People seldom know the name of the original writer."

"Hardly seems fair."

"Most of them don't take the time to learn the craft. They get a little cash and their creation gets produced. Sometimes they actually get screen credit, but not usually."

I wrapped my arms around the material, clamped my chin down on the top of it, and dreaded the thought of negotiating the outside staircase. Zelena didn't offer to help, but he did open the door for me. I had the feeling he wished I'd offer him cash for his effort, but I didn't mention it and neither did he.

The hour and a half it took to get back to San Pedro seemed like an eternity. It was all I could do not to pull off to the side of the road and begin wading through the pages. I wasn't sure exactly what I had, but I knew instinctively that it was dynamite.

TWENTY-TWO

BETWEEN MY BANGED UP KNEES, palpitating heart, throbbing head and bruised tailbone, I was a physical mess when I parked the car in front of *Donald's Dynasty.* I could hardly cross the rocks with my load of papers. I went wobbling up the gangplank and burst through the door, sweating like a teen bride. I'd straggled toward the sofa and dumped my cargo in a heap when Donald yelled from behind me, "Where the hell have you been?"

I felt married again. I whirled around, on the defensive. His face was red with anger. He was standing with his hands on his hips in front of the kitchen window (galley port hole?), his feet planted apart, chin squared. This was no Donald I'd ever seen. I wiped my hands on his shirt, stuffed my fists in his pants pockets and lifted my nose at a jaunty skyward angle. That's when he noticed what I was wearing. His expression changed dramatically. "What th' hell have you got on?" he said. "And where were you?"

I decided to ignore his questions, and turned away to organize my Zelena bounty.

"Do you know how worried I was when I came back here to an empty place?"

"Donald—" I faced him, so reasonable it was disgusting "—I'm not a child. I had a lot to do. Lane's hearing is in one week."

He sighed a long, weary sigh. A parental sigh. I hated it and started to protest, but then I noticed the slump to his shoulders as he walked toward the bedroom. I didn't have any choice but to follow him. When I said, "I'm not used to anybody giving a damn," he glanced around at me. The way he clamped his lips and dipped his head let me know that he accepted my apology.

"I got some things for you," he said, wounded. "If they don't fit, you can take them back."

There were several shopping bags on the bed. I didn't know what to say; thanks seemed inadequate. He patted my shoulder as he left the room, but the hurt was still in his eyes. As much as I wanted to dig into Kirk's files, I knew it would damage Donald's feelings even more if I didn't look at what he bought.

He'd made good choices. The four blouses were feminine but not frilly, trousers practical but not too masculine, the skirt colorful but not gaudy, and the leather sandals a perfect fit. I lay everything out neatly across the bed. I could feel him watching from the doorway. I tried again to think what to say, but the words weren't there. He turned and walked away with, "Let's see what you've got out here."

There were maybe thirty folders, each fat with notes and typed reports. I took half the stack, Donald the other half. We sat on opposite ends of the sofa with our mountain of pages between us. Kirk was right. There was nothing inspired about the content, though I couldn't help but be impressed by the amount of work that had to have gone into assembling everything. We'd put the files from Wagnor's office in front of us on the floor. As we pulled out a folder marked *See Zelena Report,* we'd dig through Kirk's folders, trying to find a match. It didn't seem there were any. Wagnor's older files that pertained to Zelena dealt almost exclusively with famous Hollywood deaths, but the newer material Zelena copied off for me had to do with methods of murder. I knew there had to be a connection, but it wasn't jumping out at me.

For instance, Natalie Wood's drowning. Wagnor's files were crammed with stories about the incident, some dated the day of the tragedy, but most of them from publications released much later, excerpts from books, entire magazine articles, and volumes of newspaper clippings from around the world. These were no doubt the clippings Kirk mentioned having gathered for Wagnor some time back. But if Zelena's newer files were on methods of murder, and yet his name appeared on a Post-it inside the cover of a Natalie Wood folder, what would be the link? Natalie Wood drowned. Catalina Island. Thanksgiving week. The method wasn't disputed. I asked Donald if there was anything about Natalia Wood in his stack of Zelena files

He thumbed through several folders, shook his head. "No, I don't see…wait a minute. Nope. Thought I found something, but it's about Bob Crane."

"*Hogan's Heroes* Bob Crane?"

He looked at me over the rim of his reading glasses. "He was murdered in Arizona, remember?"

I vaguely recalled hearing about it. A scandal of some kind. Years ago. Motel room, kinky sex.

Going back to the report he'd been reading when I interrupted, he said, "Nope. Nothing on Natalie."

The next report in my stack was on the death of Sal Mineo, actor from the '50s and '60s. The dossier reminded me that he'd been nominated for an Academy Award for his role in *Rebel without a Cause,* which I'd only associated with the late James Dean. His next Oscar nomination had been for *Exodus.* I couldn't recall seeing him in *Giant,* but Zelena's accounting said he'd had a role. I'd never get finished with whatever it was I was looking for, and I still wasn't sure what it was, if I stopped to read every summary of every celebrity murder or suicide, interesting as they might be. There were four thick folders on the death of 1930s actress Jean Harlow.

I put the file I had in my hand aside and crossed my ankles on top of the tool chest-coffee table. "I don't get it," I said, discouraged. We'd only been at it for less than two hours, but I could see spending the next three days plowing through material that didn't hook up with anything to do in any way, shape, or form with Wagnor's death.

Donald removed his glasses to pinch the bridge of his nose. "Know how Sam Cooke died?"

"The singer?"

He nodded, lifted the folder he'd been reading. "Motel manager killed him."

"Maybe Wagnor was planning to do an exposé on motels." It was surprising how many celebrities met their maker in some sleazy joint.

"Who've you covered so far?"

"William Holden, George Reeves—the first Superman—Vickie Morgan, Dorothy Stratton, Freddie Prinz, Gig Young, Jean Harlow and Marilyn Monroe. I'm just getting started." Our expressions were mutually bleak. Wagnor's secretary stole these files, or at least removed them, so that no one would see them, and it didn't make an ounce of sense.

Donald rested his head on the back of the sofa and stared at the ceiling. "You say Zelena was working for Wagnor at the time of his death?"

"He'd handed everything in, but he was still involved. Because of their financial arrangement."

"Do we know for sure what Marcie stole?"

"Well, these files on celebrity deaths, plus the newer material—Zelena's research on methods of murder."

He got up to pace again, something I was coming to realize he always did when he had a problem to solve. With his fingertips shoved into his hip pockets, he walked around the room, muttering to himself, only now and then including me. "Method of murder…information intended to be used in a screenplay that Wagnor recently bought from a novice writer. Where's the script now?"

I turned my palms up and shrugged. "We haven't found it yet."

"Let me see if I get this. Wagnor bought a script that needed work. He hired Zelena to do research on the ways in which a person can be murdered, which the polish writer was to have incorporated into the finished script. Am I right so far?" He was right. "Let's just concentrate on this newer material, what do you say? We're chasing our tail."

He joined me again on the sofa where we spent the next hour reading through reports on every manner of homicide imaginable. It was amazing how many ways there are to dispose of someone. We stopped only long enough to heat a frozen pizza and pour ourselves a glass of wine. By quarter after eleven, I felt like my eyes were going to fall out of their sockets. "Tired?" he asked, looking up from yet another file folder. He got up to stand behind me and rub my shoulders. "Knots as big as a bunion."

I put my hand over his. "You sweet talker."

He kissed the lump on my head and went to the kitchen to get what was left of the wine. When he'd filled our glasses, he said, "I'm going to read two more reports then I'm going to call it a night. So should you."

"Yes, Daddy."

He raised a warning brow.

I stifled a yawn. "Who do you think attacked me last night?"

"Frankly, I don't have a clue. I can only imagine it's someone who's scared you're onto something." He sat beside me, on the arm of the sofa.

I lay my head on his knee. He rubbed my aching forehead with rough, gentle fingertips. "I guess the real question might be who knows I'm staying here," I said.

A sound came from the deck and I felt myself go tense.

"Just the normal creaking of an old houseboat," he said reassuringly. We listened to water lapping and ropes tugging and boards squeaking for a time then he said, "You were right, you know."

"About what?"

"Nothing Marcie stole hooks up to anything that has to do with Wagnor's death."

"Well, yes and no."

"How's that?"

I wiggled around to look up at him. "In my stack of papers are four Zelena folders on poison. Method of murder. Poison."

"So?"

"So...Marcie steals folders that have to do with poison and we think Wagnor was poisoned."

He got to his feet.

"What if she did kill Wagnor? Maybe we should consider it, Donald."

"She wasn't at the house the Sunday he died, remember?"

"What was it you said the other night about slow acting poisons?"

"You know what I've been thinking about? Insurance." He clamped his lips and nodded, then went on. "We've talked about all kinds of motives that Lane might have had to kill him—jealousy, if she knew about Henny—"

"Or Marcie."

"But we've never talked about insurance. I wonder how much Wagnor carried?"

I wasn't up to exploring a new avenue of thought. Not at this hour.

He switched on the clock radio. An all-night station was playing "Slow Dancing." Donald said, "Our kind of song," and pulled me to my feet. *Slow dancing...dancing to the music...*

As we swayed to the melody, his black tennis shoes moved smoothly across the floor.

FIRST THING I DID the next morning was call Caroline. While the phone rang on the other end of the line, Donald handed me a cup of coffee and took his own to the bedroom to finish dressing for work. I'd managed to talk him into returning to the studio and, though he wasn't happy about it, he finally gave in.

"Hello?" Caroline sounded sleepy. I glanced at the wall clock. It wasn't quite seven.

"Oops," I said into the phone. "I just noticed the time. Sorry."

She yawned. "What's up?"

"A couple of things. Donald and I were wondering if your stepdad carried insurance. Life insurance."

"I know where you're headed with this. I also realize that one of the first things the police are going to try to establish is that Mom could have killed Richie for insurance."

"Did he have substantial coverage, do you know?"

"Substantial?" Her chuckle was filled with irony. "How about none?"

"Why's that?"

"When Richie was trying to put together another comeback movie for Mom a couple of years ago, he cashed it in. Every cent. It takes money to raise money. They even ended up taking out a third mortgage on the house."

"Third?"

"Richard was always borrowing, from any place he could borrow, financing various projects that never panned out. He stayed pretty heavily in debt. So, to answer your question, Katie, there's not only no insurance money coming from his death, Mom will probably lose the house."

I was glad to hear the bad news. It was one less motive for the courts to hang on Lane, but it still wouldn't be enough to save her, not with Dorothy sticking to her eyewitness account. I'd been playing with a notion straight out of *Perry Mason* and decided that, with only a week to go before the hearing I might as well do whatever came to mind. I asked Caroline if it was possible to get Michael back to town. She replied that he was on his way in later in the day. The student film he'd been working on in the Mojave had wrapped. He was going to take a few days off, maybe hang out at the Naples Island apartment with her before returning to Long Beach Community College.

"Do you need to see him?"

"I'd like to see both of you. This afternoon, if you can arrange it."

"Sure. You want to come here?"

"Let's meet at your old house." When she didn't say anything, I wondered if we'd been disconnected, or if she'd hung up on me. "Caroline?"

"Why there, Katie? With the media parked out front, I don't th—"

"I've driven by twice now and I haven't seen them. How much mileage can they get out of sitting in front of an empty house? I think they've given up on anything happening there."

"You sure they're gone?"

"I was looking down on the neighborhood from Bell Park. Later, I even circled around four or five times to make sure it's clear."

"I don't know. If anybody saw us walking up to the door, I'm afraid they'd call the newspaper and try to grab a little publicity for themselves. It's too big a risk, Katie. Can't you come over here?"

"I want you and Michael to reenact the day of the party."

She groaned. Loudly.

"I know it's a little dramatic."

"Sounds like a scene straight out of a very old, and very bad, movie."

"Trust me on this."

She gave in only after I suggested that we leave our cars at the park and approach the house by taking the path behind the seawall. I told her I'd arrive first and drop a chair on the other side for them to climb over on.

"There's a kitchen step stool in the pantry. What time do you want us there?"

We settled on three o'clock, neither of us wanting to negotiate the beach path after dark.

I'd just gotten off the phone when Donald came out of the bedroom carrying a tiny black case which he put in my lap.

"What's this?"

"A little something I picked up for you while I was buying clothes."

It hit me that it was a cell phone. I nearly dropped the thing. "Oh, no, you don't. I'm not going to be hooked to a ringing phone twenty-four hours a day."

He was shaking his head and attempting to curl my fingers over the case. "Listen to me…listen to me, Katie. Will you shut up for a second?"

I wanted to snarl. I wanted to stomp on his foot. This was going too far. Concern is one thing, but strapping me to an instrument I detest in the first place was taking matters beyond reason.

"If I can't make you stay in bed and take care of yourself, can I at least talk you into keeping in touch with me?" His expression made him look like a basset hound I once knew. When his gravelly voice said, "Please," the fire went out inside me. I wanted to rekindle it, but I couldn't stare down those basset eyes.

"Okay, okay," I muttered, slipping the nasty little thing into my trouser pocket.

He handed me a square box with holes and wires in it, along with a slender pamphlet of some kind. "Plug it in when you're not using it. To recharge it. God, Katie...you act like this just got thrown out of a UFO. It's been around awhile. It's not revolutionary."

"I know everybody else has one but, damn it, Donald, you have no idea how much I hate telephones. They're a nuisance and an intrusion. If I want to talk to somebody, I'll go see them."

"What if they live in Michigan or Ohio or across town?"

"I'll drive across town."

He was walking to the door, shaking his head. "The pamphlet explains everything. Read it." Before he walked out, he turned back to me. "And please—call me if you get in trouble. I'll be at the office most of the day. I've already programmed in the number. I'll try to get back at a decent hour. Wanna go to Seal Beach for dinner?"

I said I'd bring in something after I met Caroline and Michael. I was anxious to get back to the Zelena files. There was so damn much to try to understand. I patted my pocket and gave him the best grin I could manage. "Thanks. I'll use if I need to. I promise."

He nodded a brief nod and flipped me a half salute, then he was gone and my day was about to get underway. I'd spend up until noon reading more files, then I'd make another list, about my thirtieth one, of clues and suspects, and try to put the Wagnor puzzle into a recognizable piece.

TWENTY-THREE

I PARKED THE CAR at Bell Park and trudged along the path outside the seawall. To my left was water, to my right houses behind the stone barrier. I knew the roofline of my old home and stopped at the place I'd scaled the wall once before in the past week and a half. The boulder I'd used to make my way over was where I'd left it. I took off my new leather sandals, put them on the ledge, and dug my toes into niches, hoisting myself up and onto the other side. I dropped into my former backyard, retrieved my sandals, and paused to get my bearings.

Eight foot rock walls provided privacy from each of the next door neighbors. Paths ran along both sides of the house to gates that effectively sealed in the backyard. We'd had two dogs when we lived there; it had been reassuring to know they were safely fenced in.

I crossed to the back patio, this time armed with lock picking necessities. In fifteen seconds flat, the sliding glass door was off its track and I was standing in my old living room. It'd been comfortable when we lived there. Lane had made it glamorous. But I wasn't thinking about decor. I was realizing that this was the spot from which Dorothy claimed to have heard Richard and Lane arguing at the top of the stairs.

I followed the course she must have taken, across the living room to the arch that led to the long hallway ending at the front door. I'd gone past the door to the kitchen on my right and the opening to the family room, where Caroline and Royalee had been listening to CDs, on my left. Immediately to the right of the entrance to the house, as I stood looking at it, was the staircase. I mentally put myself in Dorothy's wheelchair. She would have rolled along from the back patio to a place directly in front of the door then maneuvered the chair around so that she could see upstairs. I stopped and shook my head. No way. She simply could not have managed it. It would have taken several attempts to get the wheelchair jockeyed into a position where she could see up there.

I stared at the landing, visualizing Lane and Richard up there arguing. As he was yelling at her, he suddenly buckled, went dead white according to Lane's account, and toppled. Caroline had commented on the perspiration on his chalky face. ("He looked dead, Katie. Ghostly white…and dead. How could he look that dead that fast? I've never seen a dead person before.") All classic symptoms of a heart attack and yet the coroner said his heart was fine. So, I mused, what are we left with? Poison. Had to be.

One week to unravel the mess…one week.

I retraced my steps to the kitchen, found the step stool in the pantry and was on my way to toss it over the seawall when Michael landed in the backyard followed by Caroline. He started to say something, but I put a forefinger to my lips, indicating the neighbors on either side. They sprinted across the grass and, together, we replaced the glass door in its track.

"Oh, my God," Caroline whispered, looking around. "I haven't been back since that day. It feels…strange."

Michael, too, seemed uncomfortable. He stepped into the living room as if seeing it for the first time. "Two weeks ago this was home."

I could see that Caroline was having difficulty keeping her emotions under control. She stared down at the gold carpet and murmured, "Who ever knows…?"

I knew I'd have to break the mood or we'd never get anything accomplished. "This is tough, guys," I said, "but if we're going to do anything to help your mom, we've got to do it now. We're running out of time."

"Where do we begin?" Michael asked.

Good question. "That Sunday. From the beginning."

Caroline pursed her lips in thought. "That would make it…what time, Michael?"

He shrugged and began pacing. Maybe pacing's a man thing.

"We were serving by two-thirty, I'm sure of that. Mom had *hors d'oeuvres* in the oven and asked me to take them out at two twenty-five. It took me maybe five minutes to transfer them to a platter and get them to the buffet table. They were the last items to go out of the kitchen."

"Oh, and the people going on to the Long Beach Civic Center from here. I know they'd commented on wanting to be out by four," Caroline put in.

"What time did the party start?"

"Two." They said it together.

"So," I said, making quick calculations, "if the others were already gone by the time it happened, it had to be after four o'clock."

Michael nodded. "The coroner's report said that Richie died around four-thirty."

Caroline added, "That was corroborated by statements made by guests."

"Henny and Dorothy?"

"Yes. And the fact that Royalee and I were more or less watching the clock. We had a TV program we wanted to see at five."

"So, let's start at four o'clock. Any idea what you were doing then?"

"I was clearing dishes from the patio," Michael said.

"I was in the family room," said Caroline, and Michael shot her a look. The kind of look siblings give each other when one of them is clearing dishes and the other's listening to CDs. Caroline shrugged. "Sorry, Michael, but you were doing fine without me."

"If we're going to do a reenactment, we may as well get going on it. Where do we begin? Michael?"

He considered my question, started for the kitchen. "This was the most central place."

A horseshoe of refrigerator, sink and stove faced us. The cooking island jutted into the center of the room, separating it from an eating nook that looked out onto a teeny slab of concrete that, using all of your imagination, might be called a patio. We'd had a chaise lounge out there for sunbathing. I saw that Lane had placed on it a potted palm and an ice cream table with two chairs. A couple of feet across the side path was the common fence between this house and the neighbor's. I walked to the sink. Curtains at the window over it were closed. The Wagnors had kept our white designer telephone. It was on the kitchen counter.

"Pretend it's four o'clock that Sunday," I said. "The people going on to the civic center are gone. Nobody's left but Dorothy and Henny."

Michael said, "I brought a tray of dirty dishes in from the patio and set them on the counter. Richard was taking a kettle of hot water off the stove."

"Where was your mom?"

"She was on the back patio, talking to Henny, I think."

Never mind *that* mental picture. "And then what happened?"

Michael thought for a moment. "He got a tea bag from a glass jar where Mom kept them and started putting together a cup of tea."

Caroline cut in. "You told me that's when Richard got a phone call."

"Oh, yeah. I forgot. I answered and it was his secretary." Caroline rolled her eyes. Michael continued. "She wanted to speak to Richie, so I handed him the phone."

"What'd Marcie want? Anybody know?"

"Yeah," Michael replied. "He said something about Marcie coming by to pick up reports that needed to be typed. Said they were on his desk upstairs. He asked if I'd let her in if I saw her coming. He wanted to get back to the last guests out on the back patio."

"Richie had an office here as well as at the studio," Caroline explained.

"She must have been someplace close when she called," I said, figuring that if Marcie had phoned from her apartment, it would have taken her at least an hour to get to the house. If that were the case, Richard wouldn't have asked Michael to be on the lookout for her since he'd be free to let her in himself by then.

When I outlined my reasoning, Michael and Caroline

exchanged looks. "I dunno," he said. "I didn't give it much thought."

"Wait a minute," I said suddenly. "I thought Marcie wasn't here that day."

"She never showed up," Caroline said. "At least I never saw her. Did you, Michael?"

"No, never."

"Go ahead with what happened next." And what the hell did any of this have to do with Marcie stealing files, or celebrity deaths, or Royalee lying about what Woody Allen movie she saw or who attacked me at the B&B and at the houseboat? I wondered. Nothing was adding up.

"Well," Michael went on, "let's see. Richie hung up the phone and I went back out to the patio to get the last of the dirty dishes."

I tried to remember Lane's account of the afternoon, as she'd outlined it to me in Onaga Valley. "Your mom said she came in somewhere around this time and that Richard gave her a peace offering. A cup of her favorite tea."

Caroline chuckled softly. "That's what he always did. Whenever he thought he'd gotten on her bad side, he'd bring her peppermint tea. It became a running joke around here."

"Yeah," Michael chimed in. "Somebody'd look at somebody else halfway crooked and we'd yell 'get the peppermint tea'!" Their laughter lasted only a second. "Well," Michael sighed, "anyway...Mom came back out to the patio and we each took in a tray of leftovers from the buffet table. When I got to the kitchen, the cup of tea that Richard had been fixing for himself was still on the counter. I figured he forgot about it when he got the call from Marcie, so I took it out to him. Then he went in the house and next thing you know, we hear this commotion coming from upstairs. I wasn't going to get in the middle of it, but Aunt Dorothy hightailed it inside fast as she could get that chair of hers in gear. Pretty soon she screamed, and Henny went running inside, too."

Caroline shook her head. "Everything's such a jumble after that. I heard Dorothy and Mom scream, but I think I heard

Richard scream first, and then that terrible sound of him crashing down the stairs. Royalee and I just stared at each other. We couldn't comprehend that it would be Richie falling. We were thunderstruck by the sounds. Then we jumped up and ran out in the hall. Royalee pushed past me and fell on her knees beside him. She was holding him…and he was…so *white…*"

"I was in the house by then," Michael said. "I could see him at the foot of the stairs. There was blood everywhere. I ran to the kitchen and called 911. Paramedics got here in…what, Caroline?"

"Four, maybe five minutes. No, I don't think even that long."

They fell silent, remembering. I walked around the room, trying not to intrude on their thoughts while trying to make sense of it all. The truth was, both Lane and Michael had plenty of opportunity to slip something into Richard's tea, the cup Michael admitted he took to his stepfather on the patio.

This was not looking good. Not looking good at all.

How did poison get inside Richard Wagnor? Was the cup of tea the source?

I was trying to imagine what would have been in plain sight that could have been added to his drink quickly and unobtrusively. If the tea bag came out of a common jar, poison would had to have been put in his cup after he'd added water.

"Describe the kitchen that day."

Caroline said, "I didn't come in much. Royalee and I had breakfast at that little restaurant around the corner. A Vietnamese man and wife own it now, but the people from West Virginia probably still had it when you lived here. After we ate, we went to the mall to get a couple of CDs."

"While Mom and I were setting up the buffet table and place cards on the patio," Michael added, sarcastically. Caroline had the good grace to blush.

"Michael?" I prompted. I wanted to mentally see the kitchen as it looked on that Sunday, April 17th.

Michael stared into space for a moment. "Well…it looked pretty much the way it looks now. The phone was where you see it, the breakfast table, chairs…same tablecloth. Mom had some fresh flowers in the center of the table. Azaleas. White. A big yellow pitcher was filled with daisies on the windowsill. What exactly are you fishing for, Katie?"

"I don't know, honey. I swear I don't." Suddenly, I wasn't sure how much I should confide in him. He and Richard didn't get along, Michael knew his stepfather was cheating on his mother, and he had more than enough time alone with Richard to slip something into his drink. I ruled out the *hors d'oeuvres,* since they'd gone on the buffet table for everyone to nibble on, just as I ruled out one of the other guests putting something into his food. There were too many people around to chance anything like that. Which brought me back to the realization that Arlene, the ex-wife, had stopped by, as had Erik and even Harmon Ermaling. Why should I suspect Michael any more than I'd suspect any of the others? I wasn't sure that I did.

"Has anybody been back in the house since that day?"

Caroline said, "The police. And the police clean-up team. To wash down the blood. I don't think they would have come back after that, do you? It isn't like they're searching for a killer. They've got Mom. Why do you ask?"

"Show me Richard's office."

We went down the hall and up the stairs. Once on the upper landing, we could go straight ahead to a guest room, to our left to another guest room, across the corridor to enter the master bedroom, or to the end of the hall, into guest room number three, the room I surmised had been turned into Wagnor's home office. I was right.

"What are we looking for?" Michael asked.

"If Marcie was supposed to pick up a report that needed to be typed, wouldn't it still be here?"

"I guess so," Caroline said. "I don't know who would have moved it."

But it wasn't there. His desk at home was as sparse as his desk at the studio had been. There was not so much as a paperclip on its surface. "Was he always this neat?"

Michael sounded disgusted. "He was a neat freak."

I opened the top drawer. Rows of staples in boxes and a tray of pens. The side drawers were empty. Not a report in sight.

I was out of ideas. Marcie was coming to pick up a report that didn't exist. What'd it mean? What would have happened when she got there? Would she have come upstairs, seen that the report wasn't where it was supposed to have been, and asked him about it? Would he have snapped his fingers and only then remembered that it was still on his desk at the studio? Or in his briefcase, wherever that was?

It could have been an innocent mistake or it could have been something else. We'd probably never know.

We left, still clueless, exiting the backyard the same way we came in, over the seawall. Terrified of being spotted, Caroline and Michael ran along the path with their heads down all the way to the park, where they waved a quick goodbye and took off in an old pick-up truck I'd never seen before.

What had I learned by doing the Perry Mason bit? Sorry to say, probably nothing.

By now it was nearly four-thirty. The day was going fast and I was getting nowhere. Once I got out on the freeway, I headed toward The Valley. I was going to drop in on Marcie and get to the bottom of those stolen files once and for all. I'd confront her with the fact I'd talked to Kirk Zelena. I'd let her know I had copies of everything he ever provided to Wagnor and his production company. What would she have to hide at that point? It made sense that she'd level with me now. Unless of course she killed Wagnor. But how could she have managed that if she didn't get to the house that Sunday?

I figured that I was on to something with the notion that Marcie stole those files because she was, as Kirk suggested, going to either produce the movie herself or, and this made much more sense, sell it to another producer willing to pay big bucks for it. If it was as good a story idea as Wagnor seemed to think it was, a producer might stoop to a little tomfoolery in order to get his hands on the script. But wait. Where *was* the script? The original one. The poorly written one. *Marcie must have it,* I thought.

Taking this premise a step further, maybe she told Wagnor

that someone else wanted to buy the story and suggested they take the money and run, rather than produce it, but Wagnor refused. Marcie, being greedy, decides to kill him and team up with producer number two. Not that it wouldn't have been simpler to quit her job. After all, you get unemployment benefits if you leave a position, but none if you murder your boss.

What if Wagnor was going to cut Marcie out of any deal having to do with the project and she killed him because of that and then went to the next producer? Still, I couldn't figure how she could have poisoned him from a distance.

The Marcie theory actually left more questions unanswered than answered. For instance, was it Marcie who attacked me at the B&B, and also at the houseboat? It wasn't out of the question. How'd she know where I was, though, in either instance? And what about Royalee's lie? What did Marcie have to do with the Woody Allen film festival? There was always the outside chance that Royalee didn't mean to lie. Maybe she meant to say she saw *Bullets Over Broadway* rather than *Annie Hall*. If so, why'd she make the comment that she'd seen *Annie Hall* multiple times? And who gave a fig which movie she saw? It didn't seem worth lying about.

Forget Royalee. Marcie had to be the one.

TWENTY-FOUR

THE PHONE RANG and I damn near collided with a truck. Jumped straight up off my dented tailbone and cursed a streak. I righted the car, returned the truck driver's hand signal, and screamed, "Who th' hell is this?" into the stupid little gadget that I had to pull out of my pants pocket. Ever have a bell go off in your drawers? Unnerving.

Donald said, "Ah, good girl. You've got the cell phone. I'm proud of you."

"Don't you ever do that to me again. I almost had a wreck."

"Where are you?"

So, this was his game, was it? I was about to learn that he was a control nut. Wanted to know my whereabouts, that's why he got me the blasted little ringer. I dodged a strip of tire in the road and said, "I'm about to cross the Tijuana border, why?"

"Did you see the kids?"

"I saw them and they saw me and I don't know any more now than I did and I'm getting sick and tired of shimmying over that seawall behind my old house."

"Why don't you go on home?"

"As in Florida or as in your private dynasty?"

He chuckled. *"Mi casa es su casa."*

I had no idea if that was proper Spanish or not. I don't speak the language. I made a turn off of the freeway, onto a residential street. "I'm on my way to see Marcie."

"Oh? Does she know about this?"

"She will."

"That's quite a haul out there. Why don't you call her first? That's what the little black thing in your hand is for." He was having too much fun with this.

"Actually, I'm going to wait until I'm closer to her place. I don't want to give her too much warning in case she decides to hightail it out of there if she thinks I'm on to her."

"How close do you plan to be?"

"Her curb would work nicely."

"How do you know she's not working at the studio today?"

"She said she was going up to wine country. Planned to come back on Wednesday. This is Wednesday."

"So it is. Be careful, Katie."

"I'll let you know what happens."

"You're going to be pretty close to my office when you leave Marcie's place. Sure you don't want to meet for dinner? Italian?"

"I've still got a dozen files—"

"They're not going anywhere. You need a break."

"Two people already tried that. First my neck then my skull."

"Very funny, Miss Marple. I gotta go. My other phone's ringing."

"See you." I hung up and folded the black creature into something resembling a wallet, but I wasn't about to put it back in my pants pocket. I let it lie on the seat beside me until I got to Marcie's street.

I'd gotten her phone number from information before I left *Donald's Dynasty* that morning. I slowed to about fifteen miles an hour as I neared her complex, dialed, and heard two rings before she answered.

"Marcie? Katie Wallace."

I don't know what I expected, but it wasn't the ice that froze my ear when she said, "I don't have anything to say to you, Mrs. Wallace. I went away to try to put this behind me. The last thing I need is to come home to find somebody wanting to drag it all out again."

"Until the situation's resolved, it's going to have to be dragged out."

She hesitated a second. "What situation? You mean the hearing? If that's the situation you're talking about, I don't see why you're calling me. I wasn't at the house the day Richard died. I don't have anything to say that would be helpful."

I took a deep breath and made the plunge. "Really? That's not what I'm learning from reading Kirk Zelena's files."

I counted. *One, two, three, four, five....* Finally she said, "What are you talking about?"

"The files you stole, Marcie. The ones you didn't want anyone to see."

"You're crazy."

"Kirk made copies for me. Very interesting." I decided to push my luck. "How hard do you think it was to put it all together? Celebrity deaths, methods of murder, the script that Kirk has a financial interest in—"

"What financial interest?"

"His time. Valuable. All he'll get is what's on the other end of the deal for him. A percentage of all those books, movies, network and cable television, national talk shows—"

I could almost hear her heartbeat. "Where are you?"

"I'm in Long Beach, but I could be at your place within the hour." I have to tell you, that was pure improvisation. I'd had every intention of letting her know I was close enough to wash her windows, but something took over and put words in my mouth. I think it's called Divine Intervention, because what happened next could only have happened if a Higher Source were involved. It certainly wasn't because of my first class detective work.

After she slammed the phone in my ear, I sat there, trying to decide what to do, when I saw her go storming out of her house, tossing the strap to her shoulder bag over one arm, sprinting toward a shed marked *Tenant Parking.* I scooted down in the seat so she wouldn't see me, but she wasn't looking in my direction and, besides, she thought I was in Long Beach. She pulled her four-year-old red Saturn out of its space. I waited until she was half a block ahead of me before easing away from the curb, following along behind. She took a left at Sherman Oaks Boulevard.

Commuter traffic was bumper-to-bumper, moving at a turtle's pace. At Osmond Avenue she made a right. Cars weren't so plentiful on this side street, so I let her gain a little distance. She slowed at California Delta Union Bank, turned into their driveway and parked under an elm. I nosed into a space at the curb behind a van. It was five after five, but she breezed right into the building and disappeared inside. Maybe she was going to withdraw funds to run away on.

I was wondering what was keeping her inside so long when she emerged through the revolving doors carrying a stack of files about the size of the ones I took into the houseboat the night before. They were probably the originals of the files that Kirk copied for me. My heart sank. She must have stashed them in a safe deposit box. Strange. Strange, because I didn't see anything in those files to warrant such furtiveness. *Well, I've come this far,* I thought. *Might as well see where she goes from here.*

She went back home. I'd done all this artful sleuthing and for what? To see her slip around to fetch what I'd already examined? Big deal. And now she was driving home. I was a block behind her, bored and hungry. I stayed with her all the way to her parking stall, where she returned the Saturn to its space, turned off the engine and got out, hauling those files from the backseat where she'd tossed them at the bank.

I'd pulled into the drive of a house with a For Sale sign in its lawn, on a street facing the tenant parking structure, far enough away that she wouldn't notice me. I watched her struggle under the bulk of the files and then she surprised me. She went to one of those big commercial trash bins like they have behind supermarkets and complexes like hers, and she heaved the files into one of them. Then she opened her purse, took something out of it, which turned out to be a cigarette lighter, and set fire to everything in the bin. She was in an alley a few feet removed from the tenant parking spaces. There were no windows that looked out onto the garbage cans.

Marcie then dashed to the sidewalk that led to her condo. I waited until she was out of sight to run to the bin. I pulled as many of the files out as I could manage, throwing them on the ground and stomping them at the same time. Paper's harder to burn than most people realize. It takes a lot to get a real blaze going, especially manila folders.

I was able to salvage half a dozen files before the flames began to spread. Once it started in earnest, it exploded into a mass of blistering yellow-orange. I scooped up the papers from the ground and sprinted back to my car as an old man pulled into a space three removed from Marcie's Saturn. I slammed the door shut on the Honda and started the engine with a feeling that maybe these files were more than a rehash of what I'd already seen, that maybe there was something else in there I should know about. As I started down the street, the old man noticed the flames in the trash bin. "Fire! Fire!" he yelled, racing toward the guard shack. People stuck their head out of windows and doors, then picked up the cry of "Fire! Fire!" as an alarm sounded. By then I'd driven nearly to the corner.

A fire truck was barreling down the street, headed toward Haven Croft Estates, when I pulled into a department store parking lot and began to read.

My hands were shaking as I dialed Donald's office number fifteen minutes later. The production assistant who answered put me through to him on the set.

"Donald," I nearly shouted into the little black monster, "you still want to do Italian?"

I LEFT MY TREASURES in the car and joined Donald at Mario's on Ventura Boulevard. It's my favorite restaurant, but tonight the singing waiters and waitresses failed to make an impression. My stomach was in knots, my heart about to erupt out of my chest. Donald arrived ahead of me. He was there to take my hand when I burst through the door. We scooted into a booth at mezzanine level, as far from the piano as possible, where I blurted out everything that had happened since our phone conversation. He listened intently, then he said, "Why don't we get something to go? We've got some serious work ahead of us."

I'd been right, of course. The files were more than what Kirk Zelena had copied for me. Donald and I read together, me finishing a page first, then handing it on to him. We didn't speak again until we'd completed the last word of the last line on the last page. It was past midnight. While we read, we'd managed to polish off two containers of Mario's excellent ravioli and an antipasto salad and now we were working on Harvey's Bristol Cream. I felt dazed, but it had nothing to do with sherry. The contents of those files were almost too much to take in. I felt myself shiver.

Donald slipped an arm around my shoulder and kissed my temple, but he said nothing. A foghorn bellowed in the distance. Everything finally made sense, but the sense it made was difficult to grasp. Like trying to understand how anyone could kill Laci Peterson, especially the way she was killed. Or how McVeigh could slaughter all of those innocent people. Our senses can take in such acts, and even accept them as fact, but we never understand the why of it. So it was with the note that fell out of one of the folders as we started to put things away. Somehow we'd missed seeing it. Donald picked it up from the floor, read it, then looked at me with an expression I couldn't decipher.

"It can't be any worse than what we've already learned," I said.

He read it aloud, slowly. When he finished, we simply stared at each other.

TWENTY-FIVE

I'D PUZZLED IT OUT during early morning, predawn, hours. Where I'd been asking myself what MacKay would have done, I now asked myself what Agatha Christie would have done, and I started making calls at eight the next morning, Thursday. By ten I'd left messages or managed to reach everyone on my list. I asked them to meet me at the Sun Beach house at seven o'clock that night. It no longer mattered if neighbors called the press. It didn't matter who saw what. It was over. I asked all but one person to leave their car at Bell Park and walk the block to Wagnor's place. The last call was the most difficult. If it didn't go the way I hoped it would go, the way I needed it to go, there was a good chance everything would fall apart. But it turned out fine. When I told Marcie that I'd pulled her files from the fire in the trash bin, but that I was willing to let her have them for a price, she didn't hesitate to say she'd meet me. Her voice was trembling when we hung up. I wondered if she noticed that mine was, too.

Donald called his office to tell them he wouldn't be coming in, which was fine with the producer since the cast and crew were out on location in Simi Valley and there wasn't that much for Donald to do as a consultant anyway.

Now it was me pacing and Donald brewing hot tea to calm my nerves. We spent the day going over plans for the night. We worked on refining the scenario, getting our facts straight and trying to anticipate every possible complication. Finally, it was time to dress. I wore the pair of pale blue trousers he'd bought for me with a new white turtleneck. He put on his white duck pants which I was kind enough to relinquish. We stopped at the door to hold one another briefly and to wish ourselves well. Then we headed out to Sun Beach to face the music. So to speak.

TWENTY-SIX

KIRK ZELENA WAS the first to arrive. He came alone, as I'd asked him to do, and seemed awkward, shy and confused. Donald showed him to the living room where he took a seat at the end of the sofa. We'd arranged it so that when everyone arrived, they'd be sitting in a circle. Donald offered him a cup of coffee, but he declined.

"Can I ask what this is about?"

Donald shook his head. "We're expecting a few others. It'll be easier to explain to everyone at the same time."

If Kirk was going to reply, he didn't get the chance. The doorbell rang. A tight-lipped Henny Thornton swept her gaze up one side of me and down the other, then she turned to Donald and repeated the process. As she breezed into the room, exuding arrogance, Royalee arrived. Her face was flushed and angry, her lips drawn into a grim line.

"What's going on, Mrs. Wallace?" she demanded, as she entered the living room. "Where's sis and Michael?"

As if on cue, they came through the doorway, apologizing for being late. Royalee glared at them, not sure whose side they were on or if they were part of the enemy camp. Caroline crossed to her and took her half-sister in her arms. Although I suspected Richard's daughter was someone difficult to rattle, at this moment it was Caroline who was the strong one. When Royalee turned to me, she said, "I don't know what's going on, but I'm grateful you didn't ask my mother to be here. She's having a hard time with all of this."

Michael shook Donald's hand, then Kirk's, and sat on a footstool in front of the dark fireplace. Caroline took the chair beside him with Royalee perched on its arm. Kirk eyed the youngsters, while the rest of us watched Henny balance on the edge of a straight-back chair, prim, prissy and fit to be tied. "This had better be good," she said tightly.

Donald introduced everyone to Kirk, while I ushered in Harmon and Dorothy Ermaling. Harmon was clearly unhappy to be there. Dorothy stopped her wheelchair to eye everyone suspiciously. She met Henny's gaze, but I wasn't able to read the message in their glance. In hindsight, I suspect that one of them had the idea, or was afraid, that the other was about to back out of their eyewitness account of the story.

Caroline and Michael refused to acknowledge Dorothy's presence. I have to admit that even though the Ermalings told me they'd attend, I was surprised to see them. I think probably that Dorothy was such a busybody she couldn't stand the thought of everyone getting together, no matter what the reason, without her being in on it. As for Harmon, it was obvious that his mission was to protect his wife.

Everyone I'd asked to arrive at seven had done so. Donald gave me the high sign that it was time to begin. I stepped to the center of the room.

"I appreciate all of you being here. Royalee, I know you've been on the road several hours to be able to join us. You're going to be glad you did. First off, let me assure all of you that the truth will come out tonight."

Michael's voice was full of cautious hope. "Go on, Katie."

"When Helen asked me to help her, she had only one request, that I find a way to make Dorothy admit she never saw Lane shove Richard down the stairs. Without her eyewitness account, the police would have ruled his death an accident. With Dorothy's statement, of course, it became murder. And the reality is this. Dorothy didn't see a thing—except Lane trying to keep her husband from falling down the stairs an instant after he collapsed."

"That's absurd," Harmon stammered.

I ignored him. "Richard Wagnor collapsed—" I paused for dramatic effect "—because he was poisoned."

The room burst into cries of disbelief. It was clearly the first the Ermalings had heard of it. I went on. "Caroline and Michael knew that Donald and I suspected as much, but we had no way to prove it. After all, even if he were poisoned and not pushed, Lane was still a prime suspect. But then, so were the rest of you. Except, of course, for you, Kirk."

I walked around the room, looking at first one person, and then the other. "Who poisoned Richard Wagnor and why? Was it Arlene, Richard's ex-wife and Royalee's mother?"

Royalee sprang to her feet, but Michael took her hand. She shot him a look wild with panic, but he said, "It's okay," and she sat back down.

"You thought it was your mom, didn't you, Royalee?" She didn't answer me, but the look on her face said all I needed to know. Now I was certain that my suspicions were right. "I couldn't figure why you claimed to have seen *Annie Hall* when it wasn't playing that night. A mix-up in movie reels. Your mom told me about it, but she had no idea she'd given away your secret. Now why, I asked myself, would you fib about something so trivial?

"Then Caroline mentioned that she confided the poison theory to you on the phone. That was last Wednesday. The day your mom returned from Mexico. Yet, when you told your mother what had happened in this house after she'd left for her cruise that Sunday, you didn't mention poison. You only told her that your father had died, that your Aunt Dorothy told police she saw Lane kill him, but that Lane swore to Michael, and later to me, that she'd reached out to catch, not shove, him.

"I take it your mom's had plenty of experience with Dorothy's interference in the past. She knew you cared about Lane, and she's one of those rare people who know how to truly love. She wanted nothing but the best for your father, even if it meant him being married to someone else. So, she called Dorothy and confronted her on the phone, demanding to know why she'd lie about something so tragic and so important. There was no question in her mind that Dorothy was using the incident to vent her hatred for Lane and to garner a little media attention for herself.

Dorothy became hysterical at being called a liar. That's when you, Harmon, took the phone from her."

"I certainly did. I won't let anybody talk to her like that. It made her physically ill. This hasn't been easy for any of us, but it was especially hard on Dorothy to have to confess that she actually witnessed her brother being murdered."

"First off, he's not her brother," I countered, keeping my cool. "And secondly, she saw no such thing. But let me continue with a straight line of progression."

I didn't allow myself much more than a glance at Dorothy, but I could see she'd turned deathly white. Harmon, standing behind her wheelchair, put his hand on her shoulder. She curled her fingers over his.

"Simply because the *Annie Hall* lie appeared to be so inconsequential, Royalee, I knew there had to be more to it. I think I have it figured out, but why don't you tell us what happened?"

She glanced at Caroline, who nodded her encouragement.

Royalee ran her tongue over her lips. I could see that she was trying to collect her thoughts. "It isn't that I thought my mother might have poisoned him, it was that I was *afraid* she might have. She taught botany. She knew about poisons, at least certain kinds of poisons. And I knew she'd never stopped loving Richie. I was so scared…" She hesitated a moment. "I wanted you to back off, Mrs. Wallace. Aunt Dorothy's lies would come out at the trial, I was certain of it. The court would discount her story and rule my dad's death an accident. But—" her voice faltered "—you just kept digging things up. If he really did die of poisoning, and if there was any way Momma could have done it…I had to stop you."

Caroline touched Royalee's arm. A brief, reassuring pat, but that's all it took for Royalee to be able to continue.

"I didn't mean to hurt you, Mrs. Wallace. In fact, I drove to Helen's house with the idea of just talking to you, but when I got there, you were pulling out of the driveway. I decided to follow you and look for an opportunity to…I don't know…to try to make you see the hurt you were causing people. Well…" She sighed heavily. "You drove to the airport. Straight to a car rental.

You'd gone there in a Le Baron, but you drove out in a Honda. I figured you were trying to outsmart the media, getting a car they wouldn't recognize, so they wouldn't follow you.

"I stayed behind you all the way to Naples Island. When you went in Caroline's apartment, I tried to decide whether or not to go on in and have the conversation I wanted to have with you in front of sis, but then…I couldn't stand the thought of even hinting that I thought Momma might have been responsible for my father's death. So, I waited outside, in the car, figuring that I'd follow you on back to Studio City, to Helen's, where we'd be alone.

"You fooled me, though. You didn't go back to Helen's. You went to the bed and breakfast. Even then I wasn't sure what I should do. I was walking toward the entrance when I saw you come out of a room, carrying a water pitcher. I ducked into the shadows and, I can't explain it…I suddenly got the idea that, if I scared the hell out of you, if you thought your life might be in danger by staying and stirring things up, then maybe you'd go away and let the law handle it. I was positive that no one but you even thought about poison. With you gone, it would never even come up. Lane would accept the court's ruling that Dad died as the result of an accidental fall. All of us would have accepted it. It would have ended right there, with Lane coming home a free woman."

"But you would have always suspected that your mom poisoned your father," I reminded her. "This way, we've learned the truth. She had nothing to do with his death."

Royalee broke down and cried into her hands. Caroline comforted her while everyone looked on, feeling helpless. Dorothy thrust her jaw into a determined square. Harmon's eyes were on fire.

"Your scenario has a major flaw," he said through clenched teeth. "Dorothy saw what she saw and her story will withstand cross-examination." His wife, swallowing back tears, looked up at him gratefully.

I said, "When I found out that Caroline had shared the poison theory with you, Royalee, and then I learned that *Annie Hall* wasn't playing the night I was attacked on Naples Island, the night you told me you were at the campus theater watching it, well, it wasn't hard to put two and two together, it just took me a while. But I made the mistake of trying to tie the attack into whoever had poisoned Richard."

Michael frowned at his stepsister, but the expression was more puzzled than critical. "I don't get why you attacked her a second time, though. Was it because she wouldn't back off?"

Before Royalee could protest, I interrupted. "It wasn't Royalee who nearly cracked my skull open outside Donald's place."

All eyes were riveted on me. Donald nodded just the tiniest nod, urging me on. I folded my arms and walked slowly around the room, inside their circle. It was becoming clearer to me as I talked it out. The pieces really were beginning to fit. It was no longer theory. Our suppositions had moved into the realm of reality.

"This second attack came on Monday night after I returned from Fresno where I met with Royalee and then Arlene. Royalee was on her way to work at the TV station where she's an intern." I turned to her. "You said you had to be there in an hour and you were running a little late." Royalee nodded, uncertain where I was going with this.

"At first I figured whoever attacked me outside the houseboat was the same person who'd attacked me at the B&B. Donald suggested it was someone else, but it didn't seem reasonable that two people would have the same idea about using violence to scare me into returning to Florida. I held to that thought all the way up until I realized you were the one who slugged me on Naples Island, Royalee. If it was you that night, I had to be looking at two different attackers, since I knew you were at work when it happened the second time."

Everyone was exchanging glances with everyone else.

"Who was tall enough to hit a five foot seven woman on top of her head? Who was strong enough to almost split her skull in two? Who else wanted me to leave badly enough to do something that drastic? After all, it was a blow that could easily have proven fatal." I turned to Henny. "Couldn't be you. You're too short, too skinny and too much of a weasel to attempt anything that brazen. The worst you're capable of is sneaking around with a married man. That's not brazen, that's stupid. I wasn't hit by a stupid person." I faced Harmon. "I was hit by a smart person."

"You're nuts," he said, but I saw the hand on his wife's shoulder begin to tremble.

I shook my head with the same degree of irony I was feeling. "Your motive wasn't unlike Royalee's. You were protecting someone you love."

Dorothy lifted a baffled face to his.

"Not that you thought Dorothy poisoned Richard. You didn't even know we were considering poison, did you?"

"I did not."

"It was what you considered to be the harassment of your wife that was tearing you apart. Dorothy wasn't used to having her word disputed. She gave her statement to the police and you accepted it as a final authority, such is your love for her. It's commendable loyalty, but misplaced."

I thought the vein in his neck might explode all over Lane's living room.

"It was the call from Arlene that made your decision for you, wasn't it?"

"She had no right," he said tightly.

"When I realized it was you," I continued, "I had to ask myself how you knew where to find me. How'd you know I was at Donald's houseboat? Care to share that with us?"

"You're doing just fine," he said. "Why don't you tell me how I think?"

"All right, I will. You think like the intelligent person you are. You saw me at the funeral with Donald, you saw me on television news with Donald, you knew that my ex-husband and I were friends with Donald and his late wife. As Donald keeps reminding me, it's a small town. Everyone knows everything about each other. Or…almost everything." I directed this last comment to Henny. She met my eyes with a glare that would cut diamonds.

"There's that two-and-two configuration again, Harmon.

Deducing that I couldn't stay at Helen's because of media scrutiny, and that I seemed to be spending a lot of time with Donald, it wasn't hard for you to find out where he lives. Maybe you didn't know I was actually staying there, but you knew that if you were diligent in your pursuit, you'd find me there at some time or another. Long enough, certainly, for you to make your point."

He was swallowing hard now, but the fire had gone out of him. I'd hit home and I hadn't been absolutely certain about my suspicion that he was attacker number two until this moment.

"You had no way of knowing that I'd already been attacked once before, and out of the same motivation, to scare me into backing off. But, once again, I was chasing myself down the wrong trail. I was still equating attack with murder, slugging me with poisoning Richard. And they are related, but only remotely, not directly."

Michael had been listening intently. Now he frowned and said, "Then who did poison Richie?"

"Ah," I replied, "I'm getting to that. Donald, I think I hear a car stopping out front. Would you mind seeing if it's—?" There was no need to finish the sentence; he was already at the door. The room fell silent as we listened to an automobile door slam and footsteps click quickly up the front walk. When a single chime sounded, Donald opened the door and said, "Right on time. Come in."

TWENTY-SEVEN

MARCIE STOOD AT the end of hall, looking into the living room, an incredulous expression on her face. Her mouth actually dropped open a bit when she turned to me.

"Come in," I repeated, indicating a chair I'd left reserved for her beside the sofa.

"What is this?" she asked in a voice both small and confused.

Donald took her by the elbow and eased her into the wingback. She was obviously having trouble taking it all in. All of these people. She knew most of them, of course—Caroline, her boss's stepdaughter, the one person who knew the truth about herself and Wagnor; and Michael, whom I would later learn she knew only slightly. Royalee was familiar to her; she'd known Wagnor's daughter since Royalee was a child. Henny was a stranger, as was Harmon Ermaling though she seemed to recognize Dorothy. When her gaze fell on Kirk Zelena, I thought she might faint. She wobbled unsteadily in her chair, caught herself, and fastened a pair of panic-stricken eyes on me. But she couldn't find her voice. All of her questions were in her eyes.

I said, "I think most of you know Richard's secretary, Marcie." There were no acknowledgments of the introduction, just more curious stares. "Marcie's a very important person in the entire scheme of things. She not only types and takes shorthand, she's a budding writer." I smiled at her, but she didn't smile back. She kept staring at me with those huge, terrified eyes. "Before we share some of her creativity with you, let's go back to the afternoon of Richard's death. The day of the garden party."

I cleared my throat and said a silent prayer that I'd make sense and that Donald and I were correct in our analysis. I glanced at him. He had an elbow propped on the mantel, fingers laced in front of him. He winked and inclined his head slightly.

This was it. The big *it.* I began slowly.

"Around four o'clock everyone had gone, except for Henny and Dorothy. Michael was clearing dirty dishes from the patio and bringing them into the kitchen. Lane was putting leftovers into containers that she'd taken out to the buffet table. Caroline and Royalee were in the family room, listening to CDs they'd purchased that morning at the mall.

"People not invited to the party had dropped by during the course of the day. Arlene, to meet Lane and see the kids and Richard, of course, on her way to board a cruise line for a three-day vacation. Erik Perez, Caroline's ex-boyfriend, also stopped by. Even you, Harmon, came in when you dropped Dorothy off. You brought an extra bag of ice, which Lane had asked you to do earlier, on the phone. All of those bodies threw me for a loop at first. Erik had a motive for killing Richard. A pretty good one, too. But as we've already pointed out, so did Arlene. And if you'd been a jealous man, Harmon, you would have had a motive, too. But that's not your nature. And so I had to eliminate three suspects, leaving us with Henny—" her gasp was a little overdone, I felt "—and Dorothy—" not a sound out of big momma "—and even Caroline and Michael, who both had motives. So did you, Royalee."

Heads were turning at an alarming rate. Everyone was checking out everyone else.

"The one person who wasn't a suspect was Marcie. Not that she didn't have cause to do Richard in, but she appeared not to have the opportunity. After all, she wasn't at the house that day, and that's the God's truth."

"You left out Lane," Dorothy snapped.

"So I did," I said. "But let me get back to those moments before Richard's death. It's important that you follow the scenario. It's a bit convoluted, but it's also perfectly logical and even rather simple, in retrospect." I paused for air. "Richard was on the back patio, chitchatting with Henny and Dorothy. Harmon was late picking up Dorothy, and Henny was still there because, well, because Henny wanted to stay as close to Richard as she could get, for as long as she could manage it. However, unknown to all but two people, there was another agenda in progress. Richard had it planned to the minute—and it was time to pick a fight with his wife."

Confusion lit every face but Marcie's. She was watching her hands in her lap.

I continued. "He began by making a comment that he knew would upset her. All it did was confuse her. She didn't know what had brought on his sudden change of attitude. He kept up the insults and kept belittling her—not where the others could hear him, mind you, just little nasty comments made to her practically under his breath. Lane began to fight back tears. Then Richard left the patio and went into the kitchen where he began preparing a cup of tea. Michael was in the kitchen and saw him take the tea bag out of the jar and put it in a cup. Watched Richard pour hot water from a kettle on the stove, into that cup."

"What the hell do we care about Richard's cup of tea?" Harmon demanded. Evidently brimstone had returned to his soul.

"I'm getting there. Be patient."

Harmon sighed and shook his head in disgust.

"Where was I? Oh, yeah...water over the tea bag. Michael was still in the room when the phone rang on the kitchen counter. He answered it. It was Marcie calling for Richard. By the time Michael had the last batch of dishes he'd brought from the patio rinsed and ready to put in the dishwasher, Richard had hung up. He told Michael that Marcie was coming by the house to pick up a report that was upstairs on his desk. He also asked Michael if he'd let her in when she arrived. He needed to be with the last guests out on the patio. Then he went back to the business with his cup of tea and Michael returned to the patio to gather up leftovers. But let me digress here for a second.

"Marcie lives in the valley, easily an hour from this house. Yet Richard asked Michael to let Marcie in when she arrived. He must have known she was somewhere in the area, somewhere close. Make sense? Sure it does.

"So, Marcie's on her way here when Lane comes into the kitchen. Richard picks up the cup of tea he had so lovingly prepared and put it in her hands. A peace offering, he told her. Peppermint tea, her favorite. He'd been rude and ugly and he was sorry. The upcoming trip to Puerto Rico had him on edge, so much depended on this film deal coming through. Lane reached up on tiptoe to kiss his cheek. And Richard walked out of the room." I pointed to Michael. "Tell us what happened next."

He was a little surprised that I'd called on him, but he came through like a champ. "Well, I came in the kitchen with a tray of leftovers. Some small containers I'd finished filling for Mom, a pitcher with a little lemonade left in it, odds and ends."

I prompted him with, "And what'd Lane do?"

"She said 'Gee, that lemonade looks good' and she poured what was left into a glass for herself." He gave me a puzzled look, shrugged his shoulders.

I nodded. "And then you did what?"

He spread his hands. "I saw that Richard had left the room without the cup of tea he'd been making for himself, so I took it to him."

I shook my head again. "Everything seemed so innocent, but what I've left out is that no more than a few minutes went by before Richard returned to the kitchen. He went at least as far as the kitchen door where he yelled at Lane to get her butt upstairs. Lane was perplexed. Hadn't Richard just given her a peace offering? What was his problem now? she wondered, as she hurried down the hall. Maybe he wanted to chew her out in private, but she couldn't figure out what had set him off again, and she couldn't understand why he couldn't wait until everyone was gone to have a confrontation, if that was his intent. He was at the top of the stairs, apparently in a rage. When she reached the second floor, he grabbed her by the wrist and twisted it, yelling at her about the quantity of pills she'd been taking."

Caroline shared a look of shock with Michael and Royalee. I continued.

"That's right, Caroline. Your mom doesn't take any kind of pills, does she? Not even aspirin. She's a bit of a health buff, in fact. It's at this point Richard gasps, turns pale, bursts out in a sweat, buckles, and topples down the stairs before Lane can stop him. This, Dorothy, is what you saw, if you saw anything."

The cockiness had gone out of Harmon's eyes, the defiance out of Dorothy's.

Michael glanced at everyone in the room, then said, "But… we still don't know…I mean, who…?"

Rather than answer him, I turned to Donald.

"Do you want to read them the pages in the folder? It's right there on the mantel."

Donald picked up a manila folder, opened it, and began.

"She was everything the public thought she was and more. She was beautiful, creative, funny, intelligent…and complex.

"For years I'd known of her delicate mental state and I'd done everything in my power to support her in her effort to return to films. It couldn't have been easy, I knew that when I married her. To enjoy the adoration of millions of fans and then, suddenly, to become an outcast must have been almost beyond my comprehension. If we've never experienced anything like that, how could we ever know? This little girl with the laughing eyes had a heart that was breaking…and all I could do was watch as it slowly helped to kill her…"

Donald read on from the folder, a remarkable, dramatic and purely fictitious, "biography" of the late, great Lane Allison… written by a grieving widower with the help of his loyal, confidential secretary.

By the time Donald had gotten to the part about how Wagnor, the bereaved husband, had caused Lane so much pain, a pain he would regret for the rest of his life, you could have heard a pin drop in the room. Actually, what dropped was Henny. Chapter Six. Richard Wagnor's ex-lover commits suicide by leaping from a Puerto Rico hotel room on April twenty-first of this year. According to the manuscript, she had followed him to the island when he took a business trip to raise financing for Lane's comeback film. When Henny realized that she couldn't persuade him to come back to her, she killed herself.

Donald laid the folder aside to assist Kirk and Harmon in

getting Henny to the sofa, which everyone else quickly evacuated. Caroline grabbed a glass of water from the kitchen. Royalee was dampening a washcloth in the downstairs half bath. Henny revived, but lay there, stunned, a washcloth on her head, heaving dry sobs.

Donald looked from me to the others. "Shall I go on?"

Michael shook his head. He put his arm around Caroline's shoulders. Royalee was seated on the floor, cross-legged in her jeans, her face a study of sorrow.

I said, "I don't think so, Donald. I think we've heard enough."

All eyes turned to Marcie.

Donald pitched the folder down on the coffee table, where everyone could plainly see the title written in marking pen: "*The Bizarre Death of America's Sweetheart,* by Richard Wagnor as told to Marcie Garner."

Marcie buried her face in her hands and turned away from us.

Kirk was still puzzled. "What'd all of this have to do with the research I did on the screenplay he—?"

Marcie turned furious red eyes on him. "There was no screenplay! Not yet."

Donald and I looked at each other. She was confirming our worst fear. I'd done bona fide detective work after all.

Marcie took a deep breath. "Richard's most successful work was his documentary on famous kidnapping cases. One day, he ran across an Internet site about sensational Hollywood deaths… Natalie Wood, Marilyn Monroe, Sal Mineo…books and movie deals that go on year after year, long after they've died. Richard got the idea that if Lane were dead, if he could create a controversy or mystique around her death, there would be book deals, miniseries, foreign sales, cable TV, interviews, speaking engagements…why, he could even produce the major motion picture he'd always dreamed of producing. Oh, don't you all get it? He'd finally be the important producer he was meant to be. He was a genius. In another era, he would have been as important as Louis B. Mayer and Jack Warner. Lane was nothing but a has-been. She held him back. He couldn't raise money on her name. No one knew her anymore, no one cared. But he could change all of that…with a powerful screenplay. After all, she really had been number one at the box office for two decades. And she really had been America's sweetheart. It was a natural. But she had to be dead for it to happen."

Her expression pleaded with us to understand, but no one did. It was sad and pathetic, and it was also about as sick as a person can get.

"Donald and I found a note in your files, Marcie. After he reads it to us, maybe you could elaborate."

Donald took a sheet of fine linen paper from a folder; Lane's personal stationary. He read aloud the typed words.

"My darlings," it said, *"don't hate me for doing this. I don't want to live any longer—the hurt is too much to bear. Know that I love you with all my heart and that I'll always adore Richie. Take care of him for me and take care of yourselves. Love, Momma."*

Caroline's hand was over her mouth, her eyes large green discs over her fingertips. Michael looked as if he might be ill. The others seemed more baffled than shocked. I folded my arms and looked at Marcie, who simply shrugged.

"Richard told me to call the house just after four that Sunday," she said softly. "I used my cell phone and I waited at Bell Park until it was time to dial his number. If he said he had a report for me to pick up and that it was upstairs on his desk, it was my signal that he'd…prepared her tea…and that I was to proceed to the house. I was to go upstairs and put Lane's suicide note on her pillow." She glanced at everyone to see if they understood. They didn't. Her voice rose. "Everyone heard them arguing. They knew she hadn't been able to make it on the screen again. Taking her life would have been the most logical thing in the world for her to do. Especially after she found out he'd been cheating on her for years. Yes…we knew it would come out in an investigation—and we were glad. It would work for us."

Michael managed to say, "What the hell was in the tea, Marcie?"

She looked at him with innocent eyes. "Azaleas. He'd cut an arrangement from the backyard as near to the time of the party to begin as possible so they'd be fresh. That was the water he used to make her tea." She glanced around the room. "Azaleas and oleander, they're deadly, you know. The fluid from their stem will..." Her voice faded as she glanced down at her hands in her lap.

Caroline considered her for a moment, then said, "Instead of drinking the tea he prepared for her, though, Momma decided to have lemonade."

Michael's voice trembled. "And the cup of tea I took to him, the cup I thought he'd left behind, was the one he'd made for Mom!"

Marcie's face crumbled. "Why didn't she just drink the damn stuff? It was her favorite! She should have drank it! None of this would be happening!"

Donald said, as he'd said so many times in the last week, "Oh, what a tangled web..."

Henny, still lying on the sofa, removed the washcloth from her forehead to say, "What's any of this have to do with me? Why was he going to...going to...?" Her voice broke.

Marcie scoffed, but there was no passion in it. "It wasn't about you, Henny. You were disposable. He was through with you. But your death would have added another element of mystery to Lane's death. Even though she would have...killed herself before you jumped out of a hotel room in Puerto Rico, the public would be left to wonder if she'd found out about you, or if your affair with her husband had anything to do with her decision to commit suicide. And yours would have kept the world speculating for years to come." She added in a tiny voice, "I thought it was a brilliant touch."

Kirk looked as if he were going to be sick. "So, the research I did for him...on poison...helped him determine how to kill his wife...and the script I'd invested time and effort into...it didn't even exist. It was going to be written later…after Lane Allison was…" He hung his head and shook it slowly from side to side. "My God…oh, my God…"

Donald used the phone in the kitchen to call the Sun Beach police department. We waited in silence until we heard them approach.

TWENTY-EIGHT

I SLEPT ALMOST all day Friday, back in Helen's guest room. Helen was with her family at Lane's Sun Beach house. Tempted as I was to stay on *Donald's Dynasty,* I needed to be alone.

Friday night I joined Lane, Helen, Michael and Caroline for dinner at Lane's place. She was the perfect hostess and looked, not happy, but more peaceful. Not that she was over the rough patches entirely; she wasn't. There was the realization that her beloved husband wasn't all that beloved, and I could certainly identify with that. There was also more media to contend with now that they were swept up in the fresh frenzy that came with the sudden turn of events. This time though, Lane said, it was easier to cope with than when they were dogging her, thinking her guilty of murder. Now there was a kind of celebration about it, as if the world were applauding her, though even that made her uncomfortable. "There's nothing about murder to celebrate," she so wisely observed.

Royalee was still grieving over the loss of her father, and now the horrible, gut-wrenching knowledge that he was also a cold-hearted killer who simply never had a chance to commit the evil deed. I don't know how Arlene coped with it, but at least she and her girl had each other. There was a measure of comfort in that.

Photographers popped bulbs in my face as I left Lane's house, but this time I didn't care. I waved at them, in fact. Katlin Wallace, woman detective. What a crock. What a *gigantic* crock.

Saturday morning I wore one of the outfits Donald had purchased for me and packed the rest along with the denim skirt and beige trousers. The brown turtleneck lost out to Wendy's mustard and was relegated to the status of dust rag, which I left in Helen's utility room.

She and I had said our goodbyes the night before when she'd elected to remain at the Sun Beach house for a couple days more. She asked me to lock up the Studio City home behind myself and to come back whenever I felt like I needed a good earthquake. Or missed having a little smog in my life. The words were frivolous, but the gratitude behind them was not.

At ten the sun was starting to break through the orange gunk in the air. I could see a patch of blue directly overhead when I went out to get in Donald's car. Michael had offered to return the Honda rental to the airport if I wanted Donald to take me to catch my plane. Which I did.

We stopped at Jerry's Deli for one of their great omelettes washed down with herb tea, then we joined the freeway throng headed mostly for the beaches of Malibu or Santa Monica. I had no desire to follow them. I had a sudden longing for huge oak trees dripping moss and long clay roads that stretch into the gentle hills around St. Seminole. I was born in Florida all those years ago, but I'd never thought about returning until MacKay talked me into it. I hadn't been back since I was a kid and never missed it. Now I realized that the child in us lives forever if we let it.

"That's some mighty deep thinking you're doing there."

I'd almost forgotten Donald was beside me.

"Sorry. I guess I'm pretty dull company this morning."

"You're never dull, Katie. You're many things, but dull isn't one of them."

A few more miles clipped by with nothing other than an easy silence between us. I couldn't put the events of the past few days behind me. There were too many unanswered questions.

"I still don't get it," I said at last.

"What's that?"

"The bit about the azaleas. Isn't that an odd means to use if you're going to try to convince people that your wife committed suicide?"

"What would you suggest?"

"I dunno. An old-fashioned gun."

"If Wagnor didn't own one, then he'd have to buy it, and that could get messy. Besides, it makes a lot of noise and—"

"Okay, okay. What about a razor?"

"How would he manage to slit Lane's wrists, do you s'pose?"

Good point, but still…azaleas?

Donald managed to change lanes between two big rigs, headed us on a steady course again and said at the same time, "There's a certain intrigue about the way he did it, you have to admit. Like Marilyn Monroe and the drugs found in her body. Only there was no drug residue in her mouth and no needles in the area. So how'd drugs get inside her? The question will never be answered to anyone's satisfaction. It'll remain a mystery—and many a writer will gain fame and fortune in endless speculation."

"There's a correlation in here somewhere?"

"Sure there is. Wagnor wanted questions to remain unanswered about Lane's death, too. All of those books he studied on Marilyn Monroe and Natalie Wood…he was trying to figure how to get the same kind of mileage out of Lane. A suicide note, their argument in front of people—"

"Henny's death in Puerto Rico."

"Exactly. He poured enough fuel on the mess to keep it aflame for years to come."

I saw his point. People would ask the same question I just asked: Why death by azaleas? Some would no doubt have speculated that Henny poisoned Lane—having been at the party that day and, with her apparent suicide in Puerto Rico a week later, a sure indicator of her guilt. A finger would also always be pointed at Dorothy once the facts became known. My God, the man was cunning. He'd have enough theories to fill volumes. And he'd become famous. He'd also be a suspect of foul play himself, I suddenly realized. And then, on the heels of that thought, another. He'd welcome the suspicion. He could play the misunderstood, falsely accused, grieving widower to the hilt. That would be good for at least one made-for-TV movie in itself.

"You have to admit," Donald grinned, "azaleas certainly would have given her death a dramatic twist."

I watched out the window without replying. It was too bizarre. Can we really live with someone and yet never have a clue that an entire other person dwells inside them? I'd no more than got the notion in and out of my mind when I saw a clear mental image of MacKay. I shivered involuntarily. Donald covered my hand with his and kept it there until we pulled up at the curb beside Tropic Airlines.

"Sure you don't want me to go inside with you?" he said.

"And spend two hours standing in a security line?" I don't know why I couldn't bring myself to open the door and get out, but I lingered.

"Can I come see you sometime?"

I thought it over for a moment. About a nanosecond. "Sure. Sometime."

"Keep that cell phone with you when you're on the road."

I threw my arms around his neck and clung to him like a child about to be sent off to summer camp. Once there, all's well, it's the parting that's such sweet sorrow. He kissed my temple. I nuzzled against him for the briefest moment, then got out of the car and waved as he pulled into traffic.

A family climbing into a Disneyland shuttle stopped to stare at me. "Hey! Aren't you that detective from Florida? We seen you on teevee!"

"That's good," I smiled back at them. Then a baggage handler said, "Afternoon, Miss Wallace. Glad you got that movie star out of the jam she was in." His face parted in a warm grin and my heart skipped a beat. Fame felt odd. Like walking naked through a public place. Everybody knew who I was, where I was from, what I was doing here…odd. The only thing they didn't know, and was none of their damn business, is that I'm a tad older than Rita Moreno—but not by much.

REQUEST YOUR FREE BOOKS!

2 FREE NOVELS
PLUS 2 FREE GIFTS!

Your Partner in Crime

YES! Please send me 2 FREE novels from the Worldwide Library™ series and my 2 FREE gifts (gifts are worth about $10). After receiving them, if I don't wish to receive any more books, I can return the shipping statement marked "cancel." If I don't cancel, I will receive 4 brand-new novels every month and be billed just $4.99 per book in the U.S. or $5.99 per book in Canada. That's a saving of 17% off the cover price. It's quite a bargain! Shipping and handling is just 50¢ per book.* I understand that accepting the 2 free books and gifts places me under no obligation to buy anything. I can always return a shipment and cancel at any time. Even if I never buy another book, the two free books and gifts are mine to keep forever.

414/424 WDN E9NE

Name (PLEASE PRINT)

Address Apt. #

City State/Prov. Zip/Postal Code

Signature (if under 18, a parent or guardian must sign)

Mail to **The Reader Service:**
IN U.S.A.: P.O. Box 1867, Buffalo, NY 14240-1867
IN CANADA: P.O. Box 609, Fort Erie, Ontario L2A 5X3

Not valid for current subscribers to the Worldwide Library series.

Want to try two free books from another line?
Call 1-800-873-8635 or visit www.ReaderService.com.

* Terms and prices subject to change without notice. Prices do not include applicable taxes. N.Y. residents add applicable sales tax. Canadian residents will be charged applicable provincial taxes and GST. Offer not valid in Quebec. This offer is limited to one order per household. All orders subject to approval. Credit or debit balances in a customer's account(s) may be offset by any other outstanding balance owed by or to the customer. Please allow 4 to 6 weeks for delivery. Offer available while quantities last.

Your Privacy: Worldwide Library is committed to protecting your privacy. Our Privacy Policy is available online at www.ReaderService.com or upon request from the Reader Service. From time to time we make our lists of customers available to reputable third parties who may have a product or service of interest to you. If you would prefer we not share your name and address, please check here. ☐

Help us get it right—We strive for accurate, respectful and relevant communications. To clarify or modify your communication preferences, visit us at www.ReaderService.com/consumerschoice.

WWL10